I0742961

Wimbledon Village thrives on the edge of a hill, the utmost southern tip of a large high plateau in South West London. Its northern border is dominated by a wasteland known as the Common, mysterious grounds teeming with wilderness. To the west, the Common spreads further like a plague, where Nature lives unruly, until it grinds against the bustling roads, the public buildings, the suburban houses of the village, where men and women live their dreams and nightmares. All along the southern ridge of the hill the Epsom Downs stretch south into Surrey and at the foot of the hill lies modern Wimbledon Town, constantly moving, growing, as it fades into the desolate urban landscape of Merton. The eastern front meets the signs of modern transportation and modern urbanisation until they all step aside to show the green triangle of Wimbledon Park, as it embraces the hill in a cuddle, as it has done since the earliest of times.

Our story starts in Wimbledon Village. But as the pages unfold, as the fog clears, and our characters come into play, it will become clear this is an alternate Wimbledon. It is a Wimbledon where you and I do not exist…

THE WYNNMAN
AND
THE CRIMSON PATHS

by
Trevor P. Kwain

Published by Threepeppers Publishing

1st Edition – July 2020
ISBN: 978-1-9993268-3-8

www.3peppers.co.uk
www.trevorpkwain.org

@trevorpkwain
#TheWynnman

To NaNoWriMo and my sister

The bells of Saint Mary's Church echoed throughout the quiet streets, and for just one minute, their ringing spread peace all around the top of the hill. If Wimbledonians listened carefully, perhaps they could hear the high-pitched murmur of devotees flowing out of the main entrance and onto the gravel path. As the churchgoers made their way through the small graveyard, the path opened up on to a grassy enclosure before reaching Arthur Road.

Like all third Sundays of the month, the green of the enclosure was full of endless lines of market stalls. They filled the space with their wonky metal tables, their shelter made out of ripped bed sheets, and their posters hand-written in clumsy capital letters. Both the shouting from the stands and the crowd seemed louder than any noise coming from the cars on the road beyond.

'What a turnout! The whole village seems to be at the fair today.' commented Dr Watkins while helping Reverend Green ease the crowd out of God's house.

'I don't think it's even a fifth!' replied the reverend dryly. 'But we have kept our number of visitors steady for three years running. I pray the Lord we keep getting new shops opening on Wimbledon High Street. Do you remember the year both the antiques shop and the Korean deli closed down? I could count the number of visitors at the fair on the palm of my hand, including you and me. New shops bring novelty, excitement…'

'…and funding.' added Dr Watkins.

'It goes without saying. God helps those who help themselves.' commented the reverend.

'Especially if their business is in the cake and sweets department.' added again Dr Watkins with another pinch of irony Reverend Green was trying to ignore altogether.

The two men had known each other for a long time, longer than they could remember. Being both members of the Wimbledon Association of Independent Shops, WAIS for short, the two men felt responsible for the local community and wanted local businesses to flourish. As well as being curator of the Wimbledon Museum, Dr Watkins was also chairman of the WAIS itself. It usually meant he had to attend each and every one of the fairs organised throughout the village during the year. The recurring one at Saint Mary's Church was relatively small but it still took its toll on him, having to organise it every month. The curator felt obliged, knowing the reverend lacked organisational skills outside what were his holy duties within the confinement of Saint Mary's Church. Reverend Green was thankful for Dr Watkins's support and always returned the favour with one or two packs of chocolate digestives, which the curator craved on a daily basis.

'Let's make our way to the fair.' suggested Reverend Green peering through the main church door to check no-one had been left behind after the service.

He and Dr Watkins were the last to leave the church steps, bringing up the rear. They followed the crowd to the green enclosure and took position in one of the wider gaps between the stalls. From there, they could admire the beauty of Saint Mary's Church in its entirety, standing alone on the top of Wimbledon Hill, distant from any house or building on every side. The church steeple stood high up in the clear blue sky of late September. The golden rooster at the top of its spire swirled round as the gentle breeze told it where to point; it shimmered at each turn as it met the high sun of noon. The grey and white pattern of the church tower, made of stone and bricks combined, seemed to shimmer too under the direct sunlight, making it all look more solid, more glorified; it was as if it shone with its own inner light. A bunch of balloons flew up in the sky, cutting across the view and rising up above the steeple and beyond. The laughter of children running nearby caught the two old men's attention for a moment.

'Despite first impressions, I must say it is quite a turn-out.' commented Reverend Green gladly.

He observed a family approaching a stall selling frames of hand-made paintings of Wimbledon. The mother leaned over, captured by their beauty, while the father dragged the two children to join them with the promise of delicious sweets if they behaved.

'Is Viviane here already?' asked Reverend Green remembering something suddenly.

'I believe so.'

'And the new fellow? The baker?'

'Well, if he's on time…'

Dr Watkins's words were cut off by the sound of tyres skidding on the asphalt followed by a melodic jingle, which played slightly in and out of tune. The music echoed from a crackling speakerphone attached to the roof of a tiny yellow Fiat 500. The tune sped up and down as the little car bumped off the main road and worked its way onto a small empty patch at the edge of the enclosure where other cars were parked. Enrico LoTrova rolled down the window and pulled himself up while keeping one hand on the steering wheel. His thick, wavy hair was held back by a pair of Ray Ban sunglasses perched on his head. He had a beckoning smile as he waved his hand to the confused crowd by the stands, some still trying to make out what was happening, some jumping back afraid of being run over. Viviane was sitting in the passenger's seat but could not help leaning over to hold the wheel before the crazy Italian baker breached all the rules of road safety.

'Easy Enrico! This is my car, and you are not at the Grand Prix of Monza!' she cried out.

'If you want to make an entrance, make it look good!' replied back Enrico without breaking his smile to the crowd.

Enrico leaned back on the driver's seat and pulled the handbrake while swerving to the left. The little Fiat 500 skidded and U-turned on itself. Viviane cringed at the screeching sound and grabbed the door handle to hold herself steady. Enrico kept his grip on the wheel, quickly straightened the car and put it into reverse gear. He then squeezed the little Fiat 500 in between two bulky Land Rovers, rear bumper first, and hit the brakes. The carillon-like music played on for a few seconds after Enrico had killed the engine. He made one last wave out of the car window while Viviane stepped out of the car a little dizzy and a little embarrassed in front of the gob-smacked crowds. She smiled to keep up appearances and dashed to open the boot as planned. It was clear to the crowds the baker's show was not over yet. The music stopped abruptly, and the baker's thick voice came thundering through the crackling speakerphone.

'Goood moorrrning, Wimbledonians! *The Wynnman* bakery is here to offer delicious bread and special pastries. Come over if you have a sweet tooth and try these fresh *sfogliatelle*!'

The boot opened with a burst of confetti and revealed a display of boxes and trays filled with bread of all shapes and sizes, plus open boxes filled with sweet and savouring delicacies. The children were the first to take a step forward, grabbing the free *sfogliatelle* from Viviane's hands and smudging their mouths with sweet ricotta cream or nutty chocolate fillings oozing from the shell-shaped layers of thin pastry. The parents tried to hold them back until they could no longer, so they too ended up joining the free tasting Enrico had carefully planned. Visitors crowded around the Fiat 500 to try and get a taste of what *The Wynnman* bakery had to offer. The other stalls could only look on with envy as his cakes and sweets were quickly devoured. After only a few months since opening *The Wynnman* bakery in

Wimbledon Village, the Italian baker had started to make a name for himself at the local fairs.

'Is he always so theatrical?' whispered Reverend Green to Dr Watkins once the initial shock faded, and the fair resumed its normal course.

'Try one of those pastries first and then you tell me if it is worth all of this!' said Dr Watkins with a wink.

The wine shop on Ridgeway was deserted when Reginald Bosham made his way inside holding a screwed-up list in his big hand. The shopkeeper shuddered and moved a few steps back behind the counter. Reginald's burly appearance, with his muscles bulging under the tight sleeves of his black top, had instilled fear in the shopkeeper from the moment Reginald pushed the door open with unnecessary force, almost pulling it off its hinges. Reginald's heavy footsteps on the bare wooden floor resounded throughout the shop, causing all the wine bottles to clink one against the other. Then Reginald stopped in front of him and slammed the list on the counter.

'Good morning!' said Reginald with unusual, forced politeness in his voice.

'Good...morning!' replied the shopkeeper as he joined his hands, still trembling. 'How...how can I help you?'

'Wine. Lots of it'. grunted Reginald.

The shopkeeper turned up his nose at the vulgar request. He ran the place with great pride, selling the best stock in Wimbledon Village, displaying the most prestigious and subtle wines anyone could offer, whether they were from the Old or the New World. He had become sensitive to the way people treated the velvety nectar squeezed out of grapes. The shopkeeper eyed the burly man in front of him. He had never seen him before. Perhaps someone passing through, on his way to a party infused with cheap alcohol.

'We are…a wine *boutique*, sir.' pointed out the shopkeeper. 'Perhaps you may want to be specific.'

'Here's the list.' answered Reginald tapping on the hand-written list still laid out on the counter. 'I am just picking up the order.'

Reginald's tapping only irritated the shopkeeper further. Yet, he still feared the burly man in front of him; something about him said it was better to keep calm and carry on. Thus, he picked up the list holding back the words he would have gladly thrown at the uncivilised wine drinker in front of him.

'Odd list, this is.' commented the shopkeeper without looking. 'Are you sure you want crates of this less refined wine?'

'Listen, I do not have all day. This is the list!'

Reginald pulled a face at the shopkeeper, making it clear he was on a tight schedule. He wanted to grab him by the collar, to make him hurry up, but his boss had warned him not to be aggressive; the last thing they needed was to attract unnecessary attention. The shopkeeper sighed and, head down, disappeared into the back.

Reginald looked around the shop while he waited, pretending to read the labels and recognise each name. Lately, he was starting to dislike these errands he had been asked to fulfil. He did not understand why he was the one who had to do it. Furthermore, spending time in Wimbledon was making him feel obnoxious. He was a fish out of water here. He felt it each time he was out and about, either for an errand or for pleasure. Wimbledon Village was no place for an ex-con like him, but the money was good. He hoped his boss's second test would soon be done. He had had enough of buying crates of wine and bottles of chemicals he had never heard of. Still, he did not understand why he had to buy all this cheap wine, each time from different stores, and then empty the bottles in barrels. He found the whole job weird. Just weird.

The shopkeeper returned a few minutes later. He barged in pushing a heavy-duty trolley with four crates stacked on it. The pile swayed a little as he parked it in the middle of the room, letting go of the handles hurriedly. Reginald could tell the shopkeeper had huffed and puffed all the way from where he had come from. The crates looked very heavy.

'Is that all?' asked Reginald, unimpressed.

'Yes!' the shopkeeper grunted as he dried the beads of sweat from his forehead. 'Four crates of the red wine specified on your list. Have you come by car?'

'The van is just across the road. I'll take this!' boasted Reginald.

He hinted for the shopkeeper to step aside and pushed the trolley effortlessly towards the entrance. Reginald was desperate to get out and be done with. He then recalled the question he always had to ask before leaving such establishment.

'Oh, almost forgot.' he exclaimed a few inches from the door. 'Do you collect empty bottles? Do you recycle stuff?'

'No, we don't.' dismissed the shopkeeper struggling to keep his wits about him. 'Is there anything else you need?'

The shopkeeper gave Reginald a forced smile, doing his best to be polite. He found the burly man irritating.

'Alright. Thanks.'

Reginald turned and opened the door to push the trolley through. He did it with such force the bottles in the shop clinked and rattled again for almost a minute.

'Excuse me!' shouted the shopkeeper behind him. 'What about payment?'

Reginald stopped in his tracks at the open threshold. The breeze blew over the stuffy air of the shop. He turned one last time.

'Who do you take me for? Cash is on the counter!' he said with a smirk. 'I even left a tip. I will come back in a sec to return the trolley.'

Reginald walked out not expecting an answer. If only the shopkeeper knew who could possibly need all this wine, Reginald thought. He crossed the empty street and reached the van parked at the entrance of a cul-de-sac. Inside, there were more bottles stacked in open boxes. He had been busy all morning going all over SW19 to make his purchases. Anyone standing behind him would think he had a drinking problem or was planning a big party. He sighed and loaded the new purchase onto the van. His head in the meantime raced onto the next thing to do. He only had to take it to the fancy house and drop it there for the two brothers to pick up. They would then take out their little chemist's tools and do whatever his boss had been asking them to do over and over again for the last few months. Results were far from close. He did not really understand what the results were meant to be, despite his boss explaining them to him more than once. That does not mean I am stupid, Reginald told himself many times. He always considered himself the 'muscle' of the operation. The two brothers had no guts but Reginald's boss, Lord Awlthorp, deemed them very essential for the second test. The one that would confirm the legend was true.

Reginald laughed to himself and closed the doors of the van. He was about to return the trolley when his phone buzzed. A message. He pulled the phone out of his pocket and raised it to eye level. It was from Lord Awlthorp's driver. Something serious had occurred that could jeopardise the operation. They had to meet urgently that same evening. At the fancy house. No further details were given.

The fair at Saint Mary's Church was in full swing after a couple of hours. Viviane and Enrico had kept themselves busy, selling bread of all shapes and sizes, finishing all their stock of *sfogliatelle* and promoting Enrico's bakery to more and more people. Dr Watkins and Reverend Green joined them by the almost empty car boot and in a moment of quiet trading took the opportunity to have a chat.

'Pleasure to have you here, Mr LoTrova!' thanked Reverend Green.

'Call me Enrico!'

'Enrico. Right. From Italy I presume? Whereabouts?'

'Somewhere central. The heart of the boot.'

'Ah Assisi, perhaps? Lovely churches there. I wish I could deliver my sermon in one of the many marvels of Italian architecture. Fascinating!'

Enrico nodded with a shy smile.

'What are you saying, reverend? Are you going to sell off Saint Mary's and move to Italy?' joked Dr Watkins.

He and the reverend, now in their later years, kept their friendship young by teasing each other without caring whether in public or private. Dr Watkins was the only one who had the courage to cut him off and pull a joke when the opportunity came. He did not fear Wimbledon's man of the cloth.

'Contrary to how churches are preserved in Italy,' continued Dr Watkins. 'our local church has been plagued for centuries with different layers of history stacking a new version on top of the old one. The first church was built in stone by the Anglo-Saxons, when they converted to Christianity around the seventh century. We don't know much about that one. A second, larger one was built out of wood in medieval times; I think late thirteenth century.'

'Is this the one?' wondered Enrico.

'What you see here is the fourth and final version, built by Gilbert Scott during the Victorian era.' clarified the curator. 'He designed the church in true Gothic architecture on top of the Georgian version from around 1780, which was built with grey bricks with a more neoclassical look.'

'When you step inside,' jumped in Reverend Green to show off his bit of knowledge. 'you should not be surprised to see old and new versions mixed together, from the Victorian tower and the entrance to the Medieval chancel roof and the Georgian nave. I bet if you look behind one of the wardrobes, you can find a Medieval stone or a Georgian plaque for sure. But I am pleased to know our church has served Wimbledonians since the Anglo-Saxons roamed this hill. Just as we receive the Lord's daily bread each Sunday, I think it makes sense you serve your daily bread here today too, Mr LoTrova. On behalf of the congregation, thank you!'

The reverend showed pride in his words. Enrico smiled politely and looked at the church in the distance. He then glanced at Viviane next to him. Viviane had showed no sign of disapproval of Enrico's little car stunt. She had played along and helped the Italian baker sell his bread with great enthusiasm. She was now smiling at him and that image meant a thousand words to him, reminding him of his rising success.

Enrico had spent the last few months, since the bakery's opening, doing everything to make his business grow. Charity bake-offs, some promotion through the local radio, and any local fair he could join. The monthly fair at Saint Mary's Church was probably the most recurring one, the one which made him feel even better with himself knowing he was helping a holy place. He worked day and night to try new recipes or improve existing ones. Viviane helped by sending him new people from her shop across the street, who slowly became his small, most trusted clientele. Dr Watkins checked with him from time to time if he needed help from the WAIS, but Enrico felt he could stand on his own two feet now that the dangers of failure were a thing of the past. Dr Watkins insisted he should have installed a new computerised till, but the Italian baker struggled to see the point of doing so. He did not trust computers. He now stood there looking at Viviane and then at the crowd enjoying themselves, tasting his food and carrying around boxes bearing the name of his bakery. *The Wynnman* still sounded like the perfect name.

'Reverend! Help! Reverend!'

The cry interrupted Enrico's thoughts and he turned around, as the rest of the group did, towards where it came from. A little boy aged around ten was running erratically through the stands, his cheeks red, his eyes wide and scared. He held one hand towards them, a girl doll hanging from his trembling fingers. It was a plead for help.

'What is it?' said the reverend.

The boy trembled and struggled to gasp for air. The reverend kneeled down to hold the child steady by the shoulders and calm him down. A small crowd gathered by the car with worried looks on their faces.

'Rosie…' the boy panted. 'I think she hurt herself…'

'Where?' asked Enrico joining the reverend at his side.

The boy lifted his finger and turned to point back at the stands, somewhere beyond them, next to the church.

'Something must have happened in the church graveyard.' commented Reverend Green. 'Charlie! How many times have I told you not to play hide and seek in there?'

The little boy lowered his head in shame.

'Let's see if we can help Rosie.' prompted Enrico giving the boy a reassuring look. 'Take us there!'

The boy's breathing was now getting back to normal. He nodded and started running back to where he had come from. Enrico nodded at the reverend and both sprinted through the stalls as the crowd parted to let them through.

The graveyard surrounded the church like the walls of a medieval fort. Clusters of tombstones, altars, neoclassical pyramids and stone angels were massed over each other in a shapeless but logical barrier around which the grass and trees had been trained to grow without disturbing the dead. The surface too was uneven. Mounds of earth had heaped for centuries on top of each other in the cramped churchyard and now a hazardous slope descended from the church towards the north side of the hill. The surface could sometimes be so steep and slippery that low walls had been built to create small terraces.

The little boy seemed to know his way through. He jumped here and there, careful to avoid the odd slippery moss or stepping onto a tomb. Enrico struggled to keep up as he followed the boy through the narrow gaps. It felt eerie to Enrico to run through the graveyard, unfamiliar as he was to English cemeteries. He wondered why they were kept in the same grounds as the church. Back home, church and graveyards were separate worlds never meant to collide. The Italian baker moved at a quick pace and could hear Reverend Green's directions coming from right behind him. 'Watch it there', 'Climb that way'. The two adults seemed to be lost in a wall-less maze, able to see where the boy was going but forced to carefully tiptoe around the silent stones of the dead. Then the area cleared slightly, and the boy slowed down to catch his breath. He walked to a lonely pine tree, held his hand against the humid trunk, and did not turn to wait for the arrival of Enrico and the reverend. Instead he kept his gaze fixed to the ground. Enrico could not see what he was looking at. In front of the boy, a solid monument stood up against the perimeter walls of the graveyard. Its inscriptions were faded, and it was larger than any other tombstone he had come across. As the two men joined the boy, Enrico realised he was only looking at the tip of the iceberg. Literally. The monument was a family vault with a pyramid-like structure and narrow steps leading to the interred crypt below. An iron gate led inside. It was ajar with its chain dangling on one side.

'What's happened here?' asked Enrico again, wishing to protect the boy.

'We were just playing.' started explaining Charlie with his eyes now fixed to the floor. 'It was my turn to find her. I had been looking for her for a while until I noticed the gate to this family vault was open. It is never open. I went in but could not see her until I heard her cries for help. I could not find her. I am sorry....'

'OK let me see.' said Enrico.

He placed his hand on the little boy's shoulder and gave a quick nod to the reverend, who offered to keep an eye on him. Enrico then went down the narrow steps and opened the gate. The gate creaked, and the rusty chain fell hard on the dusty stone floor. The clamour disturbed the solemn silence in the penumbra of the small crypt. Inside, the wall opposite the entrance had marble panels bearing names, dates and a few words in loving memory. Enrico shivered in the chilling cold and could smell the strong humidity despite the fine day outside. One of the panels on the far right was cracked and misplaced. It was leaning as if someone had pulled it out but had not been able to put it back in place.

'Rosie?' cried out Enrico.

He waited and listened. Dead silence. He wondered where she could be. Then a muffled cry started to ring in the baker's ears. Sniffles and whimpers followed. The echo in the tiny, cramped crypt amplified the suffering to a ghostly lament.

'Rosie? Is that you?'

A word or an incomprehensible moan interrupted the sniffling. A girl's voice. It was distant, and Enrico could not pinpoint where. He kneeled down in front of the cracked panel. He touched its edges looking for an easy point to grab, and then pulled an edge up a few centimetres from the floor. He moved it to one side and finally revealed a pitch-black square opening. Enrico squinted but was not able to see anything. He could not make out much. He touched the inside walls of the funeral niche and winced to the slimy touch of moss and soil. No coffin. No bones. Few cobwebs and cold earth. Up to a point. The deeper half of the narrow floor had collapsed, and an icy draught came from whatever empty space lied below. The little girl's voice was still far but crispier.

'Rosie? Are you there?' called out again Enrico.

'Yes…please…help meee…' answered the girl feebly.

'Coming to get you!'

Enrico did not know what he would find but thought it best to share his intentions and warn the reverend before he defaced the tomb of whoever was buried here.

'I am sure the congregation may twist their noses at such sacrilege.' sighed Reverend Green in response to Enrico's request at the top of the crypt steps. 'Yet, a little girl is in danger. We called the police already. Are you sure we cannot wait for them to arrive?'

Enrico cringed at the thought of meeting Inspector Baynard once again.

'Reverend Green,' he pleaded. 'the girl's voice is getting weaker. Maybe she has little or no air to breathe down there. Do you know what there is below this crypt?'

The reverend looked at the crypt entrance and then back at Enrico.

'Let me give you a torch.' he said. 'In fifty years of service I have never heard of anything lying below this crypt. God only knows now.'

Enrico returned to the crypt pleased to have the reverend's blessing. Thanks to some divine light where the funeral niche floor had collapsed, he caught sight of a narrow passage running below the crypt. It seemed endless. He sat on the cold stone floor, put the torch in his mouth and slowly slipped inside with his feet first. With both hands, he worked his way down using the sides of the hole still intact, hoping it would hold out. His feet dangled in the void for a short moment, the icy draught colder than he had imagined, creeping up to his waist. He bit hard on the torch and by clenching his arm muscles he lowered himself down into the hole. It was not as deep as he thought. He suddenly touched heaps of rubble and had to check a few times he was on steady ground before he could let go with his hands. He fell to the dirty floor below. He then pointed the torch forward. The tunnel running under the crypt was slightly lower than him and he had to crouch to proceed further.

'Rosie" I am coming!' he cried out to check with her from time to time.

'Here…' echoed the girl.

The voice was ahead of him, but the torch only saw darkness in the distance. The tunnel was made of a mix of stones and red bricks, humid and cold to the touch. A few drops of water dripped from the arched vault and the side walls. Also, a trickle of dirty water flowed unceasingly through Enrico's feet and formed puddles where scattered debris of unknown origin had piled up over time. The place could have flooded at this rate, but the water seemed to know where to flow. After a few minutes that seemed an eternity, Enrico noticed a shape crouched on the side of the tunnel. The shape looked small, fragile; it did not move.

'Rosie?' called out Enrico.

The shape was still at first and then shifted slightly. Enrico thought it may be a wild animal. He was suddenly reassured in seeing a child's tiny frame turning towards the light. She did not stand up or utter a word. Her face was petrified. Her dress was muddy and so were her ballerina shoes. Mild scratches and streaks of red showed on her tights.

'Are you ok?' asked Enrico.

She nodded quickly, wary of her surroundings. It seemed she did not want to turn her face around. Enrico moved closer until he was able to kneel right in front of her. The lines of tears on her red face could not go unnoticed.

'What are you doing here? Looking for treasure?' asked Enrico to play down her fears. 'I am Enrico. They told me your name is Rosie, isn't it?'

Rosie nodded again briskly. She stared at him, unable to look away from Enrico's face or the light from the torch. Still, she did not speak.

'Ok. Don't be scared. I will get you out of here.'

A gurgling sound echoed from deep down the tunnel. Enrico quickly flashed the torch in its direction, but the tunnel seemed to continue for miles ahead. Something caught his attention, where the light started to fade away. Another shape of some sort was lying against the side wall. He looked back at Rosie.

'Stay here. Don't move!'

Rosie's eyes widened, and she started to shake her head rapidly. Fear returned to her sweet eyes. Enrico was baffled. He looked again towards the shape lying on the floor and moved towards it despite Rosie's little hand grabbing his feet. Enrico gave her a gesture of reassurance and slowly moved forward. The second shape was still. No more sounds could be heard. As he moved closer, he realised it was long and slim similar to a human body. As the light of the torch brought colours back into his field of sight, he was now sure the shape was covered in a maroon slime, almost as hard as dry wax. It became even too clear when he recognised the shapes of upper and lower limbs, then the naked torso and stiff neck. It all became plain too obvious when his torch flashed onto the faceless head staring back at him, much to his horror. Little Rosie had found herself a dead body.

That same Sunday morning, Lord Awlthorp was enjoying his morning routine in the large private library. The old library had been extended to almost triple its size to accommodate the entire load of books, tomes, scripts and parchments Lord Awlthorp had been able to bring to his mansion over the last few months. The entire collection belonged to the Earl of Spencer and had been locked up in a vault for centuries, somewhere in the Midlands. Only the current Earl of Spencer could grant access to the vault, and Lord Awlthorp had been extremely convincing in ensuring he could borrow them for an undetermined period of time. It would save him time instead of going to the vault each time to fetch any piece of research he wished to pursue. The research he was carrying out though was more complex than anyone could imagine. All the books, tomes, scripts and parchments now on display in his library shared one topic only. The mythical legend. The one Lord Awlthorp could not stop dreaming about. Ever since the discovery of the black azalea in Cannizaro Park of Wimbledon, he had longed to shed more light on the mythical legend he had first casually read about. He needed to be sure the legend told on the yellow-stained pages he consulted day and night was true. The legend about an old great power hidden underneath the placid top of Wimbledon hill for millennia. A power strong enough to move seas and mountains.

Lord Awlthorp moved to the library with his cup of Earl Grey tea and a copy of the morning newspaper. An array of open books awaited on one of the two large mahogany tables he had arranged in the middle of the room. Some further reading would help him focus on the matter at hand. Alone and without interruptions. The solemn silence lived undisturbed in the library. Lord Awlthorp had been careful enough in planning its design. Based on the second floor, there were only two high windows, both sound-proofed and looking over an uninteresting display of thick branches and a plain green lawn that filled the entire view. He did not need any distractions by greenery that would catch his attention or the sound of chirping birds. He also removed the cogs from all the clocks he had installed in the room. He despised their ticking. It drove him mad. He only kept the clocks for their pleasant aesthetic look, like enchanted creatures chained to an unmoving, unchanging present. He did not allow anyone in here. If anyone of his few close associates had to meet up with him, it would be in his study next door. He knew he had a couple of hours by himself and there were pressing matters to deal with regarding his second test.

The latest parchment he had found talked about a drinkable potion that would help unleash this great, legendary power. The description was vague, and it could have been anything, from rainwater to some alchemic concoction. There was little detail on what should be done with it once in someone's possession. Lord Awlthorp had been at a loss for a while until he came across a recipe on a small, thin note hidden between the pages of a heavy tome on the subject of cookery in Elizabethan England. The short recipe only listed the ingredients, but not how to mix them. It was dated 1546 but it did not hint at its purpose or its origins. What caught Lord Awlthorp's attention was some of the ingredients listed. No matter how many reference books he consulted, from Old English to the Tudor era, these ingredients were never mentioned in any cookery books or journals from the sixteenth century or any other historical period. They simply appeared to have been made up; they did not exist anywhere. Lord Awlthorp became convinced they were connected to the mythical potion. All he could do was try and experiment, try and recreate that recipe, in the hope it would be a step closer to finding another item that would prove to him, and everyone else, the legend was real. Lord Awlthorp savoured the moment each time he thought about what he could accomplish with that power. His eyes glinted with greed. Even if he had nothing concrete in his hands, he had faith in his research. The black azalea, and now this potion, could lead to something.

Lord Awlthorp sat at the table and flicked through some of the notes he had written the previous day. He spent most of his time transcribing texts and drawing sketches of what he would need to do. He could not allow any of these books and scripts to leave this room. Too fragile, too valuable. He could not trust Reginald with them, let alone others on his payroll. He did not want them to fall in the wrong hands, like the Wimbledon Museum. They already owned the black azalea, which they put on display, making it untouchable. Lord Awlthorp knew at some point he had to devise a plan to ensure it returned to the rightful owner. Him alone.

One hour passed quickly. Lord Awlthorp, in his black gown, read on, undeterred by the many lines of unintelligible calligraphy from medieval to more recent times. Prophets, charlatans, priests, insignificant people from history who talked about the great power hidden under the hill where Wimbledon was founded. He did not flinch or show signs of tiredness in his eyes in the scarce natural light entering the library. Not until he heard a noise, an annoying sound of shuffling feet. It started faint, like an isolated sound from the remote areas of the large house he lived in. It then became insistent, repetitive. Lord Awlthorp closed his eyes a few times in an effort to shut out the sound. He then lost focus, and realised the sound was intended to catch his attention.

'Who dares to interrupt me?' he called out loudly to admonish an unknown presence out there.

The shuffling sound stopped.

'How many times have I told everyone? I do not wish to be disturbed in the library. Is that clear?'

Lord Awlthorp kept talking without looking or turning, trying to re-read the same sentence he had been reading for the past five minutes over and over. He could feel the presence he addressed was still there.

'What is it?' he snapped.

He then stood up and turned towards the open door leading out of the library. Just outside the threshold, a man in uniform and peak cap stood shyly. His body was rigid and did not look in the lord's direction. It was Lord Awlthorp's faithful driver. The lord frowned and lowered his accusing hand. The driver knew the rules. He was the first to obey them meticulously, to the letter. He did not dare come in. He did not knock. Yet, he had to speak to him. He had to catch his attention quickly. It meant there was something urgent.

'Let's go to my study.' said Lord Awlthorp.

He stormed out of the library, not looking the driver in the eye, and walked to the study next door, leaving the door open for the driver to follow him. The change of location was enough to signal an allowed change in behaviour. The tense driver took a deep sigh and relaxed every single muscle in his body. He took off his peak cap, put it under his arm and entered the study.

Lord Awlthorp's study was smaller than his library, filled more with enigmatic paintings on arcane wallpaper than bookshelves. It lacked modernity, but any designer would have struggled to pin down the study décor to a known point in time in history. It was anachronistic, somehow, as if taken from an alternate history nobody knew about. There was a grandfather clock in the corner, and it was stuck at three a.m. with no ticking sound. To one side of the study, there was his personal desk, layered with a lot of scribbled notes and a few reading books. Opposite the desk, more notes and coloured strings were pinned to the wall, forming an ordered chaos, an unfathomable pattern representing Lord Awlthorp's plans. To the driver it simply looked like meaningless gibberish. He stood behind Lord Awlthorp waiting before he could make his urgent announcement.

'What seems to be the problem?' asked the lord taking off his gown and revealing his morning suit, still in shades of very dark grey as was his custom.

'Good news or bad news first, sir?'

'Let's start with the good news.'

'The deeds have been signed, sir. It is official as from tomorrow.'

'The title has been transferred?'

'Yes, sir. Undisclosed identity as you requested. The public information act can only state the title has been purchased and transferred.'

The driver thought for a moment he could glimpse a jubilant expression across Lord Awlthorp's corvine face. Yet, it still looked sinister against the glint of evil in his eyes.

'That is good news, indeed.'

Lord Awlthorp sat down at his desk and scribbled something on a notebook. He then turned his attention back to the driver, his hands joined and placed under his chin. His look was more austere now, preparing for the next question.

'What is the bad news then?'

The driver wet his lips. He did not fear his boss. He was worried for him and the people he hired. After the failure in hiring Eric Quercer, it was clear they had to tread carefully not to expose Lord Awlthorp and his activity to the public.

'A terrible accident at the house. We need to act and cover our tracks.'

'Mr LaTuerva, how happy to see you…again!' said Inspector Baynard, wondering what could be worse: the unexpected Sunday 999 call or crossing paths with the crazy Italian baker.

'LoTrova!' corrected Enrico as he always felt obliged to. 'Nice to see you too!'

He became so accustomed to Baynard's mispronunciation of his surname that it almost felt part of his daily life in Wimbledon. Strangely, he had missed it.

Inspector Baynard's sarcastic grin could not go unnoticed. He stared at Enrico in his usual manner. His icy stare, his unflinching, light grey eyes, his finely trimmed and stern-looking goatee. He paid no attention to the paperwork being handed over to him while the baker was in his presence.

He had learned to keep police matters close to him ever since the events in Cannizaro Park.

'My men told me it was you who found the body, correct?'

'Yes, I found it by chance when looking for the little girl called Rosie.'

Baynard's eyes quickly checked his notes. They both stood by the gravel path outside the entrance to Saint Mary's Church. All around them the police constables had cleared the area, so the police could work undisturbed. They had also cordoned off the graveyard, especially around the family vault where Rosie had been found. Reverend Green and the little boy Charlie were being interviewed at the same time a few feet away. Enrico glanced beyond the police perimeter and spotted a reassuring nod from Viviane and Dr Watkins mingling among the curious crowd.

'I see you are quite the children's hero this time, Mr Lortova.' continued Baynard stroking his silver goatee as he listened to Enrico's recounting of how he had found Rosie and the body.

'LoTrova.' Enrico corrected him one more time. 'Little Charlie over there came to us crying for help. I did what I had to do, inspector.'

'Yes, you did. You always do. Mind you, I have two girls as well and they are friends with Rosie. I would have done the same.'

'Is she ok?'

'She is a bit under shock and slightly bruised. We thought it best to send her to Parkside Hospital for a few checks. Parents are with her as we speak.'

'That is great!' sighed Enrico with relief. 'How about the body I found there? Did you find out who he or she was?'

Baynard gave him an odd look. It annoyed him when the Italian baker did not mind his own business. Especially when nosing around police matters.

'We have been here before. Mr Lertova. You do know investigations are confidential. Not sure how things work where you come from, but again, let me remind you, please leave this in the police's capable hands. We will let you know if we need anything. I am sure your bread is waiting for you!'

'You're the boss, inspector.' smiled back Enrico with irony. 'You tell me though how many men or women that size turn up in a tunnel covered in that purple or brown mess. If you need me, you know where my bakery is. Come round for a free loaf anytime!'

The inspector sneered, not really paying attention to the invitation. The Italian baker could remember all his customers and he knew Baynard was not one of them. He preferred to buy it elsewhere rather than to be forced to meet the baker more often than he wished. Enrico could not blame him after their brief feud during the investigations at Cannizaro Park. Once the questioning was over, Enrico and Inspector Baynard dismissed each other quickly while keeping up their appearances and going their separate ways. Their relationship always ran on a thin line.

Baynard walked over to a man in white overalls busy comparing a few sealed plastic bags. Each one with a clearly visible label.

'What do we have?' he asked.

'Strange, inspector. The man appears to have suffered third degree burns.' answered the crime scene investigator.

'Are you certain?'

'I wouldn't if it weren't for the traces of charred skin found in the burnt, coagulated blood.'

'Come again?'

'You heard, inspector. I need to complete the analysis. However, I am sure this man was covered in thick blood from head to toe before he was burnt alive.'

'Oh Jesus…' exclaimed Baynard.

'Inspector, we are in front of the church…' whispered the crime scene investigator noticing the reproachful eye from the reverend a few feet away.

'You call me when you have more. I want to be the first to know.' carried on Baynard acting normal.

The inspector's thoughts deepened after hearing the new piece of evidence. It troubled him that a new, more shocking event could be coming his way. He looked at the crowd, whispering and staring, and asked a nearby police constable to disperse them as soon as possible. He told him it was better to keep things under wraps until they knew more. The memory of the explosion at Cannizaro Park months ago was no longer headlines news. Yet, the inspector knew it was fresh in people's minds as much as it was for him.

Outside the police perimeter, the fair was still ongoing thanks to Reverend Green's efforts to ensure his precious guests would not be put off by the accident. Less people, though, moved through the stands and the thick crowd was now just a glorious memory. Enrico had left the church premises and was returning to the Fiat 500 to pack things up. Viviane left Dr Watkins and moved away from the crowd to quickly catch up with the Italian baker.

'Enrico, are you alright?'

'Yeah. Just confused.'

'You're a hero. Not just a baker.'

Viviane tried to cheer him up.

'For the *sfogliatelle* or for saving the girl?' chuckled Enrico.

He was happy Viviane had come round to check on him. He was in debt to her for her support. She was his first friend after all. Viviane and Dr Watkins were his only true friends.

'What did Inspector Baynard have to say?' asked Viviane out of curiosity. 'He did not give you a hard time, did he?

'*Niente*. Nothing. Police secrets.'

Viviane looked at Enrico suspiciously. She knew this was not Enrico talking.

'Do you have one of your hunches again?'

'Mmm…I don't know…' sighed the baker.

He sat on the edge of the open car boot and stared at the bell tower of Saint Mary's Church pointing up in the sky. Viviane could tell he was brewing something.

'I think I might bake some *focaccia* for tomorrow…' Enrico said almost absent-minded.

'What is it?' insisted Viviane. 'Come on, spill the beans!'

She had learned by now that when her Italian baker friend started planning batches of bread, it could only mean something was on his mind.

'The body.' replied Enrico in a low voice, careful not to be heard by others. 'Completely covered in that purple and brown coating. As if burnt and covered by molten lava like in Pompeii, except for the colour. Horrible death.'

'Maybe the body has been there for a very long time.'

'Perhaps. It didn't look decomposed enough to me. And that gurgling sound still gives me the creeps.'

'What sound?'

'Something from the end of the tunnel. The unexplored part I believe. Reverend Green himself did not know where it led or that the tunnel even existed.'

'Didn't he say this church was built over and over again on top of old buildings?'

'You're right. Perhaps Dr Watkins would know more.'

'Are you being the *ragazzo curioso* again?' groaned Viviane. 'Remember what happened last time. Please Enrico, can you let this one go, and stay out of Baynard's way?'

Viviane knew though Enrico could not find peace until his curiosity was paid off.

'Do you have time for a late lunch?' proposed Enrico pretending not to hear what she had just said.

Sergeant Jeremy was drawing imaginary circles on the blank notepad. He held it upright, hiding the pages from the lady opposite. Anything to show he was taking every word she was saying very seriously. He smiled, pretending he was listening with interest to the lady's story. If he remembered well, it was the thirteenth time he had heard the same story. He played a little game in his head where he could anticipate which part of the story she would come to. The bathroom part came now.

'…and the vibration can also be heard in the bathroom. The sink, the toilet, and even the bathtub, vibrate all together when I hear the tremors…'

'Mrs Biggins,' interrupted Jeremy with a professional look which did not imply he was trying to shut her up. 'do you know if any of your neighbours are doing some renovation work? Or do you know of any planned gas works on one of the roads nearby?'

'I know what my neighbours are up to, young man. The tremors I hear just come and go. They are not constant.'

'And they are not always at the same time, right?' added Jeremy, happy to know he remembered how Mrs Biggins's story carried on.

The lady, who lived on Rectory Orchard, off Church Road, had been coming to Wimbledon Police station every Sunday for the last month or so, complaining about a tremor. It was an imperceptible and gentle vibration which cursed her house every day, especially at weekends, as if the London underground had finally decided to pass right under her house. Jeremy had sent more than one unwilling constable since then to check the house and it became clear from the very beginning she was probably imagining it. The Council had a few planned works across Wimbledon Hill but nothing that would make houses shake. Mrs Biggins's neighbours even confirmed they could not hear any tremors at all. However, nothing stopped Mrs Biggins from turning up every Sunday and ask to speak to whoever was in charge. That person was picked on rotation and that Sunday it was Jeremy's turn, for the thirteenth time.

'Listen to me, young man. I have been living here almost all my life and I have never heard tremors in my house. I need you to send someone to check the house.'

'Again?' groaned the sergeant.

He then covered his mouth wishing he had not spoken his mind.

'Pardon me?' asked Mrs Biggins suspiciously.

It was not clear to Jeremy whether the lady realised people made fun of her each time she turned up to report tremors. Still, he reminded himself and others not to act disrespectfully. They represented the police force after all.

'I meant, again? Is it happening again?' blurted out Jeremy, changing his voice to a deep, professional tone. Mrs Biggins, I will do my best and send someone later this coming week to check. We are dumbfounded on what it could be. We will do the best we can.'

Sergeant Jeremy scribbled a smiley face on the notepad and stared convincingly at Mrs Biggins to reassure her he had put it down on his to-do list. The lady uttered a sound which to Jeremy could only mean acceptance and satisfaction.

'Let me walk you to the front door, Mrs Biggins.' continued Jeremy to avoid hearing the story for a fourteenth time. 'It is a fine Sunday out there. I suggest you make the most of it while we look after things.'

Mrs Biggins eyed Jeremy suspiciously once more before Jeremy took her gently under his arm and led her to the way out of the police station. Once he was finally alone again, Jeremy sighed at last, impressed at how he had been able to contain his patience. Almost. It must have been the amount of time he had spent with Inspector Baynard that had made the sergeant so resilient. The sergeant glanced at his watch. He had spent one full hour and a half talking with Mrs Biggins, or rather being talked to. And he was surprised to see the inspector was not back yet from Saint Mary's Church, but he knew reports had been coming in. Something macabre. Something worse than tremors, for sure.

'Sarge!' shouted a police constable behind him.

'What is it?' replied Jeremy.

'The crime scene investigation team is here. They brought the body into the lab for forensics to look at. Care to join?'

'Is Baynard back?'

'He's still interviewing a witness at Saint Mary's. I tell you, what a mess it is! We have a burnt cadaver.'

'Jolly good!' exclaimed Jeremy with a hint of sarcasm.

He followed the police constable through to the lab where forensics had already laid out a white plastic bag with a zip running up the middle. A man in a white lab coat was preparing to open it up and start the autopsy. The sergeant had been exposed to a few dead bodies before, enough to be familiar with the concept and the procedure. Yet, most of the dead bodies he had seen were always natural deaths or victims of unfortunate accidents where the police were required to run an autopsy. Murder hardly touched Wimbledon.

'I have not read the reports yet. What do we have?' asked Jeremy.

'Adult Male. Badly burnt beyond recognition.' said the man in the white lab coat.

Jeremy gulped. A disfigured dead body was probably a first.

'Any idea what the cause could be?' he followed, slightly nervous.

The man in the white lab coat glanced at him. His expression was one of complete disorientation.

'No idea.' he said. 'The man is burnt but his body is covered by a hardened mass of a strange maroon colour.'

He then went to unzip the white bag and suddenly the corpse was out into the open, like a mummified body taken out of an Egyptian tomb. The strange mass covering the body looked hard and burnt, fixing what was left of the flesh and bones into a locked position. One of despair, with arms slightly bent at an odd angle, as if trying to protect his face from someone or something. The strange mass shined with a weird purple colour in between the streaks of charred body, but under the neon lights it shifted to different colours depending on where someone stood. From purple to brown, then onto maroon and sometimes even crimson. The mass had melted into the flesh and it now looked like hardened sulphur except its appearance was closer to colourful stones like amethyst, with its kaleidoscopic glimmer. The whole body was now an anonymous stickman, and the hairless face had no feature at all, making any recognition impossible.

'Oh lord…' muttered Jeremy. 'What happened to him?'

The Dog and Fox pub was one of the few tall buildings rising above the modest skyline of Wimbledon High Street. It stood right at the centre where the Wimbledon Village roundabout split its traffic between north and south. The dominating Victorian aura of one of the oldest pubs in the village could not be ignored by passers-by. Its red bricks and grey façades shone vividly against the paler, lower buildings that overlooked the same roundabout. It was probably the reason the pub was busy almost every hour of the day.

Enrico had kindly invited Dr Watkins for lunch and asked Viviane to come along too. He liked the curator's company, the little bits of knowledge he shared about this tiny London village, the old-fashioned charm he always took around with him. He was sure he could learn more about the tunnel from him, hear what he made of Enrico and Rosie's discovery. They took a seat by one of the large bay windows which looked out onto the roundabout.

The internal décor was a mix of old and new, and sometimes old made into new, like the plush leather armchair Enrico found himself sinking in. The wooden panels darkened the high-ceiling rooms and sucked in the bright light from the large windows as if night lived on during the day. Sunday roast was on the menu and so they ordered three. Viviane suggested something called *Yorkshire pudding* to accompany it. Enrico did not shy away from trying the local food on these occasions. He had been busy lately; he could not remember the last time he had had a pub lunch. Trying bread or pastries from his bakery kept him full most of the day.

'Is it a dessert?' queried Enrico still reading the menu.

He sipped from his pint of beer and brushed off the creamy top left on his lips.

'No, silly.' commented Viviane sipping her glass of wine. 'It is a savoury mix of eggs and flour made in a particular round shape.'

'It goes well with the roast meat and its juices.' added Dr Watkins.

'Oh, I see! So, the Brits do have bread with food after all?'

'Sort of.' answered Dr Watkins with an amused look.

Enrico was new to the local customs and was still discovering new things day by day. He could not have had better guides.

'Whatever!' said Viviane giving Enrico the brush-off. 'I'm still waiting for the day you will take me to eat at Geppetto's!'

'Dream on. Why would I let you betray your cuisine?' said Enrico.

Enrico enjoyed pulling Viviane's leg from time to time, even though he was serious; he would never place foot in that stereotypical Italian establishment. It just did not make sense.

The Sunday roasts arrived shortly after. In between avid bites and gulps of beer, Enrico did not waste time in bringing up recent events and sharing his experience in the tunnel earlier that day. Dr Watkins listened attentively without interrupting. Viviane could see from the corner of her eye the curator was restraining himself from jumping up and down with excitement about historical, Wimbledonian discoveries.

'Interesting, Enrico!' he finally exclaimed once the baker had shared his worries. 'As curator of the Wimbledon Museum, I can already tell you tunnels are not something new on Wimbledon hill. Many have been found below over the last few decades, either when digging foundations for new houses or knocking down old buildings. The area around Saint Mary's Church has probably the highest number of tunnels since it is where Wimbledon Village has its origins.

'Have you explored them all?' asked Enrico.

'Exploring is a big word. I was not personally involved but I catalogued pictures and reports. Most of the tunnels were in a poor condition when discovered and have collapsed over time. Some carried on for quite a few miles before leading to dead ends.

'And the reason they exist?'

'I will spare you any wild run of imagination. You said the tunnel had walls made of brick and stone?'

Enrico nodded reminiscing those minutes in the dark tunnel. The sound of water trickling, the echoes from Rosie's cries, the debris on the floor.

'This is no surprise.' continued Dr Watkins. 'The tunnels have been built and used by different people over the centuries. The purpose though never changed. The Lord of the Manor, when he used to reside in his manor house in Wimbledon, relied on underground passages to allow servants to reach different areas of the estate without having to go through the front door during official events or across the lawn at night. It was common practice to have a network of tunnels built under castles or palaces, especially from the Middles Ages onwards. They were renovated during the Georgian and Victorian periods and this explains why sometimes we ended up with botched-up architecture. Like Saint Mary's, where a fourth is medieval, one is Victorian, one is Georgian, and one is Anglo-Saxon. In the end, these tunnels don't lead to secret treasure rooms if this is what you are after.'

'Where are these tunnels exactly?' asked Enrico.

'I think two or three run below or near Saint Mary's. One goes down to Wimbledon Park if I am not mistaken. Entrances have been found in a dried-up well in Arthur Road, in the basement of houses between St Mary's Road and Leopold Road. Their sites have been covered up by new house builds for many years now.'

'Here you are, Enrico.' remarked Viviane eating a small potato in one go. 'It all leads to a dead end.'

Enrico paused.

'Nothing starting from the cemetery?'

'You probably stumbled upon a section of the tunnels Dr Watkins just mentioned.' Viviane tried to explain while busy mopping the gravy from her plate.

'And the water?' insisted Enrico.

'Wimbledon hill lies on a water spring well protected under its clay soil.' answered Dr Watkins calmly. 'I don't expect things to be totally dry down there. What are you getting at Enrico?'

'The body, Dr Watkins. How did it get there?'

Dr Watkins paused before picking up a slice of beef. He then leaned back and shrugged.

'Enrico, I don't have the answer to that, but you'd better leave it to the police. Occam's razor principle teaches us to accept the most obvious of explanations.'

'See?' exclaimed Viviane triumphantly. 'There is nothing weird about the whole thing.'

She pointed her fork at Enrico to make sure her point had been proven.

'Didn't you say this at Cannizaro Park too?' challenged Enrico.

Viviane gave him a look of contempt. She made it clear there was no point answering or even comparing. Dr Watkins kept eating his roast while chuckling to himself in between mouthfuls.

'Come on!' insisted the Italian baker raising his hands in the air in frustration.

He almost knocked his glass and cutlery off the table. The gesture did not go unnoticed across the room.

'So, plans for the week?' led on Viviane returning to her plate and glass of wine.

For her the discussion was closed. Enrico sulked and mumbled something.

'How's the museum going, Dr Watkins?' she carried on, taking the lead on the conversation and ignoring Enrico's mood.

'Same old, same old. Not a lot of visitors, as per usual.'

'How about the black azalea? And the diary we found? Didn't that attract some attention?'

'Not as much as you'd expect.' shrugged the curator. 'We had the few presentations. We even had someone from the Trust attending. Slim pickings though.'

'Did you hear from the British Museum?' asked Viviane, recalling Dr Watkins's plan to make their discovery in Cannizaro Park known to the most notorious archaeological establishment in Britain.

Dr Watkins sighed recognising he was the bearer of not-so-good news once again.

'Well, as much as I love Wimbledon, a lava rock cannot beat the Egyptian mummies or the Greek classical statues of the British Museum. They have not returned my calls or my emails apart from a weak promise to get back to me at some point in the future.'

'What a pity!' spoke Viviane sharing her disappointment with the curator.

Dr Watkins nodded and yawned, quick enough to politely cover his mouth.

'Pardon me!' he apologised

'Tired?' asked Enrico.

'My sleep is a bit rough lately. Between the WAIS meetings and helping with the fairs, I find myself restless at nights sometimes.'

'Insomnia?' asked Viviane, worried.

'Not at all, fortunately. Every once in a while, though, my nights are filled with dreams and nightmares of all kinds. Do you remember the Hilary Wilson's diary we found in Cannizaro Park, where she said she could not sleep? Sometimes I feel like her, waking up in the middle of the night for no given reason. Those dreams and nightmares just knock me out the morning after.'

'Don't tell me you believe that story of hers around the Black Azalea and her sleepless nights!' Enrico laughed out loud.

'Of course not. I am a man of historical facts!'

'Then listen to me, Dr Watkins!' exclaimed Enrico and leaning closer to share a wise tip. 'Take it easy and remember to always pursue la *dolce vita*!'.

The curator could not help himself giggling at the refreshing joviality of the Italian baker.

'I will. I will.'

The lunch came to an end. The pub still buzzing with people and excitement, making everyone forget what time it was. Dr Watkins was the first to leave the moment he put his cutlery across his plate.

'Leaving so soon?' said Enrico.

'Being the WAIS chairman and the curator of the Wimbledon Museum brings its duties and responsibilities. I'd better enjoy the rest of today and get some rest before another week starts.'

The curator bid farewell to both Enrico and Viviane. On his way out, he had to stop at one table to greet what could have been an old-time friend or maybe a WAIS acquaintance. His blue navy jacket and silver hair were instantly recognisable across the pub. Probably, most people inside the Dog and Fox knew who he was and had known him for years. The Italian baker wished he could reach that status one day.

A young lady came to pick up their plates and left a copy of the dessert menu on their table. Viviane could not help noticing Enrico had not touched his last bits of roast lunch. She felt Enrico's brain at work like a buzz in her head.

'Hey, *ragazzo curioso*!' called out Viviane the way she knew Enrico's grandma called him. 'What on earth are you thinking?'

The Italian baker pulled a smile and leaned back. He put an elbow on the back of his chair and stroked his belly, fully satisfied with the meal. He was now looking out onto Wimbledon High Street, watching the Sunday strollers going up and down. Families, couples, children.

'It must have been terrible for that child, Rosie, to see that disfigured body.' he said.

'It does not happen every day.' commented Viviane.

'Precisely!'

Enrico was quick to get his assumptions confirmed.

'What are you trying to say?'

'Nothing…' shrugged Enrico.

'I wonder how her parents feel.' carried on Viviane. 'I know the mother well. She comes to my shop often to pick flowers for their front garden and we always have a nice chat.'

Enrico pricked his ears.

'Are you on good terms?' he asked. 'I mean, with the mother.'

'Yes. I'd like to think so.'

'Then perhaps you should go and visit her and her daughter. They are at Parkside Hospital, aren't they?'

The Italian baker returned Viviane's gaze. Viviane held her glass of wine a sip away from her lips. She hesitated on what to answer. Something in

Enrico's attitude made her doubt about his real intentions, although she did not question Enrico's kindness.

'Yes, they are at Parkside. What are you saying, Enrico?' asked Viviane, puzzled now that the focus of the discussion had turned to Rosie's mother.'

'Let's go this afternoon!' exclaimed Enrico. 'Make sure they are ok. Bring them a nice bouquet of flowers.'

'Actually, I was thinking of paying a visit.' said Viviane.

'That is a brilliant idea!' exclaimed Enrico with a knowing smile.

Viviane was about to finish her wine, but she stopped again and narrowed her eyes at Enrico. She then realised what he was up to. The Italian baker may have been big hearted, but his kindness always came with an insatiable curiosity.

'You are really not letting this go!' she challenged him. 'You want me to ask Rosie who or what she really saw down there, don't you?'

Enrico did not say anything and simply gave her wink.

Viviane lit a cigarette nervously. Her one bad habit, her lone pleasure. She massaged her temples and fiddled once more with the flower bouquet to buy some time. While listening to Enrico, she leaned on her yellow Fiat 500 and looked at the main doors of Parkside Hospital opening and closing. She simply looked for the right words to say once she went inside to greet and comfort Rosie and her parents.

She adjusted her pulled-up auburn hair and rearranged, for a fifth time, the mixed bouquet of flowers she had put together hastily in the back of her flower shop. She had been a florist for many years now and she was able to pick the right combination and the right colours very quickly to reflect each occasion, whether it was for a happy and glorious moment, or perhaps a more sombre one. She was as proud of her work as Enrico was of his. She did not feed the world with bread, but she brought colour and joy with flowers.

She simply could not say 'no' to Enrico. His idea of bringing flowers to Rosie and her parents was indeed a good idea, especially after what the little girl had been through. Maybe Enrico's real intentions made her feel she was betraying them. He was convinced there was more to the disfigured body than everyone led to believe, and Rosie may have some answers. In the end, she felt obliged to help him. Ever since her first encounter with Enrico, she had felt she was coming closer to him as a friend.

'Are you ready?' repeated Enrico, standing in front of her.

'If you are in such a rush, why don't you go in there on your own?'

'You know what happened last time I went in on my own…'

'Well, this time we are not getting into trouble, are we?' she replied giving Enrico a reprimanding look. 'This is a hospital visit. Pure and simple.'

Enrico grunted. He put his hands deep inside his trouser pockets and shivered. Viviane could tell he was feeling a little chilly in his usual white chef jacket

'Don't you ever take that off?' she commented in self-amusement.

'Why should I? It is a trademark, no?' said Enrico.

Viviane coughed as she heard those words. The cigarette smoke caught her throat and disturbed her thoughts. She put out the half-smoked cigarette against a nearby bin and then threw it away, reminding herself she would quit someday. She then glanced at herself in one of the rear-view mirrors. Her skinny trousers wrapped her skinny legs into a nice slender shape up to her waist as it blossomed finally in her flowery blouse. Another touch at her hair and then she took a deep breath before making a move towards the hospital. She was ready.

The two walked into the reception. A soothing calm seemed to reign inside. They approached the reception desk, nonchalant. The nurse looked up as Viviane announced their arrival.

'Hi! My name is Viviane Leighwood. This is Enrico LoTrova. We are friends of Fanny Rutherford. I was not sure whether her daughter, Rosie Rutherford, had been discharged already.'

'Not until tomorrow, I believe, but doctors said she is doing much better already.'

'Is it still visiting times? We wanted to give these flowers.'

'Visiting times are still open. If you could sign here, please.'

Viviane and Enrico took turns to fill in their names. The nurse kept a close eye on Enrico, which made him uncomfortable.

'Aren't you the baker of *The Wynnman*?' the nurse said later, when taking back the forms.

'Yes…' hesitated Enrico, hoping this did not mean trouble.

'Oh, I love your bread and pastries. They are delicious!'

Enrico exchanged looks with Viviane and let out a deep sigh of relief.

'Second floor to the right.' said the nurse pointing to the lifts beyond reception. 'There are some balloons outside the door. You can't miss them!'

Viviane and Enrico thanked her twice before heading on. The corridor on the second floor was a little busier. Nurses and doctors walking up and down, mixed with visitors in their footsteps listening attentively to experts' medical advice. A janitor passed by quickly mopping the floor. Nobody minded Viviane and her flower bouquet. She was probably the umpteenth florist to walk through those corridors bringing colour and perfume to patients stuck in sterile, white rooms. The Italian baker watched warily around him, somehow still scarred by his last visit at Parkside when Eric Quercer almost framed him. He pushed away the thought.

'There it is!' said Viviane spotting the red and yellow balloons.

They moved to the side to let a nurse pulling a trolley pass. Viviane grabbed Enrico by the arm.

'So, what now?' she asked him.

'Well…we ask Rosie what she remembers.'

'Is this your plan? You bring flowers and ask about a disfigured corpse?'

Viviane kept her voice low. The word 'corpse' could sound inappropriate when shouted out loud in hospital corridors. She could not believe what Enrico had set her up with.

'You do the talking, then.' suggested Enrico, looking at her in the eye. 'Trust me: we are not doing anything wrong. What happened in that tunnel is no ordinary crime, and it is something no child should bear to witness!'

Enrico knew he was asking a lot from Viviane and he hoped his gaze would make the florist realise that he cared for Rosie. Viviane looked at him and could sense mixed feelings swirling inside her mind like electric eels. She could not ignore the feeling of betrayal, of using people. She was not a journalist or a policeman; she had no place to enter the room and ask what Enrico wanted her to ask. She hesitated, asking herself whether she should do this because of Enrico's hunch or because Enrico was her friend. Viviane then recalled Enrico's tale of the disfigured corpse covered in a brown or purple coating. It all sounded too strange for Wimbledon.

'Fine!' she dismissed, a twinge of disapproval in her voice. 'But I cannot promise results!'

Viviane stormed off in the direction of the balloons without giving Enrico a chance to answer back. The Italian baker knew Viviane's feistiness would bite back once they were out of the hospital. He quickly followed her not saying another word.

Viviane, still fuming inside, walked towards the balloons, trying to act normal and bring back the air of tranquillity she needed to portray. She thought of moving her ear close to the door before rapping gently on it. Enrico stood a few inches behind her. Voices inside. Chatting, discussing.

She thought of waiting, although it felt awkward and even creepy to stand outside the door. She wondered how she could start the conversation; they may not give her any opportunity to ask questions. Maybe they would get suspicious of her questions. Maybe Rosie was asleep.

'Hello?' said a voice. 'Can I help you?'

Viviane and Enrico almost jumped. A man in his late forties stood next to them with a paper cup of steaming coffee. He had short hair, a little grizzled at the sides. His face was clean-shaven, but the baggy eyes showed signs of fatigue.

'He-hello!' said Viviane.

'I am Nigel, Rosie's dad.' said the man. 'Hold on! Aren't you Viviane Leighwood? From the flower shop?'

'Yes. We wanted to give these flowers to Rosie, after all she went through. If it is not a bad time, of course.'

'Oh, they are lovely.' exclaimed Nigel. 'They will definitely cheer her up. Fanny always talks about your flowers.'

Viviane had never met Rosie's father, but something told her fame preceded her. Nigel shook her hand. He then looked at Enrico.

'Wait a second! Aren't you the baker of *The Wynnman*?' Rosie's father added. 'You are the man who saved my little girl!'

'"Saved" is a bit too much, sir.' Enrico said shyly as the father shook his hand. 'I was just at the right place at the right time. Is your daughter ok?'

'Much better! Thanks for asking! But why don't you ask her yourself? She is awake. Let me take you inside so you can give the flowers to her in person!'

Viviane and Enrico thanked the father and composed themselves from the unexpected surprise. The door opened up to a brightly lit room with large windows to one side overlooking the thick foliage of treetops outside. The next-door mansions could hardly be seen. A hospital bed stood against the wall to the right. Rosie was sitting on the bed's edge facing the windows.

The little girl had a few plasters on her face, shoulder and legs, and her expression showed traces of someone who had been unwell. A woman in a grey jumper, jeans and high leather brown boots stood in front of her. She must have been the same age as the father. Her face lit up the moment she recognised Viviane.

'Viviane! What are you doing here?' said Rosie's mother.

'Fanny! Nice to see you. We just came to visit. This is Enrico.'

'Oh, you are the man who saved Rosie!' thanked Fanny.

'Please. Don't mention it!' said Enrico trying to play down his bravery.

'Look Rosie! Someone has brought you beautiful flowers!' said Nigel loudly, filled with joy.

He joined her daughter to give her a soft kiss on her head. He took an empty glass next to the bed and quickly placed the flowers inside. The daughter gave a weak smile. She did not speak, as if she would rather keep herself to herself.

'Who are they from?' asked Fanny looking at her husband and then at Viviane.

'On the house, Fanny!' Viviane replied trying not to sound too commercial. 'I was there at the fair this morning when it all happened. It must have been horrible… How are you holding up? How's Rosie?'

'Well, thank you for the thought. It was a big scare, but we are glad it is all over. Rosie, did you see the colourful flowers Viviane brought from the flower shop? What do you say?'

Little Rosie looked at Viviane and then at her mother. She seemed to wait for her cue, but someone forgot to tell her what it was. The mother prompted her with a kind nod. Rosie looked at her and Viviane, hesitantly. Viviane could tell she had had a rough experience. The florist now dreaded what she had to do next.

'T-thank you!' answered Rosie shortly after, through a broken smile. 'I like flowers.'

'Good girl!' added the mother.

'You will be fine, Rosie.' added Enrico. 'Trust me!'

The little girl smiled again shyly. Viviane cringed at Enrico's benevolent comment. She hesitated for a second. Their time would be up soon before it became inappropriate to linger for longer.

'What a shock it must have been!' repeated Viviane turning to the parents.

'It was! We also had the police in about an hour ago.' said Rosie's mother. 'They asked a few questions to Rosie. They said they are cordoning off that tunnel she fell in until they identify that man or understand what happened.'

'We got a great scare, indeed!' replied the father wrapping his arm around his wife's waist. 'But we followed doctor's orders and did all the necessary checks. The good news is the doctor confirmed there is no need to stay overnight. Time to go home soon and put this behind us. No more scary men coming from underground…'

'Nigel!' interrupted the mother.

'Oh, Fanny, what's wrong in hoping for the best?' protested the father.

'But we should not mention…'

'The scary man was in the well…' spoke Rosie out of the blue.

The couple's bickering stopped in its tracks. Enrico and Viviane watched Rosie curiously. The little girl seemed to be in a trance, uttering her words to an invisible person between Fanny and Viviane.

'Not again!' sighed Fanny, rolling her eyes.

Her tone showed signs of mortification or some sort of recurring despair, a nuisance that maybe dated back to before yesterday's events. Viviane knew there and then she could not do what Enrico had asked. She just could not do it. This family had gone through so much already. She thought it best not to get involved in personal matters.

'Maybe this is not a good time.' said Viviane to excuse herself at such delicate moment. 'We'll leave!'

'What's the matter?' said Enrico softly to Rosie, not really following Viviane's intentions.

The florist watched him carefully and gave a nervous smile to Fanny and Nigel, who looked a little dumbfounded by Enrico but seemed to trust him after what he had done for Rosie. The little girl looked at Enrico, sulking.

'It is the scary man that won't go away.' she said.

'The scary man is gone, Rosie.'

'But he will come back…'

'…and the police will catch him so he can no longer hurt you!' reassured Enrico.

The Italian baker smiled to give her a little courage. He then exchanged a glance with her father and they both knew it was best to give the little girl and his mother some space. Nigel offered to walk them out of the room. Fanny stayed behind, saying goodbye to Viviane and thanking Enrico again for his bravery. She then returned her attention to Rosie, caressing her daughter's hair and looking into her small weary eyes. She muttered words of reassurance to her as if casting away nightmares. Viviane saw Rosie smiling once more and hugging her mother before the door closed behind them.

'Sorry about that!' said Nigel once outside, back in the bustling hospital corridor. 'It has been a few rough months for us.'

'Is Rosie alright?' asked Viviane showing real concern.

'Yes, she is. Just worried about her cuts and bruises.' he replied.

Nigel hung his head low and spoke as if he had a burden he wanted to get off his shoulder.

'Everything ok at home?' asked Enrico, squeezing his hand on Nigel's shoulder.

'You are both very kind!' sighed Nigel lifting his head up and looking at Viviane and Enrico. 'Children can be very imaginative. The reason Rosie went into that tunnel is due to a mania she has been having lately. Something about a scary man in the fake well in our basement back home. She had these nightmares about him for some time, and she thought she recognised the same man in the tunnel this morning, while still burning. Children's fantasy, eh?'

'A fake well?' echoed Enrico.

Enrico was not at all interested in people's house architecture. Instead, Dr Watkins's tales about the old tunnels under Wimbledon started to flash back. He specifically recalled something the curator had said over lunch, something about how some entrances to the tunnels were now buried under people's homes.

'Some old collapsed well we found when renovating the foundations to make our new basement.' explained Nigel. 'Sounds strange, I know. The Council told us it is normal to come across such findings in a Wimbledon house. They belong to old collapsed tunnels, apparently, and need to be checked and covered up for safety.'

'Why would Rosie think she saw a man coming out of the well?' wondered Viviane.

'We've had some workers in for a while as part of the renovations. They are quite slow, to be honest! They sealed the access to the basement for health and safety, but they tend to come and go all the time, always brining new crates or leaving because they forgot something. I would not be surprised if Rosie got a little scared of them and thought she saw their faces everywhere she went. She probably slipped in when they were working, perhaps to see what the fake well looked like. She is a curious girl!'

'I know what you mean!' commented Viviane glancing at Enrico.

The dad chuckled. It was a way of exorcising the family drama he had just left in the room.

'Well, thanks for the chat and the flowers! Let me go back and check on my girls.'

Nigel was about to say goodbye when Enrico asked the final question, pretending to be casual.

'Sorry if I ask but, where do you live in Wimbledon?'

Rosie's father smiled. He did not mind the odd question.

'Not far from Saint Mary's. 24 Arthur Road.' he replied.

Dr Watkins looked out of the window from the top floor of his house on West Side Common. Sunday was coming to a close. The pale evening sky hung over the vast space that was Rushmere Green and could see its shades of blue reflected in the flat mirror surface of Rushmere Pond. The sky was unsure whether to let night in completely or whether to allow the fading sunlight to linger a little longer.

Dr Watkins himself was unsure as well, whether to tell Viviane and Enrico more about his dreams and nightmares or whether to leave it all to a good night's sleep. The curator sat on his armchair under the golden hue of a tall lamp. The radio played a few chilling tunes in the background. The steam from his cup of tea coiled lazily towards the ceiling. He enjoyed the tranquillity and solitude of his humble abode, especially after the dramatic events at Saint Mary's Church. The event had shaken him a bit, and hearing some of the ghastly details from Enrico had left him stunned. He wondered what the local papers would say tomorrow. Wimbledon was not ready for such gruesome headlines. He dreaded what members of the WAIS would say.

Tunnels. Tunnels. The story of the old tunnels running under Wimbledon Hill had stimulated the curator's grey matter. He could not recall the last time there had been an update or a discussion. He pulled himself up and went to check his bookshelves. One book in particular reminded him what he and the museum records had known all long. 1948; when the first surveys were run to map the extent of the tunnels and confirm their existence. 1972; the year when the works for building Park House Middle School near Vineyard Hill had to be interrupted because of a tunnel crossing the space where they had planned to build the foundations. 1984; when a speleological society explored the tunnels to great length only to find many passages blocked as far as Wimbledon Park to the north-east and Lake Road to the east. Since then, the tunnels had been hardly mentioned in local news, historical essays, or museum exhibitions. There was simply no reason to discuss or challenge their existence. Dr Watkins suddenly felt drawn to them. A forgotten admiration somehow came back to life; one the curator could not explain or was merely his excitement for history.

He yawned. His eyes felt heavy in the diffused light of his bedroom. The excitement, or maybe the shock, was too much. The claws of sleep were ready to snatch him from reality. He put his book down and sat on his bed, rubbing his eyes and yawning even more. He watched with one eye closed the cup of tea by the armchair across the room. The steam was still rising to the ceiling, thickening like magical clouds, swirling into many shapes, now evaporating across the room. Dr Watkins was not sure whether he was awake or asleep. It was as if a fog was wrapping around him, and the furniture in his bedroom became the ghost of its former self. He could feel the bed under his fingers, but he could no longer see it clearly. The armchair, the tall lamp, the cup of tea, the books, they were all gone, sinking inside the fog. The quietness of the room evaporated as well, replaced by the sound of a rushing river. Dr Watkins looked down and he found himself in a long corridor, dark, made of bricks, with crimson water flowing under his feet, and then rising up to his ankles, cold to the touch. His eyes knew it was a dream, or worse, a nightmare. The curator though felt powerless. He looked up and down the corridor, and the more he did so, the darker the corridor appeared to be. It was an underground tunnel. A voice echoed deep in one direction. Dr Watkins wondered if that was Rosie's voice, the same way Enrico had heard it. The voice though was deep, hollow. Power. Revenge. The voice kept repeating these two words. Dr Watkins tended his ears; he then felt his legs go colder. The crimson liquid, darker, thicker, was rising to his waist. He tried to move forward, but the liquid slowed him down, and no matter how far he walked, the corridor never seemed to reach an exit. The crimson ooze rose up further; it wrapped around his chest, his neck, and touched the tip of his chin. Dr Watkins lifted his head, trying to stay afloat, trying to breathe, telling himself it was another of those nightmares. Power. Revenge. The deep, hollow voice continued calling out to him. The curator could still hear the voice when the crimson ooze swallowed him. Power. Revenge.

The evening came along, bringing dark clouds and a fine drizzle. The streets emptied as people rushed home and a random car passed through the quiet residential area every now and then. The breeze from the afternoon was blowing stronger. It made the trees quiver, almost a lament of solitude to the almost abandoned neighbourhoods. The High Street was the only bustling place alive. The blaring car horns, the bus headlights, the bright shop windows, the chatty pubs. Away from it, through the side streets of Wimbledon Village, between the lit-up windows of residential homes, all was quiet, bred in constant solitude. It was as if the buzz from the High Street was a product of his imagination. A dream left behind on the way home.

The old-style black saloon car passed unseen from the back roads of Wimbledon Hill, through Bathgate Road and Burghley Road, and it sped quickly down Church Road before entering a private road lined by trees on each side. The driver carefully slowed once the tyres hit the wet gravel, keeping the sound to a minimum as his passenger had instructed. The tiny drops on the recently polished surface glinted in the early evening light. The driver was nervous, all his earlier car polishing had been for nothing. The driveway led to a large black iron gate. It opened automatically with the pressing of a button from the driver's key holder. The lines of trees came to an end followed by a high hedgerow with scattered trees along what was the southern tip of the property border. The gravel driveway expanded to a larger, round space with a statue in the middle. It was large enough for more than one or two cars to manoeuvre and park. The black saloon car pushed on until the large mansion known as the Old Rectory came into view to the right. The mansion had no lights and was silent with its solid and ancient stance. The dark sloping roofs, the short battlements across the middle section, and a low turret to one side, gave the house a hint of medieval times in the dark of the early evening.

The car came to a stop outside the main oak door entrance. Nobody opened the door to welcome the arrival. The mansion appeared to be vacant. The driver got out of the car carrying an umbrella and opened the backdoor to let his passenger out without getting wet. He wore heavy black cowboy boots and a large black overcoat. The leather gloves and the stick gave him a noble air and the same could be said because of his stiff upright posture and tall, head-high figure. The driver was a bit shorter and struggled to keep the umbrella high enough to avoid discomfort. And the fact his passenger wore a black top hat as well did not help.

'We are here, sir. Let me walk you inside.' announced the driver.

His tone was servile and apologetic for the poor weather conditions he knew he could not control. The passenger did not say a word and grabbed his overcoat to protect himself from the light wind blowing over the hedgerow behind him. They both walked on the crunching gravel and walked up the few wide steps to the main door. The driver opened the door and let his passenger in while he traced back his steps to lock the car. He knew well his passenger was not in a good mood. He could sense Lord Awlthorp's disapproval, his hate, just by listening to his deep breathing in the car, without uttering one single word. He could sense it in the sound of his stick hitting the gravel like a pickaxe and then his heavy steps up to the mansion like a small hammer constantly beating a bell.

The inside of the Old Rectory was cold. Despite its name, it looked like any ordinary large dwelling handed down from private owner to private owner over the decades. Lord Awlthorp shivered and flicked the switch and all the lights in the entry hall lit up. From the high ceiling the chandelier with electric light bulbs shone the most and made him thank modernity for not relying on old fashioned candles. The dark ebony from the wooden wall panels and the central staircase reflected a warm glow as if radiating with its own light and heat. It suddenly brought the idea of warmth back into the empty house. The man in black called the driver behind him to get the heaters going, cursing the fact they had not been turned on already. The driver quickly disappeared into one of the back rooms on the ground floor.

'Are you here?' Lord Awlthorp called out.

He looked towards the drawing room, adjacent to the entrance hall. The interior French oak doors were wide open but the light from the hall only carved a few feet inside the semi-darkness. The man in black could barely take in the shape of armchairs, vases and paintings. One shape stood out more than the others. He knew it was there. He could feel it moving, shaking, panting.

'Answer when I call.' repeated Lord Awlthorp with a stern and malign tone.

The shape moved and then a short man in dusty overalls came out of the darkness. He still did not answer but nodded trembling, maybe because of the cold or more probably for fear of the man in black in front of him. Lord Awlthorp looked at him for a while until the silence started to become eerie, unbearable. The short man could feel the guilt gripping his insides, tearing them apart. He expected the worse.

From the back of the house, the sound of doors and cabinets being slammed shut echoed one after the other through the house and then a spine-chilling gurgle followed from within the walls confirming the heating had been turned on. Suddenly, all the lights on the ground floor turned on at once, scaring the daylights out of the short man as if the lights pointed at him like accusing fingers. He felt his heart jump when the driver showed up out of nowhere right behind him. He met the driver's impassive look, and felt like a prey caught in a trap, ready to be eaten alive. He knew the man in black and the driver came here to judge him and trial him for the serious glitch in the plan.

For a moment he thought the driver would stab him in the back. The driver then looked away, ignoring him, and moved past him to re-join his master. Lord Awlthorp chuckled. A sinister chuckle that could fool anyone into believing the storm had passed. He took his top hat off gently and then did the same with his overcoat before handing it all to the driver. His face was mature but strong and powerful, with defined jawbones and a well-shaped nose. His corvine eyebrows cast a game of shadows across his serious, almost indignant, expression. Two deep black eyes watched attentively, almost without blinking. His short and curly corvine hair was slicked back and only streaks of white and greyish hair running back from above his forehead broke the dark spell against his olive-like complexion. He wore a black suit and a grey shirt with a black tie. The whole image did not instil faith in the short man who was unsure what to expect next. He knew they had done what they could; they had tried their best.

'Mr…' mumbled the short man.

The lord shook his head and closed his eyes, incapable of bearing the insolence. He frowned and then looked somewhere to the side of the hall.

He took his eyes off the short man, who kept still, and then clicked his fingers at the driver.

'Turn that off!' he ordered.

The driver moved across the hall and the short man heard a metallic clang before he saw the driver return to his position. He held a cog in his hand, the one he had just stripped from an old baroque clock hung on a wall. Lord Awlthorp hated the ticking of time. The ticking noise of clocks and watches, the imperceptible sound of time passing, annoyed him greatly. He had removed all cogs from all clocks in his house so that they did not tick. He expected the same here in the mansion.

'Could you please tell me, Mr Claymore, why that clock was ticking?' admonished Lord Awlthorp speaking to the short man. 'They should all be off here.'

He pointed to the place where he previously asked the driver to intervene and turn off the ticking sound.

'It goes without saying I don't want to hear a single one again.' he added.

'I can't...keep track of time when we are...down in the...' stammered the short man.

The man in black slammed his stick on the floor, interrupting whatever excuse Mr Claymore was planning to give.

'Mr Claymore, what happened to good manners, eh?' resumed the man in black. 'Last time I checked, you and your brother were hired to complete the experiment as per my instructions. Isn't that the case?'

The short man hesitated.

'Well...Mr...'

'How dare you?' cried out Lord Awlthorp slamming his stick on the floor. 'I am not "Mr" to you, Mr Claymore. It is "Lord".'

'Sorry...' said Mr Claymore.

Toby Claymore was not used to manners or polite conversation. He was a chemist-turned-criminal who all his life had dealt with low-life drug lords and second-rate bombers. A mercenary at the service of uncouth, uncultivated criminals who did not understand anything of the magic he and his brother Henry had made. Yet, this man dressed in black, this Lord Awlthorp, was different. The way he looked, the way he spoke, the way he even talked about the subject. He made them feel like rookies who had no idea what they were doing. Lord Awlthorp's strange behaviour around clocks was also hard to live with. Toby could not grasp how he and his brother could run an experiment without knowing the time. There was no sunlight down there.

'And please ensure the place is warmed up before I arrive.' added Lord Awlthorp. 'Keeping you here at my expense is not a problem for me as long as you get the job done unnoticed. My problem is when I get a call at my house and I have to come over here to fix your mess. Which part of 'get the job done' and 'unnoticed' do you not understand, Mr Claymore?'

Toby Claymore did not know where Lord Awlthorp lived; he did not know much about the man who dressed void of colours. Before he and his brother Henry were approached by his henchman, the soldier-looking type called Reginald, they had never heard, seen or met Lord Awlthorp. Henry, though, who had always been the smart boy of the family, said it would be the job of a lifetime and convinced him they should accept Lord Awlthorp's offer. Until today, Henry had been the one dealing with Reginald and on occasions Lord Awlthorp. Now, it was Toby's turn to lead the conversation. Before he could even speak or explain, he already felt inferior. A dim-witted peasant before the aristocratic criminal that Lord Awlthorp appeared to be.

'Complications, Mr…erm, sir!' replied Toby carefully not to feed the lord's anger. 'It is true we had to stop a few weeks ago. Workers came in to do work on the mansion unexpectedly. We stayed low in the basement as instructed but we could not run the last phase of the experiment without making noise until it was safe to resume. Henry and I made further progress last week.'

Toby Claymore had always thought the mansion he and his brother were using for the experiment was the property of Lord Awlthorp but apparently it was not. He was not really sure who owned it; or who actually sent builders in from time to time to fix the roof, decorate the rooms, replant the garden. It made no sense to them why this house had been chosen for the weird experiment the Claymore brothers had been commissioned to carry out. However, the pay on completion of the job was a figure they had never dreamed of, so if they had to hide and work in the basement to get it done, so be it. It was worth the hassle. Until what happened a few days ago.

'We managed to run the last experiment. However, Henry suffered severe burns. You didn't say the mix would come out like it did!'

'What was the outcome of the experiment?' interrupted Lord Awlthorp.

Toby widened his eyes in disbelief and felt his lips quiver. The emotions ran fresh in his mind at the last image of his brother, just before he went beyond recognition. Before he could no longer recognise him. He swallowed hard and tried his best to push down the loathing he had started to feel towards Lord Awlthorp and his goons.

'The liquid...' stammered Toby holding himself together. 'The liquid...maintained its consistency. It was stable for longer. Until it all went out of control...'

'Stable? Did you say "stable"?'

'Y-yes...' confirmed Toby with the little courage he had in front of the man in black's inspecting eyes.

'Well, this is a step forward, Mr Claymore.' exclaimed Lord Awlthorp. 'Your formulas never came one inch close to "stable". We can say this last experiment yielded very good results. Wouldn't you agree?

'Yes...sir. A step... forward... but... Henry though came too close to the liquid and he...suffered...severe burning...'

Toby tried to stick to the script. He knew it was more than just burns.

'Henry is dead…' he quickly added although he was sure Lord Awlthorp knew this already.

The man in black did not bat an eyelid. He was not concerned about loss of life. He moved slowly towards Toby.

'I know.' said Lord Awlthorp calmly. 'I heard about the incident from my driver the moment you called him. But we also heard it from the police. Nasty work, Mr Claymore. Careless upmost. It will be taken care of. You will take care of it!'

A knock came from the main entrance. The driver went to open the large door and the burly figure of Reginald Bosham appeared at the threshold.

'You are late, Reggie!' said Lord Awlthorp holding his gaze for a second before returning to grill Toby Claymore with his threatening glance.

Reginald hated the nickname.

'Don't call me Reggie!' he moaned. 'I was following protocol. We must never come to this fancy house at the same time, as you clearly instructed.'

He then turned his attention to Toby Claymore.

'What has this idiot done?'

Reginald Bosham was a man of few words. The strong, square-shouldered man spoke only if spoken to or if he had to give orders. He was mainly a man of action. His muscled arms and heavy jaw had tensed the moment he saw Toby Claymore. After receiving the alert via text, he knew something bad had happened. He was now cracking his knuckles. His massive figure and shaved head looked brutal and could have intimated anyone unfortunate to cross his path.

He gave Toby a despising look. Reginald took every opportunity to make Toby feel inferior. He knew the Claymores were smart people, especially the older brother Henry, and he did not like that. He had been reminding them all along that they answered to Lord Awlthorp and him. They were not equals, not even in the criminal world.

'Where is Henry?' Reginald asked, having not heard the news yet.

The atmosphere in the entrance hall was cold, colder than it had ever been, despite the heaters being on for once.

'He is dead, Reggie.' said Lord Awlthorp, curt and heartless.

'What?' exclaimed Reginald. 'And where is the body now?'

'Yes, Toby. Where is the body now?' repeated the man in black.

Lord Awlthorp played along. He knew already the answer, based on police reports filling the air waves earlier that day. He wanted to hear it from Toby's lips. He could see the short man fiddling with his hands, lost for words.

'I don't know…' said Toby.

'What do you mean you don't…' interjected Reginald.

Lord Awlthorp raised his gloved hand asking Reginald to stay calm.

'What do you mean Toby you don't know?' the man in black repeated with a fake, sinister calm that made Toby's blood curdle.

Toby felt exposed. Lord Awlthorp was one step ahead. He knew Toby was not telling the whole story.

'Henry was too close to the pool… The liquid burnt him…'

Toby let it all out in one breath. Emotions running wild.

'I did not know what to do… I tried to pull my brother to safety…'

'Speak properly, you retard!' cried out Reginald impatiently.

'Enough!' spoke out Lord Awlthorp.

'I swear, if you and your brother…' insisted Reginald.

'Enough!' shouted again the man in black slamming the stick down, short of Toby Claymore's feet.

His eyes glinted with wickedness as he glared at Reginald. His face and muscles clenched, and then relaxed. He could not get rid of Toby Claymore as of yet. He had to first find out what they had done and what had happened. The experiment was all that mattered since its results would help him complete the second test. The stakes were high, and they could not take the chance and simply ignore Toby's puzzling statements. What the short man said intrigued him. The liquid was stable, although he could not explain how the brothers had done it. Henry Claymore probably was a step closer to the breakthrough he was expecting. Lord Awlthorp trusted Henry more than Toby, being the brains of the two. Yet, Lord Awlthorp knew someone smarter than him could still bring trouble. He had to find out what had happened. With Henry gone now, there was little chance Toby could step into his older brother's shoes. He knew he would have to pick up the pieces at some point. The man in black retracted the stick and resumed his smooth talk.

'I need to see this for myself, what this babbling idiot is saying.' sneered Lord Awlthorp glancing at Reginald. 'Lead the way!'

Reginald nodded and walked over to the shiny wooden panel installed right under the stairs to the upper floors. He pulled a key out of his pocket and stuck it inside the polished wooden material with great force but without damaging it. He then turned it and the clacking of a locking mechanism echoed briefly in the silent hall. A secret door opened inward, leading into a dark passageway. What was left was a cut-out frame into the perfect wooden panel, one that would be hard to notice even if you knew of its existence.

'Are the gates to the driveway closed? Lord Awlthorp asked turning to the driver.

'Yes, sir.' nodded the driver. 'There were no building works scheduled over this weekend. We will not be disturbed but I will stay here and keep an eye.'

'Good! Now, let's go and check the basement.' ordered Lord Awlthorp, narrowing his eyes at the trembling figure of Toby Claymore.

The short man in overalls blinked a few times, unsure of what he was expected to do once in the basement. Afraid of what the man in black would say or do, he moved away from where he stood and walked to the understairs door which led to the basement. He and Reginald were the only ones with a copy of the key that would allow them in and out, and it was the only way down to where the Claymores had been stationed in secret for the last few months while the world on the surface carried on with their lives unaware.

Toby Claymore was the first one in. The passageway opened up to a spiral staircase made out of rough but solid stone. It spiralled down into infinite darkness, with no lighting. The short man took out his torch. He heard the steps of Lord Awlthorp following behind. He then saw another beam of light merge with his as Reginald joined them from the rear with his own torch. Despite the sudden brightness, the stone felt cold just by looking at it. Toby went down the stone steps. The rising warmth of the mansion stayed behind and the cold, damp settings of the basement took over once again. He could no longer stand the humidity, whether it was in the basement or in the tunnels. Lord Awlthorp had strictly forbidden them to live in the main living quarters of this large mansion, apart from the basic use of the bathroom. The Claymore brothers had therefore spent weeks away from the sunlight to get the experiment going. Toby wondered if the damp conditions or maybe the absurdity of the experiment itself had been draining his energy and his brother's, affecting their efforts, their focus, their sanity. The thing he saw did not make sense.

He thought again about what Lord Awlthorp would be expected to hear once there. He did not know what to say, where to start from. There was hardly any success to celebrate for, yet another failed experiment, and he wondered why his employer had not raised an eyebrow when it was mentioned. Both Toby and his brother had been subject to abusive words from both Reginald and Lord Awlthorp as weeks passed by with no sign of progress. This time the reaction had been milder than usual. Perhaps the fact the liquid had become stable for the first time in a hundred attempts, if only for a short period of time, was the turning point his employer had been waiting for. He knew little of what Lord Awlthorp wanted to achieve. All the man in black cared for was that they recreated the mixture made up of some sort of unknown liquid. Lord Awlthorp had originally given them a recipe he had written without any information on dosage, and Toby and Henry tried to guess the right quantities as they went along. Each time the Claymores provided feedback from one of their failed experiments, it appeared Lord Awlthorp re-invented his list of ingredients and came up with new estimated doses. Reginald came over every weekend, bringing large quantities of what was first pure ethanol, then spirits, and then cheap red wine, together with chemicals and herbal extracts of all sorts, which changed week after week. Toby could not really explain the complex formulas or even keep track of the changes. He simply executed them. These formulas were something he had never seen in his life. Henry, on the other hand, understood them and had led the way through each iteration of the same experiment up to the last one, test after test. In the last three weeks or so, the mixture had become incendiary and explosive. It scared the living daylights out of Toby, and he had warned his brother. Ultimately, the last experiment had taken Henry's life. This was no longer an ordinary job.

The basement was a little bit larger than the mansion's ground floor. It was a rectangular shape, split into sections by stone walls. Each section was filled with shelves full of dusty silverware and cobwebbed antiques. There were stacks of old furniture and chairs clustered against the wall, forsaken by whoever owned this place. The three men walked to the southern end roughly below where the mansion turret could be seen from the outside. Lord Awlthorp watched Toby carefully ahead of him, his stocky figure, his wavering steps. In the dim light of the basement Toby looked like a goblin of the underworld. Lord Awlthorp felt confident he could still hold the plan together, but he had to check the state of the experiment. The word 'stable' buzzed in his head and gave him hope. The three reached the opposite end of the basement, which had been cleared of all junk to make some space for the Claymores to work in. Toby led them in and with his feet he pushed aside some of the tools he had left in the middle of the floor. To the left, a few old bulky barrels filled one corner. Along the wall, open boxes containing full bottles and jars were neatly stacked up, while empty ones laid scattered at their feet, either standing upright or on their side. The smell of stale wine, mixed with an herbal fragrance like thyme, filled the damp air of the basement. In the middle, a rusty machine stood against the wall, still on and bleeping, its dial indicators wavering, its lights off, except for a constant bright green one. A low-pitched buzz coming from the machine rang monotonously throughout the basement. Lord Awlthorp walked past Toby to take a better view. He quickly glanced to check there was no broken glass at his feet. He then looked at the wall in front.

'Is this thing still noisy?' asked Lord Awlthorp pointing at the machine.

'I am afraid so, mister…sir!' apologised Toby.

'And is this your last batch of ingredients?' asked again the man in black pointing at the heap of boxes and barrels.

'What is left from last weekend.' interjected Reginald. 'I have the order from today in the van, ready to unload.'

Lord Awlthorp nodded, not giving away whether he was pleased or annoyed. He disliked the way the Claymores kept the area given to them to run the experiment. He looked at the dirty sleeping bags and thin mattresses in another corner, with an electric lamp, a few books and some tinned food next to them. The man in black hoped the area next door had been kept immaculate as instructed. Last time he had spotted some food and some tools lying where they should not have been.

'Take me to the chamber!' asked Lord Awlthorp.

To the right, an old beige dust sheet hung against the wall acting as a temporary door. Lord Awlthorp watched Toby walk up to it and pull it to one side, revealing a half-knocked down wall. Broken and mouldy bricks lay on the floor immediately inside what was a narrow corridor leading them to a lower ground. The corridor did not have any steps and once inside, it did not match the basement structure. Bricks became cut stones and then natural rock. The short corridor led to a small round chamber with a raised pool in the middle. The pool was roughly one metre and a half deep. The stone was smooth all round, a perfect work of stonemasonry which indicated it was man-made, but there was hardly any décor or etchings of any sort. At one point on the raised edge of the round pool a small statue stood out. It was the abstract representation of a cross or a bird, with a perfectly symmetrical shape. Its two extending arms curved at the extremities like wings and were inscribed with an odd jumble of signs, figurines and geometrical shapes. The enigmatic piece of artwork leaned slightly inwards over the pool. The basin was almost empty and only a miserable puddle of dark thick liquid lay at the bottom. The liquid was as thick and dark as molasses, but its surface shimmered with hues of crimson.

'Ouch…' swore Reginald, almost tripping over as he came last out of the corridor.

Lord Awlthorp and Toby turned around to look what happened.

'A-hem…be careful please…watch out for the cables!' called out Toby.

Reginald snorted. He had already been down to the small chamber before and he still came across more hazards on the floor. Although some camp lamps had been laid out in the corridor from the basement to the chamber, the two cables that ran from the rusty machine to the round pool were almost invisible. Black, rubber ones, with the occasional yellow rim. They were necessary for the electrical output the Claymores needed and ran all the way down into the chamber. The two cables now hung over the pool and its two plugs were laid down inside, a few inches short of the puddle of dark liquid.

'What a messy layout!' sneered Reginald, taking position to one side of the small chamber.

He pointed at the table the Claymores had laid out, full of dirty tools and glass tubes now opaque by constant use. Lord Awlthorp held back his judgement. He was checking the basin and the few dregs of its content. His eyes focused on the extremities of the two power cables.

'Are the cables meant to be in the pool?' commented the man in black.

'This is…what…Henry was testing. The spark…I think he called it.' stammered Toby trying to remember his brother's words without the pang of grievance.

Lord Awlthorp processed the information but he wanted to know more. The liquid had become stable through some sort of electrolysis. It did not mean anything useful to him, but he had to admit the ingenious mind of Henry Claymore was marvellous. Despite the chaotic setup, the man in black still recognised the Claymores were as good at chemistry as he could have wished. Still, he struggled to understand what the aim of this new version of experiment was. Lord Awlthorp knew he could not rely on Toby, the less clever brother. He had to read through the formulas himself and compare them with the last one. First though he had to ensure the loose ends from Henry Claymore's death were dealt with. This was the reason they came here in the first place.

'Now, tell me Mr Claymore!' started Lord Awlthorp moving closer to the table where Toby stood. 'How did your brother end up where the police found him?'

Toby almost choked and glanced submissively at Lord Awlthorp. The man in black was now coming directly at him.

'Henry ran the machine in the morning to do the experiment.' spoke Toby. 'The tremor shook the chamber as it always does. He then poured in the latest mixture he had prepared and threw the cables in.'

'How did he get severe burning?' interjected again Reginald.

'Do not interrupt, Reggie!' admonished Lord Awlthorp giving a shot at him.

He returned his gaze at Toby. He was keen to listen but there was no mercy in his eyes. Toby knew.

'He… he…' hesitated Toby.

Toby promised Henry not to tell.

'He hurt himself in the process. He was…too close to the basin…when the charge started…'

Lord Awlthorp had had enough of the short man's games.

'Your brother didn't hurt himself by accident.' he interrupted. 'He tried the experiment on himself, didn't he?'

Lord Awlthorp's eyes were again stern, threatening. Toby widened his eyes, struggling to find the words to explain, asking himself how Lord Awlthorp knew. The short man looked the other away, unable to deny the horrible truth and scared to cross Lord Awlthorp's evil gaze once more.

'He lowered himself into the pool? Isn't that right? Your instructions, Mr Claymore, were very clear. Collect the ingredients I gave you, find the correct order and chemical balance to recreate the mixture. Then you would call me. Nothing else. Did you disobey my instructions? Is this how Henry burnt himself up?'

The man in black knew the answer already.

'Sir, we work with chemicals on drugs, bombs, food fraud.' pleaded Toby, his lips quivering. 'But we are not scientists…'

'Enough!' said the man in black with a hand raised. 'Was the experiment ready?'

He was no longer looking at Toby. He was now staring to the pool. His eyes glinted with greed.

'I…well…'

'Was the experiment ready?'

'No! Henry thought it was and wanted to show me. He was curious to know what you were up to. I knew the ingredients were not working. They were simply not right. No matter how many bottles we poured in, none of them did the job. A useless experiment.'

The man in black grimaced at the comment. The short petty criminal in front of him was a fool not to believe in the experiment. His brother though seemed to have understood something of his plans. How Henry Claymore had found out, puzzled Lord Awlthorp greatly to the point it disturbed him. Even if the brother was now dead, Lord Awlthorp could not stand that Henry or anyone could be on the same level as him or even a step ahead of him.

'Did you take the body out of the pool?' asked Lord Awlthorp, coldly.

'No. I couldn't. Shortly after he immersed himself in the thick liquid, his whole flesh set on fire, burning him alive. Then there was another tremor, a surge of power from the machine. One I could not explain. At that point the mixture became unstable and a small blast followed that knocked me out for a bit. When I woke up, Henry was gone. I followed the drops of thick liquid he left behind… They went that way, into the tunnels… But I would not dare venture that way…'

Toby took a deep breath, overwhelmed by grief, by fear, by the unknown of what would come next. Lord Awlthorp followed Toby's trembling hand pointing at a natural opening into the rock, opposite the one they came in. The tunnels, he thought. It all made sense; this is how the police had found the burnt body earlier that day. Yet, he did not know there was another entrance, a connection to the rest of the tunnel network. He wondered how he could have missed it. The man in black left Toby and walked around the round basin towards the natural opening. Another series of lamps on the floor illuminated the narrow path leading further down. There, the structure of its walls changed once again. Moving away from the natural rock and returning to uneven stone walls and red bricks.

Lord Awlthorp stopped where the tunnel ended. He could see streaks of red blood and thick purple liquid following a trail on the floor. From the chamber, they led down here and disappeared under the wall blocking the tunnel.

'What is this?' cried out Lord Awlthorp. 'Bring, Mr Claymore here!'

Reginald grabbed the short man by the collar and pulled him behind him to join Lord Awlthorp's side. The man in black pointed at the trail with his evil gaze fixed on Toby.

'What is this?' he repeated nodding at Reginald.

The burly man squeezed Toby's shoulder hard and Toby cried out in anguish.

'A trap door! It is a trap door!' Toby shouted to let the pain stop. 'Henry and I found it recently. He used it to run away!'

'How do you open it?' asked Lord Awlthorp.

'It is blocked. I tried. There's the lever!'

Toby waved his hand frantically at the wall to show he was telling the truth. Reginald let his grip go and checked a loose brick Toby was pointing at.

'It does not budge.' noted Reginald. 'It is true there is a lever, but it no longer works. Someone must have broken off the cogs. Someone from this side of the door...'

Reginald and Lord Awlthorp eyed Toby suspiciously.

'It appears you and your brother Henry had found a way out!' confirmed Lord Awlthorp staring at the silent walls. 'Henry Claymore escaped this way, out into the tunnels, but somehow you stayed behind and blocked this exit for good. And I wonder why!'

He glanced back at the wall blocking their path.

'Even if this useless trap door here keeps people out,' added Lord Awlthorp. 'we might soon see the police wandering about out there in the tunnels.'

'That is not a good sign!' commented Reginald.

'We need to act quickly!'

Reginald nodded, knowing a new important task was ahead of him. Lord Awlthorp quickly retraced his steps back to the chamber. Reginald followed, shoving Toby in front of him. The short man walked with his head low between the two men. He felt drops of sweat forming on his forehead once more. They entered the chamber and Lord Awlthorp turned around to ask an unexpected question.

'Mr Claymore, do you need more of the ingredients to carry on the work?' he asked.

'Well…yes…but…' stammered Toby, lost for words.

'I think you have a busy schedule ahead of you. Something to prove you are not as worthless as I think you are. I want you to re-run the last experiment, the one your brother Henry ran. Re-start the setup as from today. Reginald will drop today's cargo now and you will show me what your brother Henry created. I will find out what you two have been scheming! I expect a first update tomorrow. Anything else you need, you let Reginald know. And you do not leave this house for any reason at all! Do I make myself clear?'

The man in black spoke his last comment curt and cynical. Toby swallowed hard. Lord Awlthorp was narrowing his eyes at him and over his shoulder Reginald's hard stare made the short man feel lonelier than he ever was. Before he could even explain he did not have his brother's genius, or warn how dangerous the last experiment had been, Lord Awlthorp waved his hand to him, showing his disinterest in further explanations or excuses. Their meeting was over. Toby had to re-deliver the last experiment.

Lord Awlthorp walked across the chamber, heading back to the basement. Reginald followed but took the longer route, passing close by the shying short figure of Toby Claymore. The burly man pulled out his hand, demanding Toby's copy of the key to the basement.

'I will keep a close eye on you.' Reginald leered at him. 'You are going nowhere, and if you dare run away through the tunnels, I will break your legs.'

Toby froze in hearing Reginald's threats. He handed over the key.

'Call me if anything happens. Anything.' Reginald added. 'You'd better have results in a week's time. I've had enough of coming down here!'

Lord Awlthorp and Reginald disappeared into the basement leaving the short man with the cold emptiness of the ancient chamber. Despite having spent weeks in there, there was nothing familiar or pleasant about it. There was only the smell of mystery and death.

Baynard lifted his striped red and white mug and took a large sip of his tea. Earl Grey with a dash of milk for breakfast, as always. He disliked it pale or too milky and would always politely send it back if it wasn't to his liking. His half-eaten bacon sarnie lay sadly on one side on the desk. He was not very hungry today. He did not quite see the point of having either breakfast or lunch today when there was far more important work to do.

The morning traffic drove by inconspicuously on Alexandra Road, after the Monday rush hour madness, and anything visible from Baynard's office window hardly caught his attention until heavy drops of rain started to hit the bus stop cover in the street below and reminded him he had forgotten his umbrella again. As always.

Jeremy had been able to get a preliminary report on the autopsy, which had landed on his desk first thing that morning and Baynard had the pleasure of being the first to look through it. He was still scratching his head about it by the time he had taken his first bite of the bacon sarnie he had bought. The lab confirmed the third degree burns across the body which had degenerated into a complete burn-out of all tissue and most of the superficial flesh. The theory of blood covering the body was also confirmed as true with an odd twist he did not expect, nor accept. The victim was a man in his late twenties or early thirties. Before suffering the burns, he had been immerged in blood mixed with what the lab described as high levels of ethanol. Alcohol, and in high doses. Baynard humoured himself that the dead man had probably dipped himself in one of the vats at Wimbledon Brewmeister, the local brewery, rather than having one last drink at the pub before his death. A sick joke he should probably keep to himself, especially in what was going to be an odd case, whether it be suicide or homicide. The forensic expert needed more time to determine the exact time of death. Baynard though wanted to act fast. For the safety of Wimbledon, he needed to be sure whether he was dealing with dead bodies from a distant past or something more recent. The response did not please him. The burnt man's body was surely not older than a few days, but they could not be more certain until forensics came through. The body had had time to cool down and create the coagulated crimson mass that had made it unrecognisable.

In the end Baynard was left with more questions than answers. After checking missing person enquiries and even the last cold cases in arson, he felt his morning was going to be wasted. Wimbledon, and especially the village, had never witnessed macabre murders or devilish crimes. He rubbed his eyes a little. He felt rather tired after a bad night's sleep. The call from the Chief Superintendent the evening before had come out of the blue and left him worried. The Chief's words still rang over and over in his head. His role and skills had been questioned, and higher ranks had doubts he could handle another scandal in Wimbledon Village after the Cannizaro Park explosion. Baynard reassured him he would not make the same mistakes again. Ever since that Machiavellian affair at Cannizaro Park, the inspector had put his teams in line not to take the idyllic quietness of Wimbledon for granted. He thought he would reach retirement with modest robberies and parking fines. Now, with a burnt body found in a secret tunnel under one of the key churches in the area, that dream of retirement was fading by the minute.

The voice of Sergeant Jeremy brought him back to the office scene in front of him.

'Inspector Baynard?' called out the sergeant waving his hand from the opposite of Baynard's desk.

'What is it?' replied the inspector.

Baynard's mood was more on edge. Sergeant Jeremy had prepared himself before interrupting the inspector's train of thoughts. He knew how to handle Baynard.

'We finally have a positive ID, inspector.' announced Jeremy, his proud grin shining below his well-combed ginger hair.

'About time!' cried out Inspector Baynard with a morbid sense of joy.

The inspector pushed his half-eaten sandwich to the side, put his elbows on the desk and devoted his full attention to what he was about to hear. He hoped for a new lead to follow, to determine what had been happening around Saint Mary's Church.

'The burnt man is Henry Claymore.' explained Jeremy. 'Previous offender but we have lost track of him in the last year or so. He usually works with his brother Toby. They have been in and out of jail since they were teens.'

'What have they been in for?' asked Baynard.

'Henry Claymore has a degree in chemistry and used his services in the criminal underworld for bomb-making, drugs, and even food fraud. His brother Toby has no higher education. They both always worked together. Do you remember that blackmail case in Hackney a few years back?'

'Was that them?'

Baynard stroked his silver goatee and raised an eyebrow. The Claymores were the same crooks who had been able to install an irritant agent in some chocolate bars and even sell explosive washing powder at a local store in Hackney to force them to pay protection money to a local gang. Questions filled Baynard's mind and he was waiting to jump on the right one to follow up with.

'What was this Henry Claymore doing in Wimbledon? Do we have evidence of his latest activities?'

'Not much, inspector. They seemed to have disappeared, gone underground. We have an address in West London, but it hasn't been lived in for months.'

Baynard's thoughts deepened and his eyes narrowed.

'Do we have photos of the Claymores at least?'

'Not recent ones but yes we do.'

'OK. Share those internally and ask all police constables to keep their eyes open for the living brother. Send me a copy too. We need to find Toby Claymore.'

'What makes you think he is in Wimbledon?'

'You said they worked together. Assuming he knows his brother is dead, and that he was found here in Wimbledon, he may re-surface nearby.'

'Are you thinking of announcing whose body we found? Tell local press a criminal like Henry Claymore was found underground?'

Jeremy played the soft card to remind Baynard about how delicate the issue could be and how it could look to the public.

'No, not yet. But if we need to throw a bait, we may need to.'

Jeremy bit his lip. Finding Henry's body in the bizarre and cruel state it was, reminded him how the police image in Wimbledon had been close to a PR disaster when the Cannizaro Park explosion took place.

'What next, inspector?'

'I need to think. Questioning the child, Rosie, and her parents did not give much to go on. Not sure they will have more to say. There was the baker…'

'Ah, Mr LoTrova. He was the hero of the day!'

'Whatever.'

Baynard could not deny the fact the baker had saved the child Rosie. Strange how he had appeared on the crime scene again as a witness. If it were not for the lack of evidence, he would have started to have crazy ideas that he was involved or knew something. He simply hated the coincidence.

'Anything else we need to worry about?' asked the inspector moving on to facts.

Jeremy hesitated.

'I have a lady downstairs who wants to speak to you.' said the sergeant.

'A lady?'

'Mrs Biggins.'

'Oh no, no, no. I do not have time to chase butterflies or ghosts.'

'She asked for you, Inspector Baynard. She came yesterday already.'

'She comes every day now? For the same thing?'

'Yes. Tremors. She said she heard them all weekend. Yesterday was stronger than usual, in the morning, and strangely she heard them today too. Again, little stronger than usual.'

'Aren't they doing restoration works at the Old Rectory?'

'That is what I thought could be the cause, but she wants to be certain and she wants to speak to you.'

'Tell her we will send someone to her house.'

'I already did that…'

'And?'

Baynard looked at Jeremy. The sergeant sighed and widened his eyes at the inspector, hinting at what he knew he had to do. The lady needed reassurance and they were Wimbledon Police. The inspector understood the subtle message.

'Okay. Okay.' surrendered Baynard. 'Let me go in the afternoon. I will pay a visit. Rectory Orchard, correct?'

Baynard closed his eyes realising the stupid question. Mrs Biggins had been calling in or coming to the police station herself for months. They knew who she was, they knew where she lived.

Dr Watkins opened his eyes. The large window overlooking the Ridgeway framed the feeble grey light pouring in, shredded by the raindrops falling heavily on the road below. The curator opened and closed his eyes a few times. He looked around. The Wimbledon Museum was empty. He was alone. He felt like he had just woken up, still a little dazed, with an urge to yawn and stretch his arms. Those nightmares he kept having were annoying and disruptive. He tried to remember what he was doing. The morning had passed quickly but he had lost track of what he was meant to do. Looking at the weather outside, definitely not a surge of museum-loving visitors.

The curator turned around to take in the view of the museum, the glass cabinets, the archaeological findings, the models at scale of buildings long gone or still part of the skyline. He was proud of it. He remembered he wanted to contact the British Museum again, prickle their interest with another call. He asked himself what he had to do to get their attention. His thoughts went back to yesterday's events and the little research he had carried out before falling into sleep. The tunnels had not been searched or explored in a long time. Dr Watkins asked himself if things had changed down below. A crack in the walls or a geological event that had affected the tunnel. He thought it would be wise to take another look.

The curator walked to his desk by the entrance. The log file was open with the recent update on the inventory changes. He was about to put his glasses on and remind himself again of the work ahead on this grey Monday, when a knock came at the door.

'We are opening a bit later today.' called out Dr Watkins, checking his watch.

'It is me! Enrico!' said the baker with his thick Italian accent Dr Watkins had become accustomed to.

'Enrico?'

The curator opened the door and found the Italian baker in his white chef jacket in front of him. His wavy hair was well-groomed, and it framed his Mediterranean complexion and clean-shaven jaw nicely.

'Dr Watkins? *Sveglia!* Wakey wakey!' exclaimed the Italian baker, with his arms open. 'I called you about half an hour ago. I wanted to come over and ask you something.'

Dr Watkins frowned, a little uneasy that he might have forgotten something. He quickly nodded and closed the door behind Enrico. He had a blank and it was probably down to being tired. Enrico walked in, smiling, and he also took time to glance around the museum.

'I need to come here more often.' he said out loud, hands on hips. 'I am sure there is more to learn about Wimbledon.'

'I am sure it won't take long. Take a tour if you want.' replied Dr Watkins hurriedly while glancing at his phone.

He saw Enrico's number on the screen, the first on the recent calls menu. He suddenly remembered his call but not the reason why. Damn blackouts, the curator thought. They kept recurring.

'I hope I did not interrupt you, Dr Watkins.'

'Not at all. Mondays are usually slow for me.'

The Italian baker strolled past the glass case, peering through to look at pamphlets and photos. He had had an early start as always and had already baked a small batch for the day. The decision to call Dr Watkins had come unexpectedly as he stacked *filoni* and loaves on the shelves right behind the main counter of *The Wynnman* bakery. There were very few customers early Monday morning and he had time to share his idea with Dr Watkins. Not sure what Viviane would say about it, shying away from his baking duties. Yet, what Rosie and her father Nigel had told him and Viviane yesterday, made him more curious than ever. There was actually a well in their house linked to collapsed tunnels, and Rosie thought she had seen the same disfigured man coming out of it. Viviane had put the brakes on Enrico's imagination from the start. Viviane's warning about not getting involved, reminded the Italian baker he had a respectable business to look after. Yet, Viviane's efforts were wasted. He was already imagining what the link could be between the two events. He had to be certain it was simply down to Rosie's wild imagination.

Enrico stopped his thoughts in their tracks. He was staring at an empty glass cabinet not far from the one and only large window of the attic where the Museum of Wimbledon resided.

'Where did the black azalea go?' he wondered, giving a puzzled look at Dr Watkins.

He pointed at the empty glass cabinet where only the little card on the corner said what stood there before.

'Oh, didn't I tell you yesterday over lunch?' replied Dr Watkins while checking the log file, distracted. 'The Countess of Wrenbury Trust planned an exhibition on their history, and they are probably going to take it around the country, to recruit new students. They asked the museum if we could lend the black azalea and the Countess of Wrenbury's diary.'

'Oh! Well, that's good news.' exclaimed Enrico.

'Indeed, it is. So, Enrico, what did you want to ask me?'

Enrico walked over to his desk, excited about what he wanted to ask Dr Watkins. He told the curator about their visit and shared what they had learnt from Rosie and her father Nigel.

'Rosie saw the dead man burning while she was trapped in the tunnel.' Enrico said. 'What is more troubling is that Rosie, or at least what her dad told us, kept saying she saw the same man in their house for months, and more often in the days running up to last Sunday's fair. The "scary man" as she and her parents dubbed him. Apparently, Rosie believes he lived in the well and came up through their basement from time to time. The parents think it is her imagination.'

'And do you believe in the child's fairy tale?' asked Dr Watkins.

'Not sure what to believe. Maybe she was in shock and what was burning in front of her was someone else.'

Dr Watkins listened attentively once more.

'What are you *really* asking me, Enrico?' the curator questioned bluntly.

'I have been thinking, Dr Watkins.' noted Enrico. 'There is something strange that does not fit. I wanted to ask you about taking a closer look at the tunnels.'

The curator chuckled.

'You know if Viviane finds out, she may not be happy!' he commented.

'We can tell her later.' dismissed Enrico, knowing though the risk he was taking.

'Not sure it is safe down there. I also don't think I am fit enough for this kind of thing. I am not the youngest of lads.'

'One more reason to check out the tunnel entrance by the crypt before another child gets lost in there! Anyway, how deep are these tunnels going to be? You said you already have information on them. From the previous speleological expeditions. Don't you have a map?'

Dr Watkins grinned. Enrico's curiosity did not surprise or shock him. On the contrary, his comments intrigued him. The curator had always wanted to venture down the tunnels, seize the opportunity he had missed out on many years ago. Perhaps there was something buried down there which the museum could benefit from. He thought to himself he should not ignore another piece of Wimbledon history before it gets buried forever.

He went to a nearby shelf and pulled open a bottom drawer where layers of old and new laminated maps had been stacked. He pulled one out and closed the drawer.

'Here. Take this!' he said to Enrico. 'This will help you find your way. The tunnels are a closed circuit. You will find some of the paths are blocked just like they were last time someone went in there.'

Enrico looked closely at the old sketched map of the tunnels. There were about three or four ramifications, all ending up with an 'X' marking a collapsed ceiling. Enrico checked an arrow, written in a different ink, next to the sign of a cross.

'This is the tunnel access where you found Rosie.' commented Dr Watkins pointing at it. 'I marked it for you, so you know where to start. You see the tunnels don't lead anywhere? No other exit. What do you expect to find?'

'Maybe nothing. Or maybe explain why a burning man ended up in there on a Sunday morning!'

'And why did you come here first? Nothing would have stopped you to venture into the tunnels.'

Enrico grinned.

'Well, last time you told me to ask for help. Remember last time when I broke into Cannizaro Park and you had a set of keys all along. Well, here I am!'

Dr Watkins gave Enrico a weak smile.

'One piece of advice!' warned the curator. 'Be careful!'.

Lord Awlthorp was in his study, immersed in his thoughts. He sat at his desk, contemplating the array of drawings and scribbled notes pinned against the wall opposite. Most of them portrayed images of a round pool, with scanty details and notes jotted around it. They explained Lord Awlthorp's line of thoughts. These images had been buried at the back of other, more recent, pinned notes. Yet, the conversation with Toby Claymore had made him reconsider, and so when he returned home the evening before, he grabbed them one by one, checking them again and again. His night had been restless. Now, in the light of a grey Monday morning, the scene was no different. Lord Awlthorp could not ignore the fact Henry Claymore, the dead brother, had discovered something before him.

The buried Pool of Elixir, according to a Medieval script, had been buried under Wimbledon Hill to seal evil powers forever. No precise location was given of course; no treasure map existed. Just bits of texts with approximated descriptions. The legend resurfaced during Lord Awlthorp's research, roughly at the same time as he came across the drawings of the black azalea. It had become part of what he now called his second test, to prove the existence of what all these small clues from a forgotten Wimbledon history led him to believe that something beyond any man's wildest dreams existed beneath Wimbledon. It took him a year to pinpoint the location of the pool, right below the Old Rectory, left undisturbed for all this time despite centuries of building and rebuilding. It took him even longer to get access to the house itself and let Reginald and the Claymores infiltrate it. The Old Rectory had been empty for a long time and in need of renovation. When Lord Awlthorp found out there had been calls to refurbish it by local Wimbledonians and the Council, it provided the perfect cover.

Perhaps too much cover. The Claymores knew nothing about the pool's history, of Lord Awlthorp's real objectives. Their job was the recipe. To recreate the liquid or substance needed to bring the Pool of Elixir back to life, revive its power. Lord Awlthorp had to admit he had been clueless all along having no instructions to follow, apart from the sketchy fairy tales told by anonymous writers from the past and an odd recipe for an ordinary Tudor dish. He had started to believe the pool and the recipe were linked in some way, but doubt had crept in over the last few weeks. The doubt that his research was unfounded, his ambition foolish. Until the evening before, when he learned Henry Claymore had immerged himself into the liquid, Lord Awlthorp had tried to fathom why Henry Claymore would do such an irrational act, but there was only one reason behind it. Henry had found out something about the pool's history. An act that had cost him his life.

Lord Awlthorp hit his fist on the desk, filled with anger and envy. He could not tell if he hated more the fact that a stupid crook of a chemist had made a discovery before him or that he had suffered the most stupid of deaths without leaving anything behind for Lord Awlthorp to pick up. He stood up from his desk, having had enough of staring at his lifeless notes, which did not give him any clues on what to do next. He walked out and noticed Reginald sitting on an armchair on the landing, busy reading the Wimbledon Guardian. He stood up the moment he saw the silhouette of his boss against the threshold.

'Morning, sir!' he said out loud.

'Morning. Did my driver give you an update on the police?' asked Lord Awlthorp, rubbing his gloved hands.

'Yes. It seems the body has been identified and a search has been issued for Toby Claymore.'

'As a suspect?'

'Not yet. I think to ask him questions about his brother. Still, it does not sound good…'

'No, it does not.' replied Lord Awlthorp curtly. 'We need to make the body disappear.'

'To what purpose?'

Lord Awlthorp looked at him with a grim, hard look.

'The report said his body is covered in an unidentified purple ooze. The evidence could lead to our research. They could trace your purchases of cheap wine in the last few weeks. Better get rid of it.'

'Do you want me to take care of it?'

Lord Awlthorp crossed his arms and held his chin in a pensive mood.

'Yes' said the man in black. 'But make it look like Toby did it!'

'Toby Claymore will squeal like a child, give our names to the police in no time.' commented Reginald bluntly.

'Reggie!'

'Don't call me, Reggie!'

Lord Awlthorp grinned with his wicked smile.

'Reggie, who do you think they will believe?'

'Maybe you are safe. But I have a criminal record.'

'Don't worry, Reggie. I will make sure you and I stay untouched. Have you been tracking Toby Claymore's movements?'

Reginald picked up his phone and the screen showed a blinking dot in one corner of a bird's view of the Wimbledon area.

'Yes. He is locked down there as he should be. He has been busy, moving all around the place. He started working the moment I brought down all the cases of wine I had.'

Lord Awlthorp did not comment. Reginald eyed him suspiciously.

'Do you think he will deliver what you asked? Are we sure all this work is leading somewhere?'

The man in black disliked when Reginald doubted his actions. Now more than ever as he had to rely on the clumsy Toby Claymore. He felt powerless.

'Don't question my judgement, Reggie!' he snorted. 'Keep an eye on him. I hope we learn something about what he and his brother did down there.'

'Anything in particular I need to look for?' asked Reginald.

'Just make sure he does not leave the basement, first of all.'

There was no time left now that Henry's inexplicable death was in the open. Leaving the basement was of paramount importance, before it was too late. Toby Claymore had thought about it all night, as he prepared his escape. Toby's dark memories of his brother Henry, engulfed by the revived liquid, flashed before his eyes as he moved around the crates of cheap wine in the basement. In his head he remembered it bloodier, more violent. And the screams rang loud in the solitude of the basement where he and his brother had been confined. Nobody could hear them.

Toby shook his head and checked what he had at his feet. Most bottles were from Reginald's last delivery. He put them all to one side. Like hell I need them, he thought, as he imagined saying it in Reginald's face. Toby was looking for a crate he and Henry had hidden at the very back of the stacked boxes. It contained the last of six special bottles. Under the light, they all showed the purple-maroon colour of good wine swirling inside, but one in particular had this fermented juice his brother Henry had warned him never to let Lord Awlthorp find. Toby did not understand why. Its content had an extremely foul smell; he was not a wine connoisseur but felt the funny-smelling liquid had nothing to do with wine at all.

Toby found the crate with the six bottles pushed into the deep corner. It had been the perfect hiding spot, especially when Reginald always insisted on checking how much of his cheap wine was left and taking away empty creates. Toby pulled the crate out and looked at each of the bottles. Under the semi-darkness of the basement, they all looked like the same ordinary wine. It was hard to distinguish which one was the fermented juice. Toby recalled his brother Henry telling him these bottles were worth a fortune. He smiled at the memory and then moved onto placing the bottles in his rucksack so he could easily carry with him later as he escaped from this madness. Time was not on his side. With Lord Awlthorp's new hard deadline, there was every possibility he or his burly henchman would show up before he knew.

The short man glanced around the basement. His face saddened as he took one last look at the dirty sleeping bags where Toby and Henry had shared each other's company. He despised this basement. There was nothing here left to take. The other ingredients, the chemicals, the herbs, he no longer needed them. His mind was focused on getting out of this place. This had been his plan and Henry's: find a safe way out of Wimbledon, and with the money they could make on those special bottles, they could finally live like kings, retire from a life making chemical concoctions for others. That dream was now closer than ever, but he would have to live it through alone.

Toby checked the door at the top of stairs: locked, of course. He could hear the workers coming in to renovate the Old Rectory, first thing on a Monday morning. He was not bothered by it; there was another way out. He went back into the basement and clicked on the machine, its buzzing noise increasing ten-fold. The machine sent voltage into the pool to start a non-spontaneous chemical reaction. Henry was the first to understand the ingredients had to be mixed and then separated. One thing he and Henry had learned was that the electrolysis was becoming more and more unstable, sometimes against their will or calculations, creating tremors in the ground. Lord Awlthorp told them to continue regardless. Toby had the perfect idea for his escape. He would make the whole apparatus go haywire and overheat the machine. This would take one hour; enough time for him to escape undisturbed and leave Lord Awlthorp to deal with the rubble and the mess.

Toby checked the machine was running fine; he then grabbed his rucksack and moved down the natural corridor into the chamber. On the table by the pool, the laptop was on, ready to kick start the experiment, and the rest of the table was clear after Lord Awlthorp had taken all their formulas and notes. They were all outdated versions of the several tests the Claymores had carried out, most of them failures. Toby grinned and looked at a folded piece of paper in his hands. They were the last notes his brother had written; they had concealed it in the crate with the special bottles. This had been Henry's wish: ensure Lord Awlthorp would never put his hands on his final work. Toby would make sure it stayed that way, even after Henry's death.

On one side of the paper, the final recipe was neatly explained. Toby stared at it. He wondered if Henry had been right. Toby sighed and took a deep breath. He put everything in his rucksack and then turned towards the pool one last time. The dark purplish grime encrusted at the bottom stared back at him. Unlike the beauty of a park fountain with its glinting water surface, the Pool of Elixir had no water, no reflection, and smelled of death and decay. Toby rubbed his nose to clear it of the stench he could no longer stand. He grabbed the plastic petrol tank and poured the last batch of experimental liquid into the pool. The crimson liquid, with its ephemeral maroon and leaden shades of colour, oozed out of the tank and Toby ensured he filled it up beyond the threshold limit they had drawn in red on the inside wall of the pool. He then pulled the cables down into the pool, so the ends touched the thick liquid resting at the bottom. These steps were all so familiar to him; except no-one would take a dip this time. He would not follow in his brother's footsteps. He then looked across the chamber, opposite the entrance from the basement, where the natural corridor continued down towards the tunnels. The tunnels, Toby thought. In his head, he traced back the way out he and Henry had found, where to turn, which entrances to open, and which to close forever. He then pulled from his other pocket a small rusty cog. It was the missing piece that would make the trap door work. Pretending he had broken the trap door had been his idea for once. Lord Awlthorp and Reginald did not suspect he could still open the trap door and slip out of their control forever.

Toby decided it was time to go and hit 'Enter' on the laptop. Sparks started firing from the bottom of the fountain. The short man calmly walked away from the pool, stepping carefully from side to side with a watchful eye on the boiling crimson liquid. Toby felt hypnotised by the ebullient surface, with its hundred bubbles bursting and splashing, ready to reveal something underneath, something horrific. Toby felt drawn to it. For a minute, he thought something in there was speaking to him, like Henry had claimed so many times. He shut his eyes and shook his head violently.

'Wake up!' he told himself loudly. 'The voices are not real…'

The voices, that is how his brother called them. In the last week, Henry had become worse and worse, almost talking to himself, writing notes and moving things around as if following someone's directions. He knew Henry's sanity was deteriorating the longer they stayed there. In the end, Henry had thrown himself into the pool, probably to finally find some peace. Toby though would not do the same.

He pulled the rucksack over his shoulder and ran to the trap door. He fiddled with the rusty cog until he inserted it successfully. The lever behind the loose brick was now working again and it let the wall slide open. Toby ran through it without giving a last glance at the pool. The anticipated tremors from the experiment started shortly after and Toby could feel the ground vibrating under his feet. It was not as violent as an earthquake; it was more of rapid but gentle vibrations spreading through his bones and turning the rocky surfaces into a constant blur. The tremors would weaken from time to time, but Toby had removed any failsafe on purpose. Let the machine collapse and burn.

He was now in a perpendicular tunnel made of red bricks and natural rock. He found the traces of crimson liquid mixed with blood, which Henry had left behind as he had run in pain and despair out of the chamber. Toby drowned the painful memory and the guilt for not running after him to save him. He quickly followed the tracks where they led. This section of the tunnel had mostly dead ends. When Henry and Toby had first come across it, there was only one clear path leading north further down into the depths of the hill and connecting to the rest of the tunnel. Toby got his torch out and saw the traces of burnt blood running down in the dark. He then looked up where a part of the brick wall had fallen off exposing the old medieval tiles underneath.

To the cellar

What they had found at the end of this path had changed Henry and Toby's fate somehow. Toby now realised this path had to be sealed forever before he left for good. Lord Awlthorp and his goons would never find it. He put his rucksack down and took out a square pack of home-made C4 explosive. He had carefully balanced the power, enough to blow this part of tunnel but without bringing the whole hill down. He had to block this entrance behind him once and for all. He glued the C4 to the ceiling and synchronised it with his watch and the hour slot he had planned.

He then walked north, down the tunnel, away from the chamber and the Pool of Elixir. The tremors had restarted, now a little distant but still intense. He followed the traces of burnt blood on the floor, mixed with crimson traces. The strong smell of burnt blood and alcohol filled his nose. Henry had been surely through here as expected, while the liquid was burning him alive. Toby could not believe Henry had survived up to this point.

At the first intersection, the traces his brother had left behind continued in two directions. To the north, the same label as before appeared, now written in white chalk barely readable on the red bricks. 'To the cellar'. Toby knew it was a dead end; they had blocked that path a while ago. The other path, turning right to the east, was the only safe passage out of here. He and Henry had dug it out recently, re-opening an old path which reconnected this part of the tunnel to the rest of the network. It was all part of the plan. Toby could still read his own writing in white chalk.

Way Out

These tunnels were a labyrinth. Henry, in his last minutes before his death, was probably out of his mind and unable to distinguish the right way out. Toby turned right and carried on, checking his watch from time to time. As he took many turns, the vibration from the chamber returned like a soft, distant buzz. It grew in intensity and the walls of the tunnel were starting to shake. Toby hastened his pace. The more he hurried, the more the tremors seems to chase him. There and then, the whole tunnel started collapsing behind him; the ceiling falling like dominoes. Toby ran forward, panting under the weight of the rucksack. The crash of bricks roared over his shoulder. He then came across a large intersection and leaped forward before the tunnel he came out from collapsed forever. He stood still on the ground, fearing he would be buried alive, but then tremors quietened again.

That was close, thought Toby. He panted and turned around. A small section of the brick wall by the blocked entrance had fallen off revealing stone slabs behind it with a label he had not seen before.

To Viscount Standstill's Bedroom
February 1626

These tunnels did not stop surprising Toby. Each entrance carried a worn-out or hidden sign at its entrance which he remembered well from the initial exploration with his brother. More seemed to be hidden behind these old, mouldy bricks.

Toby reminded himself he had to be out before the hour was over. The tremors were picking up, not to forget the C4 explosives he had planted. He stood up and looked at the three new paths forking out ahead of him. His eyes went to the ground. He followed the traces of burnt blood and he realised Henry had taken the path straight ahead towards Saint Mary's Church. Probably by mistake. The right way was eastward, to his left, where the trickle of water opened a muddy path. His only way out of this mess.

Enrico's hands prickled. They always did when something was not right, when his curiosity suddenly became hyperactive. This was the moment when he wanted to knead more and more bread just to think things through.

It helped him focus. The tunnel incident alone forced him to bake two trays of *focaccia*, a batch of *ciabatte* and almost a bag full of olive oil bread buns. It helped him think more about why a disfigured body had been found in the tunnel. And now, he had the opportunity to check it out himself. He rubbed his hands in anticipation.

Enrico picked up his small cup of espresso, and sipped the fresh coffee made with his LaGaggia machine. He yawned. The early hours of baking could sometimes take their toll. He checked Viviane's shop across the road. The colourful flowers and leafy dwarf trees outside framed the shop front so beautifully and the arrangement of the décor reflected the whole Regency building above. Inside, he could barely see Viviane busy potting a few plants for a customer. He wondered if he should tell her what he was about to do. Enrico looked at the map Dr Watkins had given him. They were just tunnels, after all, with some earth worms and a couple of cobwebs. Enrico weighed the risks. He was not trespassing. He had to cross a crime scene, though. He then thought to himself there was no police on guard. He concluded he would be done in a couple of hours.

His plan was simple. He would explore the tunnel himself and look out for anything of interest. Anything out of the ordinary. Dr Watkins gave him a torch, a pair of plastic gloves and a few small re-sealable bags. Enrico wondered why, and the curator explained any search for history's sake needs evidence. He also insisted on giving him a smartphone to track his location. Enrico refused categorically. He feared technology, he hated being burdened with technological gadgets. His faithful Nokia 3310 would do the trick if he needed to call for help. Enrico told himself again the tunnels were not that many. If he was not back at the bakery or the museum before sundown, he agreed then Dr Watkins would know where to find him and send the cavalry.

The Italian baker left his bakery at once and closed the shop for the rest of the day to carry out his plan. The first hours since opening had been busy ones, with quite a few customers requesting *sfogliatelle* alongside the usual bread for sale. It had been a good day for business already. He quickly wrapped his chef jacket around him. The fresh breeze felt colder under the overcast sky of a grey Monday morning. The high street was slightly busy as per usual, with light traffic passing through to reach Wimbledon Town down the hill or Putney by the river Thames up north. Enrico checked again Viviane's shop across the road and took the long way around the traffic roundabout to make sure Viviane was not looking in his direction. He wanted to avoid any reprimands, either for what he was going to do or for the fact he was closing the shop way before the business day was in full swing.

Enrico cut through Belvedere Grove and Alan Road to reach Saint Mary's Church on foot. The green space where the fair had been held the day before was now empty and quiet, free of cars and stalls. The doors to the church were closed. Enrico walked along the gravel path and then made his way across the graveyard; he was the only living soul in sight. The narrow steps of the family vault in the deserted graveyard soon lay in front of him. The path was clear from indiscreet eyes and there were no police on guard to Enrico's advantage. He quickly descended before anyone could spot him and crossed under the police strips warning people to keep out. The steps through the niche and down into the tunnel were fresh in his memory. The sound of trickling water echoed in his ears and the icy draught gave Enrico the goose bumps. He held the torch up and faced the blackness of the tunnels once again. Almost everything seemed the same. He looked back to see where the tunnel came from. The path had collapsed many moons ago. There was only one way forward. Enrico started walking carefully, ears on the distant, echoing sounds and eyes on the slimy, brick and stone walls. He reached the point where he had found Rosie. He then moved on and slowed down near to where he had found the body. Traces of the purple or maroon gelatine covering the body were here and there in mud-like clumps. He also noticed long charred streaks of the same substance on the side of the wall, as if something had dragged itself against it. The baker kneeled to look at the strange coloured material and picked a clump up with his gloves. It smelled of burnt iron and alcohol with other acrid smells he could not figure out. It crumbled in his fingers like biscuit until it all turned to a fine powder. He took some of it and with lab-like precision put it in one of the re-sealable bags. He flashed the torch towards the rest of the tunnel where less familiar places awaited.

The walk was a rather long one, maybe up to five or ten minutes. The tunnel seemed to narrow down as Enrico ventured towards the unknown. The smell of burnt iron was stronger. Charred streaks re-appeared on the walls, again without a consistent pattern. Enrico wondered if the burnt victim staggered on his or her own or was dragged by someone. He followed the trail, passing a few larger patches of the dried substance until he came across an intersection, with three paths to choose from. The tunnel ahead of him was a dead end, except Dr Watkins's map said there were at least a few metres to walk before you hit a wall. The ceiling here seemed to have collapsed fairly recently. Enrico scanned the debris on the floor and then did the same for each wall to the side. To his right, at eye level, a small section of the brick wall had fallen off revealing stone slabs behind it. Perhaps a sign of the original tunnel walls. Enrico flashed the torch at it and could read some faded writing scribbled on it:

To Viscount Standstill's Bedroom
February 1626

A piece of history to report back to Dr Watkins maybe, thought Enrico. He then shone the torch all around to see if there was anything else he had missed until his gaze landed on a thin, dark trail on the ground. It ran from under the collapsed tunnel in the direction of Saint Mary's Church. At first,

Enrico thought it was the same trickle of water as before, but a closer look revealed it was the same purple and maroon gelatine he had picked up before. The strange substance, now almost dried up, reflected more colours under the direct light of the torch. Hints of black and crimson shrouded the substance in a deeper mystery. Enrico scratched a bit of it with his plastic glove. The smell of iron was stronger. To his horror, it resembled the metallic stench of human blood mixed with the pungent tang of alcohol. The Italian baker frowned, unable to get his head around it. He flashed the trail up and down with his torch. Stains appeared at random intervals as if it had dripped from something. Or someone. The body, whoever he or she was, had come through here, thought Enrico.

The Italian baker checked the second path heading west first. He checked for any signs at the entrance but there were none. Enrico walked a little further and reached another dead end as it was clearly showed on the map. No way out here, again. He walked back, frustrated, and returned to the intersection. Enrico was puzzled on where the burnt victim came from. He could not see anything odd, neither before his eyes or on Dr Watkins's map. He tried to understand but felt his mind could not concentrate in the penumbra. A low, humdrum buzz filled the air and the Italian baker wondered how long it had been ringing in his ears. It was some sort of drilling sound whirring nearby, sending vibrations throughout the tunnel. The tremors were faint at first and then the earth suddenly shook hard. The tunnels vibrated so much Enrico almost lost his balance and his torch fell out of his hands. The whole ground rumbled for a few seconds and the whirring sound reverberated through the walls, the ground, in all directions. It only lasted a few seconds, but it felt as if Enrico was in a cocktail shaker until the tremors faded as quickly as they had started. The annoying, low buzzing sound returned shortly after. Enrico thought it could be an earthquake although, to his knowledge, seismic activity in the United Kingdom, and in particular Wimbledon, was close to zero. He stood still for a moment, gaining back his balance, and strained his ears to find out where this low buzz came from. The vibration continued for a few more seconds and then it lowered down to a hum echoing in the darkness. Enrico was alone again in the tunnels, and he could only find comfort in the cold, damp air.

Enrico though did not accept defeat. The burnt, disfigured body. The crimson traces on the ground. These tremors from the depths of the earth. None of it made any sense to him; let alone give out answers to his questions. It just fuelled Enrico's curiosity more and more. Ahead of him was the third and last unexplored tunnel, the eastward tunnel. He picked the torch and checked the ground again. The mysterious traces of blood did not lead in this direction but something else caught Enrico's curious eye. The trickle of water made its way through it, turning the dry soil into a muddy path. Faint grooves in the mud appeared to be light footsteps. Someone had been through here recently, Enrico thought. He moved forward and flashed the torch ahead.

The path changed to a downward slope where traces of worn out steps indicated a footpath had existed before. The smell of damp filled the cramped space and the cold air Enrico breathed in came out in large clouds of condensed air, fogging his view. As Enrico ventured inside, the red bricks and the end of the tunnel stared silently back at him, almost asking him why he was there. Enrico felt a chill running down his spine. He had the nasty feeling he was being observed. My imagination, Enrico thought. He was thinking about what to do in the event of a possible encounter, when the tremors returned from deep inside the tunnel. This time the vibrations were more violent, rocking Enrico backwards and forwards. The Italian baker threw himself against the side wall to keep steady. It was as if the whole hill was shaking underground. Enrico felt the ceiling was about to collapse on him, but it did not. The tremors vanished once more like a ghost and the annoying hum returned.

Enrico hesitated. Whatever that was, he had to be quick. He came at another fork in his path. Here, the footsteps in the mud had disappeared. He glanced left and right to check whether the lines drawn on the map reflected the reality of these abandoned tunnels. On Enrico's right, a southern tunnel appeared to have collapsed a few metres inside. At its entrance, another faded writing was visible just behind a small section of bricks that had broken off.

To Belvedere House
May 1720

Enrico made another mental note. He knew Dr Watkins may be able to link these dates. He then kneeled to look at the broken chunks of brick. The ends were too straight, too perfect. Enrico was starting to believe these bricks had not fallen off by chance or by some natural cause. Someone had knocked them down deliberately.

The Italian baker looked at the northern tunnel on his left. There was no sign at the entrance. He shone his torch into it and started walking. The tunnel followed a rolling path sloping gradually downward. It was hard to tell how far underground he had gone, or where on the hill he was exactly. The map did not seem to show the full length of this tunnel but indicated that it ran towards Wimbledon Park. Enrico followed it through until it ended abruptly once more. He flashed his torch onto the heaps of debris blocking the path. His eyes then landed on the side walls where another section of the brick wall had been removed. The pattern was now obvious. Someone had been trying to expose the original signs. Except this time the job was only half-done. He could just make out another sign half-hidden by the old red bricks. Enrico could see two separate writings, though. On the red bricks, there was someone's handwriting in white chalk.

However, the sign underneath was different. Enrico grabbed at some of the bricks and pulled them with all his might. He placed his foot against the wall to gain some pressure, until the bricks fell out near his feet. The stone slab underneath showed a much older writing. Enrico could tell by the curved artistic lines typical of a Medieval font.

Vineyard and Orangerie

No date this time. Enrico concluded this was the end of the road, and his only way out was from where he had come. As he turned around, questions with impossible answers swirled in his head. Again though, he struggled to concentrate. The low humdrum buzz was again audible in the distance. Enrico placed his hand on the cold brick wall of the tunnel and felt a slight, tiny tremor vibrating through his fingers, his wrist and up his arm. A gentle, constant vibration, which probably nobody felt on the surface.

The Italian baker traced back his steps. Time to leave, he thought, there is nothing here. Then, at the height of the 'Belvedere House' sign, he felt cold air blowing softly from above. Enrico glanced up. A round, chimney-like tunnel rose straight up above his head. There was a rusty metal ladder attached to one side, which led up to higher ground. Enrico checked the map but could not see any marks or notes about it. The beam then fell on the ground and Enrico could not help noticing more broken bricks on the floor. He checked the vertical tunnel again and he could see the ceiling had been broken through, not sure though from which side. Enrico was more and more convinced someone had been playing with the tunnel structure, finding a way out or a way in. The Italian baker stood there for a moment, planning his next move. There was no harm in climbing to see where the vertical tunnel came out. By calculating the distance he had come from, and looking at the few reference points marked on the map, he was probably not very far from Saint Mary's Church and possibly under residential houses along the road.

'Hold on a minute!' Enrico said out loud.

There was a road labelled at the edge of the map.

Arthur Road

Enrico remembered what the Rutherfords had told him and Viviane. This was the same road where Rosie and her family lived. The coincidence was too much for the curious Italian baker to ignore. Without hesitation, he climbed up and lifted himself inside the tunnel until he could reach the cold metal steps of the ladder. Enrico felt the muscles in his arms being pulled down by his body weight and his palms starting to burn as they rubbed against rusty metal. He then pulled his legs up and found a solid foothold in the wall. He finally managed to grab the ladder with both hands and took a deep breath. He noticed a small sign was carved in at the base of the chimney-like rise, below the first foothold of the ladder.

Artesian Well

Enrico made another mental note of the clues he would have to ask Dr Watkins about. He pulled himself up the ladder. The tremors pulsed through the metal bars. Enrico swore the vibration was stronger here. Stones and dust crumbled from the side walls. Enrico kept his head down to protect his eyes and started climbing up. Then came what he dreaded the most. The tremors suddenly picked up in intensity again until the earth and the tunnel shook hard once more. Enrico held on tight, up against the ladder. Larger rocks started to fall from above. Enrico pushed himself to one side. Yet, he could not avoid being scratched on his arm by some of the debris. The ground shook for ten seconds or more, and then it all stopped. The tremors returned to a gentle vibration. Enrico could still feel them pulsing through his hands while he grappled for balance on the metal ladder. And then the tremors and low buzz sound were once a disturbing background noise.

Enrico thought he was going mad. The claustrophobic atmosphere was getting to him. It was time to leave. He pushed himself upwards, step after step. Five minutes in and the top was nowhere to be seen. The Italian baker sighed in desperation. It was impossible; he must come to the surface at some point. He climbed further up and then came across a side tunnel shooting off upwards and diagonally from the one he was in. Enrico blinked, trying to make sense of his position and how these tunnels were connected. He recalled Dr Watkins, and even Rosie's father, Nigel, talking about wells, some still buried underneath Wimbledon houses. Enrico knew he had to choose which route to take. It was then that the metal clang of a door echoed from all directions. Although Enrico could not see anything or anyone, the tunnels amplified the sound to exaggerated proportions as if a door had been shut right next to him. A bang came right after and this time from below his feet. The metal ladder started trembling and so did the walls around him. Enrico felt the earth shaking again but, somehow, he knew this time it was different. It was more than just vibrations deep in the earth. He grabbed his torch and flashed the light below trying to keep the beam steady while everything around kept shaking. A thick cloud of dust was rising fast from below. Something had detonated within the depths of the tunnel. Explosives, perhaps. Enrico panicked, feeling trapped. He flashed the light above and he was almost hit by a large stone falling from above with the rest of small debris. Enrico spluttered sand from his mouth and rubbed his eyes. Visibility was starting to get foggy and the tunnel still shook violently. Something was not right. It was as if the whole tunnel was collapsing. Enrico looked at the side tunnel, weighing up his safest options. Before he could make up his mind, he heard the bolts of the ladder snap and fly off the wall above him. A few hit Enrico on the head, and where he thought he had lost his balance, he realised it was the ladder that had broken off the wall and was about to collapse on itself. Cracking could be heard far above, and an unprecedented load of sand started crashing down with a terrifying rumble. Enrico needed to be quick before the flow of sand thickened and poured out like in an hourglass running out of time. Without time to think, Enrico hurled himself into the side tunnel and scrambled upwards without stopping. Enrico knew only too well he was betting his life on finding an exit on the way up. He had to get to the surface before it was too late. Before he was buried alive.

Baynard pulled the car into one of the wide drives on Rectory Orchard, a lovely cul-de-sac just off Church Road that had both the reserved, tranquil atmosphere of a British street and the expansive charisma of American driveways. The last house on the left was Mrs Biggins's, with wisteria hanging from one side of the roof. The inspector stopped the engine and checked his notes. There were not that many, apart from the repetitive complaints Mrs Biggins had reported. Tremors in the house. He peered over the solar-panelled roofs of Rectory Orchard and he could barely see the turret of the Old Rectory and the tip of the scaffolding to one side of the building. He could not remember how long the works were for, but he was sure the tremors were probably due to a builder happy playing with his pneumatic hammer or some other heavy tool.

'Oh, Inspector Baynard! How glad to see you!' cheered Mrs Biggins as she opened the door. 'Please come in.'

'Mrs Biggins.' nodded Baynard following the invitation.

Mrs Biggins lived alone. She was a divorcee with grown-up kids living out of London. Baynard guessed she was probably a little older than him. He hoped his visit would be the last; perhaps find the simplest of reasons behind these tremors, which until today he had never felt. Never.

'Would you like some tea?' asked Mrs Biggins making her way to the kitchen.

'Coffee. Black. Please.' asked Baynard.

Mrs Biggins hurried to the open-plan kitchen, while Baynard wondered in the wide living room. The two were one and the same, only separated by the change from carpet to tiles on the floor. On the northern wall, large sliding doors faced the lush green back garden. The rolling fields of Wimbledon Park appeared just over the fence, a little sombre under the grey Monday sky.

'Nice view.' spoke Baynard to make idle conversation before getting into the meat of the discussion. 'Ever get golf balls in your back garden?'

'Sometimes. They are not as annoying though as these tremors.'

Mrs Biggins beat Baynard to it by wasting no time in mentioning her tremors.

'I understand.' added the inspector to put it delicately. 'I know you have reported these many, many times. Wimbledon Police will do its best…'

'Inspector!' interrupted Mrs Biggins. 'I heard this spiel too many times as well.'

Baynard could have said the same of her story but he bit his tongue and stayed calm. He looked around, not sure if keen to find something that would tell him straight away where the tremors came from, or something that would help him lead the conversation on his own terms.

'Perhaps if we recap some of the details. At what time do you hear these tremors? Day? Night?'

'Throughout the day, up to four times in the last few weeks. Not every day though. The weekends are the worst.'

'The weekend?' Baynard asked puzzled.

'Yes. It drives me crazy. It is like a gentle vibration spreading throughout the walls and the floors. You see that silver statue there by the television? It is so fragile that it rattles as soon as the vibrations start.'

'Gentle vibrations? So, nothing falling off the shelves like an earthquake?'

'No, no, inspector. Haven't you read my statement?'

'Of course. Of course.' dismissed Baynard.

He avoided eye contact and pretended to look at the statue more closely. The peculiar thing about these tremors was their higher frequency over the weekend. Baynard was sure the chance of any construction work happening over the weekend was slim. He held that thought and asked further questions.

'Does it happen in all the rooms? Or one in particular?' asked Baynard.

'It spreads throughout, but I feel the tremors to be stronger here in the kitchen. Cups, cutlery, plates, everything vibrates at once. It is exhausting.'

Baynard walked to the open kitchen and took a sip of the fresh cup of coffee.

'Thanks.' said Baynard. 'Do the tremors happen at regular intervals? Specific times? For example, builders always start at eight a.m. and you hear drilling before nine a.m. …'

'Inspector Baynard, these tremors are not because of building work!' interrupted Mrs Biggins again.

She clearly did not enjoy being contradicted. Baynard played along. He had to find some objective proof without wasting police resources too much.

'I don't know the times, inspector. I don't keep a log. For example, one happened this morning. About half hour ago. Pretty violent as well.'

'Half an hour ago?' blurted out Baynard, almost spilling his coffee. 'Why didn't you tell me?'

'You didn't ask.'

Baynard took a deep sigh. He could murder the woman right now.

'Ok. Half an hour ago…' mumbled the inspector looking at his phone to put a time against it. 'Do you think you could log these tremors? It may help us help you more.'

Baynard tried to push the responsibility onto Mrs Biggins with the kindest of smiles, despite his icy stare making a contrast that probably did more harm than good.

'I am a busy woman, Inspector Baynard. How could I…'

Mrs Biggins did not finish the sentence. She stopped in her tracks and widened her eyes, goggling around the kitchen and the living room. Baynard blinked trying to follow her gaze. At first, he thought the lady was clearly mad, hearing or seeing imaginary things. Then he heard too what she heard. A subtle tremor starting from the sole of his feet and then running up his legs, gently and almost imperceptible. Everything in the room started trembling and rattling at once. The books, the small statues, the pint glasses in the cupboard, and Baynard swore one of the sofas almost moved an inch.

'What the…' he cursed.

'I told you!' exclaimed Mrs Biggins.

The smug expression on her face told Baynard she was glad she was right and that she had been able to prove it. The inspector just stared at her and then returned to look at the room in disbelief, one hand on the kitchen table to keep steady. The tremor built up in seconds and Baynard almost felt he could lose balance. There was one last shake, more violent. A plate drying by the sink fell into it. Both Mrs Biggins and Inspector Baynard jumped. Then the tremor quietened down until it eventually stopped. The house returned to normal.

'What…' repeated Baynard speechless.

'Here. Do you believe me now?' challenged Mrs Biggins. 'The violent shake at the end is something new. I have already lost an entire dinner set because of it.'

Baynard was incredulous. The tremor was unexplainable. There was nothing he could pin down as the root cause. No builder's drilling machine could do that, he guessed.

Both Baynard and Mrs Biggins grabbed an edge each, either of the table or of the counter, to find solid ground. They listened in to see if the vibration still permeated the house, but everything was still once again.

'You win, Mrs Biggins.' surrendered Baynard. 'I will need to report this back. To the Council too. Do you have a basement?'

'No, I am afraid.' she said shaking her head.

'Right. I hope we do not have to dig your foundations to find out where this is coming from…'

Baynard's speech was interrupted once more. The roar that followed was louder than his words. All Mrs Biggins saw were his lips moving and then twisting into fear, as they both shook once more and were then knocked off balance. The roar brought a new wave of tremors throughout the house. All at once, unexpected. No gentle vibration announced it and Baynard felt it was different. The ground was shaking, and cracks started to form along the walls of the living room. Cabinet doors opened, plates and glasses fell out and crashed into million pieces on the floor.

'God help us!' shouted Mrs Biggins, dragging herself under the table. 'It is an earthquake!'

'It's impossible!' shouted Baynard on one knee looking up in defiance to the abnormal act of nature that had fallen upon the house.

He heard the television fall off its stand and frames dropping from the wall one by one as the earth shook with the mightiest of forces. Baynard felt belittled and joined Mrs Biggins under the table.

'Do something, inspector!' cried Mrs Biggins.

'I don't know what…' replied Inspector Baynard at a loss.

And again, he did not finish his sentence. To his surprise, the earthquake stopped immediately. One last frame fell, making them both jump before the quietness of Rectory Orchard returned. The trees visible outside in the back garden swayed a little before birds returned to their branches, chirping away as if announcing the worst had passed.

Baynard moved out from under the table and walked cautiously across the room. The house appeared to be still in one piece. The cracks in the wall had deepened and ran from the wall to the ceiling in random places across the room. Someone ought to check the safety of the house.

'Come out!' he told Mrs Biggins. 'I am going to check outside. It will be safer in the event of the house collapsing.'

The lady followed the inspector into the driveway of Rectory Orchard where the other residents at home that morning had already flooded to. Expressions of fear and awe across the faces made Baynard realise it was not just them who had witnessed it. He looked back at the house and Mrs Biggins's semi-detached house was the only one showing the cracks on the outside.

'Was Wimbledon hit by an earthquake?' muttered Mrs Biggins in disbelief, her eyes wide open, her hair a little out of place, clumped and covered together in dust.

Baynard could hear the word 'earthquake' echoing across Rectory Orchard. Everyone else thought the same. The inspector thought it was non-sense. He needed to get emergency services over as soon as possible. He looked up in the sombre, grey sky. Baynard squinted and he could see a cloud of rust-coloured smoke rising above the trees beyond the Old Rectory and Saint Mary's Church. He was trying to make sense of it when his phone rang. It was Jeremy.

'Baynard!' he answered.

'Inspector, are you still at Mrs Biggins's?' he asked.

'Yes. I am. Did you feel that?'

'Feel what?'

Baynard had no intention of calling it an earthquake. Not until he had a second opinion.

'The ground here at Rectory Orchard just shook. Something I have never felt in my life.'

'What?' exclaimed Jeremy, incredulous.

'You heard me. Get me the emergency services. Mrs Biggins's house could be at risk of collapsing. I don't see anyone injured but better be safe than sorry. I also see a cloud of smoke rising. Did someone report an explosion or unusual shaking of the ground?'

Jeremy did not reply.

'Sergeant?' called out Baynard.

'Inspector, I was calling for that.'

'999 call from Arthur Road' explained Jeremy. 'Not far from Saint Mary's. A cloud of smoke was reported coming out of the old Artesian Well. Not sure yet if there is a fire but the fire brigade is on its way. I thought you should be informed straightaway. You are not that far, actually.'

Baynard kept silent for a second. His detective mind picked up on Jeremy's words. He took them in one by one, comparing them, assessing the risks. There may have been no link, but he could not easily ignore it. If something was in the air, it was only the beginning.

'I am on my way there.'

'The first response team is already there. You may want to know the rest…'

'The rest?' asked Baynard puzzled and worried.

Baynard's ears tensed for what was to come next, and so did every feature of his face. His jaws, his mouth, even his silver goatee. His icy stare hardened as he looked in the distance in deep thought.

'Another 999 call came shortly after.' went on Jeremy. 'This time from 26 Arthur Road.'

'What? That's just…that's almost next door to the old Artesian Well!'

'Exactly!'

'What was reported there?'

'A break-in. In the basement of 24 Arthur Road. The neighbours reported it. Details are still a bit fuzzy. I think you'd better go and see it for yourself.'

'On my way!'

The inspector ended the call and asked the civilians to stay out in the driveway and not return to their homes until the emergency services arrived and confirmed it was safe to go back inside. He turned to Mrs Biggins and gave her a knowing look. She had been right. Tremors or something worse had been affecting her home and Baynard started to wonder what on earth would plague Wimbledon this time.

For Toby, the climb to the surface had always felt never ending. The metal ladder, the side tunnel. It was worse when the shockwaves from the experiment reverberated throughout. That Monday, the first shockwave from the chamber hit the tunnels right when Toby was climbing the vertical tunnel leading to the Artesian Well. Some dust had formed, making it hazy to see through the torch light. He checked his watch. The last shockwave would arrive in less than thirty minutes and then, ten or fifteen minutes after that, his precious C4 would go off and cause the disastrous effect he had in mind. He had to be out of the tunnels before then and have enough spare time to gather all his things on the surface and disappear out of sight once and for all.

The side tunnel went up diagonally for a few metres until he reached a short ladder where a short climb led to a rusty cast iron grid. Toby pulled it off easily and revealed a round metal airtight door. He unscrewed the valve handle in the middle of the door and pushed up to open it. Toby's eyes were suddenly blinded by a bright white light. He cupped one hand over his forehead and landed on a grey smooth cement floor. He lay there for a few minutes, catching his breath and adjusting his eyes to the natural light coming through small rectangle windows high up on one wall. He was finally in the home basement. There were bags of cement to one side, tools scattered around, some scaffolding, and an automatic saw near him, still covered with stone dust. Behind him, the low round wall of a well, made with natural grey stones, stood against the whiteness of the basement. The airtight door at the top of the well, from which he had emerged, laid wide open.

Toby checked the time again. The Rutherfords would not be in for a while. He chuckled. He and his brother Henry had been lucky to land a job at 24 Arthur Road and convince the family who lived there they were tradesmen specialising in basement renovations and covering up old wells. Their little wimpy daughter Rosie had been a little too nosey and both he and Henry had to scare her off a few times to avoid their cover being blown. Still, nobody suspected anything, and for the last few months, their well had been one of the many secret ways in and out of their prison. It had allowed the Claymores to prepare for the escape, especially when they both realised there was more in the tunnels than Lord Awlthorp realised. All Toby had to do now was get to the van, get the rest of the bottles, leave and disappear.

The short man closed the airtight door behind him and started unpacking the contents of his rucksack. He placed the six bottles in a bulk carrier bag together with other random building tools he saw scattered on the floor. Toby stopped to listen from time to time. No sound of familiar voices. The house was meant to be empty for a while and it was the perfect time to act undisturbed. He put the recipe notes in the bulk carrier bag, neatly folded to one side. He lifted the bag and it was already too heavy. Toby checked his watch wondering if he had time for two trips. His van was parked outside a few numbers down. He did not really have much choice. He needed to grab the rest of the tools and arrange the basement as if he had done another day's work as the friendly builder.

Outside, Arthur Road was quiet. Toby acted nonchalantly as he walked the short distance to the van which had been parked out there for a few months already. The neighbours were accustomed to seeing workers coming in and out of 24 Arthur Road after the plans to refurbish their basement had been approved by the Council. Toby therefore did not seem out of place. Still, beads of sweat formed on his forehead at each glance of his watch. Soon the last shockwave would hit and then the C4 would detonate. He had to move faster. He ensured everything was in the van and quickly ran back to 24 Arthur Road. The thought that Lord Awlthorp or Reginald Bosham could be walking past the house at that very moment dawned on him, but he brushed his stupid paranoia to the side. The road was empty and to everyone he was just a builder doing his job.

Back in the basement, Toby did not waste time. He prepped up the room as if someone had been chiselling away at the walls, plastering here, painting there. He even dirtied his hands and his overalls. Once out of the house, he still had to play the part until he was miles away from Wimbledon. He started grabbing the rest of the tools he was meant to take back to the van, dumping them into another bulk carrier bag one by one. Toby heaved the bag at some point, feeling its weight, and decided it was time to bid farewell to the basement. He was about to walk up the stairs when the earth rumbled from its depth and the whole basement started shaking under Toby's feet. The short man tripped over and fell on the floor with an expression of shock and terror on his face. It can't be, he thought. He checked his watch. The clock hand for the seconds was not moving. The watch had stopped. Toby held tight and thought the worst. The plan was to be away from here when the C4 exploded and now he feared the ground would open and swallow him up again, making the tunnels his prison forever.

The earth shook for another short time but for Toby it seemed like an eternity. He curled up on the floor with his face buried in his arms, waiting for the ceiling to fall. Yet, the earthquake he had caused came to an end after only a few minutes without the damage he had expected. At least on the surface. Toby pulled his arms away and listened outside. He heard the next door's neighbours coming out to their front garden asking themselves what had happened. Toby had to flee before crowds or the police turned up outside. The short man stood up and grabbed his bulk carrier bag without checking everything was inside. He then heard a metal clang coming from the airtight door covering the entrance to the well. Toby froze. The door lifted slowly. It took a few times before the hand that emerged was strong enough to push the door wide open.

Enrico gasped as he drew in clean air for the first time and hurled himself out of the stone well with the last of his strength. He rolled onto the hard floor, his heart beating fast. The Italian baker was happy to touch solid ground. He sat up. The bright white light was strong and blinding, and Enrico put his hand over his eyes to check where he was. The room was a white basement in the process of renovation. The smell of fresh paint still hung in the air. Someone's house by the looks of it. He looked over his shoulder at the stone well he had just come out of. It dawned on him this could be the same well Rosie had mentioned. The same well she saw strange men coming out of. He could be at 24 Arthur Road.

Enrico kept looking around to take in his new surroundings, when a wooden door in the far corner creaked open. Enrico glanced up and caught a glimpse of the short and stumpy silhouette belonging to Toby Claymore staring back at him through the gap of the wooden door.

'Oh damn…' cursed Toby Claymore feeling exposed.

'Wait…' shouted Enrico with a weak voice.

Toby had no intention of staying and listening to the strange man in a chef jacket that had just come out of the tunnels. He was surely someone working for Lord Awlthorp, Toby thought. He shot out of the room and Enrico heard him fleeing up some stairs. He did not recognise the short man, nor did he understand what he was escaping from. It definitely did not sound right to Enrico. He quickly got up and went after the short man. A brief flight of stairs brought the Italian baker up to a ground floor landing of a large detached house. The main door was wide open, but nobody had been alerted by the commotion. Whoever lived here did not seem to be in.

Enrico dashed out to get answers to his questions. He ran half-way onto the patio outside and found himself in a medium sized garden facing the main road. The clean outdoor air filled his lungs once again. Saint Mary's Church tower was visible in the distance beyond the row of detached houses. What caught Enrico's attention though was another shape towering above the houses, almost as high as Saint Mary's spire. It was an enormous cloud of fine copper-coloured dust rising up in the sky from a short, domed turret-like building a few doors down. Enrico could not ignore the obvious fact the collapsing tunnels underneath had caused some damage above ground. Moreover, he suspected it was no natural cause. The short man in overalls probably knew something but he was nowhere to be seen.

A car door slammed. An engine revved frantically nearby. Enrico blinked and raced out of the garden, through the gate and out onto the main road. There was no traffic on Arthur Road, except for a black van speeding up the road towards him. The Italian baker recognised the short man at the wheel. Toby hit the accelerator grinding his teeth at him. Enrico threw himself out of the way and fell over the hedge and onto the front garden. The van hit the curb and swerved back onto the road without any intention of stopping. Toby Claymore then sped ahead, without looking back, and disappeared down the road. He had to get out of Wimbledon as quickly as possible.

Enrico groaned with pain and sat up in surrender on the soft grass. His breathing was heavy, his muscles aching, yet his brain hadn't stopped. The short man, whoever he may be, had just tried to run him down. Something was wrong. Police sirens blared in the distance. That did not sound good either. The Italian baker did not waste time to get up on his feet again. It was time to go back to Dr Watkins and report back what he had found in the tunnels.

'Do you need any help, young man?' boomed a serious voice from behind.

Enrico spun around to face a man with a moustache and a pipe hanging from his lower lip. Behind him, a woman, presumably the wife, stood at the entrance of 26 Arthur Road with a disgruntled look on her face. They both studied from head to toe the odd man in a chef jacket that had landed on their well-cured front garden and smashed their petunias. The Italian baker straightened himself up and smiled as if nothing had happened. He slowly walked back out into the road under the watchful eye of the man with the pipe. He then ran off before they asked any questions and before he could make more a fool of himself than he already had. The police sirens were now growing louder beyond the tall treetops. It was time to make an exit before he crossed paths with Inspector Baynard too soon.

'He's moving! This time faster!' alerted Reginald checking the blinking dot on his phone.

The driver slowed down the car and looked at Lord Awlthorp in the backseat. He nodded to let him know he waited for his instruction.

'How fast?' Lord Awlthorp asked Reginald who sat in the front seat hunched over his phone.

'Fast! He must be driving a car and he is definitely rushing somewhere important.' Reginald replied.

All three of them were already on alert when the tracker they had put on Toby started to wander away from the chamber and zigzagging under the hill, presumably through the tunnels. Now, Lord Awlthorp was starting to lose patience with the mad chemist.

'Where is he headed?' asked the man in black.

'He left Arthur Road and he is moving like a madman down towards Vineyard Hill and Leopold Road.'

Lord Awlthorp did not comment and kept his composure. The driver scrutinised him through the rear-view mirror. The black corvine eyes were lifeless, and the corrugated forehead cast shadows which barely hinted at the storm brewing inside. Lord Awlthorp was not happy.

'Let's follow him closely and the moment he stops we put our hands on him. I hope he acted alone. He has become a liable loose end!'

'I told you, sir. He is useless.'

'Why Arthur Road?' asked Lord Awlthorp.

The question was more to himself. Toby Claymore must have found a way out without telling them. Not even a day had passed, and that mad chemist had taken the opportunity to flee. Toby must know something Lord Awlthorp did not. The mystery and the uncertainty gnawed at him. They had to stop Toby getting away.

The driver had picked up Lord Awlthorp's signal to hit the gas and catch up with the chemist. He cut through Marryat Road and then Burghley Road, speeding straight through to Saint Mary's Road and then Church Hill. Reginald kept him updated on Toby Claymore's movements.

'He is crossing the bridge, taking Gap Road.' he explained.

'If he turns north at the crossroad, go via Wimbledon Park.'

The driver nodded.

'How does that help?' said Reginald.

'We can get to him quicker. No traffic lights.'

Reginald shook his head in disagreement and kept a close eye at the blinking light, hoping for no unexpected turns. The driver pushed through Lake Road and stopped at the crossroad with Leopold Road.

'Why are we stopping?' exclaimed Reginald.

'Check Reggie!' ordered Lord Awlthorp, keeping a calm but stern tone of voice.

Reginald monitored his phone. He then saw the blinking light turn north onto Durnsford Road.

'He is turning north…' he muttered in disbelief.

'Luck is on our side. Let's get him!'

The driver put the car in gear and sped through the quiet side streets of Wimbledon Hill. Vineyard Hill. The western end of Arthur Road. He crossed the bridge over the rail at Wimbledon Park, right when the blinking light had stopped at the traffic lights down the road, where their paths finally crossed onto Durnsford Road.

'He went the long way round, didn't he?' commented Reginald.

'He is panicking.' added Lord Awlthorp. 'Something did not go according to his plan.'

'He is turning right now.' continued Reginald reporting Toby Claymore's movements.

'There is an isolated car park there, just by the train depot.' interrupted the driver, his eyes on the traffic as they slowed down towards the intersection with Durnsford Road. 'Plenty of garages to rent too.'

'Make sure he has reached his final destination!' advised Lord Awlthorp without looking outside.

The driver nodded and slowly turned right once the traffic light turned green. He and Reginald could now see Toby's vehicle in plain sight.

'He is in that van!' exclaimed Reginald, checking the movement he saw in the real world were the same as on his phone.

'Just be sure it is him inside!' warned Lord Awlthorp, not ready for another bad surprise.

Toby Claymore parked the van in front of one of the many nondescript black garages. He and Henry picked it as the best and closest location for their hide-out. Inside, they kept their tools, and above all they stored what Toby could use to make himself rich and finally quit a life of crime. Unfortunately, Toby Claymore would now have to live out his brother's plan on his own.

He stepped out and lifted open the garage door in a hurry, worried in case the police or the strange man in a chef jacket would be onto him. He then returned to the vehicle and quickly parked the van inside. The strange man he had encountered had seen the van and probably the neighbours in Arthur Road were now making all sorts of connections. He had to paint it another colour or get rid of it. Toby stepped out again, ready to close the garage door behind him when a gun barrel squeezed against his nose, cold as steel, unforgiving as death itself.

'Hello Toby!' sniggered Reginald, pressing his gun harder against Toby's terrified face.

'I can explain…' he pleaded.

'Shhhhh, you mad chemist. Best not draw anyone's attention, or you may join your brother Henry before you know it!'

Toby's face hardened. He despised Reginald now more than ever, but he felt helpless. He then noticed a black saloon car parked across the exit of the garage. The driver looked at him impassively as he opened the back-passenger door. Lord Awlthorp emerged with his black suit, over a dark grey shirt and black tie, and a stern, merciless expression. The short man stuttered, trying to say something, but nothing came out of his mouth except babbling sounds filled with fear.

'Mr Claymore, we meet again!' started Lord Awlthorp with an eerie sense of cheer. 'Is this your second home perhaps?'

There was no laughter echoing in the cramped garage. Lord Awlthorp moved next to Reginald and held his gaze at the short man for a few seconds. He then turned to check the garage. There was little space in there with the van parked in it, except for one corner where three or four crates of green bottles lay neatly stacked. The man in black frowned and made a step forward to take a closer look. The bottles were full of a burgundy colour substance, that same purple and maroon blend typical of red wine.

'Mr Claymore, stealing the wine Reginald bought perhaps?' he teased while the logic in his head worked furiously to understand what game Toby Claymore was playing. 'If you wanted wine, you could have asked Reginald to get some for you to drink in your spare time.'

Lord Awlthorp chuckled to himself. He checked inside the top crate and picked up one bottle at random. He then realised something was different. The label was slightly worn out and yellowed as if aged considerably. Reginald had been buying cheap wine, with new white labels, not this kind of old bottles. The bottle in his hand seemed to come from somewhere else. He popped the cork open. The aroma was sweet and pleasant to the nostrils. He could tell a good wine from the scent, no acidity. He looked again at the label. Only two words were written on it, framed in a square where grapes, vine stems and roots were intertwined with each other.

Cecil 1590

'Where did you get this bottle, Mr Claymore?' he asked, still staring at the label.

Toby swallowed hard, unwilling to say anything.

'The boss asked you something, you idiot!' shouted Reginald.

Toby glared at him, silent but filled with anger. He had enough of being the push-over.

'If you don't answer right now, I swear...' threatened Reginald.

'Open the van!' interrupted Lord Awlthorp.

Reginald stopped in his tracks and blinked at the man in black. He did not like the interruption.

'Open the van, Reggie!' repeated Lord Awlthorp. 'The answer must be in there.'

'I don't like being called Reggie!' stated Reginald pulling the gun away and waving at Toby to slide the large side door of the van.

'You won't find anything in there…' started Toby, stalling as he turned around.

'Shut up!' bellowed Reginald.

'Mr Claymore,' spoke Lord Awlthorp. 'we will be the judge of that. You escaped the confinement of the chamber and I believe you took something with you that belongs to me. I don't know what, but I am eager to find out.'

The van side door slid open revealing the mess of tools Toby had flung inside before running away from 24 Arthur Road. Lord Awlthorp pushed Toby out of the way and Reginald pinned him against the driver's door.

'Let's see.' said Lord Awlthorp peering inside.

One of the bulk carrier bags had fallen to one side. He pulled it towards him, catching an empty bottle of wine before it fell out.

'Oh, what do we have here? More tools, and five empty bottles of wine. Picking up a bad habit, Mr Claymore? What were you meant to do with these bottles?'

'None of your business.' protested Toby. 'And you can't even count. There are six…'

'It is my business!' interrupted the man in black. 'And you are the one who can't count. There are five bottles. Your right back door is loose and ajar. One must have fallen off when you tried to escape!'

Toby's eyes panicked, wondering where the sixth bottle had gone. Lord Awlthorp searched deeper inside the bag. He picked up the note and waved it in Toby's face. Toby hang his head low in defeat. Lord Awlthorp had found Henry's last notes.

'I thought we took all your notes last night, Mr Claymore. Why did you keep this one from me? Did someone offer to buy my formula off you and your brother, you petty criminals?'

Toby growled with clenched teeth. Reginald pushed the gun against Toby's nose again to remind him who was in charge.

'The sooner you tell me, Mr Claymore, the sooner we will be out of your way…'

Lord Awlthorp chuckled but his expression froze when his eyes landed on the recipe. It looked like his, but not to the letter. Something was different. The handwriting, even the content. He glared at Toby.

'What is the meaning of this? Instructions were to follow my recipe by the letter after each fine adjustment and share any modifications. What did you and your brother do? What did you find?' he questioned with a cruel voice.

His manner had changed. No more eerily light-hearted. Coldness instead engulfed his corvine eyes and Toby felt they were daggers jabbing at him. The short man did not say anything.

'Sir,' interjected the driver standing by the car. 'I've just picked up the police airwaves.'

The driver touched his earpiece once more. Reginald turned to him to learn more while Lord Awlthorp kept his cruel gaze on Toby Claymore.

'Police in Arthur Road.' carried on the driver reporting back. 'They have identified the van but not the number plate.'

'Sir,' exclaimed Reginald. 'it is not safe to stay here!'

Lord Awlthorp's lips thinned and his eyes narrowed at Toby Claymore, merely a few inches from him. He then gave his orders.

'Get these crates of wine and the carrier bags. Put them in the car and lock this garage. Let's move out and take Toby Claymore with us. He will tell us more back at the house.'

Lord Awlthorp moved away towards the black saloon car. The driver stood still and exchanged looks with the man in black.

'Aren't you opening the door?' asked Lord Awlthorp.

'Two men have been identified by witnesses.'

Lord Awlthorp's forehead burrowed, concerned.

'A man looking like one of the Claymore brothers.' added the driver.

'And the other?' asked Lord Awlthorp puzzled.

'Someone you may know. A man in a white chef jacket.'

Baynard leaned on his car as he observed the long section of Arthur Road carefully, which had been cordoned off. He was trying to determine where the real problem lay, and whether all these happenings were connected or not. To his left, where Arthur Road disappeared towards Saint Mary's Church, he could see the Artesian Well from which a cloud of dust or smoke had emanated and dispersed into the air up to half an hour ago.

The low turret with its domed top, known as the Artesian Well, had been there at 20 Arthur Road as long as he could remember, part of the landscape but never glorified for its historical importance. The Artesian Well now belonged to a private residence, but he did not know who the owner was. A member of the Council, a woman named Lorraine, had turned up and was now sharing her dissatisfaction with Baynard.

'Inspector, the Council will not be pleased.' she complained. 'This is clearly an act of vandalism and poor civic duty in such tranquil neighbourhood. I mean, inspector, what has this town come down to? Explosions again?'.

'Nobody said there has been an explosion. This is not Cannizaro Park all over again. We don't know the causes yet, ma'am.' reassured the inspector.

Baynard told himself and his men to avoid references to explosions and earthquakes, and demanded experts to be sent on site as soon as possible. He did not want to start spreading unfounded rumours.

'I have noted down that the Artesian Well and the residence were both empty at the time of the accident.'

The woman nodded.

'I will ask the firemen to confirm the status of the building to ensure it is still safe and stable.' he concluded to dismiss her. 'Now, Lorraine, you turned up to represent the Council on behalf of the owner of the Artesian Well. Who should I contact for further questioning? You or the owner?'

'The private residence and the Artesian Well belong to the Lord of the Manor of Wimbledon, inspector.'

'Is that George, 9th Earl of Spencer?' asked Baynard.

'Not anymore, inspector. The title was bought last week by a new individual who prefers to stay anonymous. Hence, I am here on behalf of the Council, to ensure his property is safe and that we avoid another drama like Cannizaro Park. You can ask any questions to me.'

The inspector knew she would not leave until he had done so. Yet, she could not be very helpful from the start. He asked the minimum possible and then allowed her to go. He took down a few notes, though. The whole basement of the Artesian Well had apparently collapsed but the building had stayed intact. He underlined the need for a geologist and a surveyor to get their opinion on what had happened below the Artesian Well. He then looked to the row of houses in front. Sergeant Jeremy was in the front garden of 24 Arthur Road, busy talking to the Rutherfords, who had a feeling their house had been broken into. The inspector would have normally treated the whole thing as a burglary. Two things though made no sense. Nothing had been stolen, and the wimpy kid with them was Rosie, the little girl who had found the burnt dead man the day before. Baynard was trying to see the link but the scene in front of him told him nothing.

Next door, the neighbours at 26 Arthur Road waited eagerly on the front lawn for their turn to be questioned after giving their details to one of the police constables. Baynard had agreed to interview the couple the moment he heard them shouting they saw who did this. The inspector gathered his thoughts, choosing his questions carefully. Then he closed his notebook and melted his icy stare temporarily to put their only witnesses at ease from the start.

'Hello, I am Inspector Baynard. I understand you were here when the presumed burglary happened, and you claim you saw something here in the street.'

'Someone, inspector.' corrected the man holding his pipe in his hand.

'Two of them.' added the wife next to him.

'I see. Let's start from the beginning. What made you come out of the house?'

'The earthquake.' cried out the wife.

Baynard eyed her suspiciously. He knew what she meant, having experienced it personally, but assumed he knew nothing.

'Could you please be more specific?' he asked.

'I was in the kitchen when I heard a big bang under my feet.' explained the wife. 'The whole ground shook for a short time. Thank God, nothing broke. I looked out of the window and called out my husband, who was already out in the garden wondering what had happened. A thick cloud started to come out of the windows and the top dome of the Artesian Well. He saw the smoke rising so I joined him outside. Then one of the workmen from Arthur Road came rushing out of the house and onto his van parked outside.'

'Can you describe him?'

'Short man in dusty overalls. Short hair, messy. He looked scared.'

'Had you seen him before?'

'Of course.' interjected the husband. 'He was one of the two builders at 24 Arthur Road. They had been doing some work in their basement for a few months. They were always in and out of the house. They had the keys.'

Baynard frowned. Nothing stolen and the one man seen coming out had keys to the house. If not a burglary, he wondered what the motive could be.

'Was the man carrying something?' asked the inspector.

'A bulky bag with tools in it.' continued the husband. 'He just hopped in the van in a hurry. He looked scared.'

'You said there was a second person. When does he or she come to play in all of this?'

'He came out of the house right after. He ran into the street and then the worker tried to run him down before driving away.'

Baynard's inquisitive stare returned. He could not help it. Putting the events together was like building a puzzle using pieces from different boxes.

'Can you describe the second man?' asked Baynard.

'A man with wavy hair. Average height. Quite handsome.' answered the wife.

'Handsome but weird.' added the husband to play down his wife's praise. 'He was wearing a white chef jacket. Not that white though. He looked as if he had come out of an underground mine.'

This last comment made Inspector Baynard flinch. There were not that many people in Wimbledon going around in chef jackets, and he could certainly narrow it down to a few. He simply hoped the jacket in question did not belong to Mr Enrico LoTrova.

'He mumbled something about the Wynnman bakery, an offer or something, and then stormed off. On foot!'

Baynard froze. The description fit perfectly. He wondered why the Italian baker was here. He did not like the sound of it.

'And the builder tried to run him over?' repeated Baynard to get his facts straight.

The couple nodded.

'And did you actually see them arrive and go into the house?'

The husband and wife looked at each other. The inspector noticed a puzzled look on their faces. Not about the question. Something else had dawned on them.

'Now that you mention it, inspector.' said the wife. 'I don't recall the man in a chef jacket arriving at the house… Let alone the builder. His van was here overnight.'

'Unless we weren't paying attention…' commented the husband playing devil's advocate.

Baynard took the last few notes. He had enough leads to pursue for now. Any further questions would only lead to speculation. He glanced over his shoulder and Sergeant Jeremy beamed at him from the police car. He was done too. Time to compare notes.

'Thank you both for your co-operation.' said Inspector Baynard. 'We will let you know if we have any further questions. We may ask you to come down the station for a formal statement.'

He bid farewell and let one of the police constables to complete the formalities. The fire brigade had arrived to inspect the Artesian Well and the houses nearby. A small crowd had gathered at the edges of the cordoned street, having heard the sirens. Baynard disliked attracting attention, especially when unusual events took place. To make things worse, two unusual events had happened one after the other. The inspector had a nagging thought at the back of his head, telling him the burnt dead body, the shaking ground and the two men running out of the house, were somehow related.

'What have you got?' asked Baynard hinting at the few pages of notes Jeremy had written.

'Listen to this, inspector.' replied Jeremy with a glint of satisfaction. 'The family at 24 Arthur Road looked a little nervous and disturbed. Apparently, the door had been left wide open. Yet, nothing was missing from the house. Whoever broke in simply left a big mess in the basement.'

'And how does this help us?'

'Nobody had broken in. The door was locked and was opened from the inside. Yet, there is no sign of breaking and entering anywhere else in the house. Except…'

'The basement.'

Jeremy grinned at the inspector's intuition.

'I assume you heard about the workers.' added Jeremy.

'One of the two people the witness reported seeing is a short man in a dust overall.' nodded Baynard. 'One of the builders hired for the work in the house basement. They had a key apparently. Are you thinking of an inside job?'

'There is more to that, inspector.'

Baynard paused and Jeremy winked at him.

'The family at 24 Arthur Road hired two builders to redo their basement. Apparently, when they extended the basement last year, an old stone well cropped up which they thought would be best to close up. They were afraid Rosie would fall into it.''

'I am not following.'

'The builders were two brothers. A tall and a short one. I thought there and then to show Toby Claymore's picture. Guess what? The Claymores had been hired under a false name to do the work under their house. The father recognised Toby Claymore from my photo.'

'Are you sure?'

'Double sure. What is going on, inspector?'

'I don't know, but the fact his brother, Henry Claymore, is the person we found dead in an underground tunnel not far from here, tells me there is something underneath our feet that had attracted the Claymores' attention. We must get the basement checked, and I need a geologist's opinion on whether the cloud of dust and the tremors are perhaps controlled explosions from the deep bowels of Wimbledon.'

'What would be the motive? The Claymores do food fraud, not robberies. They don't even seem the speleologist types.'

'I don't know. A geologist assessing the grounds, and also the damage inside the Artesian Well, may help us shed some light. But we must find Toby Claymore as soon as possible for questioning. Any sign of the van?'

'We know the make but not the number plate. I passed on the details to the station, so they can be shared with all constables on patrol. He cannot be far.'

'I hope so.'

'Are those all the leads we have? What about the second person the neighbours saw?'

Baynard recalled the neighbours' remark on the chef jacket. It buzzed in his head like an alarm. The jacket was dirty with soil, as if he had been crawling in the mud of an underground tunnel.

The inspector could not suppress his hunch that the man running after the presumed Toby Claymore was surely the Italian baker himself. He had to verify the neighbours' statement. If true, he needed to know why the baker's name always cropped up again whenever strange events occurred. Enrico LoTrova was the one who found Rosie and the dead body in the tunnel yesterday. Today, he was the one chasing Toby Claymore out of the house where Rosie lived. Baynard dreaded it was Cannizaro Park all over again. There was only one thing left to do.

'I need to check the description. A white chef jacket. It was a bit too fuzzy for my taste.' said Baynard vaguely to Jeremy.

'You don't think it is…'

'I don't know. Let's catch up at the station after I have more information. Are you ok to handle it and wrap things up here?'

'Yessir!' confirmed Jeremy with pride. 'Where are you going now?'

'I just need to buy some bread first.' winked Baynard.

Enrico ran back to the bakery. His pace fast; his head peering over his shoulder from time to time. The echoes of police sirens and ambulances resonated in the empty side streets that stood between Saint Mary's Church and the High Street. He took the same care when approaching the bakery, throwing a furtive look both ways. Wimbledonians walked up and down the high street still unaware of the chaos that had just happened a few streets from here.

The inside of the bakery welcomed the Italian baker with a comfortable silence, a temporary solatium from what he had been through. Collapsing tunnels, horrific blood traces, and a short man who had all the intention of rubbing him out. Enrico leaned against the counter and took a deep breath. His muscles ached all over, especially his arms and legs with all the grappling and leaping he had done. He then noticed how dirty his chef jacket was, soiled patches everywhere like sinful stains against the original, pure white. He had better change into a new one, and even put on a clean pair of trousers, before he went to see Dr Watkins. Enrico loved his chef jacket so much that he took extra care in buying five identical versions of the same. He kept them all in a wardrobe in his studio flat on the first floor. Playing with flour and dough meant having a constant change of clothes at hand, although Enrico would never have thought he would need to change because of mud.

The fresh smell of clean clothes soothed Enrico's senses and made him forget the aches and pains in his body. He lifted the lapel of his new white chef jacket and breathed in deeply for as long as he could. The ring of the tiny brass bell on top of the entrance door chimed from downstairs and brought Enrico back to reality. The sign still said 'closed', he thought. He quickly rushed downstairs and in front of him, against the glass frame of the entrance, stood Viviane. The florist wore a puffy black and red blouse, and a pair of white cigarette jeans. She had her arms crossed and held one foot forward in a pose that meant anything rather than a pleasant visit.

'Ciao Viviane!' exclaimed Enrico casually. 'How are you?''

He leaned on the counter nearby as if checking something on the shelves. He could feel Viviane's stare on him.

'Working, I suppose?' asked Viviane.

Enrico mumbled a 'yes', wondering if Viviane had seen him arriving at the bakery and whether there was any point keeping up appearances.

'I see. Just stopped by to see how your bread business went. My morning was busy. Plenty of new orders for the week. How was yours?'

Viviane walked towards the other section of the counter and leaned forward on her elbows to look across at Enrico in the eye. Her auburn hair was delicately arranged in an up-do hairstyle with lovely, curled tendrils falling over her rosy cheek. It framed her deep brown eyes and full red lips, highlighting the fierce trait of her expression and indeed of her character. Enrico had no intention of playing games. He gave her a cheeky smile and walked behind the counter, tidying up a few loaves in display, until he was opposite her, as if she was the next customer. He leaned over to her and held her gaze. There was something beautiful about Viviane, now that he looked at her closely, something he could never put his finger on. He beamed at her wondering what had brought her to the best place for bread in all of Wimbledon.

'Same old, same old. Baked a batch early this morning…'

Enrico did not finish his story. Viviane's hand had reached Enrico's earlobe and he could feel her pressing hard on it.

'Ouch!' cried Enrico in pain pulling away. '*Mi fai male*. It hurts. What did you do that for?'

'You are a pathetic liar, Enrico.' she grinned.

Enrico grumbled massaging his ear.

'Don't do that again!' he protested.

'Then don't tell me you were at your bakery today. I work across the road.'

Enrico avoided her glare.

'I did bake a batch early this morning.' he added in a soft voice.

'Yes. At five a.m. Where have you been this morning when you could have made some bread business instead? New customers?'

'What are you? My accountant? My mother?'

Viviane sighed and held her hands up. She knew she may have overstepped the mark, caring about Enrico's business too much. She wondered whether she cared too much for him perhaps.

'I saw you in your chef jacket. It was filthy.' explained Viviane. 'Where did you bake? In the mines?'

Enrico chuckled to himself at the irony of Viviane's comment. He hesitated on what to tell her. He knew his escapades would not go down that well with Viviane, who always told him he should focus on making his bakery more known. He was looking over her shoulder, through the shop window and out in the streets, in search of inspiration or advice on how to best explain where his curiosity led him. Wimbledon was normal as always. Enrico had thought he would hear cries of help in the streets by now, but the high street was as calm as always.

At first the Italian baker did not notice it, at least not until the muted deep blue tint of the police siren was right in front of his line of sight. Viviane saw the surprised reaction on his face and spun around. They were both looking at a police car which had just parked with two wheels on the pavement, almost blocking the entrance to the bakery. The biggest surprise was seeing Inspector Baynard stepping out of the car. He looked in their direction and then cupped his hands to check inside. His inquisitive stare froze both Enrico and Viviane and his faint wave of hand to say 'hello' did nothing to put either of them at ease.

'What did you do, Enrico?' asked Viviane.

'Why you say that?' protested Enrico, even though he knew too well Viviane was right. 'Maybe he wants to finally buy some bread from the Wynnman bakery?'

Viviane shot a look at him in surprise, not sure what he meant. The chime of the bell killed any chance for Enrico to explain his last comment. Baynard finally appeared at the threshold. His trench coat was unbuttoned and loose. His grey eyes scrutinised Enrico and Viviane, while he caressed his goatee.

'Good morning, Miss Leighwood. Mr Liriva.'

'LoTrova!' commented Enrico, not impressed.

'Morning, inspector. How have you been?' replied Viviane pulling off her flowery charm. 'Did you find out what happened to that poor man Enrico found dead?'

'Ongoing investigation, Miss Leighwood.' the inspector said. 'I hope to find some answers very soon.'

Baynard gave Viviane a pursed smile and sat at one of the small coffee tables, a bit unkempt. He put his hand in one of the deep pockets and rummaged inside.

'I stopped earlier, Mr Larrova.' continued Baynard while he kept searching his pocket, biding his time.'

'LoTrova!' replied Enrico.

'Yes, yes. Well, I saw your shop was closed on a Monday morning. Pretty unusual.'

'It is normal in Italy for small shops.'

'Right, right. I thought maybe the baking business wasn't going well for you.'

Enrico grinned politely at the sarcasm. The inspector was probably here to chat rather than buy bread. However, he knew Baynard's chats were always linked to his police work. Enrico knew he was in trouble. Viviane was turned towards Baynard and he could not exchange glances to warn her what she may soon find out.

'Personal affairs to attend to.' answered Enrico quickly to satisfy or perhaps dismiss Baynard's questioning. 'I can afford a break now and then. The big sale of the *sfogliatelle* after Saint Mary's fair proved to be a good idea. Would you like a taste? Oh, I am sorry. I have not asked you how I can help you. Would you like to purchase some bread? Would you like a coffee?'

Enrico knew well Inspector Baynard was not a customer at *The Wynnman* bakery. His politeness though was not about gaining a new customer. It was more an attempt to minimise collateral damage and make sure he did not go against Baynard again.

'I am here as part of my investigation. The incidence at Saint Mary's.' explained Baynard finally pulling out the notebook from his pocket.

'Oh, I understand. Still, would you fancy a coffee? A tea?'

Inspector Baynard seemed uncomfortable with the pleasantries or maybe he was pressed with time and rather get to the chase.

'If you insist, Mr LeTrovi. Americano. Black, one sugar.'

'LoTrova!' echoed once more Enrico. 'So? What questions do you have for me?'

The Italian baker moved to attend to his LaGaggia coffee machine and plated up a *sfogliatella* to sweeten the deal. With the corner of one eye, he gave full attention to Baynard's inquisitive stare.

'Could you please tell me your movements after Sunday? Both of you actually?' asked Baynard.

'Oh…Well…' started Viviane as she stood up from the counter gathering her thoughts. 'We had lunch. We both went to see the little girl, Rosie, to see how she was. We brought some flowers. Then I was at the flower shop this morning.'

Enrico listened to her version of Sunday. Close to the truth, and actually the whole truth itself, without the inconvenient hint of suspicion as to why they went to see Rosie. Viviane was clever. Enrico knew he had to be careful to stick to the same truth for most of his story but not tell the whole tunnel adventure. He needed to reconcile with a new version of the truth from a different angle justifying his whereabouts near 24 Arthur Road. Enrico thought quickly while he walked from behind the counter and served Baynard his black Americano and *sfogliatella*.

'Thank you!' replied Baynard. 'How about you, Mr Larava?'

'LoTrova! Please do try the *sfogliatella* first.'

Enrico was buying some time. He smiled at Viviane, playing along as the cheerful baker, unaware of his mischievous deeds. The florist observed Baynard and then Enrico. Something did not add up. She found it odd the inspector had come here to ask questions, unless there was a reason. After all, Enrico had found the burnt body. She bit her lip, unsure what to think.

Baynard hesitated and then took a small bite of the *sfogliatella*. It did not crumble at all and both the pastry and the cream melted in his mouth. He could not deny it was nice. He had to keep a cold smile, though, to remind Enrico this was still police questioning.

'So?' added Baynard sipping his Americano.

'I had lunch with Viviane and we both went to see Rosie.' said Enrico while he glanced outside, pretending to gather his movements. 'I had to bake early this morning and then I had some deliveries to follow up on this morning. Hence, the shop was closed.'

'Deliveries? You deliver bread now?' chuckled Baynard, astonished.

Viviane thought the same thing.

'A new idea I have been testing.' said the Italian baker.

Enrico dared playing hard ball.

'And where did you deliver?'

'Mostly Arthur Road.'

'Did you happen to deliver at 24 Arthur Road perhaps?'

Upon hearing the address, Viviane tried hard to stay detached and expressionless. It was the home address of Rosie's family, and Baynard's newly interest in it could only make Viviane's intuition tingle. Something was going on. She listened in as a quiet witness, knowing Enrico would have a lot to explain once the inspector had left.

'Yes. The door was open.' Enrico continued. 'And as I walked up the patio, I found myself facing a short man in overalls. He pushed me aside and ran away in a van. I was a bit surprised. Once I noticed there was no-one at home, I chased him thinking he was a burglar. He tried to run me over...'

Enrico swallowed hard while keeping a straight face. If he knew Baynard, he knew what would come next. The inspector stared at him. His face hard but not angry, his light grey eyes impenetrable.

'How come you did not call the police?' questioned the inspector.

'I came face to face with the neighbours and I panicked, thinking they would presume I was the burglar. My mistake on that inspector. Was that wrong? Did something happen?'

Baynard took a deep sigh. His inquisitive stare moved back to his notes, his posture relaxed for a brief moment. He stroked his goatee in thought. He was not sure what to make of Enrico LoTrova's statement. It sounded right but the neighbours claimed they saw nobody arriving at 24 Arthur Road. Someone was inaccurate or lying. Baynard felt he had been caught unprepared by the Italian baker's casual honesty.

'Would you be able to recognise or describe the man?' the inspector carried on.

'I think so. Quite short, stocky. His hair was short, a bit messy. A puffed face, and slightly chubby arms and legs.'

Baynard took out the picture of Toby Claymore he borrowed from Sergeant Jeremy.

'Is this the man?'

'Yes. That's him!' exclaimed Enrico, smiling at both Baynard and Viviane.

The Italian wanted to show as much as possible he was helping the police. Viviane grinned at him with what was more of a mocking smile than a cheering expression.

'Could you come down to the station to make a statement? Tomorrow maybe?' asked Baynard putting away his notebook and the photo.

'Sure! Is something wrong? Did someone get hurt?'

'No. Just a house robbery and we are making enquiries. A witness saw a man wearing a chef jacket and I was checking with chefs and bakers in the area. Glad to know it was you as a passer-by and did not get hurt.'

Enrico wondered what game the inspector was playing at. He was clever and did not believe everything easily.

'Is the man in the picture the burglar?' continued Enrico, now his turn to get information out of the inspector.

Baynard wet his lips and limited his answer to what his diligence as a detective inspector demanded.

'He is suspect number one.' he warned. 'His name is Toby Claymore, brother of the disfigured body you found. Please stay away from him. If you see him, contact me immediately.'

Baynard then stood up and swiftly moved on, changing the subject.

'You will be happy to know the little girl Rosie is safe and back home.' said Baynard. 'Thanks again for your help! How much for the coffee and pastry?'

'On the house, inspector.' answered Enrico. 'Glad we could help.'

'Are you bribing me with coffee and pastry?' commented Baynard, his icy stare making tough to tell if he was joking or accusing. Enrico gave out a fake laugh to let the uncomfortable moment pass. Viviane joined him too.

'On the house, inspector. Honestly.' Enrico repeated. 'I will come tomorrow for the statement. Is that ok?'

Baynard nodded. His stern, inquisitive stare hid the doubts floating in his mind. He did not know what to make of the cheerful Italian baker in front of him. Once before, he had played a trick on him. He eyed the florist briefly as well. She seemed unaware of Enrico's movements, except past experiences told him otherwise. He needed to think this through and compare notes with Jeremy.

Enrico and Viviane showed Baynard the way out, while small talk filled the silence between them. From the grey Monday weather to when the next fair at Saint Mary's Church would take place. Viviane suggested Baynard should come with his family. The inspector nodded vaguely with a shy smile. He then walked off to his police car and turned to both, keeping the same straight face and icy stare he always had.

'I will leave you two to your business.' he said. 'Remember, it is always an advantage to cooperate with the police. Call me if needed.'

The inspector then said goodbye to both and stepped inside the car. Enrico could tell Baynard was on to him. His last sentence was not a threat but a warning not to interfere with police work. He watched the car drive away until it disappeared from view.

Enrico thought the storm had passed. He was about to go back inside the bakery when Viviane blocked his way. She was standing still in his way, hand on hip and foot tapping on the concrete pavement. Her deep brown eyes demanded answers. She showed eagerness on her face to hear Enrico's excuse this time. Her presumed anger though was a mask of worry towards the Italian baker's reckless curiosity.

'What did you do?' she asked in a harsh tone Enrico had not heard in a while.

Lord Awlthorp crouched over his ivory desk in concentration; his wicked grin sparsely lit by the light of the large oil lamp in one corner. Otherwise, the room was shrouded in pitch black, no windows. Even if there had been more lights, there was nothing to see in the cubicle-sized room he was in, except bare walls, a red rug and burnt out candles scattered on the floor. His concentration room did not allow distraction. The only door out was a heavy pressurised metal door with a valve as handle, which he only could open from the inside. His inner sanctum required complete isolation, complete concentration for pure thinking. No clocks, no time.

The man in black had two small notes in front of him, laid out neatly on the ivory desk, next to each other and perfectly aligned. They were almost identical if it were not for the calligraphy and the content of each line being slightly different, Lord Awlthorp could not deny the fact Henry Claymore had done his research and had been clever at concealing his work. The man in black picked up the note to the right. It was his own transcription of the original list of ingredients he had found.

Juleep

Aqua majorane cum musco

A Succat

Manus Christi pulvis

A date had been written by Henry Claymore next to his list. It said 1546. Lord Awlthorp had the time to look it up and he was horrified to learn this recipe had been well documented by historians as a common medicine, one which was administered to Henry VIII when he stayed at the Old Rectory, in Wimbledon, due to sickness, on 20th December 1546. Lord Awlthorp could picture Henry's smug face as he made note of Lord Awlthorp's amateurish mistake.

The man in black snorted at the thought. He then picked up the second note on the left, comparing line by line with the first note.

Juleep

~~*Aqua majorane cum musco*~~ ***wrong!***

~~*A Succat*~~ ***wrong!***

Manus Christi pulvis

Alkimiae mulsi

Sangui venerarius

Lord Awlthorp sniggered at Henry Claymore's arrogance transpiring through those simple correction. Yet, he had to admit Henry Claymore had indeed found new ingredients he had not come across in any of his literature. The entire collection of Spencer manuscripts in his library had failed to even mention one of them and Lord Awlthorp felt his last two years of book research had been for nothing. For that, he despised the Claymores even more.

On the back of where Henry had written the list of ingredients, there was a personal recount of Henry's latest findings. Here, the clever one of the two chemical brothers openly criticised Lord Awlthorp's approach. The man in black found it even more irritating as his harrowing eyes read through it a second time, with mixed feelings of awe and jealousy.

> *The ingredients baffled me at first as they were not existing chemical compounds in the modern sense of the word. The ones overlapping with Lord Awlthorp's list appear to be ingredients for a traditional medicine from the Middle Ages. Lord Awlthorp could try and tweak it as much as he wants but all he will get is*

a cough syrup or a remedy for the common cold many times over.

The last two ingredients are the missing pieces to the formula, and it is something I have never heard before. Online translation from Medieval Latin into Modern English are vague and meaningless. So far, I have been able to understand one is 'fermented juice', or something like that, and the other refers to blood, which gives me the creeps.

My latest calculations suggest wine, or a similar form of ethanol, would work as a replacement for 'mulsi'. Lord Awlthorp has been supplying a good amount, meeting our demands. At this stage, though, we have no proof this mix, once prepped and run through the electrolysis, will work. We don't even know what to do with the final product. Rinse our body with it? Drink it? Burn it as if it were a hocus pocus witches' brew?

No matter how bizarre it may sound, it dawned on me this is what Lord Awlthorp may be after. The anonymous writings we found in those old, empty bottles are my only proof. Yet, it escapes me how, whoever wrote them, knew how to source these ingredients, or what the recipe was for.

The note ended with a few equations and the doses to use. Lord Awlthorp focused on the text, reading it over and over in disbelief. He had finally found how to recreate recipe for the potion he was after. Yet, even though he now knew how to make the potion, he still did not know what to do with it, or what it meant. He looked at the two special ingredients he had not been able to identify until today.

Mulsi was the Latin name for 'mead', a low alcohol beverage made out of fermented honey, very popular in Medieval England before wine took over.

It was an old way of turning natural produce into alcohol, except in this case *alkimiae* did not refer to honey but something else, still unknown. The answer was probably in the wine, as Henry Claymore had assumed. Wine after all was the product of fermented grapes, and the result was a higher level of alcohol. The liquid Henry Claymore's body had been covered in was indeed high in ethanol and helped the combustion that led to his death. Wine though did not burn so easily or not at all, unless it was some special kind of wine. Lord Awlthorp could not yet see a clear link between the ingredients and Henry Claymore's untimely death.

Sangui venerarius on the other hand was indeed a reference to blood. Yet, the Claymores did not have access to Lord Awlthorp's extensive reading material. For a moment, Lord Awlthorp's ego felt vainly superior. He knew the ingredient meant 'sacred blood' literally, and probably held a more figurative explanation than scientific. 'Sacred' could be more openly translated as 'privileged', which meant human sacrifice or blood offering. This was a clear reference to a ritual of some sort, and one he wanted to know more about. In fact, despite clearly stating he was oblivious about the purpose of the potion, Henry Claymore had decided to immerge himself into the pool, while the experiment was running, and was burnt beyond recognition. Lord Awlthorp could only guess Henry knew more than what he had shared in his notes. Why would Henry Claymore, a more rational man than his brother Toby, want to commit suicide. Perhaps Henry Claymore's source of information, those 'anonymous writings' he mentioned, could reveal more about the rituals revolving around the potion, if only he knew where these writings were. Perhaps Toby Claymore would know. He hoped Reginald, meanwhile, had been able to extract information from him. His attempt to escape with bottles of wine puzzled him. Toby Claymore had witnessed everything his brother did. He must know something, he thought to himself.

Lord Awlthorp looked up in the dark confinement of his concentration room. The feeble light in the cramped square room was enough to let Lord Awlthorp read Henry Claymore's notes. It could have been day or night outside but in the windowless space he could not tell and did not wish to know the time. His mind had to stay focused on his search for the old great power hidden underneath the placid top of Wimbledon hill; a power strong enough to move seas and mountains, as he had read many times before. He had already put a lot of effort into trying to prove it existed and he could not walk away now. Lord Awlthorp closed his eyes for a minute remembering how he came to learn about the legendary power, how he wanted such legend to be true. It all came down to the story he heard as a child; the story of an old village on the hill left to its own device at the outskirts of Londinium, and how a local man, a sorcerer of sorts, promised he could lead the village to new highs. He had the power to transform nature and have control over life and death. He claimed he could create wealth beyond the villagers' wildest dreams. That sorcerer's promises were destroyed before he could fulfil his prophecy. All that was left now was a fairy tale, a children's story, and the same old village with a crumbling history nobody cared for. Lord Awlthorp knew that if he could find that power, learn it, harness it, he could then lead Wimbledon to new, glorious highs. All he had to do was prove to himself and the world the relics existed. The old manuscripts from the Spencers' vault had led him to the two tests he had set himself. The first test proved simple; proving the existence of the black azalea, that simple, innocuous lava rock, was an easy task. He thought the second test would be easy as well; find the potion in the Pool of Elixir. Yet, all he found was millions of recipes and an old Anglo-Saxon fountain with no direction on what this potion looked like or what it was for. He was now convinced Henry's notes and his final actions pointed at some macabre, complex ritual that would open a new door in his quest. Lord Awlthorp had always thought such legendary power existed beyond life and death. To prove its existence, to really pass this second test, he now believed it was not just about finding a potion. He had to go beyond and find out what led Henry Claymore to immerge himself into the Pool of Elixir. In pursuing what Henry Claymore had discovered, the man in black knew he could share the same fate as him. Yet, deep inside he was willing to dare reproduce Henry's plan even if it meant death. He could not miss the promised powers that lay beyond. This was no longer a mere second test. It would be the ultimate test.

Lord Awlthorp took a deep sigh. He then placed the two notes he had been staring at in one of the drawers of his ivory desk. He stood up and walked up to the pressurised door. He opened it with little effort. The artificial neon lights glared strongly, and the shocking brightness of the plain grey room outside caught him off guard despite it now being a daily habit of his to visit his inner sanctum. From outside, the inner sanctum was a metal soundproof box at the centre of a larger room, blending with the grey colour of the walls around. The pressurised door closed behind Lord Awlthorp and the touchpad flashed the word 'locked', echoing a dull sound across the grey room.

This was Lord Awlthorp's lab, accessible to him alone. He had set it up as a place where to test his ideas, run his experiments, analyse the evidence drawn from the forgotten knowledge which lay hidden in the heavy tomes in his library. On one side, the five bottles taken from Toby Claymore stood on the long counter running around the perimeter. A row of ceiling lights shone directly above the running counter where his research notes and old parchments were laid out alongside vials, microscopes and test tubes.

Two of the five bottles had already been opened as Lord Awlthorp had tried to unlock their secret and understand where they came from, and why the Claymore had been stacking all these bottles in their rented garage. He had expected the bottles to contain the discards of their failed experiments, or perhaps fake grape juice being passed for real wine. The Claymores were famous for their food fraud after all. Instead, Lord Awlthorp found it to be an extraordinary wine. A round, full-bodied texture; smooth and velvety when he tasted it. It was a good vintage, almost invaluable. Nothing to do with the less prestigious wine Reginald bought for the experiments.

All the bottles bore the same label: Cecil 1590. The name 'Cecil' written on it was familiar. Based on the Wimbledon history he knew well, the Cecils were Lords of the Manor between 1588 and 1639, a title held first by Thomas Cecil and then later his son Edward Cecil, Viscount Standstill. Lord Awlthorp, however, knew very well there was no proof the Cecils ever made wine; no-one could make wine here in Wimbledon. The climate was simply not good enough. The year too had been dubious from the moment Lord Awlthorp laid his eyes on the label. No wine could last that long, in such pristine condition. Lord Awlthorp was convinced these bottles, despite the good taste and smell, were likely to be a perfect scam the Claymores had come up with as part of their escape plan so they could make some money out of all this. Shops across the country pay high prices for such a local vintage wine, thought Lord Awlthorp. Yet, how the Claymores managed to produce it so perfectly still eluded him.

Lord Awlthorp's thoughts quickly moved to the mission at hand. He had to check if Reginald had made any progress. He turned to a short flight of stairs and at the top the wall slid to the right, taking him from the grey walls of his lab back to the enigmatic paintings and arcane wallpaper of his study. The top floors were quiet, as they should be. He took the mahogany staircase and walked up one floor, to the attic. From behind the closed door, he could barely hear Reginald's cries and Toby's muffled whimpers as he was beaten up, fist after fist. He hoped Reginald, being the muscle in an interrogation, would have made more progress in breaking the only man standing between him and greatness.

The door opened onto a low attic, void of furniture, and with a few electric lamps hanging from the ceiling. Toby sat tied up to a wooden chair in the middle. His head covered in a black hood, dangling to one side in defeat. Reginald stood to one side, drying his hands from sweat and blood. The air was musty, the smell of pain too strong to ignore. Lord Awlthorp could only find it empowering.

'Did you break him?' asked the man in black.

'He has spilled some of the beans.' commented the burly man.

He pulled the hood off.

'Hey, scum! Repeat what you just told me.'

'I can't…'

Reginald slapped him hard across the face.

'I can't hear you!' mocked Reginald savouring every moment.

Toby Claymore coughed and spat blood and saliva. His right eye was puffy, and he could hardly feel his jaw. He turned to get a better view of Lord Awlthorp, his dark silhouette barely standing out in the penumbra of the attic. The wicked smile stood out and his small corvine eyes, more frightening than another of Reginald's fists on his face.

'The wine. We found it!' confessed Toby, giving way quickly.

'You found it?' asked Lord Awlthorp. 'Don't fool us with one of your scams! Do you want to make us believe you found wine from the 1500s?'

'No. No. I swear.' repeated Toby. 'We found it. In the tunnels.'

'In the tunnels?'

'It was Henry. He was the one who found the trap door. It was his idea to explore the tunnels. We always asked ourselves why you were so interested in that pool, why it was there…'

'Everyone knows all tunnels under Wimbledon are dead ends. What did you find down there?'

Toby tried to catch his breath, rushing to confess what they wanted to know.

'When the first tremors from the experiment caused some bricks to collapse,' explained Toby 'we were able to find out where each tunnel led to. This included one blocked tunnel. A faded sign, hidden behind the bricks and rocks, said 'To the cellar'. Since that tunnel led north where the hill sloped down and was closer to the surface than the other tunnels, Henry had the crazy idea there was another entrance and thought these cellars were still accessible.'

'Are you saying you found the wine cellars belonging to Thomas Cecil?' questioned Lord Awlthorp with an air of scepticism. 'Is that where the wine comes from?'

'Yes…' gasped Toby, sounding desperate.

'Sir, I don't think we can trust this information.' warned Reginald.

'I'll be the judge of that, Reggie.' replied Lord Awlthorp bitterly. 'Where is the other entrance?'

'I can take you.' panted Toby. 'It is accessible from Wimbledon Park. We went there a few times, escaping through Arthur Road, and then smuggling out the wine we found, still bottled in cellars that had not been accessed in centuries.'

'Why would you smuggle the wine?' insisted Lord Awlthorp. 'Was your plan to sell it and make money?'

Toby sighed and dropped his gaze in surrender. He then looked up at Lord Awlthorp, pleading.

'That was the original plan!' confessed Toby. 'We could not make any progress on your stupid formula and we knew you would kill us if we didn't. We agreed to stock up all of the Cecils' wine left, store it in the garage, and then the time was right we would seal access to the cellar forever, run away and sell the vintage wine on the high street. Everything was ready until a few weeks ago something changed. Henry started saying he had cracked the enigma around your recipe, your formula. He believed the wine was the missing ingredient for the experiment…' said Toby.

Lord Awlthorp tried to control his surprise in hearing the short man's pathetic story. The man in black was taken aback by the revelation. This special wine was perhaps the missing ingredient, the *alkimiae mulsi*, the missing link to make the leap towards greatness. He could not believe his ears. Reginald, instead, looked doubtful. The burly army man did not trust the short man. He searched Lord Awlthorp's gaze and then looked at Toby's puffed face.

'How could Henry be so sure?' asked Reginald.

'Something he found.' panicked Toby. 'Something he read …or someone told him…'

'Someone?' repeated Reginald with scorn.

'I don't know.' said Toby. 'Lately, he talked about hearing voices in the tunnels. He claimed he had found what the formula was meant for and knew what you two were up to.'

'And what was I up to?' challenged Lord Awlthorp.

'I don't know, sir. I swear.' pleaded Toby. 'He never told me. Henry did not share those details with me. He told me to setup the experiment and said we could finally deliver. I thought it was a cover-up for our escape. Last thing I know, he immerged himself in the pool, and…'

Toby hung his head low. The memory of Henry was biting back, and he felt sadness. He hoped by saying what they wanted to hear he would make this nightmare go away.

'That is all I know.' he cried in despair. 'You need to believe me. I just trusted Henry. He was my brother.'

Lord Awlthorp's face was hard and emotionless. He had no pity for Toby Claymore, but he had to spare him until he got to the end of what Henry had learned about the potion and the ritual behind it. He knew the answers lay in the cellar. Thomas Cecil's wine cellar. It seemed the bottles of wine in his lab were indeed four hundred years old.

'And is there any wine left? In the cellar, I mean?' he asked Toby.

'Most of the barrels and bottles in there were empty when we found the cellar. We took what we could. There may be a few bottles left.'

'Your brother mentioned some text, some writings he found in some old bottles. He wrote it in his final notes. Are these in the cellar too?'

'I don't know…' whispered Toby, still in pain. 'And I don't want to know! I do not want to end up like my brother…'

Lord Awlthorp's moved closer. His tall figure was now bent over the frail short man. He was in full control, as judge and executioner. Reginald pulled Toby's head up by the hair so that Lord Awlthorp could look into his eyes.

'You won't.' said Lord Awlthorp.

His voice was bitter and evil, and yet eerily soft spoken like a priest at confession.

'You will help me finish my work.' he continued. 'You will tell me everything your brother did, whether you like it or not. Starting from tonight. You will take us to the entrance to the cellar and prove to us you are telling the truth.'

'Yes! Yes! Will you then let me go?' whimpered Toby.

Lord Awlthorp did not answer and shook his head. He then turned to Reginald.

'Make sure he remembers who is in charge! I will see you tonight!'

Lord Awlthorp then left the attic, leaving behind him the muffled sound of Reginald's fists beating Toby blow after blow. Once the door closed shut, the rest of the house was quiet once again as it always was. He went back to his study, his mind still thinking about Toby's confession and the Cecils' wine. Lord Awlthorp's interest though was beyond oenological purposes; if what Toby told them was true, he knew there could be something in the old wine that could help identify this mysterious *alkimiae mulsi*. And if the grapes used for the Cecils' wine were indeed native to Wimbledon, despite every history book or research paper out there stating the opposite, it could only mean something powerful beyond knowledge of man had been able to create the impossible. The ludicrous idea flashed before Lord Awlthorp's eyes and the childish stories of sorcerers roaming the hills of Wimbledon with the promise of power and glory somehow started to ring true.

'I can't believe it…' cried out Viviane in shock.

The florist leaned on the desk, her legs and arms crossed, and her head cocked to one side, trying to make some sense of Enrico's story after hearing it a second time. Her voice resonated against the glass cases which crowded the Museum of Wimbledon, and luckily the entrance door to the museum was closed.

'How many times do I need to tell you, Viviane?' shrugged Enrico easing off any guilt from his shoulders for the second time. 'I went into the tunnels to find out more about Rosie's story. That's all!'

'And trample over crime scene after crime scene just like that?' insisted Viviane, even if she was saying the same thing for a second or maybe a third time. 'Are you out of your mind? I feel like we are reliving what happened in Cannizaro Park again!'

'*Non c'era nessuno.* There was nobody at Saint Mary's!

'Well, it did not take Baynard long to figure out you had been there.'

'Ah, the inspector has nothing on me.'

'That is not the point.' pleaded Viviane to overstate the obvious. 'You could have been killed down there…'

She did not know why but she cared very much for the unpredictable baker. She could not believe Enrico's tale of what he had been through. Blood traces. Collapsing tunnels. When she heard his story the first time at the bakery, she had to interrupt him in the middle of it in outrage, maybe due to his carelessness, or maybe because he had kept her in the dark. Hearing it a second time here at the museum, the aura of déjà vu filled the room. She did not like the matter one single bit. The simple fact a dead body had already been found told her they were getting involved into something too dangerous to handle. More dangerous than Eric Quercer and his mad plans.

'Easy, boys and girls.' interjected Dr Watkins. 'Let's not lose our minds. Nobody got hurt fortunately.'

The curator popped his head out from behind the open storage room door and gave Enrico and Viviane an apprehensive look. He had been listening to Enrico's quick summary of his story while he brewed some tea and was keen to learn more of it in detail. He was not going to have an argument about it, and so he quickly appeared with a tray, on which a steaming teapot of freshly brewed tea and a plate full of chocolate digestive announced his way to settle any quarrel. No wonder he was the chairman of the WAIS, where his stoic patience came in handy when dealing with heated debates on local issues.

'I do not even understand why you let him go!' Viviane told Dr Watkins as he put the tray down on the desk. 'Why such an interest in these tunnels all of a sudden?'

'I will take the blame, Viviane.' replied Dr Watkins with an innocent smile. 'I couldn't ignore the chance to learn more about some of Wimbledon's underground past. I was simply not expecting Enrico to destroy half of Wimbledon Hill.'

The curator winked at her openly for Enrico to see.

'I am here, Dr Watkins.' said Enrico. 'I did not touch or do anything down there. I followed your map. How was I supposed to know Wimbledon was about to be hit by earthquakes?'

'Earthquakes, right?' commented Dr Watkins and patted Enrico on his shoulder with a patronising attitude.

He then poured the tea for the three of them and took his seat behind the desk, nibbling at a chocolate digestive and making sure he had their attention.

'What surprises me the most,' said Dr Watkins. 'is how Enrico dug himself out of the same house where the Rutherfords live. 24 Arthur Road, isn't it? Viviane, we have to recognise that is too much of a coincidence!'

'Too much of a coincidence, I say!' said Enrico with excitement. 'I think we are onto something!'

'Remember you are not a detective!' reprimanded Viviane without looking at him. 'I think Baynard said it better than me. Cooperate with the police. Tell them what we know.'

'What *do* we know?' exclaimed Enrico.

The Italian baker moved away from the bookshelf and wondered in circles around the space in front of the large attic window. Dr Watkins coughed and hinted at him to grab the cup of tea waiting for him on the desk. Enrico stretched his arms and back, muscles still aching from the morning. He wished the curator had something a bit stronger than tea.

'Let's clear our heads about the whole thing.' said Dr Watkins. 'Then Enrico may have something useful to tell Inspector Baynard when he gives his statement at the police station tomorrow.'

Dr Watkins exchanged looks with Viviane, whose hardened smile confirmed she agreed with the idea. The curator then looked at Enrico and handed him a digestive biscuit. The Italian baker looked at it and could not help letting out a chuckle, wondering how Dr Watkins was able to keep calm so easily. The museum was quiet, and so was the rest of the Wimbledon Society building on this seemingly idle Monday. It seemed the relics, the artefacts, the decade-old documents were ready to listen.

'So, where shall we start from?' prompted Enrico.

'I'll start.' replied Viviane, determined to get the story straight for the police. 'Did you find out where the burnt body came from?'

'From the point where Rosie and I found him, there were traces of that material. I found more, deep inside the tunnels.'

Enrico pointed at the re-sealable bag on the desk. The sample was smashed into smaller pieces and now a fine dust, where the violaceous and ashen highlights could still be seen and almost glittered in the bright light. Dr Watkins leaned forward to examine it once more. He was unable to make out what it was.

'The man must have been going crazy in there.' Enrico carried on. 'It seemed as though he had run back and forth, perhaps he was injured.'

'Didn't you say someone could have dragged the body already dead?' commented Viviane.

'I thought so. Then I saw the mixed traces of blood and charred streaks on the wall too, as if someone had held himself against the wall. But at some point, the traces disappeared into thin air. I could not piece together all his movements in the tunnels.'

'How many tunnels are we talking about?' said Viviane.

They all approached the desk to check the map Dr Watkins had given Enrico. The tunnels branched out in all directions across the piece of paper.

'Can you list again what the faded signs said?' asked Dr Watkins. 'Do you remember them all?'

'*Certo!*'

Dr Watkins took out a handful of colourful post-its and placed them on the map as Enrico traced his steps in his memory. Each time the Italian baker mentioned a faded sign, the curator jotted down the exact text and a few notes, including the tunnel entrances where no signs had been visible. Enrico and Viviane noticed he was grinning.

'Are you laughing, Dr Watkins?' commented Viviane incredulous.

Dr Watkins nodded impassively. He waited until the baker had finished before he stood up without saying a word.

'Dr Watkins?' called Enrico puzzled by his actions.

The curator moved past Enrico and Viviane, and crouched by a stand nearby, full of postcards, local leaflets and pictures of old Wimbledon. He opened a cabinet at the bottom and flicked through a long stack of laminated sheets of paper. Viviane glanced over Dr Watkins's shoulder and noticed compass symbols, topography of mountains, quadrants overlaid over rivers and roads. They all appeared to be maps of different sizes and styles, possibly of the Wimbledon area. The curator slipped one out and laid it on the desk right on top of the map of the tunnels.

The laminated sheet was transparent showing only lines, dots and squares. Enrico and Viviane looked at each other. The markings and the labels did not make sense at first. However, as Dr Watkins slid the laminated sheet around, each marking and label moved accordingly and in the blink of an eye they seemed to align with the map of the tunnels.

'Ok.' Dr Watkins started to explain. 'If I follow what you describe, we should be able to pinpoint what was on the surface corresponding to the same point you were underground.'

Enrico and Viviane looked at Dr Watkins in acknowledgement. They then took a second glance at the new combined map in more detail. With the help of a small compass drawn in the top right corner, they made their way through the map calling out loud the name of the places, checking with each other they were on the right track. Wimbledon Park. Church Road. The straight stretch of road to the High Street, the roundabout, the Dog & Fox. The road up north to the Common. The one to the south where a wavy street led down the hill until it crossed the more symmetrical roads of modern Wimbledon. Additional dashes and dotted markings popped here and there, especially around the village, with short annotations or dates next to roads and buildings that used to be in one place or the other. It dawned on the baker he may be looking at Wimbledon's past in a two-dimensional format.

'Is this old Wimbledon, drawn on the laminated sheet?' asked Enrico.

'Sort of.' replied Dr Watkins. 'It shows contemporary roads and buildings as well as old ones we know stood there at some point in the village's known history.'

Enrico and Viviane both nodded. Their eyes were glued to the map, their fingers moving along, their minds wild with childish excitement. Enrico noticed a cluster of large buildings he was sure he had never seen in the area all around Saint Mary's Church. Some of them overlapped public roads and private gardens which he knew existed today. Arthur Road, especially, snaked through two of these large buildings. One seemed to dominate the northern slope of the hill when coming from Wimbledon Park or Home Park Road. Surely a building that size could not be missed but last time he had checked only the green of the ninth hole and more modest mansions were there. The building he saw on the laminated sheet was as a big as a palace, shaped in a perfect 'H'.

'What are these?' asked Enrico curious to know what the cluster of buildings around Saint Mary's Church represented.

'They are Wimbledon's five manor houses.' replied Dr Watkins. 'They no longer exist, unfortunately, save one. They were either destroyed by fire, or by the neglect of local government.'

Viviane winced at the curator's harsh comment. She wondered if he expressed the same candour when the public visited the museum. She then saw Dr Watkins starting to draw on the laminated surface with his black felt pen. Enrico and Viviane's mouths almost dropped. Dr Watkins saw their reaction and stopped for a second to explain to both the map was a duplicate of the original and he would never deface museum property.

'Let me point out Saint Mary's.' explained Dr Watkins, circling the church where Enrico had entered the tunnels from. 'This is where your tunnel starts, moving in a north-eastern direction. Your straight tunnel seems to lead ahead to where the third manor house was built in the late sixteenth century. The one by the slope looking over Wimbledon Park. A magnificent

Elizabethan palace of large properties facing the stretch of Wimbledon Park, which was way bigger back then and more of a wild stretch of land. The Cecils built it around 1588 and Edward Cecil, the second Lord of the Manor, lived in the palace after inheriting it from his father Thomas in 1623. Edward Cecil is the Viscount Standstill you read about.'

'I take the nickname is of a depreciative nature?' checked Viviane.

'Indeed.' confirmed Dr Watkins. 'He was a man incapable of making decisions, who brought about a failed attack on Spain in Cadiz. An embarrassing act King James I preferred not to talk about. Hence, the nickname "Standstill".'.

'So, the tunnel was a secret access to his bedroom?' asked Enrico making his own conclusion about the importance of the tunnel.

'Maybe.' chuckled Dr Watkins. 'More a secret escape, perhaps. It is common to find one in Medieval and Tudor palaces. However, this one would probably lead nowhere since the Elizabethan palace no longer exists.'

'What happened to the palace?' wondered Viviane.

'It fell in disrepair and was put up for sale in the late seventeenth century. Around 1675, I believe. A French Huguenot called Theodor Janssen came to live in Wimbledon and bought what was left in 1717. He was a businessman, and even Director of the Bank of England. He demolished the Elizabethan palace to use its bricks to build his own manor house, the third one, in a more appropriate Georgian style.'

Dr Watkins pointed to a house called 'Belvedere House' across the street from Saint Mary's Church, towards Wimbledon Village.

'This explains the meaning behind the third faded sign he saw.' continued the curator. 'Tunnels in the 1700s and 1800s were built for servants to communicate with different parts of the house or the estate. Both Janssen's third manor house, called Belvedere House, and the fourth manor, built by the Duchess of Marlborough in 1733, made use of existing tunnels or built new ones to serve whichever purpose they required at the time. This is the main, and most accepted, link we found between the tunnels. The Duchess of Marlborough, for example, used them for servants to take food from the kitchens in the servants' house to the dinner room in the manor house. Incredible how we are piecing history together here!'

'What do you make of the last tunnel then?' challenged Enrico.

His eyes were fixed on the last blocked tunnel he explored, where the faded sign had been half-covered by another, contradictory label. On the surface, there were no markings. Just the vast space that surrounded the Elizabethan palace at the time. A beautiful garden that stretched all around the hill and as far north as Putney. Dr Watkins wet his lips, unable to hide his excitement.

'I remember this tunnel.' said the curator. 'It was believed to stretch down the hill as far as the artificial lake in Wimbledon Park, perhaps as a source of water, but no one ever managed to reach the end of it. It had collapsed half-way, water trickling everywhere. From what you saw, Enrico, the tunnel collapsed even further.'

'But what does "Vineyard and Orangerie" mean?' insisted Enrico. 'Another nickname or secret code?'

'I think it is simply what it says it is, Enrico.' answered Viviane. 'Although I am not sure grapes and oranges grew around here…'

They both searched for Dr Watkins's gaze who playfully observed the map. He looked up and smiled.

'I am a man of historical facts.' admitted the curator. 'I can only speculate on what we gather from the old drawings dating back to 1600s, the only proof of how the Elizabethan palace looked. The sketch, done with a primitive three-dimensional view, shows a large estate next to the manor where vineyards and orange trees were grown.'

'*Non è vero*! Are you joking?' exclaimed Enrico incredulous. 'In this climate?'

Enrico was stupefied by what he had just heard. The notion of grapes and oranges growing on British soil, like in France, Italy or the Mediterranean was a bit far-fetched.

'England is so cold.' continued the Italian baker. 'How could you grow oranges and grapes? I have heard they have vineyards, to make wine. For all I know it is just rubbish. It must have been the same four hundred years ago!'

'Hey mister! We do have a nice English sparkling wine!' called out Viviane, showing some pride.

Enrico was about to draw on his pride for the long tradition of winemaking in Italy, but Dr Watkins rolled his eyes and stopped him before the conversation exacerbated to chicken on pizza or green pesto on bread.

'I don't know if wine was ever grown here.' the curator interjected. 'The sign is just an indication of where it led, whatever that may have meant for Wimbledonians in the Elizabethan era. It has historical value even if we may disagree on the gastronomic value.'

'I'll be damned if wine has anything to do with the mess we're in!' joked Enrico.

'We'll see, *ragazzo curioso…*' bit back Viviane, good-heartedly.

Dr Watkins took a step back and looked at the map with all the arrows and circles drawn. He fixed his eyes on it for a moment. With the felt tip pen he retraced the lines drawn and moved to where Enrico had come out at 24 Arthur Road.

'The well under the house, the one you used to leave the tunnels, was a secondary exit of the old Artesian Well nearby. When you started your climb, you were actually below the Artesian Well. It is the domed turret-like building next door, where you saw the cloud of dust coming out of!'

'Is this Artesian Well as old as the Elizabethan palace?' asked Enrico trying to keep track of timelines.

'No. It was built by the Second Earl of Spencer in 1763 as part of the fifth manor house. Now, only the well remains and it is privately owned. It didn't really work back in its heyday and was closed up by the Earl of Spencer and left in decay for many many years. The falling rocks and sand were probably its bottom sinking further down. Although it doesn't happen just like that…'

'*Giusto!* You are right.' followed Enrico. 'I kept feeling tremors and then the whole ground underneath shook. Can you tell me then whether Wimbledon gets earthquakes of some sort or not?'

'As much as the United Kingdom is a hot country and the most favourite tropical destination in the world!' joked Dr Watkins.

'Then what would explain the tremors and the sudden collapse? Did you feel anything Viviane?'

Enrico sought her friend's opinion. Viviane looked back and frowned, biting her lower lip in thought.

'I didn't feel anything like what you describe, Enrico.' she admitted. 'When Baynard came to the bakery, he did not mention the dust cloud you saw rising from the Artesian Well, or any explosion for the matter.'

'Someone may have tried to make the underground tunnels collapse…' trailed off Dr Watkins, his head down on the multi-layered map now a mess of notes, colours and signs.

Enrico and Viviane looked at each other perplexed. Dr Watkins then resumed his drawing, leaving his sentence half-done. Maybe he did not have an answer to his theory, or maybe the answer was too obvious not to see it. Enrico and Viviane observed his felt tip pen tracing Enrico's steps, to where the crimson traces had vanished.

'Was this the tunnel where you lost track of the charred streaks on the wall and the trace of the strange-looking dried gelatine?' asked Dr Watkins. 'The one labelled 'To Viscount Standstill's Bedroom'?

Enrico nodded.

'This tunnel was not blocked at this point.' continued Dr Watkins, thinking out loud. 'It had collapsed a bit further down from the entrance, and even then, it did not lead anywhere. The blocked entrance must be recent. Now, if we look at the tunnel without any signs, the one leading north away from 24 Arthur Road…'

'That was another dead end!' interjected Enrico.

Viviane checked what Dr Watkins's pen was pointing at. There were no marks where the northern tunnel stopped abruptly as Enrico noted. Not far from it, though, on the surface, a tiny building sat in between Church Road and Saint Mary's Church, labelled 'Old Rectory'.

'Dr Watkins,' stepped in Viviane. 'does that building still exist?'

'Indeed.' replied the curator while he drew a circle around it. 'The first manor. A historical building which unfortunately has been a private house for many decades now. I wish it was a public historical building, opened as a museum maybe.'

'It is not as big as the later ones.' commented Enrico. 'If you say it still exists, I don't even remember seeing it. Are you sure it is a manor?'

'A "manor" used to describe the land held by a lord. As far back as 1086, we know Wimbledon was just a small farm with a few houses on the top of this hill. It was a place of no importance that belonged to the actual manor house at Mortlake, near Putney. In Medieval times the farm was where a bishop or a vicar appointed by the Church would reside, collect taxes for the manor and look after the congregation. Such residence was called "parsonage house", or more appropriately "rectory". "Rector" was another name for "bishop". The Old Rectory, although not as majestic as future manors in the strict sense of the word, became the centre of power in Wimbledon as the village grew and rose in importance. After the Reformation, bishops and clerics were stripped of their possessions, their "manors", which included all farms and the land around them. The Old Rectory passed onto a new Lord of the Manor of Wimbledon, appointed by

Henry VIII himself. The Old Rectory was technically the first manor of Wimbledon, until the Cecils built their own manor, the majestic Elizabethan palace I just told you about. It is a shame the Old Rectory was then lowered to a status of stable or servants' home, dwarfed by the new manor houses built around it over the centuries. Ironically, it is the only one that has lasted in the end.'

Dr Watkins said these words with a hint of melancholy at Wimbledon's lost past. He did not raise his head, but the pen kept hitting the centre of the circle he had drawn, marking the shape of the Old Rectory on the map with tiny, idle dots.

'Why are you telling us all this, Dr Watkins?' prompted Viviane with a puzzled look.

The curator raised his head. A stern, more serious look met Enrico and Viviane's curious gaze. He cleared his voice before speaking.

'Apologies for my historical digression. It has helped me discard all the leads that have gone cold so far.'

He then turned the map towards them and pointed again to the same area he had been focusing on for the last few minutes.

'Enrico, you said the charred streaks and the blood traces came from a tunnel that, I can tell you now, had no exit at all.' carried on Dr Watkins. 'Therefore, where did they come from? Now, all the tunnels we examined so far are linked to old manor houses one way or the other. Yet, these manors no longer exist. The only obvious link which still exists today, which we could explore, is the Old Rectory. If there is a connection, something that could tell where the burnt body came from, we can only find it there. Maybe in the basement of the Old Rectory.'

Viviane was incredulous upon hearing the curator's suggestion.

'Dr Watkins, have you lost your marbles too?' she exclaimed in stupor. 'Are you now considering breaking and entering too?'

Dr Watkins gave a pursed smile and raise a hand in reassurance.

'Don't worry, my dear!' he replied, amused. 'We will go through the motions. Let me find out through the WAIS or the Council who owns the Old Rectory, and we may be able to get some sort of permission to access.'

'Do you think it still belongs to the Lord of the Manor?' wondered Viviane looking at the many magnificent mansions that once thrived across the hill

'Does Wimbledon still have a Lord of the Manor?' teased Enrico.

'Funnily enough, the title still exists although just on paper.' explained Dr Watkins, his love for history coming out once more. 'Yet, we no longer know who owns the title, since the last Earl of Spencer put it up for sale fairly recently. However, I am not sure whether the title still gives him or her ownership of the Old Rectory outright. As I said, the building is now privately owned like any other residential house.'

Enrico and Viviane watched how the curator took his time to explain and how he had been doing so since they started examining the map together. They both thought they could sense Dr Watkins's sadness, or maybe his disapproval, at a long gone past of which little was left to admire and for which nothing had been done by previous councils to keep. Wimbledon was probably suffering from amnesia, not remembering what a beautiful past it had.

Inspector Baynard munched over his tuna sandwich with utter disinterest. He held each bite in his mouth long enough to chew more than the twenty times he had to, lost in his thoughts on how the case he had on hand had turned complex and almost absurd. He sat at his desk, slouching on his chair in a moment of weakness, drained of all his energy. He blamed it on the Italian baker and his nosey attitude. It was not the lying in the inspector's face that drove Baynard crazy, neither was his suspicious behaviour or movements. The inspector simply could not follow the baker's line of thought and understand his secrecy if the baker had nothing to hide. Witnesses' statements had put him on the heels of Toby Claymore. Baynard had been wondering for the past hour why Enrico LoTrova was chasing something or being chased. He and Jeremy were definitely convinced he had not been delivering bread at all but could not explain why Enrico LoTrova happened to be at 24 Arthur Road. Again, there were still some facts unknown to him that had not been shared. Baynard could only hope the Italian baker's statement the next day would help him dig deeper.

Outside, the grey clouds had not moved, and they filled the whole sky, flattened as far as the eye could see, beyond the roof tops of Wimbledon Town. Baynard checked his watch. He was waiting for Sergeant Jeremy to report back on the evidence picked up at Arthur Road. He hoped something new had cropped up that could help. In the meantime, he flicked through the geologist's report on his desk. He had read it twice already and Baynard knew he could not get anything more out of it. The UK, let alone Wimbledon, was not a seismic area. The earthquakes had been ruled out easily. The report carried on about the tunnels under the hill and how they may have become weak over time. An inquiry would be organised in due course. Baynard bit his lower lip. If he had not witnessed the shaking earth himself at Mrs Biggins's house earlier that day, he would have accepted the geologist's conclusion. He knew though he could not let it go that easily. Perhaps learning more about these tunnels would help him understand what the Claymores were up to down there.

'Inspector!' called out Jeremy.

Baynard snapped out of his thoughts and looked up at the sergeant annoyed.

'I see you have not finished your sandwich. You have been holding it for more than ten minutes, inspector. Something on your mind?'

Jeremy was probably the only police officer in all Wimbledon Police who dared throw arrows of sarcasm at a man whose icy glance and inquisitive stare were renowned as something not to joke with. The sergeant beamed at Baynard, his ginger hair almost bright and shiny in the dullness of the office.

'Easy with the jokes, Jeremy, or I'll downgrade you to traffic warden.' replied Baynard to set the bar. 'I hope your interruption is justified.'

'I checked with forensics and learned something I had never heard before.'

'Hold it there. I have enough mysteries and puzzling questions.'

Jeremy hesitated.

'Well,' he started. 'they could only isolate some of the elements that made up the creepy maroon or crimson gelatine covering Henry Claymore's body. Apart from traces of flesh and blood, some of them remain largely unknown and will take time to analyse. Overall, the substance had the corrosive effect of acid and the burning effect of gallons of gasoline.'

Baynard did not flinch. Deep inside though he wondered what those two mad chemists had been up to this time for Henry Claymore to suffer a death as ignominious as his.

'A few things came up, though, during the search at 24 Arthur Road and also the street outside.'

'Such as?' said Baynard.

His inquisitive stare prodded Jeremy to go on and not waste time with quizzes.

'The Claymores' fingerprints were all over the basement, the walls, the tools. They had been working there for quite some time. We found them on the airtight door to the well. Unfortunately, the explosion or tremors, or whatever you want to call them, made the well collapse on itself and it is no longer accessible...

'Jeremy, give me something I can follow up. Not dead ends.'

'Some of the fingerprints bear traces of blood and ethanol, similar to those found on Henry's body, except it is not Henry's blood.'

'What?' exclaimed Baynard. 'Are you sure?'

'As much as we can be for now. Forensics need time to identify it, if at all possible.'

Baynard's inquisitive stare hardened. He feared another corpse could pop up at any moment.

'I need to learn more about the tunnels the geologist's report talks about. Anything from the Artesian Well?'

'No.' said Jeremy shaking his head. 'The Artesian Well building has not been a well for more than century. It was filled in and turned into a private residence as you know. The tremor simply made the bottom collapse and sink further, taking everything with it.'

'I still struggle to understand what the Claymores were up to. Even if the tremors were explosions and the Claymores intended to blow up the hill, it does not really make much sense at all. No motive. You said their speciality were explosives and…food fraud?'

'Yes.' Jeremy confirmed

The sergeant then put his finger on his chin. Something had dawned on him.

'That may explain the bottle.' he added.

'What bottle?' exclaimed Baynard, about to lose his patience.

'We found a bottle of red wine in the street, under one of the hedges. Surprisingly, it was intact.'

'Perhaps it fell out when they were sorting their recycling.'

'It was full, sir.'

Baynard knew that was strange. No person was insane enough to throw away a full bottle of wine.

'How does that help the investigation?' he prodded.

'Well, here's the thing.' said Jeremy. 'The bottle dates back to 1590!'

The inspector blinked incredulous.

'Come again?' he said.

'It must be the smartest fraud scheme, inspector. Horrible wine from the smell, believe me, but the label and the glass appear to be genuine. We could not find traces of tampering, and forensics of course warned not to drink it.'

Baynard scratched his head. The case was becoming more and more a game of Chinese boxes.

'Do you think I can have the bottle? I may drop at a local wine shop this afternoon. I want to see if I can get a quick opinion before forensics putting it under examination. We do not know how long it will take them.'

'I thought you might. Forensics are busy with the body, so we could use some help.'

Jeremy put a plastic bag on the table, sealed at the top with a red tape and a label on it identifying it as evidence. The bottle inside was an ordinary seventy-five centilitre in size. The glass was opaque, impenetrable, in part for its dark crimson content, but also because the glass itself was old with stain and no longer shining. Dry mould encrusted the bottle in a few places. The label was ripped at the edge and faded almost beyond recognition, no longer yellow but a thin, invisible greyish paper on the verge of being illegible. Only two words could be read on the label, framed in a square where grapes, vine stems and roots were intertwined with each other.

Cecil 1590

Baynard stood in disbelief. The clues he was coming across by the hour were all things he did not expect. Tremors, criminal chemists, burnt bodies. And now a five-hundred-year-old bottle of wine. He could not predict what else could come. Just the thought made him edgy. He needed to act fast.

'And you said the smell is terrible?' asked Baynard still checking the bottle.

'Yes. Maybe it has aged too much. It no longer resembles wine. It made most of us retch.'

'Fingerprints?'

'Recent ones, belonging to the Claymores.'

Baynard cursed under his breath. He looked at his half-eaten tuna sandwich. Appetite was gone. Only the craving for truth lingered in his mouth. Savoury but with that bitter aftertaste of not feeling satisfied.

'What next, chief?' prompted Jeremy seeing the inspector perplexed.

He was stroking his silver goatee with fine precision. His inquisitive stare looked at his desk. Each item on it pulling a thread he desperately needed to find an end to.

'I am forced to issue an arrest warrant for Toby Claymore. With immediate effect. Find him. Find the van. I'll go and get some answers about this mysterious bottle.'

'What should I tell the Chief Superintendent if he asks?'

The Chief Superintendent. Baynard had almost forgotten about him. Ever since the shocking events at Cannizaro Park, he had been clear to Baynard about keeping sensational crimes in check. He had also asked him to ensure civilians, particularly the Italian baker from 9/b High Street, did not get involved in police investigations. Wimbledon was a tranquil, family place, he preached to the inspector many times. Baynard could not agree more. Yet, he struggled to find the right words to explain to the Chief Superintendent that another strange event had occurred in Wimbledon. One that was unfathomable, unexplainable, unpredictable. A body burnt beyond recognition had been found in a tunnel. A mad chemist was on the run after collapsing tunnels, and forging bottles of wine along the way. And Enrico LoTrova was somehow again in the midst of all this.

Dr Watkins woke up in the tunnels. The crimson liquid he thought he had drowned in had just disappeared. He tried to remember how he had ended up there. Last thing he could recall was watching Enrico and Viviane leave the building together and walking back to the High Street. The curator stared at the darkness in both tunnels, and then picked one at random, dragging his feet in the thickening mud. He kept being slowed down as he tried to pick up speed.

The tunnels did not look strange to him. Perhaps familiar from the many pictures he had seen of the 1984 expedition. He squinted, not in an attempt to see further, but to understand whether this was a dream or a long-forgotten memory. There seemed no end to where he was going. He called out, but his voice came back many times over, stuck with the echo, until it died out again.

Dr Watkins pushed on. He noticed his breathing was getting a little heavier, his chest feeling tight. The curator knew he was adequately fit despite his age. Yet, at every step his legs became weaker and weaker. Dr Watkins wondered if this was why he had asked Enrico to venture into the tunnels and not himself. He then tried to remember if he had suffered the same problems when he first visited the tunnel. Or perhaps he had never visited the tunnels. This was all a dream or a nightmare. Dr Watkins shouted, and no voice came out of his mouth. Just a feeble gasp.

A rush of wind picked up in the narrow passage of the tunnel, blowing against Dr Watkins with all its strength. Dr Watkins felt the walls becoming as high as a cathedral, the mud becoming huge dunes. He realised he was getting smaller and smaller inside the tunnel. He then looked up and saw a giant version of himself standing over him. It looked malignant. Dr Watkins could no longer speak and as the seconds passed by, he felt all his bones in his body crush and his whole body collapsed on itself, as if he had no flesh, no muscles. The wind blew over him once more, and it seemed to cry out two words to him. Power and revenge.

Click. Dr Watkins opened his eyes. He rubbed his eyes and gave out a big yawn, overdue from the long talk he had had over the map. He was looking out of the window of the museum and he saw Enrico and Viviane disappear behind the corner. The curator tried to remember when they had left. He glanced at his watch and realised only five minutes had passed. He then realised he had had another dream, another blackout, and during the day this time. He was tired. He needed to get some sleep. He owed some background research to Enrico and Viviane, though. He struggled to remember if he had done it. He then turned to check his desk. The two had left both the map and sealable bag with him. Yes, the curator clicked. He remembered. He had to find out who owned the Old Rectory.

At first, he thought of phoning the Council but then again Reverend Green was probably a faster source of information. Dr Watkins picked up his jacket and locked the museum behind him to take the short walk to Saint Mary's Church. The High Street in Wimbledon Village teemed with people and brought some joy despite the grey clouds hanging over them. He passed *The Wynnman* bakery and saw Enrico busy attending to customers. Viviane across the street was doing the same with a handsome man looking for flowers for his partner. They did not notice him passing and he thought he would stop by when he had more news to share.

The steeple of Saint Mary's Church pricked the grey clouds like a mighty sword rising at the top of Wimbledon Hill. It stood quietly in all its glory. Dr Watkins always felt belittled as he approached the oldest church in Wimbledon. It was not Westminster Abbey or Notre Dame de Paris. Still, its slim, high rise to the sky, visible as far as Southfields, lifted the spirits of Wimbledonians, regardless of their belief.

Dr Watkins stepped into the church. The doors were closed but not locked so anyone could visit the house of God. The creaking sound boomed ten-fold in the echoing silence common to every church. He knew Reverend Green would be in his office above the atrium. A narrow spiral staircase took him one floor up to the mezzanine, near the large pipe organ directly facing the altar and presbytery, typical of Georgian churches. The reverend was in his small office, typing away on his tablet.

'Oh, Dr Watkins.' he exclaimed from above his reading glasses. 'I did not hear you coming in. Were we meant to meet up?'

'Not at all, reverend.' said Dr Watkins. 'I have something to ask of you, and I thought I'd take a short walk and pop round in person.'

'You did well. Our Monday meeting has been cancelled this morning, and I have not yet spoken to a living soul today.'

'No police came round this morning after yesterday?'

'No. Thank God! The police line is still up for now. I did hear police sirens nearby this morning. Something on Arthur Road. Burglary, I think I heard? I don't know. I saw smoke from the Artesian Well. It looked like an explosion to me.'

Dr Watkins listened curiously. It fitted Enrico's story.

'I am sure the police will come to remove the police line here at the crypt,' continued Reverend Green. 'and put a new one up in Arthur Road. What is happening to Wimbledon? Ever since Cannizaro Park…'

'Sign of the times, reverend. Things change but hope stays.'

'You should be running my sermon this coming Sunday, Dr Watkins. You would enlighten people more than I manage to.'

They both chuckled.

'So,' asked Reverend Green. 'what was it you needed to ask me?'

'Yes, yes. Do you happen to know who owns the Old Rectory? I know it is privately owned but its current owner escapes my mind.'

The reverend eyed Dr Watkins with a mocking glare.

'I thought you knew. Julian Alberon bought it one or two years ago I believe. It has been a while now.'

'Julian Alberon. From Alberyx Enterprises?'

'The man himself. The best local businessman Wimbledon has ever had.' boasted Reverend Green, unable to hide his admiration for the self-made entrepreneur.

Dr Watkins was not surprised. Julian Alberon had been involved in improving Wimbledon business ever since he started promoting local shops and local events. One of the first funding the WAIS received came from Julian Alberon himself. He became so influential that he was able to set up his own company, Alberyx Enterprises, here in Wimbledon. It specialised in anything from tech and pharmaceutics, to food and merchandising. It also provided venture capital to support anything new and promising to come out of Wimbledon. Dr Watkins was somehow relieved to find out Julian Alberon had bought the Old Rectory. It was as if the historic building was protected, safe from further shame.

'Is he still in Wimbledon nowadays?' asked the curator.

'Last time I heard Wimbledon was now his HQ. Unless he is travelling, you might be able to get an appointment at his house. Being the chairman of the WAIS, I am sure he will find time for you. What is your interest in the Old Rectory?'

Dr Watkins considered the reverend his dear friend. Keeping secrets from him might have come across as disloyal. Yet, the curator thought it best not to drag the reverend down a path he himself did not know where they led. He had promised Viviane to get the facts they needed and pass them onto the police.

'The interest was mere curiosity.' explained Dr Watkins with a distant voice. 'I came across a few old books and photos the other day. I wondered if a chance to open the Old Rectory to the public was at the door.'

Dr Watkins yawned and caught himself in the act, covering his mouth in apology.

'Pardon me, reverend.' The curator excused himself. 'I feel a little tired. I had strange dreams in my sleep last night.'

'Still finding it difficult to sleep?' asked the reverend.

'Sometimes.'

Reverend Green watched the curator. His mouth twisted in a smirk.

'Why are you laughing?' said Dr Watkins puzzled.

'Remember, you are not a young explorer anymore!' reproached the reverend with a chuckle.

Dr Watkins cocked his head to the side. His furrowed forehead told the reverend he did not follow. The curator always joined the dots of the conversation. Yet, this time he found the reverend's words a little cryptic. Reverend Green's eyes blinked a few times, and then escaped Dr Watkins's gaze for an instant as if he realised something was not right. The reverend chuckled again to brush off his hesitation.

'Excuse me!' continued the reverend, quick to correct himself. 'What I meant is that you are always chasing and exploring opportunities. Like in 1984, when you joined…I mean…when you hoped something would come out of the speleological expedition and then everyone came out empty handed.'

'Well, maybe if I had joined the expedition…' suggested Dr Watkins.

'You would have discovered something!' continued the reverend, relentless. 'Yes, Dr Watkins. You told me that before. Or take a few months ago, when that lava rock that was discovered in Cannizaro Park. Since then you have been trying to get some response from the British Museum. Or what about the many protests to the Council and calls to arms you sent to English Heritage in support of your cause to protect what was left of historic Wimbledon…'

'I get it, Reverend Green. And isn't that what the curator of the Museum of Wimbledon should do?'

'Of course!' approved the reverend on a peaceful note. 'It gives hope. A stable kind of hope as things change for better or for worse.'

'You are now stealing my lines, reverend.' chuckled Dr Watkins.

'I am just reminding you not to lose hope in the search for a truth. Use your love of history as a means to inspire Wimbledonians with hope.'

Inspire Wimbledonians with hope. Reverend Green's statement rang in Dr Watkins's head for a while after he left Saint Mary's Church, and accompanied him in his thoughts as he made his way back to the high street. He had not expected advice from the reverend when all he asked was a piece of local information. The curator wondered what the reverend was hinting at. Perhaps to take it easy and to choose his battles. Losing hope probably meant losing the strength to carry on. He asked himself what he really expected to find in the tunnels and in the Old Rectory. The strange dreams he had had at night, even those he experienced during the day, popped into his head like scattered photos across a table. Snapshots of a reality known to him, but somehow new. Dr Watkins felt tired all of a sudden. He let out a yawn and again held his hand to his mouth. The excitement was taking its toll on him. Once this matter was over, he ought to get some rest. First though, he had to call Julian Alberon's office today and make an appointment for at least tomorrow.

Dr Watkins strode down the high street, past the Dog and Fox, the shops, the cafés. He then stopped outside *The Wynnman* bakery. He glanced at the sign at the top, and before moving on, he yawned once again.

Baynard stopped the car with an abrupt halt, parking on the pavement. The screech of the brakes scared the few passers-by walking along the parade of shops at the beginning of the Ridgeway. The inspector flashed the blue light of his siren to calm everyone and ensured he had left enough space for local traffic to pass through.

The wine shop he had parked in front of was open and the owner stared oddly at the police car from behind the counter. Seeing an inspector walking through his shop entrance left him a little dazed and a little worried. He then noticed a bag in his hand, which the inspector placed on his shop counter with a loud thud as if he was dropping a sack of coal. The shopkeeper ignored his poor taste in manners; he would never get used to bad manners. His attention, however, was quickly grabbed by the bag. Keeping it upright, Baynard slid the bag over the counter. The shopkeeper recognised the vague shape of a bottle inside.

'And hello…officer?' said the shopkeeper.

'Baynard. Inspector Baynard.' replied the man from Wimbledon Police.

The shopkeeper was surprised. He had had police constables coming over a few times to question him about under-age drinking reported in the area, but an inspector entering his refined wine shop was a first and he hoped it was not slippery slope for his reputation.

'Oh, Inspector Baynard. Nice to meet you. I am the owner. How can I help you?'

'I am looking for a quick expert view. Can you check this bottle of wine for me? I am interested in knowing the source. The age too, perhaps, to confirm what the label says.'

'With pleasure. I will do my best to evaluate the quality of such wine. Part of your own collection? Do you know the grape…?'

'It is police evidence, sir.' interrupted Baynard with his inquisitive stare. 'You probably want to speed up your evaluation and keep it to yourself. If you may.'

The shopkeeper turned his attention to the bag. His mind raced as he imagined a blood-stained bottle, one perhaps used as a weapon in a local homicide. His expectations were drowned the moment he realised the bottle, sealed in a police evidence bag, was a normal seventy-five centilitre bottle.

'Let me open it for you.' said the inspector.

Baynard took a pair of gloves to open the evidence bag so the shopkeeper could take a better look. He then pulled the loose cork to let him smell it. They both waited for the full-bodied aroma of wine to come out of the round bottle neck. Baynard had not yet experienced the foul smell Jeremy said he had experienced, and he did not make much of it. Wine, when aged too much, could turn vinegary. Yet, he and the shopkeeper were not prepared for what their nostrils had to endure. The foul smell no longer resembled anything like wine. It was a mixed, retched smell of rust iron and mouldy herbs. The shopkeeper pulled a face in disgust and put his hand over mouth and nose. He could feel his eyes watering. Baynard moved back from the counter instead and coughed loudly, as if to spit out the horrible smell.

'Oh lord, what the hell is it!?' he cursed, unabashed to express how vile the contents of the bottle were. 'This is not wine!'

The shopkeeper tried to keep his self-composure, suffering deep inside and at the same time cursing the person who had thought this could possibly be wine. He reached for the cork and closed the bottle. It took a minute or two for the air around them to be breathable again, although Baynard could still taste the smell in his throat.

'This is not wine indeed!' concluded the shopkeeper, stating the obvious. 'My nostrils have been exposed to cheap wine in my time, but it smelled and tasted better than this.'

'What is it then? Is it a cheap attempt to make wine? Food fraud?'

Baynard knew he was leading the question. He bit his lip for rushing. He was pressed for time though.

'It smells like fermented liquid, but no grape was used. Maybe honey and herbs like mead. Still, it bears no resemblance to that either.'

'Would you be able to say how old it is? Or at least the bottle?'

The shopkeeper hesitated after hearing the inspector's request. He would normally be able to give an approximate evaluation if he dealt with wine. The contents of this bottle could have been poison, for all he knew.

'I am afraid, inspector, I won't be able to help you further or tell you anything about the contents of this bottle.' The shopkeeper explained. 'This is not wine. And if it were, it would require tasting and, believe me, that is out of the question.'

'An educated guess perhaps?' insisted Baynard.

The shopkeeper then crouched over the bottle and analysed it from all angles, comparing it with the thousands of bottles he had seen coming through his shop on his trips to Italy and France. The thickness of the glass, the faded label, the words inscribed on it. Baynard watched him stare at the mysterious bottle, hopeful he would come out of the wine shop with something more than a bad taste in his nose and mouth.

'Well, inspector,' concluded the shopkeeper after careful reflection. 'I cannot be fully sure, and I would advise a more scientific analysis of the glass. However, the glass is authentic. It has aged naturally in a cellar. See the crusts inside and outside, from mould and dust. If this was food fraud, they still used an old, genuine bottle. At least two hundred years old. Perhaps not as old as the date stated on the label but I would not dismiss that. It could be possible.'

Baynard listened to the shopkeeper attentively. Forensics would need more time. Time he did not really have, unless they found Toby Claymore first.

'Thank you.' said the inspector putting the bottle back into its evidence bag. 'Have you got anything on what is written on the label? "Cecil 1590"?'.

'Cecil…Cecil…I read this somewhere…' muttered the shopkeeper.

The shopkeeper searched his memories. Then his face lit up.

'Ah yes. Now, I remember. You might find your answer next door.'

'Next door?' repeated Baynard.

'The Museum of Wimbledon. I read this name there some time ago. I am sure Dr Watkins, the curator, could shed some light.'

Dr Watkins, thought Baynard. The curator who helped Lady of Cannizaro during the strange events of Cannizaro Park. He had not met him since that tragic night. The Italian baker had been there too. For a second, Baynard had the faint idea Dr Watkins may know more than just historical names and dates. He wondered if he was helping someone this time too. A paranoid thought more than a hunch or a suspicion. He guessed it would not harm to pay the curator a visit.

'Thank you for the tip, sir.'

'You are welcome. Would you care for some wine?'

'No thanks.'

The inspector bid him farewell and rushed out, taking the bag with him. The shopkeeper lowered his shoulders in disappointment. He did not understand why it was hard to get people interested in real wine. Not cheap versions of it or horrible concoctions claiming to be real wine.

He watched the inspector leave his shop and at the same time he saw another customer coming in. He quickly realised he was a habitual customer. The burly, army-like man had returned with his awful etiquette and weird bulk order of cheap wine. He seemed nervous this time; hesitant in his movements. The shopkeeper thought he saw angst in the burly man's face as he watched the inspector walk past him and off along the Ridgeway in the direction of the Museum of Wimbledon.

Reginald Bosham held his breath when he crossed paths with Inspector Baynard at the threshold. He moved his burly figure to the side and let the inspector through, keeping the door to the wine shop open with his burly figure and square shoulders. Baynard passed through unaware of his suspicious gaze. For Reginald, the disquieting encounter with the detective inspector of Wimbledon Police at the wine shop was not a good sign at all, especially at such a critical time.

Dr Watkins woke up. He thought he had been sleeping, instead he was standing by the bookshelf. He looked around, a little dazed. He still felt tired. The museum was empty, and the entrance door locked. It was past closing time and time to go home. He had his phone in his hand and the recent calls menu was open. He then quickly remembered calling Alberyx Enterprises's main office.

'Julian Alberon is more than happy to meet you, Dr Watkins.' said the personal assistant on the phone. 'Is tomorrow late morning, at his house alright for you?'

'Perfect!' replied Dr Watkins.

'Do you have the address?'

'Still on Parkside?'

The personal assistant confirmed.

'I'll text you the address, so you have it.' she added.

'Lovely. I hope I am not disrupting Sir Alberon's busy schedule at such short notice.' apologised Dr Watkins.

'Not at all, Dr Watkins. Julian Alberon always has time for the chairman of the WAIS.'

The curator was unsure whether that was true or just clever marketing.

'May I ask the purpose of the meeting?' asked the personal assistant.

Dr Watkins could hear her fingers type away on the keyboard, ready to fill in the appointment details on Sir Alberon's agenda. He mulled over what to say.

'The Old Rectory.' said the curator. 'I believe he owns the property.'

'That is correct.'

'I just have a few questions on behalf of the museum.'

'No problem. All booked in for you. See you tomorrow.'

'Thank you. See you tomorrow.'

The curator glanced at his phone. He had ended the call about ten minutes ago. He struggled to remember what he had done since then. He yawned again and cursed under his breath for being tired. Time to go home indeed, he thought.

Dr Watkins glanced at the desk. The map and the sealable bag were on the desk, where Enrico had left them. He was tempted to stay longer and have a look at it more closely. The thrill of it made his head spin and the curator grabbed the edge of the table to hold himself steady. No, he insisted. Too tired. Better look at it in the morning. He grabbed the key and locked the door to the museum behind him. He went down to the ground floor and made a small detour to the cafeteria of the Wimbledon Village Club. Frank, the man always behind the bar, nodded to him as he wiped a few mugs clean. He bore a long, bushy moustache, which he pulled and twisted at one thin extremity. There were no more than two or three people sitting in the lounge.

'One for the road, Dr Watkins?' asked Frank with a smile you could only tell from the way his moustache twitched oddly upwards.

Dr Watkins checked his watch. After six p.m. the cafeteria became a licensed bar. The idea of a stiff drink was as tempting as reading more into the case of mysterious tunnels and burnt bodies. He thought it best to get some rest.

'Sorry, Frank. Long day.' he apologised.

'You may need one. Someone's here to see you.'

Frank nodded behind him. Across the room, Dr Watkins saw a man sitting at one of the furthest tables, his face buried deep behind a newspaper. Frank poured a single shot of brandy for Dr Watkins and winked at the curator to reassure him it was on the house. Dr Watkins blinked at him. He then turned around and the man had lowered the newspaper. The inquisitive stare of

Inspector Baynard beamed across the room, making the relaxed atmosphere now heavy and oppressive.

'Dr Watkins, I presume. I am Baynard, Inspector Baynard.' said the inspector.

He folded the newspaper neatly on the table, next to his cup of cold black coffee, and beaconed the curator to take the seat opposite.

'I know you, inspector. We have met before. Last time probably in the most tragic of situations.'

'Oh…the Cannizaro Park case? Yes, tragic indeed.'

'I have never seen you here. What brings you to the Wimbledon Village Club?'

'I was actually keen to see the museum, and more specifically speak to you.' explained Baynard.

Dr Watkins's senses heightened. The presence of Inspector Baynard here, out of everyone who could have come and visit, was suspicious. He feared the police may have already found what he and Enrico had been up to.

'Me, inspector?' said Dr Watkins sitting down. 'How can a dotard like me help the lead detective inspector of Wimbledon Police?'

The curator sat slowly at the table and took a sip of his brandy, steadying himself to hear the reason for the inspector's visit. He quickly remembered the sealable bag with the crimson remains Enrico had found and the tunnel map with all the notes were still upstairs. He tried to stay calm.

'We were investigating a burglary in Arthur Road earlier today…' started Baynard.

'Burglary? I thought I heard an explosion.' corrected Dr Watkins pretending to know.

He recalled his conversation with Reverend Green. Baynard's inquisitive stare did not flinch.

'No explosions.' dismissed Baynard quickly. 'The imagination of Wimbledonians can run wild sometimes. While searching the burgled house, we came across something I would like to get your opinion on.'

Dr Watkins leaned forward and waited for Baynard to explain. The inspector glanced sideways with suspicion.

'Is there a more reserved place where we can discuss? Your museum, perhaps?' he asked.

Dr Watkins thought quickly again of the sealable bag and the map. He could not let the inspector see those and yet he had no excuse to refuse his suggestion. He did not protest and asked the inspector to follow him up to the second floor.

The curator's mind raced as he walked a few steps ahead of Baynard, enough to buy a few extra seconds. He had to hide anything related to the tunnels. He jogged up the stairs, casually, and could still feel the inspector's eyes on him. He quickly unlocked the door and excused himself for the mess while he tidied the mess of papers on his desk. Dr Watkins pushed the sealable bag to one side and let it slide off into the waste basket behind the desk. He then grabbed all the papers, including the map, and stacked them neatly so the desk appeared free of clutter. Before he turned around to welcome the inspector, Baynard was already inside the museum glancing around, observing the glass cases.

'I need to bring my girls here. They may like it.' spoke out Baynard moving off topic.

He circled around the museum, biding his time, while Dr Watkins leaned on the desk, his arms crossed, waiting to learn what Baynard needed from him,

'Hey, is this where the infamous black stone from Cannizaro Park is showcased?' pointed out Baynard, standing by the empty glass case where the label read 'The black azalea of Cannizaro Park'.

'The black azalea, yes.' confirmed Dr Watkins. 'A nice addition to the collection. Currently unavailable. We lent it temporarily to the Countess of Wrenbury Trust.'

Baynard nodded without further comments.

'So, inspector.' resumed Dr Watkins. 'You mentioned you are here on police business. Surely, you are not interested in local history. How can I help you?'

'You will be surprised. May I?'

Baynard held up his plastic bag and hinted at the desk as suitable surface to show what he had brought. Dr Watkins smiled, holding his nerve, and showed him an empty space furthest away from his stack of paperwork. He was wondering what Baynard's plastic bag contained.

The inspector proceeded with the same steps he had performed at the wine shop. Pulling down the bag now upright on the desk, putting his gloves on, opening the evidence bag and letting Dr Watkins look in awe at the old bottle rising out of it. Baynard did not say anything, ready to play his cards carefully.

'What is this?' asked Dr Watkins with his eyes already glued on the bottle.

The curator could not hide his interest. A bottle of wine. The label was barely legible apart from the words 'Cecil' and '1590'. He went to pull the cork and Baynard held his hand back.

'I would not do that, Dr Watkins.'

'Is this not wine?'

'Smell is awful. Worse than sewage.'

'Where did you find this?' asked Dr Watkins looking at Baynard.

'My team at the lab believes it is genuinely a five-hundred-year-old bottle. I would love to hear a second opinion, if you don't mind.'

'I look after a museum, inspector. I am not a wine maker.'

'The wine shop nearby is where I am coming from.' sighed Baynard. 'They advised me you could tell me more about the name and the date. Could you tell me if there is a connection I am not seeing here, Dr Watkins?'

The curator frowned at the bottle. The Cecils. The family that built the second manor of Wimbledon, the great Elizabethan palace. The first connection was plain to see for him. The one you could read in the books or photos on display here. The one he went through with Enrico and Viviane.

'Do you have a few minutes?' prompted Dr Watkins.

'I have all the time in the world.'

Dr Watkins took the time to explain the story of the Cecils, father and son. He went on to add how the Cecils had relied on the fertile grounds of the hill to build a vineyard and orangery on the north-eastern side of Wimbledon Hill, not far from where Saint Mary's Church and Arthur Road exist today. The vineyard and orangeries stretched out from the side of the Elizabethan Manor House, built in 1588, but the only evidence were a few drawings from the seventeenth century. There is no solid proof, but some claim the British climate back then could have been warmer before the cooling down period of the last three hundred years or so.

'English wine, Dr Watkins?' exclaimed Baynard baffled.

'A theory inspector. And if your team at the lab finds out the age of the wine inside is as old as the date on the label, the bottle at least would date back to the time of the Cecil family. I cannot stress how important this is historically.'

'Not so quick, Dr Watkins.' reined in Baynard while processing the bits of information he just heard. 'This is still evidence and not another of your museum artefacts. Assuming this horrible wine, or should I perhaps call it awful crimson waste...'

'Crimson, did you say?' interrupted Dr Watkins.

The adjective caught his attention. Crimson were the traces Enrico had found, crimson was the gelatine covering the flesh of the disfigured body, crimson was the liquid he had dreamt of. Crimson. The word swirled in his head like wine in a large glass, leaving rings of clear alcohol that never dissolved. Dr Watkins had his eyes fixed on the bottle while his mind got carried away.

'Dr Watkins?' called out Baynard.

'Oh…sorry.' mumbled Dr Watkins as if waking up from a reverie. 'You were saying?'

Baynard frowned and then carried on.

'Assuming this horrible wine is as old as we think, could someone be searching for such a bottle? I mean, is there a financial value to it?'

'Priceless, inspector, priceless.' confirmed Dr Watkins with a serious face.

Baynard smiled. He could easily be holding a glass bottle dating back to Elizabeth I's reign or perhaps one of the Claymores' worst food fray yet. Either way, there was enough reason to believe the motive was lucrative. Perhaps the brothers had turned on each other. Baynard thought there and then he could ask the curator's opinion on the tunnels.

'What can you tell me about the tunnels running under Wimbledon?'

Dr Watkins shifted nervously and by mistake knocked the stack of papers down to the floor. He cleared his throat and quickly grabbed all the papers in one large sweep before Baynard offered to help. He could not see the map at first glance, probably well hidden under his boring museum reports.

'Are you ok, Dr Watkins?' checked in Baynard with his inquisitive stare.

The curator found it hard to decipher. He could not tell if the inspector observed him out of concern or out of suspicion.

'Are all these questions still related to the burglary, inspector?' asked Dr Watkins, quick to compose himself.

Baynard shrugged, wise enough not to give away too much information. Dr Watkins wondered if the question was on purpose or a mere curiosity.

Perhaps the inspector needed a good reason before he removed police lines at the tunnel entrance in Saint Mary's churchyard. The curator could not ignore what he had been up to in parallel with Enrico and Viviane. The adjective 'crimson' popped into his head again. It felt as if someone had just whispered it in his ear.

'Dr Watkins?' insisted Baynard, unclear how to take the curator's bizarre fixed gaze.

'Erm…just gathering my thoughts…' he excused himself.

The curator went on to explain the tunnel history. At least, the public version of it, and the many attempts to map the many dead ends with the few historical facts at hand.

'You will be pleased to know a well was found at 24 Arthur Road. Unfortunately, filled in.' added Baynard.

'Plenty of those around the houses in Wimbledon Village, especially in that area.' Explained Dr Watkins, pretending not to be that excited by the news Baynard shared.

The curator yawned again. Dr Watkins could not hide his frustration at being so tired.

'Terribly sorry, inspector. Today has been tiring, strangely enough.'

'Don't mention it!' replied Baynard wrapping the bottle and placing it in its double bag. 'Very kind of you to take the time and explain the historical value of this bottle. Thank you!'

'My pleasure.'

Dr Watkins went to open the door for Baynard, and before walking out of the museum to take the stairs, the inspector turned to him. His inquisitive stare eased off the hardened feature on his face. A cold, empty gaze was left. He gazed at Dr Watkins and then decided to share some heeded advice.

'I see you like your job, Dr Watkins. I know you would not risk your respectability as a representative of the WAIS, your much-loved Wimbledon Association, and curator of the Museum of Wimbledon. I will put it across as clearly as possible. If you happen to find out anything, and I mean anything, please let me know.'

Baynard then flipped a card out of his pocket and placed it in Dr Watkins's hand. The curator beamed at him, forcing himself to hide his doubt about Baynard's cryptic advice. Viviane had mentioned Baynard's last words to Enrico earlier that day, before leaving the bakery. Baynard was not that stupid to ignore the fact Dr Watkins was in touch with Enrico and Viviane. The curator had a nasty feeling the inspector was getting closer to the trail Enrico had stumbled upon.

Baynard disappeared down the stairs and Dr Watkins stayed in the museum a little while longer. He walked to the only window overlooking the Ridgeway. He saw Baynard step into his police car and drive away with this five-hundred-year-old bottle. Dr Watkins watched the clouds above the rooftops. The grey overcast sky which had dominated the whole day was now breaking up, letting the crimson glow of the oncoming sunset pierce through. Crimson, thought Dr Watkins again. The colour seemed to glow in his head. He recalled the dream he had had the night before, when he drowned in crimson-coloured liquid. A nightmare, or a forgotten memory, or the memory of a forgotten nightmare. Dr Watkins felt dizzy. His face was troubled. He had felt tired before but not like in the past two days. He could not pin it down to what it was; he had better get some rest to be in his best form for tomorrow. He grabbed his phone and texted Viviane and Enrico about tomorrow's meeting with Julian Alberon before he forgot. He told them Julian Alberon was the owner of the Old Rectory now.

The Old Rectory. Such an important building in the century-long struggle between the Church and the English Monarchy, it was now back at the centre of attention after being forgotten for so long. Yet, Dr Watkins could not even fathom the secrets waiting to be revealed and his mind was buzzing again. He felt light-headed, his eyelids heavy. He felt a voice calling out. The curator turned but the museum was empty. He looked at the glass case where the black azalea was meant to be. He suddenly remembered something he had to do.

He walked back to the small waste bin and picked up the sealable bag Enrico had brought back with him. The dried crimson powder shone in his eyes. Despite feeling sleepy, the colour mesmerised him and seemed to come alive. Dr Watkins wondered whether he was still awake or dreaming again. His legs felt heavy and numb as he walked across the museum floor, away from the entrance and into the small storage room at the opposite end. He looked for something among discarded relics and dusty rags. From a nearby shelf, he pushed a few books aside and touched the wall to look for the fake panel. He thought someone had told him where to look for it. He could not remember who. The panel was roughly a size larger than his hand, so that once opened he could type a code on the digital keypad behind it. The secret door next to the shelf made a soft sound and was now ajar to reveal its existence. The flickering of lights from inside, as they turned on automatically in the room beyond, reminded Dr Watkins it was time to work. Across the space, on a long counter, the black azalea shone on a short pedestal under a surreal violaceous light. Dr Watkins gazed at it and suddenly felt sleepy again. He walked inside the room, sealable bag in hand, listening to the voice in his head.

Enrico spread the dough in four directions, pressing lightly against it and playing off its plasticity. The dough fought back retreating to its original small circle and Enrico pushed it harder against the tray. The smell of baked bread filled the basement from the early morning batch now on display upstairs. He did not need to make more bread. Yet, this batch gave him the opportunity to focus and think things over. Making dough, with the energy and patience it required, helped him concentrate. His focus was on the *focaccia* he was preparing and on the face of the short man in overalls. He had scared the life out of him. He had tried to run him over. This short man alias Toby Claymore had been in the tunnels and Enrico wondered what his business there was. Baynard talked about burglary but this motive sounded ridiculous to the Italian baker. Toby Claymore was up to something else.

Enrico picked a small brush and brushed the square, thick dough with some olive oil. He then sprinkled some salt and rosemary. The right dose, the right balance. For him, precision was important. He was not just making bread; he was helping people enjoy the art of bread. When things were fuzzy, unclear, he would not accept it. Life, like bread, needed clarity and precision. He wished Viviane understood that. He could not simply accept loose ends. Unfinished business was like a recipe half-done, a loaf of bread half-baked. No flavour, and hard to digest.

The rest of the day soldiered on, and Enrico spent it between the counter work on the ground floor and getting ready for tomorrow's early baking in the basement-turned-into-kitchen. Without stopping once, closing time came fast and by the time he turned the lights off, the high street had slowly emptied. He sat at one of the small tables with his *focaccia* warm from the oven and a refreshing glass of sparkling water to contemplate the street outside in the dying twilight, shortly before night fell altogether. Late summer was starting to wane, and shorter days were upon them. Shadows engulfed Enrico and stretched inside the empty bakery with only the few lights from outside to feed them. Across the street, Viviane was taking her pots inside and starting to lock up as well. Enrico followed her silhouette from the darkness of the bakery. She moved lightly in and out of the shop, like a fairy breezing through the thick foliage and colourful flowers of her shop. The immaculate white cigarette jeans and flowery blouse gave her an artistic flair to what she did. The way she held the watering can, or the way she seemed to whisper tender words to a bouquet of lilies.

Enrico thought about what to do for the evening. He could go back to his studio upstairs, unexciting, uninviting. The buzz from his expedition in the tunnels still reverberated in his body and mind. Dr Watkins's text about his findings on who owned the Old Rectory, made Enrico even more restless and thirsty for more. He thought there and then he would not mind proposing a drink to Viviane. Or even dinner.

The knock on the glass of the door almost made Enrico fall off the chair. Viviane cupped her hands and called out through the closed door.

'What on earth are you doing, Mr LoTrova?' she joked. 'Checking me out?'

She then pushed the door open and Enrico quickly straightened himself up, not to expose the slight blush of embarrassment forming on his cheeks. He glanced over Viviane's shoulder and across the street. She had already closed the shop. All the flower vases and small trees had been brought inside, safe and a little warmer.

'Don't scare me like that!' said the Italian baker, nervously. 'I...I was... admiring your work.'

Viviane beamed at him with a pursed smile and enjoyed the brief pleasure she felt from putting Enrico on the spot.

'Wrapped up for the day?' she asked.

Enrico stood up and opened his arms in an Italian fashion to indicate the obvious around.

'Drink?' she then followed up.

Enrico thought she must have read his mind.

'Well...why not?' he replied.

'Let's go then. Dog & Fox?'

Enrico made a gesture with his hands to note he was not bothered where. He finished off his last piece of *focaccia* and joined Viviane in the fresh air outside.

'It will be autumn soon, Enrico. Colder months, you know. Still wearing a chef jacket?' she asked him, shaking her head.

'Of course.' admitted Enrico, not at all concerned by colder weather. 'An extra layer underneath will keep me warm.'

He pretended to flash open his chef jacket to her. Viviane played the game and pretended to look away. The two laughed and started walking up the High Street, passing in front of the closed shops and the bustling restaurants.

The Dog & Fox welcomed them with a warm air and the aroma of the dishes being ordered by hungry folk. They took a seat by the bay window again, looking over the roundabout in the evening lights. Every now and then the headlights of red buses and black cabs would cross each other's streams and throw a blinding light towards the guests inside the pub. Viviane sipped her glass of red wine, and Enrico opted again for that British ale he had learned to appreciate.

'Don't you have a coat or something?' asked Viviane with another insisting look at Enrico's chef jacket.

He had it on, unbuttoned and loose as if it were an ordinary jacket. A dark green sweater was visible across his chest.

'I like it. It keeps me cosy. Inside or out.'

'Were you wearing that when you went in the tunnels?'

'Yes. But not the same one. I have a few and I wash them daily. I am not a dirty person, Viviane. I know the one I have on is not immaculate but...'

'Usually I would expect Italians to be dressed in Armani suits...'

Enrico groaned at Viviane's joke on stereotypes.

'I am more curious and nosier than your average Italian probably.'

'That I believe. Would you gossip with people from your village in the town square?'

Enrico smirked. Viviane eyed the Italian baker curiously. His wavy hair was impeccable and not a speck of flour dust had messed up its dark colour or ruffled its natural flow.

'Where do you come from again? I always forget.'

'A small town in the heart of the boot. Too small to be on the map.'

'I can check it here on my smartphone.'

Enrico stared at Viviane. She was rummaging in her bag, pulling out keys and pack of tissues in the process. He was impressed to see how her updo hairstyle never fell out of place. Her auburn hair took on a strange dark caramel tone against the warm indoor lights of the pub.

'You know me. I am not fond of technology.' commented Enrico, before Viviane could take out one of the many technology gadgets Enrico could simply not stand.

'Ah yes. Is that why you have a phone from the Eighties. What are you? Allergic?'

Viviane was always in a playful mood with Enrico. Teasing him about his habits when she was not complaining about his careless curiosity.

'I just get itchy all over. And to be honest, my Nokia 3310 is not that old. Anyway, what did you want to talk about?' asked Enrico changing the subject.

'I see.' Viviane interrupted with a tone of disappointment. 'I thought we could chat about the weather or weekend plans, or do you prefer to talk about these tunnels again? Disfigured bodies, old manors. It is a mania, Enrico, and Dr Watkins only fuels the fire. What pushes you so hard to find out?'

'It is the way I am, Viviane. *Ragazzo curioso*, you know. I've spent my life seeking things, getting to the bottom of them. I came to accept that whenever I come across stones unturned or bottomless tunnels, I need to find the truth.'

'Is this from back home in Italy? You never talk much about it.'

'It does not matter where I come from. Which town, which street. Seeking led me to places and it finally led me here.'

'For what purpose?'

'To make bread and make people happy.'

'And what do the tunnels have to do with this? If you keep closing the bakery for your adventurous intervals, you will be left with no bakery at all.'

'When mysterious deaths shake your daily life, what will happen to happiness? All the bread in the world will not solve that. Tell Baynard.'

Enrico uttered these words staring out at the evening as he sipped his beer. Viviane thought it was the first time the Italian baker shared something deeper, bordering on melancholy. It was moments like these that made her realise that the people with whom we spend most time, are more like strangers in the maddening crowd. And it was a fast moment, just before the headlights turning at the roundabout washed the dim, warm colours of the pub once more and the awkward atmosphere returned to evening chatters and everyday smiles.

'You probably saw Dr Watkins's text.' resumed Enrico. 'He found out who owns the Old Rectory. A man called Julian Alberon. We have a meeting tomorrow. I assume you are joining us, right?'

'I'd better even if it costs me an hour's work. You and Dr Watkins could get up to more mischief without me. However, how could I miss meeting the famous local businessman? Wow, Julian Alberon! He is very popular around here. Wimbledon Village is definitely in debt to him. Me included.'

'Really?' exclaimed Enrico stupefied and curious.

'Yes. He gave the WAIS the funds for the first loan for my shop years ago. He is a local businessman who focuses on local interest. That is his motto, I remember. Julian Alberon is a major player in funding works and initiatives across the hill. He rebuilt old buildings, broken roads and churches, helped new shops and restaurants open without the burden of the local council. Dr Watkins thanked him many times for giving the first funds that would pave the way for the WAIS.'

'I didn't see any of that when I opened the bakery.'

'You did, Enrico. Indirectly. The fair at Cannizaro Park was sponsored by Alberyx Enterprises. It is his company, headquartered here. The funds you received to open the bakery and get your first customers were thanks to him. Julian Alberon helps everyone.'

'Wow! I did not know. Well, let's see if he helps us tomorrow.'

'I am sure he will. He is a person with an open mind. Are you going to see Baynard as well, tomorrow afternoon?'

'Yes. He kindly asked me to go to the police station to report my official statement about the short man and all the events from this morning. I owe him that I suppose.'

'Do you think he is suspecting you again?'

'I don't think so. He knows I was at the scene, but I was not the burglar, so I am in the clear this time.'

'And became a witness instead.' pointed our Viviane with a raise of her glass. 'You did not tell him much about the tunnels.'

'We both kept our cards close. He did not mention any tunnel explosions but if he was at 24 Arthur Road, he could not ignore the blocked well in the basement, the collapse of the Artesian Well, the tremors that came from underground. Didn't you feel anything?'

Viviane shook her head, picturing her inert pots and vases and not the slightest tremor to recall.

'Well, it was scary down there. Baynard is not ignoring it. That man is clever.'

'Do you think you are cleverer?' challenged Viviane.

'Me? I am just a baker.' he replied on a lighter mood.

The two laughed and clinked their glasses without looking into each other's eyes. Enrico downed the last foamy layer of beer and offered to buy dinner. Viviane accepted, hinting that it was the least he could do. Enrico rolled his eyes and disappeared into the crowd around the bar. Viviane stared out of the bay window, her lips on the glass, drinking her wine slowly as if the sweet, velvety red nectar deepened her thoughts into a comfortable numbness. She convinced herself she did not feel any tremor that morning. The earth did not shake at all at Wimbledon Village but from the way Enrico described it, it seemed a danger of gargantuan proportions right under their feet. Mr Claymore was drilling holes under the hill, she thought. To find what, she asked herself. Enrico's curiosity was becoming contagious.

'Done.' boomed Enrico's voice as he sat opposite her. 'Steak and ale pie for both us. More drinks?'

Viviane blinked at him and she realised she had downed her wine without thinking. She could feel it going to her head.

'Do they have wine belonging to the Cecils?' she laughed.

'English wine?' groaned Enrico again. 'Come on, what Dr Watkins said was a stupid idea!'

'Is the *ragazzo curioso* not tempted to know?'

Enrico glanced at Viviane knowingly.

'Are you teasing me? You know you may regret it! Remind me again, the Cecils were Lords of the Manor, right?'

'Something like that.'

'And that title still exists today!' said Enrico, his reaction still in awe at the years of Wimbledon history behind them. 'This place will never stop surprising me.'

'We don't know who owns it. For all we know, it may have been sold off or more probably it became extinct, like many other noble titles across the United Kingdom.'

'Do you think this Sir Alberon will be able to help us?'

'Having friends in high places can have its advantages. Who else could help you in your crazy cause? And why don't you start calling him Julian? He is a friend of the village. He is a caring philanthropist to whom we owe some generous donations.'

'Is that so?' said Enrico unconvinced. 'What is the plan for tomorrow then?'

Enrico did not know what Dr Watkins had in mind for their meeting with Julian Alberon. Not knowing the local businessman and never having met him in person, made Enrico uneasy about sharing their story, their suspicions. The Italian baker was in the hands of Dr Watkins and Viviane who spoke highly of Julian Alberon. A possible ally. Enrico had to trust his two friends this time, especially if he needed to feed his curiosity and find out what secret lay in the tunnels underneath Wimbledon Village.

'Dr Watkins invited us both to the meeting at his house.' explained the florist. 'I guess our dear curator will know what to ask. He seems over-excited by all this.'

'True. For once, I am following orders.'

Viviane cocked her head to the side.

'OK then.' she replied in a flat tone. 'If we see there is more trouble ahead, we'll ask Dr Watkins and Julian Alberon to put the matter into police hands, alright?'

'Your wish is your command!' confirmed the Italian baker with a powerful, serious voice and pretending to bow to her.

He knew Viviane implied no more running around playing detective or looking for trouble with Baynard.

'Don't patronise me!' Viviane scoffed.

'Sorry for being cheeky and stubborn. I will play it safe. I promise!' apologised Enrico with a tight lip smile.

'You don't have to apologise.' answered Viviane apprehensively. 'You remember how the events at Cannizaro Park pushed us to the edge. I don't want that again. You are a baker; I am a florist. We are not heroes. Plus, I am worried about Dr Watkins. He said he is not sleeping well lately. I just hope his health is not impacted, and he does not get too tired running around to solve this puzzle. Your puzzle.'

'Dr Watkins will be fine.' cut off Enrico. 'I did not see him fall asleep in the middle of our conversation. Surely, he yawns a few times, but I think deep inside he gets a kick out of all this.'

'Does a disfigured body, found by a terrorised girl in a filthy tunnel, sound exciting to you?'

'I was referring to the history, Viviane.'

Enrico looked at her in the eye and sat up straight in his chair.

'Don't you want to know what really happened down there?' he then added.

He let the question hang in the air and gave Viviane a friendly smile as a sign of truce. The florist looked at him, first with suspicion, then she warmed up to him with a nervous smile.

'You could have died in those tunnels. The same way you almost got shot in Cannizaro Park. Don't make decisions on your own. Please.' she spoke.

Enrico understood what she meant by those words. Viviane knew being curious was his nature and that she could not change who he was. Enrico on the other hand understood she cared for his safety and that she was there to help him stay out of trouble. As the light traffic outside played merry-go-round once more on the roundabout of Wimbledon Village, headlights flashed again inside the pub. In an instant, the bright light melted the warm, cosy orange glow inside the Dog and Fox. In an instant, it blinded the lads talking loudly in one corner and the girls giggling in the other, relieving them briefly from their alcohol-induced stupor. It was an instant that made Enrico and Viviane stone cold sober, made them realise someone or something out there could change things forever. For better or for worse. Both Enrico and Viviane understood they would need to watch each other's back going forward if they wanted to know how deep the rabbit hole went.

Home Park Road was dimly lit at night. The only light came from the houses on one side of the quiet, suburban street. The glow stretched across the road like thin, bony fingers, and scratched in vain at the impenetrable obscurity in which Wimbledon Park was shrouded.

Lord Awlthorp rubbed his gloved hands, impatiently. He looked out of the black saloon car, in the direction of the obscurity, waiting for something to emerge from the empty park. The iron gate railings fencing the park were almost invisible if it were not for the light casting dim reflections against the shiny metal. The darkness seemed like a cloud ready to swallow everything up and never return it.

'How long have they been away?' asked Lord Awlthorp to his driver.

'Forty minutes, sir.' confirmed the driver, tapping his fingers on the wheel and checking the road every now and then. 'I do not think you should have come out here, sir. Toby Claymore could be setting up a trap for us.'

'He is not smart like his brother.' disagreed Lord Awlthorp. 'In any case, us being out here and not with Reginald and Toby does not make us accomplices.'

The driver tapped his fingers fast, still nervous about the whole idea. Under his stiff, expressionless face, the driver brooded over what had happened in the last forty-eight hours.

'Sir,' asked the driver, still peering out at the emptiness of Home Park Road. 'if the location Mr Claymore revealed really exists, what do you plan to do?'

Lord Awlthorp stopped rubbing his gloved hands and leaned against the black tinted passenger window. He peered outside and took in the black nothingness that was Wimbledon Park to put his thoughts in order.

'If true, by tomorrow we will have what we need to recreate the potion and I will know more of what Henry Claymore actually did. Completion of the second test is within our grasps.'

The driver did not turn around. He glanced at Lord Awlthorp through the rear-view mirror and met his knowingly, wicked smile.

'Do you think Henry Claymore found out about your second test?' he asked.

Lord Awlthorp did not reply straight away. He had not yet shared with the driver the possibility that the second test may demand more than just recreate a magic potion.

'Be ready for all possibilities. There are details from Henry Claymore about a ritual I need to investigate further. I care to say we are now entering unknown territory and our success hangs on a very thin thread.'

'What do you mean, sir?' wondered the driver, finding Lord Awlthorp's reply disturbing.

'What I mean is, the police are starting to stick their nose where they shouldn't, especially after that idiot of Toby Claymore caused the tunnels to shake and collapse today. Reginald also saw Inspector Baynard, of Wimbledon Police, at the wine shop today. He did not know why, but we have to assume they are closing in on us. They identified the body already and they are looking for the brother, so we need to keep Toby Claymore out of sight.'

'What do you have in mind?'

'I am thinking we ought to find a place where we can lock him up while being of use to us...'

Lord Awlthorp's trailed off. His gaze caught a change in the light reflections outside. Towards the park, he could now see two thin shadows in the dark fast approaching. The driver immediately recognised Reginald and Toby rushing towards a small secondary park gate and then dash back to the car up the road before anyone spotted them. The driver glanced up and down the street very carefully until the two were inside the car. Toby Claymore sat at the back, trembling next to Lord Awlthorp. Reginald sat in the front passenger seat. The driver then nodded to Lord Awlthorp and drove away.

'So? Did you find it?' prompted the man in black.

'We did.' admitted Reginald. 'Towards the south-western tip of Wimbledon Park, not far from the fence that divides the residential gardens belonging to the houses on Arthur Road and Rectory Orchard. There is an underground electrical substation accessible through a manhole. From there, the Claymores cut through the reinforced concrete and a short tunnel takes you to a grate…'

'I am not interested, Reggie, how you got inside.' hissed Lord Awlthorp. 'Did you find the wine cellar?' hissed Lord Awlthorp.

There was a moment of silence.

'Yes.' answered Reginald in short. 'I had to see it with my own eyes to believe it all. The wine cellar is there, deep underground. It is about two or three times the size of the Old Rectory's basement. There are small and large barrels everywhere. Plenty of crates of empty bottles.'

'Is there any wine left?' asked Lord Awlthorp.

'One last crate.' confirmed Toby Claymore.

Reginald turned around raising his hand at him

'You speak when you are spoken to!' he threatened.

He then sat back in his seat and carried on answering to Lord Awlthorp.

'The last crate in the wine cellar has some full bottles left. That is all. The rest of the Cecils' wine is in the Claymores' rented garage and then there's the five we have back at the house. There were a lot more bottles in the cellar. They are all empty now. Not sure who drank them all. Probably these two pissheads!'

'Easy, Reggie!'

'Don't call me, Reggie!'

'At least we found out this "pisshead", as you call him, told the truth.' grinned Lord Awlthorp. 'And tell me, did you find the writings Henry Claymore mentioned?'

Reginald searched his jacket and pulled a rolled parchment from his inside pocket. It was not the same paper from the recipes; it was much older and fragile. He handed it to Lord Awlthorp.

'Here are the two texts!' he said. 'Toby, please repeat what you told me!'

The short man swallowed hard the moment the attention was on him.

'These are…These are the two texts my brother read over and over…after we discovered the cellars.' added Toby Claymore, in the hope of Lord Awlthorp's clemency towards him.

'There were other minor notes, sir.' continued Reginald. 'Scraps of paper with handwritten quotes. However, they were all gibberish. Nothing about potions or recipe ingredients as you asked. That Henry Claymore must have drunk all the wine and really lost his marbles in those tunnels…'

Lord Awlthorp was not listening. His attention drawn to the two parchments unrolled on his knees. The intermittent light from the streetlamps washed the yellow-stained paper, revealing the old handwriting bit by bit. The two pages were the size of a notebook and the side of each was torn as if it had been ripped out from somewhere. A few salient words stuck out. Whoever the author was, he wrote in relatively modern English, explaining the steps of mixing the four ingredients from Henry Claymore's final recipe. Lord Awlthorp knew he must replicate the steps at once that same evening, back at his lab. He had to be sure. The second page showed the same calligraphy, but it was more of a jagged scrawl and it was hard to read in the scarce light. Lord Awlthorp knew though he was on to something.

The black car moved out of Home Road and made its way the long way around the silent hill, via Dora Road and then onto Leopold Road. At the roundabout with Alexandra Road, the car met the scarce Monday evening traffic and the driver merged with it towards Wimbledon Town centre. Passers-by and other cars moved on, unaware of the events unfolding around them. Lord Awlthorp's face blurred in the myriad of lights from shop windows and pubs and neon signs as he watched them fade away in the night. He then heard Reginald breaking the silence of his concentration.

'What next, sir?' called out Reginald.

Lord Awlthorp squeezed his eyes to sooth his irritation. He needed time alone in his lab to plan the next move.

'Let's go back to my house. If my revised plans for the second test are correct, tomorrow, Reginald, you must go back to the cellar, grab the last full bottles and do Mr Claymore here a favour by blowing up the entrance to it.'

Reginald nodded.

'What about me?' spoke up Toby, out of his depth. 'I told you everything I knew and now you know it is the truth.'

'You did. You did.' muttered Lord Awlthorp, still looking outside.

'Will you let me go then as promised?'

'In due course, Mr Claymore. We are not finished. I told you we will help me finish my work. You will complete what you and your brother started, what you two were paid to do.'

'What does that mean?'

'We will take you back to the Old Rectory basement tomorrow, where a job half-done awaits you. You will be provided new instructions and we will make sure you do not escape this time!'

'What? I am not going back…' protested Toby in vain.

Reginald pulled a gun straight at the short man. Toby could feel the cold barrel aimed at him, without even seeing it. Lord Awlthorp stood impassive at the scene.

'Your brother almost took an opportunity away from me, of which you cannot even imagine the importance, Mr Claymore. You will do what we tell you, and next time you go astray, you will pay with your life!'

Lord Awlthorp's eyes glinted with evil. He uttered his words in a deep voice and then silence returned inside the car. Toby did not reply. He felt he no longer had a voice on the matter. He had his back against the wall and there was no escape but just an uncertain future. The fate of Toby's life was back in the hands of the man in black. Lord Awlthorp would not let him go until he had satisfied his morbid curiosity. He seemed consumed by it, just like Henry, and Toby wondered if Lord Awlthorp too had perhaps heard the same voices his brother Henry claimed to have heard throughout the long-forgotten tunnels, the echoes from behind the large barrels in the wine cellar, or the whispers rising from the crimson depths of the Pool of Elixir.

Dr Watkins yelped in his sleep and woke up suddenly, drenched in his sweat. Around him, the tranquillity of his bedroom emerged from the fog of his sleep. The nightmares or visions were still vivid in his memory and the curator desperately tried to grasp them before they faded in his wake. He struggled as the reality of his home on Westside Common brought back familiar things he could see and touch. This time he had not dreamt of abandoned tunnels or of drowning in crimson liquids. He could only recall the vague sight of a rock sparkling in a halo of blue and violet light, and a thin crimson dust scattered around, both glowing and slowly melting into each other. Nothing else around him; no details of where he was.

These haunting dreams had been recurring more and more frequently, and some of them had been more intense in the last two days. He vaguely recalled Hilary Wilson's diary. His thoughts went back to those pages where she said she also suffered from bad sleep. Yet, the idea that a lava rock could influence anyone's sleep made Dr Watkins chuckle. Enrico had been right then: it was just the imagination of a young woman who believe in fairy tales. The curator knew he was just doing too much and getting tired too quickly. It was all the excitement from the last few days.

Dr Watkins sighed, surrendering to the fact that another night's sleep had been disrupted. He pushed himself to the edge of the bed, feeling tired already, and turned the bedside lamp on. The bedroom, washed in the warm glow, appeared surreal in its normality. The shadows retreated into the corners and crevices of the furniture, warning they would return.

The curator buried his face in his hands and gently woke himself up. He only had himself to blame for getting too involved in this tunnel business. He peeked from behind his hands and glanced at the book open at the page he was reading. He had been reading again about the 1984 speleological expedition. Definitely not giving myself a break, thought Dr Watkins.

He put his glasses on, his slippers, and walked down to the ground floor. A cup of tea would help him get back his much-needed sleep. He yawned again as he dragged his feet across the living room to the kitchen. Piles of books on the coffee table reminded him of the extensive reading he had been doing. Perhaps it was all down to envy or jealousy he had been growing deep inside all these years. He had wanted to be part of that speleological expedition so much, but the chance had not been given to him then, and now he was no longer fit to do it even if Wimbledon history was at stake.

The steam from the boiling water as he poured it into the mug clouded his glasses and his thoughts. He found it soothing, as he did almost every night now. It somehow freed his mind and memory from the burden of these nightmarish visions, allowing him to think more clearly. He walked back to the living room and stood there for a moment to contemplate the silence, a chance to meditate and pray for sleep to come back. Tomorrow was a big day. Meeting Julian Alberon could be a turning point in getting some of

Wimbledon history back on the local agenda. What Enrico discovered in the tunnels was astounding. Dr Watkins recalled the map and the sealable bag with the dried crimson powder. A worrying thought dawned on him. He could not remember where he had put them. The more he tried to remember, the more he realised he had little recollection of the last hours of yesterday, especially after meeting Inspector Baynard.

Dr Watkins could not hide the slight surge in panic he felt rising from his gut. The lack of sleep was starting to affect his daily routine as much as the night-time, with black-outs and forgetfulness. His eyes searched with haste around the room in the hope something would remind him. A reassurance this lapsus was just a blip. He then noticed the small noticeboard by the phone. There was a post-it written in thick, black characters, which stood out of the many leaflets, vouchers and other reminders.

Sealable bag sent to the DCSR at the British Museum
Reminded them about the black azalea too!

The curator pulled the post-it off the board and re-read it with a sense of relief. Glad he had put a reminder somewhere. He had forgotten about it. He snorted at whether the British Museum would reply at all, or if the dried crimson residue would deem some attention. It had been weeks since his last request to try and catch their interest about the black azalea.

He shrugged and made his journey back to the bedroom upstairs. Outside the window, the moon-less night made Dr Watkins shiver, as if he could feel the cold wind outside, announcing the arrival of autumn. The curator took another sip of the tisane to keep warm and put it on the bedside table with the intention to drink it slowly and let sleep gradually seep in. He jumped back into bed, pulling up his covers. He thought of the tunnels once more with the hope to live pleasant dreams until the following morning, or nothing at all. The steam from the mug next to him faded some time later under the warm glow of the bedside lamp. The half-full mug turned cold, left unattended. Dr Watkins had fallen asleep already. A deep, deep sleep.

Lord Awlthorp woke up. He had closed his eyes temporarily to focus. He was back in his concentration room. The red candle flickering in the corner of his ivory desk. This time in front of him the two parchments found in the cellar. Same calligraphy but not signed anywhere; he wondered who the author was. Dark crimson ink had been used. Definitely oily and varnish-like; that type of ink could not date further back than the sixteenth century most likely. He did not have time to verify the age that same evening, but it would suffice to go through the mysterious content.

The first text clearly showed the steps of how to mix the ingredients in the right order. The ingredients were meant to be added into an electrostatic pool. Although it did not mention electrolysis or even electricity explicitly, the author talked about a very similar process, explaining it in very rudimental terms.

First *juleep* and then *Manus Christi pulvis*. The former was today's equivalent of an infusion of rose petals and mint leaves, the latter a strange mix of sugar, cinnamon and golden leaves. The author mentioned he had used substitutes replacing those common to the Tudor era. Perhaps this was a clue he was writing at the same time as the Cecils or perhaps later. Lord Awlthorp frowned and carried on reading.

The next step was finally addressing the *alkimiae mulsi*. The author warned about pinching one's nostrils for the smell of such foul mixture is intolerable. It resembled a stench of fermentation, low in alcohol, and he stressed the importance to pour it into the mixture as he had found it. Found it, repeated Lord Awlthorp in his head. It meant this substance naturally occurred or was readily available to him. Lord Awlthorp strongly believed it was the Cecils' wine. It could not explain yet how, but it was the only fermented liquid in the cellars. He knew he was getting closer. He read on.

The third step required to brew the mix, stir it until the purple colour of the liquid turned maroon. Then the galvanisation process would make the potion stable and ready, turning it a vivid crimson. The last ingredient was poured at the end, and it was indeed blood, but the blood from a human being, to which Lord Awlthorp shuddered.

The man in black paused for a moment. The author never mentioned the Pool of Elixir directly and only vaguely referred to a 'pool'. Pointing out when or where this note had been written was not easy. He put it aside and move to the second parchment, the one with the jagged writing. Its disturbing content and the deranged tone of voice transpired through the pages. It would have terrified any living soul, but Lord Awlthorp found it mesmerising instead. The text had been scribbled hurriedly, across uneven, irregular lines, completely different from the previous one. Only the calligraphy proved it was the same hand. The author seemed to have been taken by hysteria as he tried to jot down his thoughts. Lord Awlthorp read again those few lines in the middle of the page.

First thing you hear are the voices. The same that haunt every single drop of alkimiae mulsi. *The voice will speak to you as the crimson liquid starts to form and boil. It will make you feel the pain, the sorrow, the inadequacy. It will call upon your thirst of power and revenge.*

The temptation will be strong enough to give in to the voice, listen to its instructions. Giving in would mean self-immolation. Burn as if you had opened the gates of hell…

Lord Awlthorp was perplexed by the way the author described what must have been his or her own first-hand experience. Looking beyond the outlandish biblical and apocalyptic style of narrative, he could not dismiss the importance of this first-hand testimony. Toby Claymore himself had said his brother started to hear voices in the tunnels, and if Lord Awlthorp factored in what happened to Henry Claymore, the pattern was beginning to emerge. He had immerged himself into the pool to sacrifice himself. It was suicide after all. The Pool of Elixir opened something. Lord Awlthorp deep inside knew it would lead to the sorcerer's secrets. Yet, what lay beyond did not give him much to go on, except contemplating a horrible death and questioning whether this is where the second test was meant to lead him to.

He sighed in frustration and picked up the two parchments, rolling them up into one. He rubbed his eyes to shake off the tiredness. He had read enough, and it was getting late. It was time to check the tests on the wine. He opened the pressurised door and stepped outside into the outer lab. The five bottles of wine were still lined up on the running counter, all uncorked. He had spent all night vaporising the wine, exposing it to X-rays, putting it under the microscope, not to mention further distillation and even electrolysis at a small scale. Nothing. It was just ordinary vintage wine. No foul smell from it or nothing even close to how it had been described in the parchment. The only conclusion he was able to come to at such a late hour was that the wine was indeed dating back to 1590, and the wine's taste had remained intact as if bottled only a decade ago. Lord Awlthorp did not care though. He needed to find the *alkimiae mulsi*. Perhaps the last bottles left in the wine cellar held the key to the mystery. Another thought popped into his head as he moved from one microscope to the other. Something at the back of his mind has been nagging him. Henry Claymore's body. It had been dipped into the pool, apparently full of the vivid crimson liquid. He could only assume Henry had been that smart to follow the steps given to him to the letter. If so, a small tissue of his disfigured body could perhaps help him isolate and synthesise the *alkimiae mulsi*. If time was the essence, the body itself could also be a vehicle to replace the missing ingredient. Lord Awlthorp knew he had to have both the bottles and the body.

Lord Awlthorp bit his lower lip. Without delay, he walked up the short steps, out of the lab and back into the study. The house was quiet except the noisy chortling from Reginald downstairs. He quickly summoned him and the driver up to the library with a clap of his hands. There was no time to waste. Time was indeed of the essence.

'Sir, we thought we would not see you until the morning.' noted the driver as he watched Lord Awlthorp take a seat in one of the high chairs.

'I have been thinking it through and we now have a revised plan.' said the man in black. 'I will take you through it step by step.'

Reginald listened to Lord Awlthorp carefully.

'Tell me, Reginald, what did you find out at the wine shop when you went there this afternoon? What did the shopkeeper say about the bottle you showed them?'

Reginald was taken aback by the question and tried to recall the conversation he had, right after he saw Baynard walking out.

'He confirmed one of the bottles we found on Toby Claymore is indeed a five-hundred-year-old bottle, sir. He wanted to pay me an exorbitant amount of money. Why do you ask…?'

'The wine is indeed old as my tests have proven and, as you rightly said, worth a lot of money. It will be our scape goat to frame Toby Claymore; it will be his motive.'

'I don't understand, sir…' replied Reginald scratching his head.

'It will be his motive.' continued Lord Awlthorp turning to the driver. 'The police have already identified Henry Claymore, and the fact you found one of their inspectors asking questions at the wine shop worries me. They may know more than we think they do. You will need to make sure the Cecils' wine leads to Toby Claymore alone. This will put the police off our scent.'

'Consider it done, sir.' nodded the driver. 'What about you? Is your second test considered done?'

'Not yet.' warned Lord Awlthorp. 'We have what we need though to re-run Henry Claymore's experiment!'

'But sir…Henry Claymore suffered a horrible death. We cannot allow you to risk the same!'

'Henry Claymore is the key here!' insisted Lord Awlthorp impatiently.

The driver flinched. Confusion swirled in his head in hearing Lord Awlthorp's words.

'We must retrieve his body.' continued the man in black. 'He holds the missing ingredient to the formula. His body is held at the forensics lab in Wimbledon police station, sir. Reginald, I will need you to retrieve it, tomorrow!'

He crossed eyes with the burly man. Reginald sucked his teeth, weighing up the task at hand.

'Infiltrating the Wimbledon Police forensics' lab should not be a problem.' replied Reginald in short, to the point. 'Where should I bring it?'

'At the Pool of Elixir.' confirmed Lord Awlthorp.

'Are the basement and the chamber still intact and accessible after today's tremors?' questioned the driver.

'I checked today.' replied Reginald. 'No damage to the Old Rectory reported by the restoration workers. I can run a quick check on the status of the chamber at dawn, before the workers arrive. I don't see any problems. If you think about it, it will take time for the police to link Henry back to the basement and the chamber. The deeper tunnels have collapsed thanks to Mr Claymore's demolition plans. That was the only trail leading to the chamber. We have bought ourselves some time…'

The driver fidgeted with his hands and tried to contain his nervousness about the whole thing.

'Sir,' continued the driver, now addressing Lord Awlthorp. 'you heard the police radio waves and the news. You said it yourself. They have already identified the body and they may be already onto us. We cannot allow them to track us, perhaps risk that they identify Reginald and then find out who you are.'

'We can handle the police.' reassured the man in black. 'We can pull some strings. You know that!'

'I was more worried about the other people involved. For example, there is this Italian baker…'

'Please!' interrupted Lord Awlthorp. 'Why should my plans be concerned about a stupid baker?'

'I don't know, sir.' confided the driver. 'His presence troubles me. Something about him does not add up. Second time he stumbled into our plans, like a constant spanner in the works. First with the black azalea, now he threatens to interfere with your experiments.'

'He won't bother us.' dismissed Reginald. 'I can deal with that Enrico LoTrova again if needed. I am more worried about Toby Claymore. You said you want to frame him. What do we do with him until then? He is back in the attic, tied up until further instructions.'

'He will do the leg work for us while we set him up as a scapegoat for the police. Take him with you tomorrow, keep him tied up in your van. Once you have collected the body and dealt with the wine cellar, you bring him to the Old Rectory as instructed. You will ask him to re-run his brother experiment for me!'

'When?' asked Reginald

'Tomorrow night!'

Reginald frowned. What had started as months of planning were now crunching into the last twenty-four hours. He hoped Lord Awlthorp knew what he was doing.

The driver listened in silence. The fervour of his boss was not something new. He understood and shared his ambition. Yet, the rush of his act towards an outcome that could seriously harm him worried him greatly, and the unreliability of Reginald and Toby in the big scheme of things could prove damaging to Lord Awlthorp.

'Sir!' prompted the driver again. 'If I may, I think we may be rushing into things…'

'There is no time left.' Lord Awlthorp cut short. 'We have been waiting for too long. Now, if you excuse me, I prefer to be left alone once more. Tomorrow is an important day. I will see you in the morning.'

The man in black dismissed them both and shortly after he was alone in the library, shrouded in darkness and silence. A clear moon-less night was seeping through the scattered clouds and through the large windows. The square patch of spectral light onto the solid floor stirred Lord Awlthorp's imagination. He stood up and dragged his feet to the window, thinking about the Pool of Elixir. He wished he was already where he wanted to be. He quickly reminded himself to be patient. He gave out a long yawn; he needed some sleep for the day ahead. He looked out of the window and the moon-less night stared back at him like a mirror. In the framed black void, Lord Awlthorp glimpsed at the reflection of his soul, in that instant almost void of sanity, consumed by his search for answers. His search for power and revenge in the hope Wimbledon one day will regain its glory.

Tuesday morning did not start well for Inspector Baynard. Not even the sunny spells and blue skies piercing through the broken clouds seemed to cheer him up. Not even his morning sarnie that lay miserably on his desk.

It all started as early as eight thirty. The office mood was still in full swing with police officers catching up with reports from the night crimes or from the investigations they had been trying to close for days. Baynard sat at his desk, thinking of where to start from on the Claymore case before he met with Jeremy. He was re-assembling his thoughts and notes from yesterday, in his mind and on paper. The disfigured body. The chemist brothers. The stinking wine imitation. The Italian baker.

His eyes wandered around the office. His inquisitive stare bore the marks of tired eyes. Last night's sleep had been poor. The Claymore case was constantly on his mind. He had seen murders before, but the ghastly death of Henry Claymore daunted him on what could be landing on his desk next. Another death, maybe, or another explosion, or a giant volcano erupting out of Wimbledon Hill. His thoughts were interrupted when the phone rang; Baynard repeated to himself to keep it together and picked up the receiver promptly and professionally as he always did.

'Wimbledon Police. Baynard speaking?' he answered.

'Oh inspector. Nathan Glenn here.'

'Who?'

The phone line crackled. Baynard did not recognise the voice.

'We met a few weeks ago.' repeated the caller.

'I am sorry. I did not catch your name. Could you please repeat? Where exactly did we meet?'

'Nathan…Glenn…' repeated the caller in a mumbling voice. 'We met…outside the clothing store in South Wimbledon…for that burglary. I was just calling to check everyone was ok in Rectory Orchard and Arthur Road. Those tremors must have been…'

'Mr Glenn? From the Wimbledon Gazette?' blurted Baynard the moment he was able to catch the name of the speaker.

The voice did not respond, although Baynard could hear the man's sigh, having been exposed.

'Inspector,' finally spoke Mr Glenn. 'I was just calling to hear your thoughts on those hideous tremors felt in Rectory Orchard. I believe you were there… with a Mrs Biggins…'

'No comment, Mr Glenn. And please do not call me directly again.'

'You don't care what the Wimbledon Gazette reports about murder and explosions suddenly hitting Wimbledon twice in less than a year? What are you hiding?'

'No speculation, Mr Glenn. Whatever happened at Rectory Orchard is not related to the accident at Saint Mary's, and not even to the incident at Cannizaro Park earlier this year.'

'Do you have evidence to prove this?' fired back Mr Glenn, his voice insisting. 'What is your explanation?'

'Goodbye, Mr Glenn.' interjected Baynard, hanging up.

He slammed the phone down, causing a few heads to turn in the office. Baynard's mood was known, especially his icy stare back at them, reminding them to mind their own business.

Nathan bloody Glenn, he thought. The journalist was taking the route of sensational news. It was not a good sign. Fine when petty crime was being reported but complicated matters like the Claymore case would send Wimbledon in a spiral of panic. Panic he was happy to have defused after the incident at Cannizaro Park. The next worst thing was for the Chief Superintendent to show up and tell him local newspapers were already breathing down his neck. That is when the second call came.

'Baynard speaking. Who is this?' he answered.

The inspector breathed heavily down the receiver. The caller could probably feel his frustration at being interrupted again.

'Is that how we answer the phone, inspector?'

The caller's voice boomed on the other side. Baynard flinched and his jaw dropped.

'Chief Superintendent!' he called out in an uncertain, cheerful mode that did not sound like him.

He cursed himself for not foreseeing this and not checking the caller display on the phone.

'I was just getting rid of some reporters on the phone.' clarified Baynard. 'Speculating news…'

'On that comment, inspector, I am seriously concerned about the events of the last two days.' said the Chief Superintendent in an apprehensive mood. 'The Council called me last night about a few complaints in regard to these "tremors". One lady specifically said you were present when one of them happened. Do you care to explain?'

'The geologist's report says the underground could be unstable. We recommend the Council arranges an enquiry with the fire department…'

'And that has been issued?' interrupted the Chief Superintendent.

'No, sir. The tunnels could be linked to the Claymores.'

'And on what grounds?'

Baynard had to give facts the Chief Superintendent would be able to accept and take to his superiors or to the Council. There was little to go on except the most obvious line of investigation; one Baynard himself found hard to believe.

'We believe the Claymores may have been using the tunnels for food fraud activities. Cheap wine, I believe.'

'In the tunnels?' exclaimed the Chief Superintendent. 'Last time I heard, labs were more convenient for this. Have we learnt anything from the dead body? Henry Claymore?'

'Waiting for the time of death and I will check today on the latest.'

'Is it fair to say his brother could have killed him?'

The Chief Superintendent was rushing to a conclusion Baynard respected but could not concur with. Not before they had put their hands on Toby Claymore himself.

'Possibly, sir.'

'Remove the "possibly", inspector. Wrap this up before the end of this week. Tomorrow if you can.'

'I'll do my best.'

Baynard could imagine the Chief Superintendent's smirk in hearing Baynard's detached agreement, not yet fully committed. The inspector hated the unnecessary pressure, blind of the complicated evidence they were facing.

'And another thing, inspector?'

'Yes, sir.' sighed Baynard again.

The Chief Superintendent knew him well and simply soldiered on with his stern voice, issuing his orders.

'I heard a baker was seen by witnesses in Arthur Road and this was Enrico LoTrova, from the bakery at Wimbledon Village.'

Baynard confirmed, knowing what would come next. On this matter, the two probably agreed for once.

'I don't know what this Enrico LoTrova thinks of police investigations, but I demand that civilians are kept out, and I mean out of police work. We do not want vigilantes in good old, peaceful Wimbledon.'

'I will see to it, sir.' Baynard confirmed again. 'Anything else?'

'Don't take it lightly, inspector. Your job could be on the line if you don't restore order!'

Click. He ended the call as abruptly as Baynard started it. The tone in the Chief Superintendent's voice did not sound good. He asked for a second time the impossible and Baynard was gob-smacked at how it all seemed to be happening again. Wimbledon was doomed to be involved in mysterious shocking events, and all under Baynard's watch. The inspector clenched his teeth and narrowed his eyes, unable to accept under any circumstances being toyed around with, whether by his superiors or a nosey journalist, nor would he accept defeat. The Claymore case needed closing.

The phone rang a third time. Baynard looked at the number on display. He did not recognise it. London area but not Wimbledon. He glanced around suspiciously as if the caller was in the room. All officers did not dare look in his direction. The persistent ring seemed to echo pending doom. Baynard cut it off by lifting the receiver again. It was one of the forensic experts.

'Inspector, we may have some developments earlier than anticipated.'

Baynard rolled his eyes in relief, thinking whom he should thank for the gods-send.

'Tell me.'

'Henry Claymore's body is about three to four days old.' she explained over the phone. 'He died a very slow and painful death. We identified ethanol on his flesh which made the combustion easy.'

Baynard listened carefully.

'We then tried to isolate all the substances we could find in the burnt flesh and his coagulated blood. Most of them are still unknown, but for now we found traces of chemicals. A lot of iron, more than we would expect. And then, believe it or not, wine derivatives.'

'Did you say wine? Are you sure?'

'Affirmative, inspector. I found that odd too.'

'Anything else?'

'These are the current results of the autopsy. Some elements came out as unknown and I don't think we will find out anytime soon...'

Baynard grunted in dissatisfaction.

'...but we have more on wine derivatives.'

Baynard's face lit up all of a sudden.

'I am still listening.'

'Well, I have been to Hampton Court...'

'Hampton Court? To see what?'

He could feel the forensic expert was hesitant to share the revelation. Baynard leaned forward, about to issue an order and ask her to quit stalling.

'The Great Vine.' explained the forensic. 'One of the oldest and longest vine roots in the world that has been here at the Royal Palace of Hampton Court since the late 1700s. I had to check with a local viticulturist and compare my notes. The wine derivatives we found on Henry Claymore's body are older than the Great Vine.'

'Older? How much older?'

'We do not know. Much older.'

'Before 1590?' asked Baynard remembering the date on the bottle.

'I thought you may ask that. Probably older. Hard to pin a date down. The range could be from 300 AD to 1200 AD. And hear this: these wine derivatives contain the same minerals mentioned in the first geologist report on the tremors. They are still checking the results.'

'I am not following.'

'The traces of wine derivatives we found on the body are from a grape grown on the side of Wimbledon Hill because of the unique minerals found in its soil. These derivatives could have originated from grapes grown on Wimbledon Hill, long before Henry VIII was king…'

Baynard almost fell off his chair. Not for the historical wonder, but because he had no idea how he was going to link this to the case.

'Is that possible at all?' asked the inspector.

'In theory, yes.' carried on the forensic expert. 'I am more of a gardener than a wine-maker, but minerals absorbed by a plant can still be found in any liquid form obtained from that plant. Not just wine, of course.'

'Right.' mumbled the inspector. 'Now, going back to this Great Vine…'

'The longest and oldest root, inspector. And I quote the viticulturist … "Planted by Lancelot 'Capability' Brown himself, one of the best landscape gardeners of the eighteenth century." Guess what? He also designed the gardens of an old Elizabethan Manor that used to exist on Wimbledon Hill. These gardens are now Wimbledon Park, I believe.'

Baynard wished he had the curator Dr Watkins with him. He scribbled another note.

'And how long again has this big root been at Hampton Court?'

'Since 1768.'

'And our "grapes" … I mean… our wine derivatives come from grapes older than this Grape Vine by, let's say, a thousand years...'

Baynard could not believe the words coming out of his mouth.

'Yes.' confirmed the forensic expert.

'…which means our "evidence" from today contains wine made from the early Middle Ages?'

'Yes!' repeated the forensic expert.

Baynard rolled his eyes. He admired her conviction. He was more concerned if this would hold as evidence when presented to the Chief Superintendent.

'And are we sure it is not a fake? Food fraud, for example?'

'If it is, inspector, then they were bloody good!'

Baynard did not find the answer reassuring. It meant the Claymores may have pulled off one of their biggest scams. The inspector though was not interested in the historic links to Wimbledon. He needed to explain why Henry Claymore was dead, and his suggestion that the Claymores wanted to profit from the sale of fake aged wine seemed obvious to follow. How they did it hardly mattered.

'Not sure this visit to the viticulturist produced the results I expected.' confessed Baynard.

'You asked for a quick turnaround on the results, inspector.' explained the forensic expert, annoyed by the inspector's dissatisfaction. 'We managed to pull it off in such a short time, and you can see the outcome left us as perplexed as you are now.'

'How about the bottle with that foul liquid? Any results from the analysis of that?'

'Not yet. It is still in progress at the lab at Wimbledon Police Station.'

'Do you think it will contain some of the same wine derivatives, or whatever you call it?'

'Possibly. We had to order more resilient masks to be able to run analysis on it. The stench is unbearable to work with.'

'Is it wine gone off?'

'Unlikely. It could be a failed attempt to make wine in the first place.'

Baynard's line of enquiry seemed to point more and more on the Claymores' mad experiments. Toby was the man they had to find at all costs.

He thanked the forensic expert and then called Jeremy.

'Yes, inspector?' answered the sergeant.

'Just got off forensics and their crazy theory on the oldest wine in Britain.' said Baynard. 'My gut feeling is Toby Claymore orchestrated a very clever scam making us believe this wine is old. He could have killed Henry Claymore just for greed.'

'First time I hear you say it out loud.'

'It does not mean I am convinced. Any news on finding Toby Claymore?'

'Nothing. He seems to have disappeared. The van he escaped with, the one he tried to hit Mr LoTrova with, is nowhere to be found.'

'Speaking of the baker, is he coming to give his statement?'

'Yes. He is meant to be here later this afternoon.'

Baynard was not sure whether the Italian baker could shed more light on this. At the back of his head, the idea the owner of the Wynnman knew something more still gnawed at him. A feeble suspicion was brewing behind his inquisitive stare as he looked out of the window.

Sir Julian Alberon's mansion was on Parkside, the stretch of road which ran from the corner of the Common at Rushmere Green and ran straight north beyond the parish borders and into Putney. His mansion was one of the many large properties lining the eastern side of Parkside, while across the road, the thick trees of the Common created a long and impenetrable green barrier.

The driveway to Julian Alberon's mansion was large enough to make Viviane's Fiat 500 feel smaller than it already was. Despite two large cars, a bulky off-road and a slick Jaguar, there was enough space to park multiple Fiat 500. The mansion was a modern interpretation of Victorian and Edwardian styles and architectures. The red brick, which echoed those used throughout the buildings of Wimbledon Village, called out its history from the ornamental pinnacles placed in an asymmetrical fashion across the roof. The mansion tried to break away from the standard rectangular shape. From the traditional façade with its porch and white windows, the structure erected upward and grew into odd shapes as if it were a living plant or creature. The mansion took on the appearance of a remote castle on the edge of a cliff, unbalanced, off-centre. Its unusual patterns made it easily visible from the road. Wimbledonians could not miss it each time they passed it.

'Eccentric guy, this Julian Alberon?' commented Enrico slanting his head to grasp the confused structure. 'How come he does not live at the Old Rectory if he owns it?'

'Aren't all business tycoons eccentric?' added Viviane. 'He probably owns more than one house.'

'We are in debt to this man so please behave!' interjected Dr Watkins. 'We are guests. Let me do the talking.'

Dr Watkins explained on the way there that Julian Alberon had Wimbledon at heart and would be open to listen to their story from a cultural and historical point of view. Enrico and Viviane quickly learned Wimbledon was part of a conservation area aimed at protecting buildings, funding local development and safeguarding public spaces from any modernisation that could tarnish or even ravage Wimbledon's history and legacy. Julian Alberon was a member of the conservation committee and he would support any preservation effort under the advice of the Museum of Wimbledon and other local associations. Dr Watkins was convinced their story would sound more credible if presented as such. Sir Julian Alberon was not the type to get involved in illegal activities if it compromised his image or Wimbledon's. Dr Watkins would do the talking since he made the appointment but also knew the history of the tunnels, and the local manor houses. Enrico and Viviane could not agree more.

The lion-shaped door knock welcomed them onto the porch and its suspicious, lifeless eyes invited them to self-announce their arrival. After knocking, the sound of footsteps came up to the door. The man who opened the door was tall, well-groomed and clean shaven. He wore a red velvet dressing gown about three quarters in length. Chest hair was visible at the height of the surplice neckline, a sign that he was not wearing a top or a shirt. He wore a pair of jeans with slippers a shade darker than the gown. His eyes were dark and deep. He could have been forty years of age or maybe younger. His relaxed and perhaps flamboyant appearance gave him an active and outgoing look as he stood on the threshold with a casual but welcoming smile on his face. He held a Bloody Mary in his hand.

'Dr Watkins!' he exclaimed with a grandiose voice. 'How do you do? Nice to see you, to see you nice. I see you brought a team of advisors with you!'

Julian Alberon laughed and shook their hands one by one. His attitude made Enrico and Viviane feel at ease despite his odd look, of which he did not seem at all embarrassed or the least worried. His handshake was energetic, firm, as intense as his eyes. He swiftly invited them in.

'Please make yourself at home. I asked my staff to arrange the living room for our meeting. Follow me!'

Julian Alberon opened the door wide to let the three enter a spacious atrium with a high ceiling and solid, hard wood flooring of the finest quality. Large baroque paintings hung against yellow and green striped wallpaper. He led them through to the living room, double in size and decorated with a different style altogether. A maroon wallpaper with tiny golden fleur-de-lis changed the mood of the room; neoclassical paintings and sculptures were placed alongside the latest modern gadgetry, such as a flat screen TV and a well-designed sound system. It became clear Julian Alberon was the eclectic type, mixing his love for the aristocrats' antiques and embracing the lifestyle of a businessman always in touch with the modern world. A small brass coffee table in between two long sofas invited them to take a seat and help themselves to an extensive choice of teas, coffee-filled pots, biscuits, freshly squeezed orange juice, jams and buttered toast.

'I hope you are hungry and don't mind me choosing a small, eclectic selection for you all. I was not sure if you were in a breakfast or elevenses mood. Please, if there is something else you would prefer, or if you have allergies, please let me know. Dr Watkins, I have a plate of chocolate digestives just for you.'

Dr Watkins wet his lips in delight like a school kid. Enrico, still in awe at the unusual surroundings, glanced around to see the rest of the living room which extended to the back where there was a grand piano and a pool table. The staff was nowhere to be seen. Sounds of cupboards and plates, and a tiny murmur of voices, echoed beyond a single door at the back. The house was bigger inside than he thought, especially as he still could not see the windows looking over the back garden.

'So, Dr Watkins, my personal assistant said you had something interesting to report, something to bring to my attention.'

'Thank you for meeting us at such short notice, Sir Alberon.' said Dr Watkins as the group sat on the two sofas. 'Did she fill you in?'

'Please. Julian.' corrected Julian Alberon with a smile while offering a biscuit to Viviane and passing a cup to Enrico. 'And your friends are…?'

'My name is Viviane. I own the flower shop on the High Street. Let me thank you for giving me the opportunity to let me start my business…'

'Oh please. No need to thank me. I am glad I could be of service to the community. I remember the flower shop. Pleasure to make your acquaintance personally.'

Viviane blushed a little in front of Julian's charm. The businessman returned his welcome smile once again. Enrico gave him an odd look, not sure how to take the eccentricity of the famous Wimbledon businessman he had been hearing about.

'And you are? Let me guess. Pastry chef?' joked again Julian as he addressed Enrico in his chef jacket.

The Italian baker was not impressed.

'*Buongiorno!* Enrico LoTrova. Nice to meet you.' he replied with a less enthusiastic tone than Viviane.

Enrico knew he was bordering apathy and thought again he owed the success to this man. Plus, he was under direct orders from Dr Watkins and Viviane to behave and did not want to disappoint.

'I own The Wynnman bakery.' he added.

'Oh, Mr LoTrova. *Piacere.* Is that right? Your fame precedes you. I asked my staff to buy from you after finding your bread so lovely. Fresh, crispy, what a flavour!'

Enrico could not help blushing at a compliment he did not expect. He did not remember Julian Alberon being a customer of his. Still, he did not know who Julian's staff were. Maybe his prejudice towards the businessman was unjustified or too hasty.

'Oh *grazie!* My pleasure. And as Viviane said, thanks for giving me the opportunity to start my business…'

'Please, Enrico and Viviane. I am no royal on a pedestal. I am a friend of Wimbledon as much as you are. This makes us all friends. Treat me as such.'

He beamed a warm, reassuring smile. Dr Watkins was already scoffing a few digestives, and Julian gave them the time and space to settle, fill their bellies if they wanted to, and feel comfortable.

'Well, we have drinks and food. Why don't we get down to business?' he asked shortly after.

Julian Alberon set the scene for the meeting and gave space to Dr Watkins to tell the story they agreed to tell. The curator mentioned the events near Saint Mary's Church to start with. He was clever enough to focus on what was discovered in the tunnels, the paths that presumably led to the old manors, and the idea that there was probably more below Saint Mary's Church than the museum and the community generally thought. He did not waste time to show their interest in the Old Rectory.

Julian Alberon listened throughout, hardly interrupting. His outgoing mood turned into a reflexive and deeply interested one, carefully nodding at every word from Dr Watkins and never losing eye contact when serving himself with a piece of toast or a sip of his Bloody Mary. Enrico felt more puzzled by his habits. Viviane on the other hand was fascinated to be there and witness the conversation. She saw Julian as the local celebrity and was staring at him in awe.

'We believe these tunnels may have a connection to the Old Rectory, which we believe to be a property of yours. We were wondering if it was possible to give us access or show us the building to give an initial confirmation of our theories. With your permission, of course.'

Julian was pensive for a second.

'Your query comes at interesting times, Dr Watkins. The museum is one step ahead of me this time. Great return of investment, I say.'

'In what way?' asked Dr Watkins.

'You said it yourself, Dr Watkins.' carried on Julian with genuine excitement in his eyes. 'The loss of Wimbledon's majestic manors over the centuries, from the Elizabethan palace to the Spencers' house, has always been a painful memory in our village past. I know both of us personally share this stigma, Dr Watkins. You will be delighted to know I am happy to give you what you need and help you unearth any mysteries. This can be great for Wimbledon Village, an opportunity to shine again and find some form of old glory still meaningful today. Now, I heard of these "tremors" yesterday and my first thought went to the possible damage in Saint Mary's and the Old Rectory. It is good to know nothing was damaged on the surface. I wonder though what may have happened below. Imagine, Dr Watkins, we could finally find out more about what we have lost over the centuries and perhaps rebuild the history of some of these manors and majestic buildings. Get archaeology back on the map here in Wimbledon! Wouldn't you agree?'

'I could not agree more!' smiled Dr Watkins with pride. 'The British Museum still has not returned my calls…'

'See?' chuckled Julian, understanding Dr Watkins point of view.

'Is that why you bought the Old Rectory?' interrupted Enrico.

'Precisely, Mr LoTrova. To give it back to Wimbledon. Restore it where possible but with the intention of returning a piece of history to the community.'

'That is so generous of you.' commented Viviane.

'Excuse my ignorance!' continued Enrico, skipping the pleasantries. 'What terrible things could have possibly happened to these manor houses?

I heard Dr Watkins talking about it and I hear you echoing a similar painful history.'

'Dr Watkins?' asked Julian, polite enough to allow the curator to show off his knowledge.

'I think I owe you and Viviane a better explanation. The Elizabethan manor house was a great feat in its time, as I told you. Surprisingly, it was not destroyed by wars or fire. After Edward Cecil's death, it passed through the hands of members of royalty, careless noblemen and temporary guardians. Over time, it fell in disuse and parts of its land were sold off for money. A French Huguenot named Theodore Janssen, who was a refugee from France and founding member of the Bank of England, purchased the manor in the early 1700s. He dismantled it to build a new manor near Saint Mary's Church in the fashionable Georgian style of the time. This is how Belvedere House came into existence, covering the area from Saint Mary's to the High Street. Janssen literally used bricks from the Elizabethan house. Years later, Sir Theodore Janssen went bankrupt because of the South Sea financial crisis. The bad management of his finances forced him to sell most of his possessions and was buried at Saint Mary's with nothing left of the wealth he had hoarded. He was barely able to buy back Belvedere House.'

'Is he buried here in Wimbledon?' added Viviane.

'Of course. He was a Wimbledonian after all.' interjected Julian. 'Ironically, the tomb is now made of bricks. A dark reminder of how he died in almost absolute poverty. Belvedere was sold off and knocked down to give space to modern housing. This is why we now have a conservation area, to avoid the foolish annihilation of Wimbledon heritage.'

Julian's last sentence was proof to Enrico and Viviane of his key role in the commission and how the matter was dear to him, as much as it was for Dr Watkins.

'The Duchess of Marlborough took the title of Lord of the Manor from Janssen.' continued Dr Watkins. 'She built her manor, the fourth one, south-east of Saint Mary's, roughly twenty years later. She did the same as Janssen: used bricks from what was left of the Elizabethan palace to build her new manor in a different location, until there were no traces left of it.'

'Was the fourth manor house also knocked down?' guessed Viviane.

'No. It burnt down in a fire.' Julian answered. 'Most historical buildings suffered a similar fate. Windsor castle included, if you think about it.'

Enrico counted in his hand how many manors had existed in Wimbledon, trying to get his head round such a complicated local history. Julian though was not yet finished.

'We then have the last one built by George, Second Earl of Spencer, of the Spencer-Churchill family…'

'Churchill?' interrupted Viviane. 'Same as *the* Winston Churchill?'

'Indeed.' exclaimed Julian with pride and satisfaction. 'They belong to the same aristocratic family. Let's not forget that the Duchess of Marlborough was married to John Churchill and makes her George Spencer's great-great-grandmother. The Spencer family has held the title of Lord of the Manor in Wimbledon for around three hundred years.'

'Who owns the title now?' wondered Enrico, guessing it was Julian Alberon himself given his status.

'I don't know at present.' said Julian.

He pursed his lips to his own disappointment for not having an answer.

'The title was sold by the last Earl of Spencer' he added. 'and was in the public domain for a while. Only this week I heard it had been bought.'

'By who?'

'Nobody knows. The purchase details of the title are private, under the wishes of the buyer.'

Dr Watkins eyes widened.

'We have a Lord of the Manor and we do not know who it is?'

Julian shrugged.

'Nobody pays much attention about noble titles nowadays. The title of Lord of the Manor does not give you much control on Wimbledon outright, anyway. It is just a title on paper.'

'Wow!' spoke Viviane, overly excited. 'The historical links to Wimbledon are more important than I thought. How come no manor house is left?'

Dr Watkins and Julian looked at each other with a resigned look.

'Unfortunately, the last manor, Spencer House, was sold off. Again, for monetary reasons. The last owner was the Council who knocked it down.'

'House development again?' commented Enrico in tune with the recurring theme. 'Now I know why you are so touchy about this subject.'

Dr Watkins nodded, digestive biscuit in hand.

'I am so excited about this!' added Julian. 'New tunnels leading to or from the Old Rectory? What a great theory! I am more than happy to help you with what you need. I tell you what. Why don't I take you to see the Old Rectory right now? The place is a little construction yard. However, I can quickly call the team on site and inform them of our arrival. You can then check out the theory for yourself!'

'That would be wonderful!' thanked Dr Watkins.

'Let me get changed and ask my staff to prep the car.' added Julian, unable to hide his enthusiasm.

He excused himself and disappeared in the atrium.

'Happy with the result?' asked Dr Watkins turning to Enrico once the three were alone again.

'The man has a weird taste.' pointed out Enrico bluntly.

'He is the local tycoon that makes the impossible possible.' defended Viviane in a low voice. 'Why does it matter if he is a little bit eccentric? Have you seen his house?'

Viviane glanced around in renewed awe. There was a man-sized Corinthian column on which a precious Ming vase stood, a small bronze replica of a Donatello standing beside a rough model of a humanoid robot.

'You really admire this guy?' said Enrico baffled.

Julian Alberon's over-the-top lifestyle made him feel less successful and a little envious.

'I didn't know you were the jealous type.' teased Viviane ruffling Enrico's hair like a pet dog.

The Italian baker leaned away to keep his pride and hide how he felt about Julian Alberon.

'Do we feel he can tell us more than we already know?' Enrico asked Dr Watkins.

He went back to a straight, professional face under the effect of Viviane's amused look.

'He can give us access to the Old Rectory.' replied Dr Watkins finishing his cup of tea and downing the last digestive. 'It's a start!'

Earlier that morning, Reginald realised he faced a long day ahead. He slammed the door of the van and checked his watch. He had been awake since the break of dawn and there was still a lot to do. He listened in and could not hear Toby Claymore's muffled noises from inside the van. The sedative he had given him was quite heavy and would leave him out of play for a good part of the day until his services were required again.

The Old Rectory was just behind him, standing tall and bright in the fresh Tuesday morning. A completely different view from the dark building rising from the shadows as the first rays of sunrise hit its sloping roofs, its short battlements and turrets. He had been in the basement since then to check the status of everything after the tremors. The rusty machine, required by the experiment for the voltage, had all its fuses and part of its wirings blown up; he mended it with some of the workers' supplies available on the first floor. The chamber itself was surprisingly still intact, as if nothing had happened. The Pool of Elixir had come out unscathed. Only a few rocks had fallen onto the natural path leading to the trap door. That reminded him to secure that trap door once and for all. He could not afford to let Toby Claymore wander through the tunnels again, even if all links to the exits had collapsed. He ripped out the small cog from the level, where Toby had shown them, and threw it out into the tunnel before closing the trap door forever.

Reginald could not stand being down in the basement any longer. The damp smell, worsened by the purplish sludge at the bottom of the pool, was unbearable. The fact he had to guard Toby Claymore down here daunted him. Lord Awlthorp wanted him to re-run the experiment early that evening, once the workers had left the Old Rectory. He had given Reginald the steps he expected Toby to go through. Reginald did not make much sense of it. His boss was paying for him to do so and he would make sure he delivered. He quickly ran a few more checks. The cables, the basement, the stock of chemicals and herbs. Once he was happy it was all set, he traced his steps back up the stairs.

The hall was empty. The workers would come soon, and he had to be in position before the place became a working site again, like any other day. His mind though was on his plan for the afternoon to retrieve the body of Henry Claymore and then the last bottles of wine in the Cecils' cellar. He was thinking it over one more time. Then his phone rang with a loud echo in the silent hall.

'Reginald!' called out Lord Awlthorp on the other end of the line. 'Is everything under control in the chamber? Is the Pool of Elixir still intact for the experiment?'

'Yes, sir. Ready to take my place now here in the hall as per usual.' explained Reginald.

He then went through his plans again. Lord Awlthorp was more than satisfied.

'Fine. I asked our inside man at the police to ensure your access to the forensics' lab goes undisturbed but try not to let the police recognise you when you break in at the police station. We already have them looking for Toby Claymore!'

'How about entering Wimbledon Park?'

'Yes, you have the same necessary cover to come and go undisturbed. Once you have retrieved all the wines from the Cecils' cellar, blow the place up. Nobody needs to know it ever existed.'

Reginald grunted in agreement.

'Good. I'll see you tonight.'

Reginald grunted again and the line went dead. The sound of gravel crunched by tyres could be heard outside as vans and trucks moved into the driveway. The chief project manager was the first to open the main entrance and enter the hall with its hard, white helmet and yellow jacket.

'Good morning, Mr Bickingham.' he announced, pushing both doors wide open for his workers.

Reginald had already hung up and set himself straight in front of the secret door, auricular in his ear and black shades over his eyes despite the utter darkness.

'Good morning.'

'How was the night?'

'Quiet. I had to do a double shift after hearing of a burglary on Arthur Road yesterday. You cannot be too careful with a place like this.'

'That is true.' replied the chief project manager. 'We got scared yesterday when the ground sent these gentle vibrations. People talk about earthquakes. Nonsense!'

'There are strange people out there!' noted Reginald.

'Well, I guess that is why Alberyx Enterprises hired you, Mr Bickingham, I suppose. To keep this place safe. I still can't grasp how you manage to keep guard for day and night. What is your secret? Coffee?'

'Army training, sir.'

'Sounds way too hard for me.'

The chief project manager from Alberyx Enterprises waved his hand at Reginald and went to his position to review the plans for today. He always had a friendly chat with their security guard when he arrived first thing in the morning.

Workers started going about their work with poles and tools and cables. They did not look up or stop for a chat. They sped in the direction they were meant to work that day. Reginald scanned them as any security guard would do. He also ensured they did not suspect what was going on underneath their feet.

'What are you covering today?' asked Reginald.

It was important to know their whereabouts at all times.

'North-west wing. We have to put an external scaffolding to reinforce the upper wall and the roof.'

'Good. Please proceed. Are you aware we all need to leave at four p.m. today?'

'Yes.' the chief project manager nodded. 'We saw the note from the fire brigade about them checking buildings after yesterday's tremors. My men will be happy to leave earlier for a pint.'

He started giving directions and sharing copies of plans and schematics as the workers spread throughout the building like ants. Most of the restoration work was on the upper floors but their coming and going through the hall became a constant flow as they picked up or returned their equipment. Reginald realised today, out of all days, was a busy one, and found it slightly unnerving.

A couple of hours passed, and Reginald had been standing in the same position ever since the workers arrived. He continued to scan them as they came in and out, playing his role as security guard. His mind though was on his afternoon plan. Police station, body, park, wine. Piece of cake.

'Mr Bickingham?'

The voice echoed in his head. He then tapped his earpiece.

'Yes?' he answered quickly.

'Julian Alberon's personal assistant here. Just to let you know the boss decided to come over to the Old Rectory.'

'What for?' spoke out Reginald, suddenly concerned.

He did not like the sound of that. It was unusual for Sir Julian Alberon to come down here during the works. This could jeopardise his plans.

'He needs to check something out. He is bringing a few guests. He thought you may want to know.'

The personal assistant clicked off. Reginald's face was hard, serious, not letting any emotions come through. Someone unexpected was coming.

Julian Alberon decided to drive himself to the Old Rectory and offered to give Dr Watkins a ride. Viviane and Enrico followed in the Fiat 500. The florist struggled to keep up with Julian's bulky off-road as it twisted and turned through the back streets of Wimbledon Hill to avoid unnecessary traffic for what was just a five-minute journey.

From Parkside the road followed the plateau on which Wimbledon stood. The road then adapted to the slopes gradually rolling down off the hill and to the plains of Wimbledon Park and the River Wandle. As both cars winded up and down, the steeple of Saint Mary's Church was the only point of reference visible in the distance. It rose above the trees and rows of houses covering Wimbledon Hill to the south. Enrico could not help noticing that a church or a place of worship was always the centre of the community, the beacon of salvation; it was the same here in Wimbledon like in Italy and the rest of the world.

The Old Rectory was hidden away, between Saint Mary's Church and where Church Road bent downward towards the bottom of the hill, in the direction of Southfields and Wimbledon Park. Enrico and Viviane followed Julian's car curiously as it steered right into a narrow road marked as 'private'. At the bottom, an open iron gate awaited them. The two cars moved past it and entered a gravel driveway protected by lines of trees. Such an entrance almost resembled a secluded rite of passage to access a secret garden. Once through the gate, the driveway opened up onto a wide roundabout. The trees disappeared and were replaced by a tall hedgerow blocking the northern view of the hill. Across the roundabout, the Old Rectory stood silent, with Saint Mary's towering steeple visible in the background. It was as if they were driving through a portal and were now in a different world or planet, without any contact or reference to the world they had left behind, the one outside, beyond the gate, beyond the hedgerow.

Enrico and Viviane could not believe such a big place was hidden away so well in the small space between Saint Mary's Church and the residential houses on this side of the hill. From the road, the Old Rectory was almost invisible.

Despite showing bundled parts of old architecture and clear signs of modern restoration, the Old Rectory had its peculiar charm and bore no resemblance to a religious house or castle, or even one of those modern mansions they had passed on the way there. It was timeless.

The two cars parked by the wide steps leading to the main entrance. A few vans and trucks were parked at the bottom of the driveway.

'Apologies for the crowded parking.' said Julian to excuse himself. 'Our restoration work is underway and each day the workers section off different areas of the house that need urgent repair work.'

'What kind of restoration?' wondered Dr Watkins in awe at seeing the Old Rectory in front of him once again.

'Mainly fixing the modern, shameful additions from previous owners. We are trying to bring out the old brickwork and make everything look as closely as possible like the original floor layout. Not an easy task. I called my contact in charge of security and told him we were coming. It should be safe for us to walk around but I have been told the upper floor is not accessible. Hopefully, this first tour can still be of good use.'

The businessman led the way up the stairs, followed by his guests. Julian had changed into a more appropriate attire bordering still his eclectic taste. Dark blue jeans, a light turquoise shirt and a grey suit jacket. Enrico and Viviane looked in awe at the building towering above them. They followed Julian and Dr Watkins inside where it was a little darker despite the curtains being pulled apart and the light of midday shining through. The dark wood of the wall panels and the beams exposed under the sloped ceiling sucked any bright light pouring in. A fresh smell of polish filled the whole ground floor trying to cover a musty old smell and the powdery whiff of builder's dust. Specks of the same dust left traces, visible across the floor in the reflection of the light from outside.

A strong man with square shoulders greeted them in the atrium. He did not smile when shaking hands. He maintained a professional stance, constant eye contact with Julian and his three guests and spoke only the bare minimum. Enrico found the man's towering appearance intimidating.

'Hello. Welcome. I am Agent Bickingham' Reginald said.

'Hello, Mr Bickingham!' replied Julian. 'My chief project manager talks a lot about you. Thank you for taking the time to meet us. I was hoping my

PA called you just in time. I did not want to cause problems with the work going on here.'

Reginald shook his head to reassure him it was not a problem.

'This is our security guard.' explained Julian turning towards his guests. 'He is in charge of security while the restoration works are underway. We at Alberyx Enterprises hired him to oversee things when we chose the building contractor.'

Julian thanked Reginald again and beckoned at his guests to follow him through. Enrico glanced at the security guard. He thought for a moment the guard had been staring at him while Julian Alberon spoke. Yet, he did not remember seeing him before.

The Old Rectory did not seem to be in such a bad state of disrepair. The main features targeted by the restoration were the obvious signs of modernisation carried out in recent times. While some were necessary to keep the house up and running to living standards, most of it had nothing to do with the history of the Old Rectory as Dr Watkins had told Enrico. Julian was swift in taking time to explain what he had learned about such a historical place for Wimbledon. From time to time, he would seek Dr Watkins's nod of approval or a few additional words on the fine details of history they could recall from the fine wooden decor of tables and chairs, or the faded colours of old paintings. The curator followed Julian with the excitement of a young scholar entering the Vatican Archives or perhaps a young boy visiting Disneyland for the first time.

"…The Old Rectory had been around since the mid-to-late Middle Ages and was built for the purpose of providing a place to live for the local parsonage. It had passed through different hands and owners and had seen little change over the centuries until it was sold to private owners in 1861 who then started adding new rooms and extensions. The battlements, the wooden beams, the turret, the sloped ceilings, the perfectly squared windows, they all hint at the era of Henry VIII and the English Renaissance.

Most of them though were repaired or replaced, perhaps in line with the fashion and lifestyle of the twentieth century, focused on comfort as well as meeting health and safety standards…"

Enrico followed the speech and paid attention to those items he could tell did not belong to English history. A CCTV camera here, an electric air conditioner there. Dr Watkins was probably horrified by the butcher's job carried out by unconcerned billionaires. Enrico could read his expression as they moved from room to room. They saw the ground floors, the vast living and drawing rooms, the kitchens, the cavernous fireplaces.

Enrico knew Dr Watkins's interest was in the underground section of the house. He had to wait until the curator put the matter forward, whenever that may happen. The Italian baker was losing interest by the minute. He was not sure they could find something here that would help them. On their way back downstairs, he glanced the polished floor with its specks of dust and the traces of small wheels or footprints coming in and out. It then dawned on him not all of them went from the main door to the stairs. The reflection from outside showed a thin trail of footprints going towards the security guard's feet and against the wall panels. Enrico found himself staring at the trail when he looked up and met the gaze of this Agent Bickingham. Burly man, square jaw and bulging muscles. He was looking at Enrico from where he had been standing. The stare was not the friendliest. Enrico looked away and followed the group as they moved to the bottom of the stairs. He kept his back to him to avoid his disturbing gaze.

'Well, this is the Old Rectory from the inside.' concluded Julian Alberon.

'Does it have a basement by any chance?' asked Dr Watkins.

Enrico was relieved. He could not wait any longer.

'Yes.' said Julian. 'You can access it from the garden. Very small to be honest. I thought there would be a larger one.'

Enrico thought he heard Reginald's feet shift on the floor. He then heard his monosyllabic answer boom behind him.

'It is accessible if you really need to check it.' he spoke.

Enrico looked over his shoulder, the burly figure looming over him.

'Good.' confirmed Julian with satisfaction. 'Shall we?'

The group left the security guard and moved through the kitchen to the outdoor garden. Enrico caught up with Viviane and hunched next to her so as not to be heard by Dr Watkins or Julian Alberon.

'That security guard gives me the creeps…' he confessed.

'He needs to Enrico. He is a security guard after all.'

'Something about him does not seem right.'

'Another one of your hunches, Enrico? Can we worry about one thing at a time?'

Enrico groaned in response. He met Viviane's expression; one he had seen many times when he was crossing the line. Her eyes then softened.

'You can't see mystery and danger everywhere. Let's see first if Dr Watkins's lead actually takes us anywhere.'

The garden was roughly the same size as the front driveway. A high grey wall opposite the house showed its dull colour to the world, stripped of ivy and other climbing plants. It was a neat divider from Saint Mary's churchyard and the neighbouring houses to the north of which you could hardly see the rooftops. The garden itself was simple, kept to a minimum for easy maintenance. Low bushes and well-kept shrubberies of roses and lavender were dotted around the gravel pathway. There was little grass except for a small patch near the building. The most striking feature was a dense foliage at the far end, stretching from the centre to the south of the garden. The vivid green leaves belonged to a line of old fig trees running along each side of a stone path. Their branches met half-way in a loving embrace and over the years, a natural arch had formed.

'Are those fig trees?' exclaimed Enrico nudging at Viviane while she checked the state of the roses.

Viviane looked up in Enrico's direction.

'Yes, indeed. It is called "The Fig Walk".' confirmed Julian as he followed through the garden of the Old Rectory. 'One of the two fig walks left in the United Kingdom. They do produce fruits sometimes, in those rare hot summers, but the main attraction is the beautiful colour they add to this place.'

'No vineyards?' joked Enrico.

He casually dropped a clue into the conversation. Dr Watkins shot him a look of disapproval. The focus was on the basement without raising too much suspicion.

'Vineyards, Mr LoTrova?' acted Julian surprised. 'Maybe not here now but we cannot ignore the fact they may have existed on this side of the hill.'

'I referred Enrico to the old drawings from the sixteenth century.' interjected Dr Watkins to explain Enrico's comment. 'The one where vineyard and orangeries stretch out from the side of the Elizabethan Manor House. He is fascinated by the fact that vineyards may have existed on this hill and the Cecils may have produced wine, although if such a thing would be remotely possible, he does not believe English wine is any good anyway.'

'Ah, you are Italian!' commented Julian. 'I can understand. There is no solid proof, obviously, but some claim that more than three hundred years ago or so the British climate could have been warmer than it is today.'

Julian motioned them to follow him as he led the way to the basement. They turned round a corner of the Old Rectory and Julian pointed a double door on the ground.

'Care to help me open it?' he suggested.

Enrico offered to lift one of the heavy wooden double doors. The musty closed smell of a basement whiffed out and the opening revealed a short flight of stairs to a basement right under the ground floor. It was small in size, probably as big as the hall, and it was empty.

'Is this it?' blurted out Enrico, expecting more.

'As I said, this is what we have.' said Julian.

Enrico and Viviane glanced towards Dr Watkins who had stepped inside with them. He turned around and checked the stone walls. He did not seem disappointed or at least it did not show.

Enrico frowned. The basement was the whole point of coming here. There was definitely no tunnel here, inviting them in. He joined Dr Watkins in touching the walls. For a moment, he believed he could hear tremors in the cold stone.

'Everything ok?' Julian asked, confused from their odd behaviour.

'Yes, yes.' dismissed Dr Watkins wiping his hands. 'We wanted to know if the old tunnels ran below the Old Rectory. Apparently, this is not the case.'

'I understand. We have not found anything larger. If you are looking for tunnels, you may have better luck via Saint Mary's. Have you heard about that girl on Sunday? Didn't she get lost in a tunnel?'

'Yes. We were there, shocking news.' replied Viviane. 'Do you think that tunnel leads anywhere?'

'I doubt it.' said Julian.

'What makes you think so?' wondered Viviane, trying to probe with the question she knew Dr Watkins would want to ask.

'Unless you are interested in hearing about old legends from ancient folklore, there is nothing special about the tunnels.'

'Ancient legends?' echoed Enrico and Viviane, their curiosity suddenly prickled.

'We are not here to hunt legends!' reprimanded Dr Watkins cutting them off.

The curator walked out of the basement and back into the gardens, showing his disinterest in the new conversation. Julian shrugged with a smile on his lips. He then followed the curator outside, but Enrico and Viviane wanted to know more.

'What legends?' insisted Viviane while they closed the double doors of the small basement.

'I am a man of local history.' said Dr Watkins out loud from behind the corner building. 'Legends are just a waste of time.'

The curator had moved on already and taken one of the garden chairs to sit on. His frown showed clear dissatisfaction. Enrico and Viviane understood Dr Watkins wanted to find an entrance here at all costs; to find some hard evidence that would explain where one of the blocked tunnels led to. Instead, it was just a dead end.

In the meantime, Julian had gathered three more chairs and invited Enrico and Viviane to take a seat while the weather was pleasant. He did not mind Dr Watkins's outburst, and seemed to share the curator's disappointment.

'Dr Watkins is indeed a man of history, my friends.' said Julian to put everyone at ease. 'I know that, and I vouch for that…'

'Thank you, Sir Alberon!' added Dr Watkins.

'…but let's move away from the history books for once!' continued Julian with a cheeky wink to the baker and the florist. 'Wimbledon was an Anglo-Saxon village. We don't know much about its past since there are no written records until the Domesday Book of 1086. Right, Dr Watkins?'

Julian put forward a kind smile to the curator's stern face. Dr Watkins shifted in his seat and just nodded to let him go on.

'Thank you, Dr Watkins. Now, I am no historian. But most people who have been to the Museum of Wimbledon know that hardly any valuable remains have been found to this day on our Anglo-Saxon heritage, and historians stay vague about it.'

Julian eyed Dr Watkins again to check he was in line with the official stance on Wimbledon history. Enrico and Viviane listened on, captivated by Julian Alberon's oratory skills, and keeping quiet as if they were sitting around a camp fire. The businessman then arched his body pretending to be a deformed hunchback. He grinned the moment he stepped out of his professional look.

'Old Anglo-Saxon legends across England talk about sorcerers and potions and monsters.' he started narrating. 'Sorcery may have been at the heart of this hill, which at the time was isolated from bigger villages in the area as far as today's Putney and Merton. This isolation is believed to have been created on purpose due to a local sorcerer, or wizard, or whatever you call them. He spread fear, not because of his threat but because of his deep knowledge of dark arts. Surprisingly, the Christian missions passed through but never stopped here permanently. *Wimbedounyng,* as the Anglo-Saxons called Wimbledon, used to be just a place to rest from their journey. Here, Christian missions used to convert local farmers and spread the word of God when they could, before carrying on towards bigger villages as their final destination.'

Viviane chuckled at his theatrical voice. Julian was now playing with them with grand gestures and looking far in the distance as a well-trained thespian.

'Priests scared of some black magic?' humoured Enrico.

'Who knows.' carried on Julian. 'The sorcerer who lived on this hill claimed to have control over life and death of living things, and even master his or her own immortality. All we know is that at some point Saint Mary's was erected as the official village church. Despite the village having no more than two, three houses, people walked all the way here from Mortlake, Putney and Merton where the church had now been founded. We are talking about two, three miles to reach a place which had no relic or pilgrimage status…'

'Children's' fairy tales.' blurted Dr Watkins annoyed. 'What a load of rubbish!'

'Sounds more interesting though.' led on Viviane. 'Where did you hear all this, Sir Alberon?'

'Call me Julian, please.' added the businessman. 'It is indeed a fairy tale we all heard growing up. Dr Watkins knows it too, but it is something you don't read this in history books!'

'Exactly!' echoed Dr Watkins in agreement.

'You know this story, Dr Watkins?' wondered Viviane. 'How come you never told me?'

'I am a historian, Viviane!'

'Come on, what else is there?' pressed Viviane, amused. 'Does this sorcerer have a name?'

'I can only speculate here, Miss Leighwood, without upsetting Dr Watkins here.' resumed Julian. 'As you probably know, the name *Wimbedounyng* means "Wynnman's Hill". I would dare to say Wynnman is not the name of a local chieftain, as most people think, but the sorcerer's himself.'

'*Come come?* Excuse me?' blurted out Enrico. 'Did you just say "Wynnman"? Have I just named my bakery after a *stregone*…a sorcerer? *O mio dio…*'

'It is a fairy tale, Enrico.' said Viviane. 'I didn't know you were the superstitious type!'

'I'm not. I just hope people don't freak out when buying my bread. How does this fairy tale end?'

'The story goes' explained Julian. 'that the sorcerer was driven away by Christianity, cast away, but in fleeing, he left behind his elixirs and potions, some of them deemed to make any man all-powerful. He could bend nature to his will and create something out of nothing. Maybe growing vineyards or even orange trees on the side of this hill, all thanks to the Anglo-Saxon sorcerer's magic absorbed by these very grounds we stand on, where he carried out his meticulous work. The Church may have hidden all this to protect the population from heresy and maybe save their conversion of Britain to Christianity…you decide! Perhaps we will never know!'

'Enough!' interjected Dr Watkins, standing up and giving a strict look at the other three. 'I dislike such a distortion of facts. There are no magic potions and there is no sorcerer. The Wynnman was likely to be a local Anglo-Saxon chieftain. Lack of proof does not mean we need to invent something ridiculous out of it!'

'We are fooling around, Dr Watkins.' said Viviane in a calm voice, rubbing her hand on his tense shoulder. 'Maybe growing vineyards in Wimbledon could just have been the fruit of a miraculous British warm weather. None of us believes in dark magic and wizards, do we?'

Viviane hinted at Enrico and Julian with a wave of her hand to which the two did not hesitate to agree to avoid hurting Dr Watkins's feelings about history even further.

On the way back into the building, Julian and Viviane returned to more down-to-earth subjects like flowers and plants. Enrico walked by Dr Watkins's side, giving one last look around at the beauty of the Old Rectory's garden.

'No hard feelings, Dr Watkins.' said the Italian baker as a form of truce.

'None taken. I just take my work seriously. Maybe too much.'

'These tunnels are dear to you, aren't they?'

'Maybe. I don't know.'

The curator did not look Enrico in the eye and for the first time the Italian baker felt Dr Watkins was somehow detached, although briefly.

'Happy to have made the trip down here?' Enrico said quietly so that Julian could not overhear.

'Maybe.' replied the curator with little joy. 'Where did that body come from though?'

Enrico understood perfectly what he meant. Having the opportunity to come here was at the hands of their benefactor that was Julian Alberon. He did not need to know about their real motivation, or maybe not yet. Still, the small basement made him itch with curiosity as well. If the crimson traces led towards the area below the Old Rectory, but there was no apparent way out here, then Dr Watkins was right to look at the facts and ask the big question: where did the burnt body come from?

'Ah, Dr Watkins!' exclaimed Enrico in remembering. 'I think I left my sealable bag with the traces of crimson powder at your museum. Is that right?'

'Yes, yes. Not now Enrico.'

'But we could use that…'

'I sent it to the department of scientific research at the British Museum!' Dr Watkins cut him off.

Enrico was used to abrupt responses. He found it odd though from the curator himself, always calm and well-mannered. The visit to the Old Rectory had somehow annoyed him or disturbed him. He then met Dr Watkins's gaze who gave him a saddened look.

'Sorry Enrico. Just tired from poor sleep. Excuse me for being rude!'

'Nah, don't worry! You have been hanging around with me too much!'

The two joined Viviane and Julian in the hall, under the scrutiny of the security guard. Viviane was talking with enthusiasm about her flower shop and discussing business ideas with Julian, who seemed to be thrilled by it. Enrico saw the way Viviane looked at Julian. He told himself he did not mind but also found a little pleasure in interrupting the conversation.

'Are we all set to go?' he jumped in.

'Yes.' answered Viviane. 'I was saying to Julian we should meet more often.'

'Your visit has been refreshing, I must say.' spoke Julian frankly. 'Not as boring as some of my business meetings.'

'*Certo!* Sure.' muttered Enrico shyly.

The Italian baker had not made his mind up yet about Julian Alberon. He had found his fairy tale in the garden enjoyable, but the businessman came across as too sure of himself. Enrico observed his manners, his flair, his perfect lifestyle, and a tinge of jealousy crept inside him. He looked away and his eyes landed again on the footprints and the wheel traces in the dust at their feet. He was sure the one trail he had seen before was a little off-centred. He followed it with his eyes, and it led to the security guard's feet. When he looked up, he realised Agent Bickingham, the intimidating security guard, had been looking at him with suspicion all along and Enrico was again the one being looked at. He did not know Reginald had recognised him ever since they had arrived. Yet, something told the Italian baker he was no longer welcome here at the Old Rectory.

The blue patches in the sky were long gone later in the afternoon, bringing grey clouds again over Wimbledon High Street. The Regency-style buildings opposite *The Wynnman* bakery, with their red copper bricks, now appeared dull and sad. The forecast announced some rain in the evening. Autumn was creeping in very quickly.

'Do I need an umbrella?' asked Enrico looking out of the curved window of his bakery.

'I am driving you there, Enrico. My car is outside. You won't get wet. Come on! Get moving!' pushed Viviane, tapping her foot by the counter.

She had been impatiently waiting for Enrico to be ready to leave. Enrico had closed earlier so he could go to Wimbledon Police Station and she had offered to take him. Something told her he would do less damage if he was not completely on his own.

'What did you think of today's glorious meeting?' asked Enrico after jumping inside Viviane's little yellow Fiat 500.

'Better than nothing.' replied the florist, unable to ignore Enrico's sarcastic tone.

'I think he is pompous. *Un pallone gonfiato.*' moaned Enrico.

'I think Julian Alberon is modest and adorable.' Insisted Viviane. 'Not your typical careless rich man.'

'*Adorabile?* Adorable? *Non ti capisco.* What is wrong with you?'

'At least he does not go around breaking the law, Enrico.' warned Viviane with a cheeky smile.

Viviane knew she could not lose when playing the legality card. The Italian baker gave her a smirk and then looked out of the window.

She turned on the engine and drove off. She rolled down both front windows a few inches for some fresh air.

'It is not summer!' reminded Enrico, wrapping his chef jacket tight around his neck.

'Then buy a coat, for God's sake!'

Enrico found Viviane's teasing could be unbearable and at times irresistible. He looked at her again from the corner of his eye.

'Don't look at me like that!' Viviane scoffed. 'And don't change the subject: going down the tunnels after what happened, and not even telling the police what you found, is called "obstruction of justice"!'

'I just did what Dr Watkins asked me to do.' moaned Enrico.

'One more reason to drop it. This whole thing may be too much to bear for Dr Watkins. I am sure you noticed how tired he is. He is always yawning and still not sleeping as much as he should.'

'Has he always been like this?'

'Not really. Ever since the events at Cannizaro Park, I have found him a little bit more restless. Did you see how he almost lost his temper when Julian Alberon started talking about magic, sorcerers and potions?

'I did not know he could get so touchy about the subject. I hope he is ok.'

'I hope the same too. Let's be thankful Dr Watkins was able to get a meeting with Julian Alberon, whether you like him or not. Now we know

Dr Watkins's theory does not work. There are no tunnels under the Old Rectory.'

'And don't you wonder where that disfigured body came from?'

'That is something you can tell the police today.' Viviane cut it short, her eyes on the road. 'Baynard will be thrilled. Time to hand it over to the police.'

Enrico crossed his arms, unable to defend his position. He had to admit there was not much to go on. The stare given to him by the security guard, that Agent Bickingham, at the Old Rectory, still daunted Enrico. Something about the guard's stare or the footsteps Enrico saw on the floor did not add up. He had not told Viviane about it yet, and now Enrico had to decide whether to tell the police all he knew. Baynard's joy, as Viviane put it.

The little yellow Fiat 500 roared its mighty small engine down Wimbledon Hill Road and at the crossroad with Alexandra Road, Viviane turned left to park opposite Wimbledon Police Station.

'Here we are!' announced Viviane.

Enrico pushed his thoughts to the back of his mind the moment the engine died out and focused on the building opposite. Wimbledon Police Station. He thought he would never come to this place on his own accord. But lately, it seemed as if everyone wanted nothing but legality from him whether he liked it or not.

'Are you going to be ok? Do you know what you have to say?' Viviane reminded him, to show she cared.

'Yes. Yes.' replied Enrico a little annoyed of the reminder. 'Baynard and I are friendly enemies. He wants something, and I give it to him. He may have something to give back.'

'You scratch my back I scratch yours?'

'Sort of.'

'OK. That works for me. As long as we don't get too involved. I'll wait here, shall I?'

Enrico nodded. He wanted to be accompanied. Viviane gave him one last look, a merciful one, and then reached over to kiss him on the cheek.

'What was that for?' said Enrico feeling his cheeks turning a faded pink.

'Encouragement. This is what friends do.' Viviane comforted him ruffling his wavy hair to annoy him. 'Go before I regret it.'

Enrico lightly brushed his cheek, not sure whether to wipe the kiss off or keep it for longer. With a half nervous smile, he jumped out of the car. He quickly checked for incoming traffic on both sides and crossed the street with determination, to reach the police station's main entrance. He did not turn to wave, but he knew Viviane would be waiting until he had finished what he had to do.

After announcing his arrival to the guard in charge, a police constable swiftly took Enrico through the many corridors and floors of Wimbledon Police Station. Enrico knew he would get lost if he tried to remember his way back. The police constable finally led him to a door where a young policeman with ginger hair had been waiting for him. Enrico recognised him vaguely, seeing him always at Baynard's side.

'Mr Enrico LoTrova?' asked Sergeant Jeremy.

'Yes ...'

'Sergeant Jeremy. I am the sergeant in charge, and I am here to take your statement today.'

'Not Inspector Baynard?' questioned Enrico with surprise and a hint of disappointment.

'I am afraid the inspector has been called elsewhere. However, it should not take long.'

The two shook hands. Sergeant Jeremy's bright ginger hair squared his cordial freckled face. It clashed with Enrico's experience with the police and he could not help wondering if the sergeant in front of him worked with Baynard on a daily basis and if he found it a hard job. He smiled to himself at the funny thought.

Jeremy led him into a bright room with two high windows, a table and two chairs. He put a notepad and his dossier on the table, and asked Enrico to take a seat.

'This is not an interviewing room in the strict sense of the word, as you can see from the nice wide windows. The interview will be recorded. Standard procedure as stated on the form you signed with the guard downstairs.'

Jeremy flicked one switch on the wall to activate the microphone built into the room to capture the audio. An automated voice announced the recording was on.

'Definitely a more comfortable experience compared to last time…' noted Enrico looking around the room.

Enrico hinted obviously to the last time Baynard had interviewed him as a suspect in the dingy interview room in the basement. Jeremy tried to hide his embarrassment of the event.

The interview started the moment they both sat opposite each other. First were the formalities, date, place, attendees, occupation. Then Jeremy prompted Enrico to share what he knew about the incidents at 24 Arthur Road.

Reginald Bosham had finished painting Toby Claymore's van and he had even changed the number plate to remove anything that would allow identification. He had done a perfect job even though he showed his rage and impatience in the way he sprayed the plain white paint over the van.

Seeing the baker and his friends arriving at the Old Rectory with the owner of Alberyx Enterprises was the worst nightmare to wish for. Part of him wished it was an innocent coincidence; he knew though he could not be fooled more than once. Lord Awlthorp's driver was right. This Enrico LoTrova had found the body, he had bumped into Toby Claymore, and now he was nosing above the very ground where their work was being carried out. He noticed the way he looked around; the baker was onto something. He had to tread carefully and move quickly.

Reginald changed into the clothes chosen for his cover. He wore scrubs as clothes, a surgeon's cap of the same colour and a white surgeon' mask which covered most of his face. He was meant to arrive at the labs of Wimbledon Police Station under orders to pick up and transfer Henry Claymore's body. He was confident it would work, as long as the body was where Lord Awlthorp's inside man said it was. The plan was then to return here to Toby Claymore's rented garage and swap vans once again to cut off any tail on him completely so he could deliver the rest of the plan.

The burly man looked at himself in one of the rear mirrors. His disguise was perfect. He then grabbed the keys of Toby's van and moved out of the garage. Reginald's own van was parked in the garage next door. It would stay there until his return. It was time to put this plan into motion and reach Wimbledon Police Station.

The route only took ten minutes. When close to his destination. Reginald swerved away from the traffic lining up on Alexandra Road and took a side street next to Wimbledon Police Station. The freshly painted white van approached the security and Reginald flashed his fake ID to the police guard without having to pull down the mask from his mouth. He passed through undetected.

'Need to pick up a body from forensics for transfer…' he said in a muffled voice.

The police guard checked his ID, then the van. He opened the doors at the back. Mostly empty with just a stretcher in the middle. All clear, he confirmed. Reginald raised his thumb up and pushed through the barriers. He drove to the back of the building among other police cars and parked the van as close as possible to the service door at the back. His mask was still on and so was the soft surgeon's cap. From the rear mirror he could see the CCTV cameras placed on all angles; he had to ensure his disguise stayed intact until the job was done.

Reginald stepped out of the van and moved on fast. His pace hinted at a well-studied plan. First, he pulled the stretcher from the van and pulled down its four wheels; he then pushed it across the narrow car park and to the back door. He ignored the small CCTV whizzing from left to right and scanned his ID to let the door open up to a tiled atrium of a pale blue colour. Reginald's instinct was to turn right, where he knew the door would lead to the forensics lab. According to Lord Awlthorp, their inside man, whom Reginald had never met, had arranged for the body to be as close as possible to the door Reginald was now looking at. So far, breaking into the police station had been far too easy but Reginald Bosham knew only too well any mistake now could be fatal. For a moment, his thoughts were distracted from the plan and the burly man questioned why Lord Awlthorp had insisted on retrieving Henry Claymore's body. It was such a high-risk operation.

There was no time to waste. He pushed the door leading to the forensics lab slowly until it was wide enough for him to get through with his stretcher. A long bare corridor opened up in front of him, wide enough for two stretchers to pass. At the end of the corridor the sign clearly confirmed access to the forensic lab. Reginald went through the plan again and the body was meant to be there, according to the precise instructions Lord Awlthorp had received from the inside. Reginald had wondered who could be feeding such intel but for now his only concern was to get in and out as quickly as possible.

There was a metal table half-way down the corridor with a body bag on top. Reginald moved next to it and glanced at the label. Henry Claymore, it said. Reginald asked himself whether he ought to check. He sneaked a quick peek at the face. Henry's face was no longer recognisable, an empty stare of molten skin and muscles.

Reginald lifted the body bag to feel the weight. He then heaved the body onto his stretcher and felt something roll inside followed by a heavy thud. The burly man unzipped the body bag once more. He noticed a bottle of the Cecils' wine had been strapped to the body's legs. He recognised it by the familiar label: 'Cecil 1590'. Reginald was not sure what to make of it or how the police had got hold of it. Better leave it where it is, Reginald thought, and take everything with me. He zipped the bag up and moved to the other side of the stretcher to push it towards the exit of the building. He could not manoeuvre the stretcher as swiftly as before. The body was quite heavy. He pushed hard until he got back to the exit. Then the clack of a door over his shoulder put him on alert.

'Excuse me, who are you?' said a voice.

Reginald did not turn. He could not engage in a full conversation.

'Taking a body to the morgue…' muffled Reginald through his mask, leaning against the stretcher to push the door ahead of him.

After that, he thought he heard a clear request to wait. He did not wait. He used all his strength to quickly get the stretcher out of there. He broke into a brisk walk. His cover was about to blow; he knew, from now on, it was all about minimising collateral damage.

The back door leading to the car park banged against the wall when Reginald opened it violently as he rushed out to the white van. The stretcher wheels rattled against the concrete surface, as the body bag wobbled here and there. He glanced sideways without stopping and hurled the body bag into the back of the van alongside Toby, still unconscious. He knew whoever was after him would be right behind. He quickly pulled the stretcher towards him and slid it around to use it as a weapon. He rammed the stretcher into the man in the white lab coat, who had chased him outside, and the man immediately fell to the ground. Reginald had just enough time to make a run for the van and get behind the wheel. He grinned, and he suddenly felt fresh air on his face; he put his hand on his mouth and nose. His mask had fallen off in the rush to escape. He looked up by mistake and that is when the CCTV on top of the back door caught him in the act. Reginald did not stick around to wait to hear the sound of the alarm echo all around Wimbledon Police Station.

'…and you can confirm the van tried to run you down before you fled the scene?'

Enrico confirmed. He had been mainly nodding 'yes' and 'no' for the past five or ten minutes. Jeremy's questions were just a more formal re-hash of Baynard's inquisitive ones. There was no space to probe the truth and bring new facts to light, or at least the Italian baker felt he was not given the right opportunity to explain.

'To recap, you did not manage to get the van's number plate, but you could recognise the man you encountered in the house. Is that correct?'

Enrico thought this could be the most appropriate time to slip in a clue as to why he was in Arthur Road, that he was actually coming from underground, that he was looking for clues as to what really happened to the disfigured man.

The Italian baker straightened the lapel of his chef jacket and was ready to say 'yes' once more when the sound of an alarm rang loud in the room and throughout the whole building. A light by the door turned red. Sergeant Jeremy jumped up alarmed. His eyes showed a lack of readiness for such a situation and Enrico realised this was no ordinary fire drill.

'Building security has been breached. I will need to ask you to stay here until the situation is cleared. Do not attempt to leave until safe to do so!'

The sergeant was quick to pick up his stuff and leave the room. The door was locked behind him. Enrico blinked in confusion. The alarm was still whaling and ringing in his ears to deafening point. Sounds of footsteps and shouts outside made him wonder if the police station was under attack. A bit far-fetched. Someone had escaped maybe. They had a few cells, but this was no penitentiary.

Enrico got up from the chair, anxious to know what was happening. He looked out of one of the windows to see if there was any movement outside. From the floor he was on, he could see the roofs of Wimbledon Railway Station and part of the bustling traffic of the Broadway. The view down below, closer to him, showed the backstreet of the building and the police car park. All empty, he thought, until he noticed a man wearing what looked like scrubs or a surgeon's vest. The man, with muscled arms and large square shoulders, was getting into a white van and he then pulled out of the parking space at incredible speed. From the sound of screeching tyres, Enrico could only assume he was running away out of fear, escaping from something. As the van reversed and was about to hit the gas, the man at the wheel came quickly into view through the rolled down window. Enrico had seen him before. Square jaw, hard face, intimidating eyes. He was not sure until the man at the wheel glanced up, not directly at Enrico but somewhere on the wall of the police building. It was a quick glance, enough for the Italian baker to pin down who the man was. The security guard. Agent Bickingham. The security guard at the Old Rectory was now disguised as a medic of some sort by the looks of it. Enrico did not buy it. He was the one who had triggered the alarm and he was getting away. Enrico knew there and then this man, whoever he was, was not a security guard nor a doctor. He had to find out what he was up to.

The van immediately sped off out of the police car park. The Italian baker shouted and banged the window glass. He needed to get out and follow the van before it was too late. He then grabbed the chair and threw it at the windowpane, smashing it into pieces.

The Italian baker looked out of the open window. He cleared the broken glass and grabbed the black metal drainpipe close by. He checked to make sure it was solid enough to slide down and pushed himself off the window ledge grabbing the pipe with both hands. The pipe jerked slightly under his weight and Enrico started to slide down the two storeys bit by bit. The skin on the palm of his hands started burning and Enrico felt he had to alternate hands to ease the pain. By the time he had reached the ground, both arms and legs had already stiffened from the pressure of his grip.

Enrico desperately looked around. The white van had already disappeared round the corner at full speed. He heard a few gunshots and shouting. Police constables were gathering inside the car park behind him. Enrico dashed in a hopeless chase, still trying to catch his breath after the hazardous window escape. The white van had just come out onto the main road and the police barrier had been broken through; the police guard lay injured on the ground. Viviane, thought Enrico. He had to get to her, not just to check she was safe, but to go in pursuit of the white van with the Fiat 500. The fact Agent Bickingham, a security guard, had just broken in and out of Wimbledon Police Station was too suspicious to ignore. Somehow Enrico had the gut feeling this was related to everything that had been happening lately. It had to be.

The Italian baker reached the main street. The traffic was at a stall after a few cars had zigzagged and bumped into each other to avoid the white van speeding north on Alexandra Road. Police were gathering at every corner of the police building. Some were shouting out asking if anyone had spotted the number plate of the white van; others were setting a parameter to manage the crowds stranded on the street. Enrico dashed across the road.

'Hey, you!' shouted a police constable. 'Don't move!'

Enrico froze in the middle of the traffic. He knew too well the situation was not in his favour. He could not help it. Trouble always found him where curiosity had led him. The baker tried to catch his breath and act normally, so as not to give anything away to the police constable.

Viviane and her Fiat 500 were parked where he had left them. The florist had been following what was happening from behind the wheel. She could now see Enrico in an awkward position. Their eyes finally met, and Viviane understood something had gone wrong. The white van. Enrico rushing out right where the van had come out. The police station alarm going off. She could see the police constable had nearly caught up with Enrico. She hesitated. She could not leave him there high and dry.

'Ah, what the heck!' she cursed under her breath.

Viviane stepped on the gas and pulled out onto the road.

'Get in!' she yelled at the Italian baker opening the passenger door.

Enrico leaped in amid the confusion. The sound of stray bullets rang in Enrico's ears the moment Viviane put her foot down on the accelerator.

'What did you do?' cried out Viviane staring ahead.

'Drive!' Enrico shouted in panic. 'Did you see the van?'

Viviane's eyes flickered. She nodded. She had to trust Enrico's guts, even though the stakes were getting too high.

'Chase it! I'll explain on the way.'

'Ok. Fasten your seatbelt.' she warned. 'This time, you'd better get ready for the Grand Prix of Monza!'

Reginald was slamming the wheel with his hand to contain his anger. He had managed to escape but they had probably seen his face and the van. He needed to proceed with the next phase as quickly as possible, before they identified him and traced his movements up to the garage. He had put the surgeon's mask on again to at least reduce the chances of being identified by more people, although what he really had to do now was go underground before it became impossible to move around Wimbledon.

Swearing under his breath, Reginald swerved the white van right at the crossroad between Durnsford Road and Merton Road. He drove it straight into Toby Claymore's garage and wasted no time in closing the garage door behind him. Alone in the obscurity of the garage, his racing heartbeat rang loud in his ears and every deep breath he took meant a sharper focus on what he had to do next.

Without wasting time he did not have, Reginald opened the door that communicated with the garage he had rented next door. His own green van was parked in there, ready to take the load. The transfer would happen away from prying eyes. Reginald quickly pulled the body bag from the white van and lifted it over his shoulder. He then moved Toby's sedated body and slumped it over, careful not to wake him up and glad the rush from the police station had not woken him up either. He finally proceeded to move the crates of the Cecils' wine the Claymores had stored here. He could not believe the number of crates they had smuggled out from the old cellar. Reginald glanced at his watch again. He had to leave the garage behind at once.

Next step was to cram all the chemists' belonging in the white van. He then rigged the remote explosive all around it, using the spare C4 Toby Claymore had. He tried to keep his hands steady as he put everything in place and wired it altogether to destroy all the evidence. He checked the timer was set and then quickly changed clothes once more. This time he wore a dark green uniform with 'Wimbledon Park Maintenance' written in gold on the breast pocket. The second part of the plan was about to be set in motion.

Outside the garage, the open space was strangely calm. The calm before the storm. Reginald was no fool, though; he knew the police would be on his doorstep in no time.

Viviane drove like a racing driver, zigzagging through the slow traffic and trying to keep the white van in sight. The other drivers frowned at her with their dumbfounded looks as the little Fiat 500 cut corners and pushed through any space available on the road. It was a miracle she did not bump into other cars and managed to maintain her distance from the van. The Italian baker kept his eyes on the road, his back flat against the seat, his grip on the door handle to hold himself steady.

'*Piano.... Pianooo* ... easy!' he kept shouting.

'You go easy next time, Enrico. We probably have Wimbledon police chasing us now! What the heck happened back there?'

Enrico explained how he saw Agent Bickingham acting suspiciously in the police car park. He stressed many times how he had not done anything wrong; he could not just let him get away without knowing why he was there and what he was up to with the van. Viviane thought she would be furious at Enrico. As she listened to him, though, she understood the circumstances were different this time. She too shared Enrico's interest in finding out what the security guard of the Old Rectory was up to and where he was headed.

Police sirens still echoed in the distance when the Fiat 500 turned left onto Durnsford Road. Viviane accelerated out of instinct; keeping the distance from police cars was probably wise too. She knew what the consequences would be, and then she glanced at Enrico who did not seem at all worried apart from not wanting to lose sight of the white van.

'Over there!' he shouted.

The Italian baker spotted the white van disappearing over the bridge across the railway track. Viviane accelerated again, overtaking an SUV and going over the solid white line. Viviane breathed deeply; she felt the sense of danger and adrenaline was addictive. She focused ahead to where the white van had turned right at the crossroad with Merton Road into an isolated and empty open space, surrounded by low storey buildings and secluded from the traffic.

'Those are all rented garages.' commented Viviane.

'Follow him!' advised Enrico.

Viviane looked in her rear-view mirror afraid she would see police sirens coming down the bridge.

'We need to be quick!' warned Viviane. 'The police are probably chasing after both the white van and a yellow Fiat 500…'

Enrico did not reply and watched closely. The white van had disappeared into one of the garages.

'What is he doing?' wondered Viviane. 'Let me park somewhere safe.'

'Let's keep our heads down too!' whispered Enrico.

Viviane drove round a corner and then edged the car a little forward. They both had the garage in sight. Ten minutes passed by. To Enrico and Viviane, it seemed like an eternity. Then, a garage next door started opening and a dark green van drove out in reverse. Viviane was about to start the car and move further behind the corner. Enrico put his hand on her arm, asking her to wait.

'I bet you that's him!' he said.

Viviane looked over. The big face and hard jaw of Agent Bickingham came into view for a second in the car window. The burly man then reversed the dark green van towards them, then sped off and left the area.

'He is going. Go before we lose him!'

Viviane did not wait for Enrico's instructions. She had already started the car and brushed off Enrico's hand to get it into gear.

The big van crossed the intersection again and this time it went up towards Wimbledon Park underground station and the eastern slope of Wimbledon Hill.

'He went that way, Viviane.' pointed out Enrico. 'Don't lose him!'

'I can see him!' grumbled Viviane. 'Don't get over excited. We don't know what this man is up to!'

The pressure was on. She glanced left and right of the main road before reaching the intersection. No police yet. The sirens though seemed to fill the air all around them or perhaps it was just her imagination. The traffic light turned red the moment Viviane sped through the intersection, without checking the oncoming traffic. A few horns blared. She did not care; she had her eyes stuck ahead on the dark green van, barely visible in the traffic up ahead. At that precise moment, a loud explosion rumbled behind them. Enrico turned around.

'Something blew up by the rented garages!' cried out the Italian baker incredulous.

'What the h…?' swore again Viviane.

She glanced at the cloud of black smoke rising high behind her. The traffic came to a halt at the intersection as everyone stopped in shock to witness the instant blaze.

'Keep going!' said Enrico putting his hand on her shoulder. 'I told you something dodgy was going on!'

Viviane tried not to get too distracted by the explosion and kept her eyes fixed on the road. For once, she could not disagree with Enrico. The dark green van crossed another bridge, over the underground tracks. She kept her distance again. Beyond the railway bridge, Arthur Road was plain to see. It led up the steep eastern slope of Wimbledon Hill. The dark green van, though, turned right into a quiet road where the traffic was now non-existent.

Home Park Road bordered the northern side of the hill, where large houses overlooked Wimbledon Park. Viviane slowed down to match the van's speed. She knew she was exposed now, no traffic to hide behind.

'Park there, Viviane!' suggested Enrico. 'Let's see if he carries on or stops somewhere.'

The little yellow Fiat 500 came to a halt behind a big SUV and they peered out onto the stretch of Home Park Road to check on the man's movements. The dark green van had just stopped where the road started to rise slowly back towards Saint Mary's Church, not far from one of the service gates of the park. Enrico and Viviane waited anxiously with Enrico asking Viviane to describe things most of the time since she had the better view. She could understand his impatience. She shared some of it too now that she was becoming infected with his curiosity.

When Agent Bickingham stepped out in a dark green uniform, Enrico and Viviane felt another wave of shock. They now had confirmation the man Julian Alberon had trusted with looking after the security of the Old Rectory, was hiding something. Something worth protecting if he dared to break into Wimbledon Police station and blow up a white van to hide his tracks.

'Something fishy going on!' commented Viviane. 'Do you think we should warn Julian?'

'Better see what he is up to first.' said Enrico. 'What is around here anyway?'

'Just the park. Hey, is that a maintenance staff uniform he is wearing?'

'I don't think that is his second job!'

Enrico could not understand the connection in Agent Bickingham's actions. First time he spotted him, he was dressed as a doctor or surgeon.

Now, a maintenance staff uniform after blowing up the garages. These were disguises as part of a cover-up.

'Something tells me he is not even a security guard!' commented Enrico.

'So, what now?' asked Viviane.

'*Semplice!* Simple!' answered Enrico. 'We keep following him!'

'Is it that simple?'

Inspector Baynard could not believe the mess. The cloud of smoke had reduced the white van to a burnt chassis and a black blotch had formed all around it as if an ink cartridge had exploded. Even though the firemen spoke of a garage, Baynard could only see four charred, crumbling walls with the roof completely blown out.

He stared at the shapeless blotch from the crowd control barrier where he was giving swift orders to the agents on site. This last accident was not easy to digest. Another explosion in full daylight, right after the police station had been breached. It seemed the whole of Wimbledon was at war. The higher ranks would not let this go unnoticed unless Baynard moved faster in restoring some form of order. Not tomorrow, but today, as the Chief Superintendent put it across to him earlier in the atrium of the police station. The conversation was still fresh in Baynard's mind.

'What is this mess, inspector? Are we to become the mockery of the Metropolitan Police?' questioned the Chief Superintendent.

'We are working on it!' replied Baynard.

He was checking a few reports Sergeant Jeremy had handed over to him, running up and down them. He kept his eye contact with the Chief Superintendent to a minimum. He had to give the impression he had it all under control.

'How could a man come and go from the police lab as he pleases?' complained the Chief Superintendent. 'And take away a body in the process, which is actually key evidence in an ongoing case?'

'He must have had a vantage point we are not aware of.' observed Baynard.

'Such as?' leered the Chief Superintendent. 'Please illuminate me!'

Baynard was still checking the report; pretending to read important sections for the first time except he had read them more than once and now knew what they said word for word. Two men had been spotted before and after the alarm was given. One was disguised as a medic and the freeze-frame of his face, captured by the CCTV, was being compared on the police database. The other was seen running away when ordered to stop; he was wearing a chef jacket and he was seen hopping into a yellow Fiat 500. Baynard did not need to read on. He had had enough of the Italian baker causing havoc and making a fool of him and the police. His interference had to stop; his motives unveiled.

He lifted his head and looked at the Chief Superintendent. The inspector was aware he could not share such intel with his superior without avoiding another wave of criticism. He would have preferred to be out on the job. That is when the second emergency call came in. An explosion had been reported at a rented garage at the end of Durnsford Road. The conversation with the Chief Superintendent had to end there, unresolved.

Baynard's focus returned to the present, standing in front of the burnt garage. The phone rang in his pocket bringing him back to the reality. He moved away from the crowd barrier to answer in private. It was Jeremy, reporting back on status at the police station.

'All in order here, sir!' said the young man pleased with himself. 'The breach at the police station is now contained and traffic outside is back to normal. We dispersed the crowds.'

The image of chaos outside Wimbledon police station was fresh in both their minds. Unimaginable.

'Anything else missing?' asked Baynard.

'It seems the whole purpose was to steal Henry Claymore's body. We also cannot find the Cecils' bottle of wine. The one with the stinking liquid inside. It is gone. Nothing else is missing or damaged.'

'Who would find Henry Claymore's body inconvenient?' said Baynard, puzzled.

'Toby Claymore, probably.' guessed Jeremy.

'Any news on finding him?

'Nope.'

'Intensify the search. How come the body was moved out of the lab?'

'The forensic team is trying to find out who issued the order. They don't know.'

Baynard rolled his eyes, incredulous.

'And who would steal a bottle filled with that foul crimson-looking liquid?' continued the inspector with his line of enquiry. 'It does not make sense.'

There was a pause only filled by the crackling wood and plastic from the hot ashes of the garage. They tinged Baynard's icy stare with a fiery glow.

'How about the man who looked like a medic?'

'The search of the police database gave us the name of Reginald Bosham.'

'It does not ring any bell. Who is he?'

'Getting more on that. No latest address. He has a criminal record though and spent a few years in Wandsworth Prison. We also took details of the van he fled in.'

Baynard thanked his sergeant for the fresh clues he was able to gather quickly. The last few days had not been easy and today was the worst. He needed to pin down those responsible for what had happened today. A hunch told him they were probably the same people who were behind the mysterious happenings of the last few days.

Jeremy gave him make and model, and the inspector's face gloomed as he stared at the burnt chassis. He summoned one of the firemen and one of his men to check the early report they had put together after putting out the fire. The number plate had not burnt completely, and it was still legible.

'I have it in front of me, Jeremy. Can you repeat the number plate you have?'

Jeremy repeated the series of numbers and letters. Baynard checked each one.

'The burnt chassis here is the white van.' he confirmed with the policeman next to him nodding to confirm.

'You know Henry's body was inside the car…' murmured Jeremy.

The sergeant did not finish his sentence. Baynard knew the explosion was a means to destroy all that evidence. It went unsaid someone was desperately covering their tracks. Toby Claymore and this Reginald Bosham were working together, and Baynard could not believe they were capable of devising such a plan. They had to be stopped.

'Sergeant Jeremy, call me the minute you have more on Reginald Bosham or Toby Claymore. In the meantime, issue the police warrant for both their arrest. Effective now!'

'How about the other man, inspector? You know… the chef jacket? Do you wish to issue the police warrant for his arrest too?'

Jeremy did not have to mention the name, for fear the Chief Superintendent may hear nearby.

'He is on my list. I will go and find him once I wrap up here. I know where he lives.'

Baynard hung up and returned to the scene in front of him. A sparse crowd watched from across the road while the traffic tried hard to return to its pace, unable though to ignore the black mass. Another police constable walked briskly towards him. From his face, he could tell he was bearer of news. Good or bad; it was hard to tell lately.

'Inspector, we were able to check the owners of the rented garages here. The garage that blew up was rented by Henry Claymore a few months ago. The white van inside was registered in his name.'

Baynard could not believe his ears.

'Are you serious?' he blurted out.

'Yes. There is more. While the one to the left was empty, the one to the right was rented by…Henry Claymore again!'

'What?' blurted out Baynard. 'How many garages is he renting? Found anything intact from the explosion?'

The police constable shook his head.

'The one where the van blew up was filled with equipment and tools. Yet, it will take days to figure out what they were needed for. The one to the right had hardly anything in it.'

Baynard's inquisitive stare shifted from the police constable to the row of garages. He wished ashes could talk and tell him what had happened. This Reginald Bosham used Henry Claymore's van. Maybe he knew where Toby Claymore was.

'Inspector...' added the police constable.

'Yes?' spoke Baynard a little irritated that his thoughts had been interrupted.

'We have something else.'

Baynard's inquisitive stare focused on the police constable, who trembled under his gaze, hoping the news was as good as he thought it was.

'Speak up!' he ordered.

'We checked other garages here and one at the far end caught our attention. A third one rented by Henry Claymore.'

Baynard's frown deepened.

'This is getting ridiculous! Are we sure it is the same person?'

'This is the name on the register.' continued the police constable. 'We had permission to force it open and found a few empty wine bottles, wine-stained syphons and all these old bottles of wine labelled 'Cecil 1590'. Does that make sense to you?'

The inspector did not have to guess the link this time. Wine was at the heart of all this. Strangely as it sounded.

Reginald walked up the slope to reach the farthest south-western point of Wimbledon Park, following the same trail Toby Claymore had showed him the night before. Here, the short, well-kept grass easily gave way to tall, wild shrubbery, and clusters of high thick trees massing against the high fences of residential homes built against the northern side of Wimbledon Hill. It was an unkempt corner of the park.

The burly man had goggles on and a face mask pretending to run his maintenance routine as one of the staff from the park. He kept a steady pace, face looking straight ahead, eyes focused on his destination but sometimes wandering off to look at the Old Rectory and the pinnacle of Saint Mary's Church visible from where he was walking. He pushed the panic away. The sirens echoed feebly in the distance. He knew the police were probably at the garages now. Although he had covered his tracks there as much as he could, the snapshot of his face from the police CCTV would be on the front page of the Wimbledon Gazette tomorrow. The chief project manager from Alberyx Enterprises would surely recognise him. His cover as Agent Bickingham would be blown, and his real identity fully exposed. Lord Awlthorp would not be pleased. Reginald blamed the Claymores for the way things had turned out. Completely unreliable, like Eric Quercer. Toby Claymore, in particular, had become a nuisance and burden. He would have killed him already if it were not that Lord Awlthorp needed him a little longer for his damned second test. Reginald only had to wait for the order to come to finally get rid of Toby Claymore.

In a small clearing, among the thick trees, he gauged the rusty, square manhole which led to the underground electrical substation. His muscled arms pulled it up effortlessly to one side. The hinges did not creak. He gauged the size of the manhole; large enough to bring up the last crate of wine as he calculated. He descended the ladder, going from the quietness outside into the buzz of running electricity underground. Below, the only service light dangling from the ceiling failed to reach the far corners of what was a very small generator room for the lighting in Wimbledon Park. Reginald walked to the opposite far side. At first sight all the concrete walls looked solid and intact but in one corner a section had been cut out, leaving a loose block visible only to the trained eye. Reginald touched the sides of the block to get a good grip and pulled it out towards him with all his strength. He moved it to the side enough to peer through the hidden low tunnel behind it. As he slipped inside, he wondered how the Claymores had managed to be so ingenious to find this way in and at the same time so utterly stupid in getting caught. He crawled along the short tunnel and quickly reached a rusty grate at the end of it. The cold damp from the depths of the hill reminded him he was entering long forgotten caves.

Enrico was not sure whether he had been seen by Agent Bickingham ever since they had left the car. He signalled to Viviane to hold still a little longer and hide behind the trees. The Italian baker was wedged between a high wooden fence and the thick trunk of a tree. He leaned forward and kept completely still to avoid rustling the branches. The view was perfect, and he was able to see the burly man stare into the ground and disappear inside. There was indeed another tunnel entrance.

Viviane looked at him anxiously and kept nodding her head to him, urging him to quit stalling and make a move. Enrico was surprised to see she was unable to contain her excitement despite the twisted dangers they could be facing. She hardly complained when he told her his plan was to see where Agent Bickingham would lead them. Proximity to the hill and the Old Rectory and the old tunnels could not go ignored. She could see that too, and perhaps going back was not an option. Nobody would listen to them. There was not enough time to get grips on something they were both still trying to solve. They had to bring back some form of evidence.

When the time was right, Enrico beckoned Viviane to follow him. They both came out of hiding and edged against the fences, looking over the steep ground where the park's flat surface rolled up against the hill. They moved closer to where Agent Bickingham had disappeared, among the tall grass and the high trees. The manhole they found was wide open. Enrico was about to exclaim at the joy of the discovery; his hands on his head. Viviane put a finger on his lips to remind him to keep quiet. From the depth of the manhole, heavy footsteps and the sound of a heavy rock being moved around echoed up to the surface.

'Hold on!' mouthed Viviane.

She listened in and waited before she thought it safe to speak.

'Do you have a torchlight?' she then whispered in a very low voice, scared to break the silence.

Enrico stared at the ground, thinking. He rummaged in his pocket and pulled out his Nokia.

'Are you crazy?' mouthed Viviane unable to believe he wanted to light the way with that museum piece.

He then pointed at it again and then to Viviane's pocket. He was referring to the bright screen of her smartphone. Viviane sighed having finally understood. She stepped into the opening to lead the way; Enrico followed her down the ladder. They paused in between steps, lending their ears to the void below. They could hear the buzzing sound of the electrical substation; the heavy steps and other sounds had faded.

'Now where to?' Viviane commented when they both landed on their feet in the narrow concrete room filled to one side with a large metal cabinet that managed the entire electrical system of Wimbledon Park.

'Look over there!' replied Enrico.

He moved passed her to reach the opposite end. Something had caught his attention. A block of concrete was taking up most of one dark corner. Enrico squinted until Viviane walked up behind him, flashing the light from above his head. The block in front of them was the exact size of a tunnel entrance nearby, cut out of the wall as if it were the missing piece of a jigsaw. Inside the tunnel, it was pitch dark.

'He went this way!' suggested Viviane, leading in with her smartphone.

'More tunnels…great!' said Enrico, having a strong feeling of déjà vu.

The tunnel had been dug out a few metres downwards. The familiar stone and brick pattern Enrico had seen before, started to re-emerge. They were now back into the intricate system of tunnels running under the hill, coming in from another side and unsure where it would lead this time. There was no sound of water or mud on the floor. The air seemed drier until they reached a rust grate on the floor. Cool damp air rose from below. The grid was out of place. Agent Bickingham had been through here. Enrico was certain the burly man was well and truly involved in the matter. They heaved themselves down without needing to jump. The tunnel continued. The bricks and stones felt colder and colder as they moved deeper into the base of the hill. Their walk lasted a few minutes before an orange dim light ahead of them grew stronger, like a lantern in the mist. The end of the tunnel. Soft echoes started flowing towards them, amplified by the narrow path they were walking through.

'He's here!' whispered Enrico in Viviane's ear.

They tiptoed to the end of the tunnel, wary of their surroundings. The echoes were getting closer but still quite distant. Again, the sound of heavy footsteps and someone moving things around in a hasty manner. The dim light was brighter than expected. Multiple lanterns hung from the ceiling, diffusing their warm glow over a modest square room about twice the size of Saint Mary's Church. The tunnel came out to a raised level, which ran around the perimeter as if it were a mezzanine. Short steps led to a lower floor in the middle, where four rows of enormous wooden barrels lay in resting position. Low shelves stacked with bottles filled the rest of the room. Enrico and Viviane stopped at the tunnel entrance, using the darkness to their advantage, and quickly pinned where the echoes came from. Agent Bickingham was busy searching among barrels and crates, pushing away bottles and letting them rattle on the cobbled floor.

'What is this place?' wondered Viviane.

'I think we may have found the Cecils' wine cellar.' guessed Enrico, sniffing the air for that familiar smell of cork and damp, wet earth. 'I wish Dr Watkins were here!'

Reginald grumbled as he walked around the cellar to pick up the remaining bottles Toby had shown him the night before. On a worn-out table in the corner of the cavernous cellar, he had found the scraps of paper the Claymores had left behind during their escapades to the cellar. The two brothers had counted every single bottle they had taken out. They had officially drained the place of what was probably the oldest wine he had ever heard of. Lord Awlthorp had mentioned the full-bodied taste of it; Reginald could not care less. He felt cheated by the Claymores, remembering how he went back and forth to the wine shop to get cheap wine they had probably drunk rather than use for Lord Awlthorp's weird experiment.

The burly man picked up two more bottles and continued scanning the room. Enrico and Viviane watched silently from behind a stack of smaller barrels in a remote corner. The dim light of the lanterns had favoured their hiding so far, allowing them to keep their distance and sneak around the cellar undetected. They both followed the burly man's actions with an ever-increasing curiosity as he picked bottles at random from the floor. As they walked around, Enrico and Viviane reached a wine rack whose wood had seen better days and seemed to hold miraculously. There were a few bottles, some open and some with moulded corks still stuck in. All were empty. Viviane slid one out half-way and moved her nose closer to the rim. The vinegary smell of the wine that had aged too much shocked her nostrils. Enrico saw her screwed eyes. He ran his finger inside the rim of the bottle and stuck it in his mouth to check the taste. It was wine indeed. A bit acidic but it had been wine once and probably a good one.

He stared at his crimson finger. He was incredulous about the whole discovery. All this time they joked about wine being made here in Wimbledon and here there was possible proof this could be the old English wine Dr Watkins had implied existed once upon a time. Another thought dawned on him before rubbing away the dregs of wine from his finger. The colour reminded him of something he had seen before. Yes, the colour of wine. Unmistakable. Yet, there was a familiar hue. A vague resemblance to the crimson colour he had seen in the tunnels before and on the disfigured body.

Viviane elbowed him, pulling him away from his thoughts. She was prodding him to keep moving. Reginald Bosham was about to come full circle and was now standing at the entrance through which they had all come in. He was carrying a crate now with maybe five or six bottles. Enrico and

Viviane could only assume they were full, for the burly man held it with care in his big, strong hands.

Reginald put the crate on the floor. He had managed to get all the last full bottles Toby Claymore needed. It was time to let this place go to sleep forever. He traced his steps back to the lower ground and walked in between the rows of massive barrels which dominated the middle of the cellar. Reginald stopped at random intervals and kneeled to carefully push something in between the barrels. Enrico and Viviane could not see well what the security guard was doing; Enrico wished though he could get closer for a better view of Reginald's actions. The burly man had now stood up and was back at the cellar's entrance, with the crate in his hands. He was looking at the cellar one last time. Enrico and Viviane held their breaths unsure what his next move would be.

The Italian baker was still trying to understand where all the wine had gone. Smuggled out, perhaps; somehow, he figured this Agent Bickingham had something to do with it. The worth of wine as old as five hundred years, if this was the real age of these barrels, could be very high if the quality was exceptionally good.

Viviane pulled at Enrico's chef jacket again. Enrico woke up from his thoughts and followed her line of sight. Reginald had returned towards the tunnel entrance under the scrutiny of Enrico and Viviane. Enrico had already thought about what to do next. Having a look around would help him and Viviane search for clues in their own time. That was his plan until Viviane pulled at his chef jacket again. Somehow, she was looking at him as if he was not paying attention, not looking close enough at what was happening. Enrico focused again on Agent Bickingham. The burly security guard was toying with something in his hand, something small. Enrico strained his eyes. The scarce light was now playing against them.

Reginald did not stand there for long. He started running away into the tunnel, shrouded by darkness the moment he turned away. The beeping sound came after. A three-second sound which echoed in the silent cellar. Somehow Reginald had pressed a button to start it all and it only took Enrico and Viviane an instant to realise something was about to blow up. But it was too late.

Toby Claymore came round. The alarm on his brother's digital watch next to him had been beeping constantly in his ear for a few minutes. He did not remember setting an alarm. He did not even remember where he was. Then the musty air of the basement of the Old Rectory made his nose itch, a pungent smell which never seemed to go away. The grimy stone floor, close to his face, reminded him of the nausea he felt from time to time when he had been working in those disgusting conditions. Memories of his brother resurfaced, as he stared at the watch. More recent memories then returned. Being beaten up, gagged and sedated. A deep feeling of hatred sent shock waves through his body to the point he clenched his fist and tried to grab the watch and throw it, but something held him back. His other hand was handcuffed to one of the metal handles of the rusty machine. He was a prisoner in here. Again. He pulled and almost let out a cry, a shriek that would pierce the inert cold stone walls of the basement he had come to despise as much as Lord Awlthorp himself. The bully. The evil man. He started shouting thinking he may get the attention of the workers, but upstairs silence reigned. It was already early evening. Everyone was gone.

Then the secret door at the top of the stairs creaked and its echo came all the way down to the basement; the one Toby had grown accustomed to when Reginald was coming to drop supplies or expect an update. Toby waited for the burly figure of Reginald to emerge. Heavy steps could be heard walking down the solid, uneven stairs from the hall upstairs. There was a pause half-way and then the steps resumed. Heavy breathing became clearer and soon, in the semi-darkness of the basement, Reginald's hard, sweaty face came into view. He was carrying a heavy crate with his bare hands.

'Wakey wakey, sleeping beauty!'

'What the hell happened?' grumbled Toby, his voice croaky. 'What am I doing back here?'

'I am trying to sort your big mess, you idiot!' hissed Reginald, towering menacingly above Toby. 'I will make you pay! Everything in due course, though, while I figure out what to do next. Here are the last bottles from the cellar.'

He dumped the crate on the floor close to him. Toby winced at the clinking sound of the bottles as if they had just cracked. Reginald picked a crowbar and cracked the crate open. The dusty bottles popped out with each of their corks half-way out.

'The boss wants to test your precious wine.' commented Reginald lazily. 'He somehow thinks it will make the experiment finally work. I think it is a load of rubbish that just put me and all of us in danger!'

Toby gulped. He quickly recalled the events from the evening before. By now, Lord Awlthorp would have learnt about the ritual from the anonymous parchments written by a madman. Recreating the experiment was now probably easy for him. He had all the notes, he had most of the ingredients required. Save the fermented juice. The disgusting liquid that looked like wine but smelled like rotten eggs. Toby had no idea where the bottle with the fermented juice had ended up. Fallen from the van when he tried to escape, or maybe he had picked up the wrong bottles from the cellar. He squinted at the bottles to check if it was among those. It was not. Of all the bottles, it was the one needed the most. Without the fermented juice, there was no experiment. Lord Awlthorp would just kill him either way. He knew that. He had to find a means to escape.

'…Power and revenge…'

Toby blinked. He looked at Reginald.

'Did you say something?'

'I said I'll be back in a minute.' said Reginald with a menacing look. 'As you can see, I made sure you would not be going anywhere this time. Don't try anything stupid or I will kill you on the spot!'

Reginald's short trip back to the van was quick, although the burly man struggled to keep a steady nerve. Soon they would link his name to this van and Alberyx Enterprises. He was afraid he would have to lay low for a while and the only option was to hide in the basement. He had parked the van off the driveway of the Old Rectory, out of view. Eventually, they would find the van, but for now it had been the best place to unload the van undisturbed. He grabbed the last item, the bag with Henry's body, and rushed back inside the empty Old Rectory. Reginald made sure the lights stayed off. He wanted to ensure it stayed that way to any curious onlooker. He closed the secret door behind him and ran back down the stairs. The spectral silence of the basement in the dark gave him the creeps.

'And here's the last item!' he announced dropping the body bag only a few feet away from Toby.

'What is that?' asked Toby, uneasy.

'A little surprise for you.' taunted Reginald with a cruel smile.

He squatted by the bag and unzipped it from head to toe. The stench grabbed his nostrils as if it were a disease attacking him. Toby covered his mouth and nose. His eyes seemed to swell up. His lips quivered at the sight of the disfigured body, completely beyond recognition. All familiar traits gone. A complete carcass covered in a gooey crimson substance burnt into the flesh and bones. His heart sank.

'Henry…' muttered Toby.

'Lord Awlthorp thinks he can use your brother's corpse for this damn experiment. I still don't understand why your brother Henry killed himself. You were the dim-witted brother. It should have been you in here!'

Reginald's words came out as venom, slapping his resentment in Toby's face for everything that had happened. Toby's blood boiled. He felt his misery and anger blend into one, raging against Lord Awlthorp and Reginald. They had forced his brother do this to himself. They were responsible for his death.

'…Power and revenge…'

The words echoed again in his head. Toby blinked. He then closed his hands in a fist, tempted to punch Reginald in the face. He threw a punch with his free hand, but he was not close enough and missed.

'I said, don't try anything stupid!' threatened Reginald, taking a step back and pulling his gun out at the ready.

Toby scrambled back against the machine. Reginald watched him warily. He then moved closer to the body bag and detached the bottle that was strapped to one of Henry Claymore's burnt legs. Reginald did not know what it was. Another bottle of wine. Same label as the others. He was about to pull the cork when Toby's voice came back at him.

'Don't touch that!' he warned.

Reginald pulled the gun up.

'You are making me bloody edgy, you babbling idiot!'

He looked at Toby. The short man's spirited eyes took him aback. His skin was suddenly pale. He did not look good. Reginald glanced at him and then at the bottle.

'Why not?' sneered Reginald, ignoring Toby's warning.

Suddenly, he regretted it. The foul stench from the bottle had nothing to do with wine, not even the vinegary or sour versions of wine gone bad. It was disgusting.

'What the hell is this?' cried out Reginald.

'The missing bottle…*alkimiae mulsi*…' announced Toby.

There was a hint of prophecy in his widened eyes. He did not care if Reginald heard. All he cared for now was for the experiment to run.

'You are all bloody mad!' shouted Reginald. 'If you like this bottle so much, then why don't you take a sip!'

Reginald angrily stepped forward and grabbed Toby by the neck, pushing him against the wall next to the buzzing machine. He then pressed his cheeks to open the mouth and tilted his head slightly. Toby waved his free arm helplessly. Reginald pushed his body against Toby's legs so he would stop kicking. He then lifted the bottle of *alkimiae mulsi* over Toby's head to force him to drink it. At first some of the nauseous fermented juice splashed onto his face as Toby spluttered it out. Reginald then grabbed his nose and forced him to swallow. He then let go and took a step back.

'This is for having to put up with you all this time.' shouted Reginald. 'Just to remind who is in bloody charge!'

Toby fell on the hard floor, gagging and trying to spit out the violaceous fermented juice. His arms trembled and he then collapsed to his side, catching his breath.

'Now, you be quiet over there while I make a call!'

He walked away to keep his conversation private, deep into the darkness of the basement, while keeping Toby in sight. He found a dusty shelf to lean on and took his phone out.

'About time you called. Do you have everything?' answered the driver after not even one ring.

'All done! There was nothing else left at the cellar, and it is now sealed. Something tells me though we have more things to worry about.'

'So, I heard.' confirmed the driver, who always seemed to keep a tab on the police radio waves. 'You too have been compromised!'

'Compromised? I am a dead man if I step out in the streets.'

'Where are you now?'

'At the basement, with that idiot of Toby Claymore. Do you realise I cannot move from here? You can tell Lord Awlthorp to forget the wine and the body and the experiment.'

'Leave it with me!'

'Hold on…'

The driver hung up. For Reginald, the situation was getting worse and worse. Reginald disliked the idea of being stuck there with the idiotic Toby Claymore. He was trapped with him until the driver called him back. He should call Lord Awlthorp himself to tell him how things stood.

There was a groan from the other end. Reginald looked up. Toby was stirring, coughing up the bad taste in his mouth. He then sat up; his weak smile directed at Reginald.

'You are trapped…' he smirked.

The chuckle annoyed Reginald's nerves. He stepped forward, past the body bag, only an inch away from Toby's small figure, and looked down on him. He noticed Toby's expression was defiant or fearless. He did not flinch or look away.

'Do you find this funny?'

Reginald slapped him, just to be sure he knew where they stood. Toby chuckled, half-choking. His hands trembled; his nails scraped at the dirt on the hard stone. He wanted to shout out his anger. He glimpsed at Henry's burnt flesh visible through the half-opened body bag. The pain he had felt, the sorrow he had endured, was suddenly charging him with an energy he had forgotten.

'…Power and revenge….'

Toby shook the mesmerising voice out of his head. He could still hear it. The image of his brother appeared before him, brewing the concoction, preparing the electrical current. Something in his memory shifted. He remembered his brother, laughing at him. Toby squeezed his eyes. The image clashed with what he remembered. His brother never laughed at him.

Then Toby recalled something else. He remembered the voice talking to him directly, giving instructions on how to run the last experiment. It was Toby who told Henry what to do, the steps to follow. Toby's head suddenly hurt.

'…Power and revenge…'

'Shut up!' Toby yelled, as if trying to cast something out of his mind.

Reginald pulled up his gun.

'What is wrong with you?' he cried. 'You are mad like your brother. Two mad chemists…'

Toby shook his head and pulled himself together. The clashing memories vanished in a haze. Toby started laughing hysterically. He somehow saw clearly now, as if he had been blind or dormant all this time. The voice spoke to him again. His head did not hurt this time. He listened. He knew what he had to do.

'I…I…can run the experiment…'

Reginald eyed Toby perplexed.

'What do you mean?'

'I have what I need. I can run it once and for all. That missing bottle is all we need.'

Reginald raised his eyes in suspicion.

'What tells me you are not going to fail like your brother?'

'My brother did it wrong…'

'And you tell us that now? All of a sudden, you are an expert? You are an idiot, and I am tempted to slap you again!'

'I can help you get out. If we run the experiment.'

'I'd better call the boss. All this does not make sense.'

'No…'

Reginald sneered at Toby's desperate attempt to persuade him and moved away to call Lord Awlthorp.

Toby watched him moving into the darkness, his back to him. He had to stop him. He had to run the experiment. He was destined to do it; he had been chosen.

'…Power and revenge…'

The voice echoed louder in his head. Toby fumbled with the small key in his hand; the one he had grabbed from Reginald's pocket. He held his breath and stopped by the machine. He looked around for a weapon and picked one of the vintage bottles Reginald had brought. He wet his lips and controlled his breath. He imagined himself crashing the bottle onto Reginald's head. That head he hated so much, nodding as it spoke into the phone. The pain and the sorrow gave Toby a strange courage. He crept up slowly behind Reginald and raised the bottle before it came crashing down. Reginald did not see it coming and fell on the floor. Toby now had the upper hand. He would complete what he had started.

Sergeant Jeremy did his best to restore calm and order at Wimbledon Police Station so they could move on with the multiple investigations that had fallen upon the town. All police constables had been mobilised to find out the perpetrators and intensify the search of the many suspects Baynard had been adding to the list since Monday morning. The Chief Superintendent had been very clear that no stone would be left unturned until they captured who was responsible. The Chief also demanded Baynard stopped by the station. Rumours about a chef jacket did not please him, and Jeremy could read it in his face as they both waited on the office floor.

Baynard rushed into the room, thinking what to tell the Chief Superintendent. Anything to stall him and get back to running his investigation. He had to find the baker.

'Inspector, glad you are here.' said the Chief Superintendent with a hostile glance. 'I was wondering when you would come and tell me this mess is close to being solved. Your sergeant is struggling to update me.'

'The situation here is under control.' added Jeremy.

'I meant "solved", for Heaven's sake. Not just "under control".' bit back their superior. 'I have the Council expecting an hourly update. Now, what are these rumours of a chef jacket being seen here at the station?'

'If you refer to Mr LoTrova, he was here for a statement…' stepped in Jeremy to clarify.

'And escape from the back window when evidence was being stolen? Not to mention the disregard of the police order when he was asked to stop?'

Jeremy looked at Baynard, whose icy stare did not flinch at the fact his boss had been briefed in detail already.

'I am on my way to check all possible leads.' said the inspector.

'Does that include your dear friend Enrico LoTrova?'

'He is not my friend, sir. I was planning on going to his bakery as first stop, especially since Sergeant Jeremy here could not finish taking his statement.'

'Get him arrested, Baynard! Before you leave, I want him added to the list of all the suspects. The baker. Those mad chemical brothers. And this third man…'

'Reginald Bosham!' followed Baynard. 'If you let me do my job, perhaps we can find out who he is. Sergeant Jeremy?'

The inspector gazed at Jeremy without dropping his inquisitive stare off his face. Jeremy hesitated among the tension he felt between the two strong officials.

'Erm… From the one in our police database, we can see Mr Bosham is an ex-convict.' explained the sergeant. 'No traces of him in the last two years since leaving Wandsworth prison. No employment, no home address. We then cross-referenced the image of Reginald Bosham with other databases and found out one more entry. Apparently, he was hired by Alberyx Enterprises a few months ago under the false name of Ritchie Bickingham. He now works as a security guard at the Old Rectory here in Wimbledon!'

'Good God!' exclaimed the Chief Superintendent, clawing at his face. 'This has gone too far. I want this man, this Reginald Bosham, arrested before he can cause any more havoc. Is Alberyx Enterprises his target? We must warn Sir Alberon!'

Baynard quickly thought it through. He knew the Old Rectory was not far from Saint Mary's Church and Arthur Road. It was another coincidence he could not ignore. Yet, there was something more dangerous he could not push aside. The fact Wimbledon's number one business was now at risk of being involved, putting more weight on their shoulders.

'Baynard, I already have the Council on my back.' warned the Chief Superintendent. 'We do not want Alberyx Enterprises putting pressure on us as well!'

Inspector Baynard understood what his superior meant. The stakes were now higher.

'Jeremy,' said Baynard. 'I am going to Sir Julian Alberon's address right now. On Parkside, isn't it? I will stop first at the Wynnman bakery and check on the baker. Is a warrant for Mr Bosham's arrest already out there?'

'Yes!'

'Good, and…'

A loud noise interrupted their conversation. Baynard spun around. He could hear the sound of commotion beyond the doors leading to the entrance hall. Baynard nodded at Jeremy and they both sprang towards the doors, worried it could be another security breach or something far worse. The Chief Superintendent followed behind them.

In the entrance hall, Baynard saw a handful of police constables holding back a small crowd. He could recognise the woman in front, trying to barge through. Mrs Biggins, wearing her dressing gown and her hair ruffled, called out for Baynard's name. A man next to her scribbled on a notepad and turned to her from time to time, whispering to her, almost suggesting what to say. The few people behind seemed vaguely familiar. Baynard recognised the neighbours from Rectory Orchard.

'Where is Baynard?' shouted Mrs Biggins. 'We need to speak to him urgently. These tremors have to stop!'

'Yes! Where is Baynard?' repeated the man with the notepad.

The inspector stepped forward, making himself notice.

'There you are, inspector!' called out Mrs Biggins. 'We have had enough. When will the police do something?'

'Yes! When will you do something?' echoed the man with the notepad.

'Please calm down.' ordered Baynard with a gentle wave of his hands. 'What happened, Mrs Biggins?'

'The tremors. The earthquake. They happened again!'

Baynard frowned. He knew what she meant. He could not believe they had happened again. At that moment he realised Rectory Orchard was also within distance of the Old Rectory. Arthur Road, Saint Mary's Church, Rectory Orchard, they all surrounded the Old Rectory. He was about to turn to Jeremy asking to take Mrs Biggins's statement, when the man with the notepad pushed a recorder in his face.

'Inspector Baynard, this is Nathan Glenn, from the Wimbledon Gazette!'

Baynard recognised the name of the journalist who had pestered him on the phone.

'How do you explain the police inadequacy in solving a simple matter like shaking houses?' continued Nathan Glenn, his words rushing out of his mouth as fast as bullets. 'Mrs Biggins came here to report…how many times? More than ten times? Ten times, inspector! And today it has happened again while your own police building was open to the public as if it were a supermarket. What is happening to Wimbledon? Is this place no longer safe? Care to explain to the Wimbledon Gazette readers?'

Baynard flinched a few times, pulling himself together at the wave of accusations the pestering journalist had thrown at him. He took a step back and more police constables ran past him, to control the crowd and walk everyone out of the building. The inspector felt a hand grabbing his arm. The Chief Superintendent looked straight at him as he pushed him aside.

'This is what will happen but at a larger scale if we don't put a stop to the madness!' he warned. 'Cannizaro House first. Now this!'

Baynard's face hardened. He did not reply. Instead he pulled away and walked back towards the offices. The Chief Superintendent then turned to the crowd of Wimbledonians to give one of his reassuring spiels.

'Damn journalist!' swore Baynard running with Jeremy through the office floor. 'We don't need this! Not now!'

'You are right, we don't, sir!' said Jeremy. 'Better if you go and warn Julian Alberon before he hears it on the news!'

They reached one of the back doors for police use only. Baynard glanced at Jeremy.

'Get Mrs Biggins's statement about the tremors. Again.' said the inspector. 'Maybe we missed something.'

'Do you think these tremors have anything to do with the Claymores and this Reginald Bosham?' wondered the sergeant.

'Tell me if you can come up with a better idea.'

'What about the baker? Does he fit into all this?'

Baynard did not reply to Jeremy's last question. He was already getting into his police car.

Lord Awlthorp opened his eyes inside the grey room, his upper body slouched on the counter scattered with his tests on the Cecils' wine. He held a hand to his temples. There was a nagging noise ringing in his ears. His phone, buried under his drawings and sketches, had been vibrating for quite some time.

'I am listening.' he answered.

'Complications, sir.' said the driver.

'What is it this time?'

'Reginald's break in did not go to plan.'

'Did he get the body and the wine?'

The driver paused.

'He did.'

'Then what is the problem?'

'He has been exposed. Police have identified him. It won't be long before his cover at the Old Rectory is blown.'

Lord Awlthorp winced at the news. Then his eyes narrowed, cold and heartless, leaving only a deep feeling of disappointment.

'Where is he now?'

'At the Old Rectory, in the basement. He fled there after blowing up the entrance to the Cecils' wine cellar. We must tell Reginald to stay put, lock himself down in the basement with Toby Claymore until further notice. He cannot risk his face being seen around.'

'What matters now is getting that experiment done and nothing else!' snarled Lord Awlthorp. 'I need that body and that wine!

'I think it is no longer safe to do so, sir. Reginald cannot be seen with you for a while, and you coming to the Old Rectory is out of the question. Police will be over the place soon. Shall we call everything off, or perhaps delay it?'

Lord Awlthorp sneered upon hearing such blasphemy.

'I can't, and I won't. Not now that I am close enough after weeks, months, of failure. If we back down now, it will be another piece of glorious history we give away to the Council to dismantle! We have located the black azalea;

all we need now is the potion. We must proceed as planned! Show the world it is all real!'

The driver could imagine Lord Awlthorp's evil eyes staring into the void. His folly was a dangerous impulse that could have serious repercussions. The driver rarely challenged his boss. Yet, they were at a breaking point where everything may change from then on.

'And then what, sir?' he asked, pulling all his courage. 'What happens after you have your potion?'

There was a pause. He could hear Lord Awlthorp breathing heavy down the line.

'Enough!' barked Lord Awlthorp, his anger growing. 'How dare you question my vision? I did not come all this way, spend all my time and money, to come out empty handed and be judged by you. I will find a way or anyone else. Tonight, I will ensure that bloody experiment is run! And I will destroy whoever stands in my way…'

The driver stayed silent, not at all wishing to contradict Lord Awlthorp again, unsure as to how to counteract Lord Awlthorp's folly.

'I will call you back when I have a new plan!' he snarled once more.

'Yes, sir.' obliged the driver

Lord Awlthorp hung up. He sat on the high stool in his dark robe. Here was the man who wanted to uncover the unknown secrets of Wimbledon at all costs, even if lives had to be sacrificed and blood spilled. Inside, his heart hardened, and his blood boiled at the thought he had to give it all up, simply because Reginald or the Claymores had not been careful enough. He started thinking what he could do to put his hands on the body and the wine. He needed them to verify he could recreate the last ingredient, the *alkimiae mulsi*. And he needed to be at the Pool of Elixir once the experiment was under the way, to perform the ritual, listen to the voices as the anonymous note said, let them show him the way to the sorcerer's secret.

His phone rang shortly after, and Lord Awlthorp was pleased to see Reginald's number. He calmed his nerves and his impassive voice answered the call.

'Reggie, I told my driver I would call when I have a new plan.'

'Don't call me, Reggie.'

'I will call you what I want until we fix things.'

Reginald, hunched in a corner of the basement to keep his conversation private, did not like the voice of Lord Awlthorp. The driver must have briefed him already.

'I called for this reason, sir.' he continued, wary of what he was about to say. 'Henry's body is here and so are the last bottles of wine. As instructed!'

'You bloody fool! I cannot do anything with those unless you bring them to me…'

Reginald held his breath, waiting for the right pause. He did not want to upset Lord Awlthorp further than he may already be.

'There is something else.'

'What on earth is it now?'

'There was something attached to Henry's body. Another bottle.'

Lord Awlthorp focused his attention to Reginald's voice. The grey room around him stood motionless, waiting to hear.

'Did you know the police had it?' continued Reginald.

'What bottle?'

'It has Cecil 1590 written on it. Again! But what a godawful smell. The stench is unbearable when I uncorked it. Surprisingly, Toby Claymore knows about it. What the hell is it?'

Lord Awlthorp's eyes widened. The stench of fermentation. The foul smell the unknown author had described. It could only be the long sought *alkimiae mulsi*. He then recalled a small detail from the day before.

'Do you remember how many bottles we found on Toby Claymore when he tried to escape?'

'Five?' Reginald guessed, not following.

'He panicked there were only five. Normally, crates have a minimum of six. Indeed, he had lost one. A sixth bottle.'

'Well, this may explain why he recognised the bottle. He is the one who had it in the first place. He tells me it is all he needs to run the experiment.'

Lord Awlthorp was as incredulous as Reginald. Then something clicked. A stupid idea dawned on him. That he had been fooled all along.

'Toby knows…' he muttered.

'Knows what…?'

Reginald's voice crackled. An interference buzzed in Lord Awlthorp's ear.

'Reggie? Reginald?'.

A ghostly voice came up to the phone. It was new, different. It spoke slowly, void of emotions, intimidating.

'Mr Claymore?' called out Lord Awlthorp, his corvine eyes darting across the grey room. 'What is the meaning of this?'

'You will never find the Wynnman!' the voice whispered.

The line went dead. Lord Awlthorp knew there and then he had to take the matter into his own hands.

Dr Watkins opened his eyes in the white room. The light of the room hurt his eyes until they adjusted. He rubbed his eyes unsure what time it was. He was in front of scribbled notes and books. A constant knocking had just woken him up, not sure whether he was dreaming or not. At first the knocking seemed to be in his head but then it disappeared. A voice thundered calling his name and the knocking recommenced.

The curator realised someone was in the museum hall. He scrambled to the door, pressed the digital number pad, and crept out of the white room. He stood in the storage room, straightening his blue navy jacket, collecting his thoughts. He had no idea what time it was, but the shadows hinted at the onset of the evening.

'Dr Watkins! Dr Watkins!' repeated the voice, almost to the point of yelling.

There was a heavy tone of grievance. Dr Watkins leaned forward. It was Inspector Baynard scanning the deserted museum with his inquisitive stare. The inspector was looking for him, knocking on the desk to get his attention. He had no intention of desisting and leaving.

'Inspector! I am so sorry.' apologised Dr Watkins coming forward. 'I was busy moving boxes and I did not hear you at all.'

The curator walked over to Baynard, passing in front of prehistoric artefacts, medieval drawings and pictures from late Victorian times. He tried to act normal. Baynard eyed him suspiciously.

'The door to the museum was open.' said the inspector. 'I thought you would be in since you never leave without locking. Need to speak to you urgently!'

Dr Watkins watched him walk to his desk, looking around. His looks and tone of voice did not sound promising at all. The curator felt disoriented. Things had happened, and it was as if he had been asleep all this time.

'Have you seen the Italian baker?'

Baynard went straight to the point.

'Enrico? I saw him this morning.'

'Where?'

Baynard's fired questions one after the other.

'We went to meet Julian Alberon. Business meeting.'

'The owner of Alberyx Enterprises?'

Dr Watkins nodded, unsure if there was a link he should acknowledge.

'Where is the baker now? His bakery is closed again. Not a very hard worker, eh? Busy doing something else?'

'I…I don't know where he is, inspector. He was meant to go to the police station for a statement.'

'He did but he went for more than just a statement!'

Baynard explained his version of the facts as they had happened, from the police station break-in to the garage explosion in the area of Wimbledon Park underground station. Dr Watkins's attention was drawn in particular to the security guard from the Old Rectory they met this morning. Going by the real name of Reginald Bosham.

'Have you checked with Miss Leighwood?' asked Dr Watkins. 'They are good friends. She may know his whereabouts.'

'I also noticed Miss Leighwood's flower shop is closed, Dr Watkins. It seems we cannot locate either the baker or his lady friend, Miss Leighwood. However, a yellow Fiat 500 was spotted at Wimbledon Police Station when Enrico LoTrova used it as a getaway car. We just found the small car a few minutes ago, abandoned in Home Park Road. No trace of Enrico or the owner of the car, Viviane Leighwood. Two good friends of yours. I will ask you again, Dr Watkins. Do you know where your friends are?'

Inspector Baynard's disapproval said it all. He knew he had been played all along by the Italian baker. He sat on the chair behind the desk and his inquisitive stare did not relent. He guessed Dr Watkins knew more than he led to believe.

Dr Watkins panicked. He had not heard from Enrico and Viviane since morning. He worried he may have had a blackout and missed their call for help. Something told him they had probably picked up a dangerous lead at the police station, the one they could simply not let go of. However, Dr Watkins now feared their lives may be in danger.

'No, I don't.' admitted the curator. 'I really don't know.'

'Do you know if they have been working with this Reginald Bosham? Perhaps help him escape?'

'That is not true!' protested Dr Watkins. 'I have known them for a decent amount of time. They are not the evil kind.'

'I am just looking at what the facts tell me.' insisted Baynard. 'Perhaps you could tell me something I don't know.'

Baynard cocked his head to the side.

'You are terrible at covering your tracks, Dr Watkins.'

The curator looked dazed.

'But I am not here to accuse you, or even arrest you, for that.' reassured the inspector. 'Why don't you tell me more about this though? Is this your next museum project?'

He waved his hand over the desk. Dr Watkins did not notice but it was messier than he had left it. A few maps were scattered on it. One in particular caught his attention. One that probably caught Baynard's attention too when he entered the museum, uninvited. The map of the tunnels with Enrico's notes. The damn tunnels, creeping all around Wimbledon Hill. Baynard could not ignore the coincidence. It was impossible that all of Wimbledon was suddenly interested in what lay underground. He was now looking at the curator with great expectations, waiting for the curator to spill it out.

The curator sighed. He did not waste time in telling the inspector what they had been up to in the last few days, their latest assumptions and how they had drawn to their conclusions. He felt he could no longer fabricate stories, not after a second visit from the police.

Baynard on the other hand was impressed to hear of the wine references, the connected tunnels, and the dead end when they visited the Old Rectory earlier that day. Someone had been indeed working down there. The Claymores. Probably Reginald Bosham. Someone was definitely running a criminal activity of some sort, although he was not sure what sort. The inspector thought again about food fraud. It seemed the best logical explanation.

'Did you speak to Julian Alberon about all this?' asked Baynard.

'We did not talk about the burnt body or the man who attacked Enrico, this Toby Claymore. He only knows about the potential historical evidence linked the manor houses hidden down in the tunnels.'

'But you went to the Old Rectory with the intention of seeing the basement, right?'

'The basement was one room smaller than this museum accessible from the back garden. Not deep enough and with no access to tunnels whatsoever. The man you found dead in the tunnel could not have come from there despite the traces coming from that direction.'

'Maybe you did not check well, and Sir Alberon could give us a hand. He has the resources, and so do the police. Your little baker is getting mixed up in something dangerous, Dr Watkins. Again! When was he going to let the police know?'

Dr Watkins shrugged.

'We ought to let Sir Alberon know the whole story' the inspector carried on. 'His business, his estate, could also be in danger. His own security guard is a criminal! There is not one minute to lose. We need to let him know and get him to approve a special warrant to search the Old Rectory. Yet, we need to be honest with him!'

Dr Watkins understood. He glanced at his watch and wondered where Enrico and Viviane were right now. At such a late hour, he could not help thinking the baker's curiosity could come at a very high price.

'Where are Enrico and Viviane?' Dr Watkins implored 'You say you lost track of them. I now fear for their lives…'

'We have a warrant for his arrest, Dr Watkins. Alongside Toby Claymore and Reginald Bosham.'

The curator's eye widened.

'Trust me.' reassured Baynard. 'It is for his own safety. Even if he is not guilty, it is better to stop him before it is too late. Time to go!'

Baynard looked at Dr Watkins's worried look. He tapped his fingers on the desk and bit his lower lip in thought. Their one and only trail not yet cold was the Old Rectory, where Reginald Bosham acted as a false security guard. It was even more obvious now based on what Dr Watkins had told him. He asked himself whether Enrico was there now, whether Toby Claymore was there too, whether he was close to solving the case. The heat was on.

The evidence from Dr Watkins and the Italian baker was enough to put him a step ahead. It was time to make a nuisance call to the most influential man in Wimbledon Village.

There was rubble everywhere in the Cecils' wine cellar. Viviane coughed twice. She felt the pressure on her lungs and wheezed each time she tried to breathe in and out. Her eyes burnt a little under the heavy fall of dust now settling across the collapsed cellar. Enrico lay next to her, his body curved alongside hers and his right arm and leg crossing over as in an attempt to protect her. Above them, a feeble light still shone. It no longer came from the ceiling but from some remote ground floor in the corner on the opposite side. Probably the only lamp to survive the explosion and the fall. The feeble light was getting weaker and it cast scary shadows across the bombed-out ceiling above Enrico and Viviane. She was happy to see nothing had blocked their view. No debris squashed their limbs under the heavy weight of rocks fallen from above. She realised the Italian baker had thought well to throw themselves near one of the solid pillars lining the edges of the wine cellar, in an attempt to minimise the impact of the explosion.

Viviane coughed again and tried to move her arms and legs, even if just an inch. She did not feel pain or contusions. Enrico's eyes were still closed. Viviane nudged him a few times and called out his name. He did not respond. She freed herself from Enrico's deadweight, careful not to knock any debris off balance, and knelt down at Enrico's side. His pulse was still beating, thank goodness. She shook him at first, then spread him a little in the cramped space they were in to apply CPR. Nothing yet. She then pinched his lips to open his mouth and wrapped hers with his to blow air into his lungs. She did it a few times. Enrico coughed and spurted, lifting himself to one side. Viviane sighed in relief. Enrico blinked and looked around confused. He saw Viviane and then tried to make out what had happened. It took him a few seconds to realise where he was, looking at the rubble which only a few minutes before had been the bearing structure of the Cecils' wine cellar.

'Are you ok?' he asked still coughing.

'I am ok. Just a bit of dust. Nothing broken. Are you ok?' she said checking his face more closely.

Enrico checked himself and felt no pain. He blinked again and then pulled himself up. His muscles were a little sore. He could stand easily though, and then he helped Viviane to pull herself up.

'I'm ok.' he gasped. 'Thank you, Viviane. What happened here?'

They climbed out of the debris to see the aftermath. The ceiling now was just a mass of soil held together almost by magic and they could even see the fine tips of tree roots. Enrico jumped a few steps forward to find the tunnel entrance. He struggled to pin it down at first since large, heavy rocks now blocked the entrance. There was no way he could move them.

Viviane pulled out her smartphone to see if she had any network. The whole screen was smashed to pieces and the phone did not give any signs of life. Enrico pulled out his Nokia 3310; it was intact but had no network available.

'Have we been buried alive?' Viviane said in shock while she wiped the dirt off her face.

Enrico did not want to panic yet and glanced around to check if they had any other options.

'Let's move to the corner where that old worn-out table is.'

He stretched his hand out to Viviane and holding each other up they walked over the mountain of debris that filled most of the room. Enrico checked where the barrels had stood. Chunks of wood were visible here and there. No splashes of wine to be seen. Only the dry crimson and maroon stains on the wood chunks.

'All these barrels and bottles were empty.' commented Enrico. 'Where did all the wine go?'

'Was that why that man, Agent Bickingham, or whatever he's called, was here? To pick up what was left?' added Viviane.

Enrico jumped off the last rock and helped Viviane down. They landed on one of the few clear spaces left, a fresh reminder of the stone floor of the cellar.

The table used by Reginald Bosham no longer existed, split in half by a fallen column. Scraps of paper and ripped notebook pages could still be found, some on the table, some on the floor, some just in shreds. Enrico did not waste time to pick up what was left of them.

'What are you doing?' wondered Viviane. 'Aren't we supposed to find a way out?'

'Yes, we are.' replied Enrico flicking through the few sheets in his hand. 'These may hold clues about what this place is and what they were doing here. And maybe give us a hint as to how to get out!'

Enrico spoke trying to avoid her worried look. He knew they were stuck in the worst kind of way, but there had to be something there to give them a clue to what was going on with all this vintage wine. He focused on the writing notes before his eyes, sifting through them, piecing them together, tracing them back to check if he had missed something. Viviane joined him at his side. The bundle of papers were a mix of scribbled annotations and formulas, written with a modern-day pen and paper. There were separate anecdotes written by an unknown author in search of something.

> *Week 8 – Access to the cellar from the tunnels was blocked, although clearly marked. Just a few calculations around the structure of these tunnels, and Toby and I were able to find the right spot where to force an entrance from the north. This wine cellar apparently belonged to Thomas Cecil, but there was very little wine left when Toby and I found it. His son Edward Cecil, the Viscount Standstill we keep reading on the signs, probably squandered most of the wine after all his failures. I guess we will never know. All of Edward Cecil's personal papers were lost in a fire in his house in London.*

> *Week 12 – I read somewhere the Spencers asked the landscape gardener Lancelot 'Capability' Brown to check the soil of the park estate around the hill. It was about the time when they commissioned him to re-design what is today Wimbledon Park. 'Capability' Brown was the one who cured the planting of the Great Vine at Hampton Court. I wonder if the Spencers knew about the wine cellars. Maybe they produced and drank the wine. I have to test its authenticity.*

'Toby?' said Enrico, puzzled. 'Haven't we heard this name before?'

'Isn't it the name of the man behind the burglary at 24 Arthur Road?' remembered Viviane. 'The one who tried to run you over? Baynard gave us his name.'

'Toby…Claymore! Was he down here? That explain a few things.'

'Who wrote all these notes, then? The big guy who just left and buried us here forever?'

'He does not look the type. Didn't Baynard say this Toby Claymore was the brother of the burnt man I found?'

Viviane nodded. She recalled it too. They looked at each other, a knowing smile. They carried on reading, lured by the fact these notes belonged to the disfigured man.

Week 16 – All my tests and formulas finally confirmed it is authentic wine. The wine could be from local vineyards, possibly the hill itself. Yet, it is unmistakeably as old as the Cecils' and still in good condition. Sound crazy! I had to stop Toby from drinking it. He is a little grumpy lately. It must be the cabin fever, from being down here all this time.

Week 19 –There is nothing more we can do for the experiment. We run a new version each time without success. It is no longer worth the money. Instead, the wine in this cellar is worth a lot more. Toby and I thought it through. We take all the wine left and make a run for it. Retire like kings. Soon!

'So, English wine is not a myth?' said Viviane reading over Enrico's shoulder.

'Yes, and who wrote this seems to know their stuff.'

'I wish Dr Watkins was here…' commented Viviane as she focused on the earlier conversation with Julian Alberon. 'If I am not mistaken, the Spencer family was the last Lord of the Manor and built the fifth manor house. 'Capability' Brown embellished Wimbledon Park for them with amazing landscape gardens.'

'*Secchiona!* You sound like a nerd!' teased Enrico. 'Instead, I wonder how Dr Watkins will take this when he learns this Toby and whoever wrote this had the intention to make money off their historical discovery. I am intrigued to know what happened to the wine they took, and what the experiment they refer to is.'

The rest of the notes were a series of disconnected sentences and chemical formulas Enrico and Viviane could not get their heads round.

'They seem to be instructions on how to mix various ingredients.' explained Enrico reading through. 'But it does not say what the mix is for…and there is not even a list of ingredients…'

'Hey, more text here!' exclaimed Viviane.

She knelt to the floor. A couple of notes must have been dropped, but they appeared wedged under one of the wooden wine racks nearby, as if pushed under on purpose.

'Maybe it'll tell us more.' she carried on, unfolding them. 'How about a way to get out of here?'

Week 21 – Toby came to me a week before the escape, holding a crate of bottles. All bottles were empty save three. Two had some old parchment hidden inside. They looked like pages ripped off a diary or a notebook. It took a while before I realised it had a strong resemblance to the recipe of the experiment we are meant to run. I told Toby I am no longer interested, and he did not take it so well. He then insisted on showing me the third bottle, saying he found wine older than 1590. It smelled horrible. I gag each time I open it. Toby found it in the opposite corner where there is always a cold draught. The idiot thinks it is wine he could sell for a lot of money. I told him it is not wine, but he became very aggressive when I disagreed with him. The quick escapades we do to smuggle out the wine do not seem to ease his bad temper.

Week 23 – Something's wrong with Toby. He insists we should run the experiment one last time before we escape. I tried to reason with him, but he does not seem to listen to me. There are times I don't recognise him. He wanders around the tunnels like he knows the place. His head is somewhere else, talking to the shadows in the cellar or in the basement of the Old Rectory. Muttering words like 'power' or 'revenge'. He even told me he sipped the foul-smelled liquid, saying it tested like fermented juice. I slapped him for being so dumb and careless. His face was filled with hatred after that and we have not spoken since. I'd better set up some fake experiment to keep him happy and then we need to leave!

'What were these two up to down there? Can you make anything out of any of this?' said Enrico.

Enrico folded the papers they had read and put them in his pocket. He hoped he could bring them to light once they found a way out to the surface.

'The notes talk about an experiment and "fermented juice". They even mention the basement of the Old Rectory. I don't think it is the same as what we saw this morning.'

'I agree…' replied Viviane distractedly.

She had learned enough from the notes and had started to wander around the cellar for more clues in search of a way out.

'Where does it say Toby found that extra crate of bottles?' she asked.

'Over there…' pointed out Enrico.

Enrico and Viviane turned their attention to the opposite side and move closer to take a better look.

There was an archway leading to a separate corridor blocked as well by large boulders and debris. The baker noticed brickwork similar to what he had seen previously in the tunnels. He moved closer and he could tell this was the tunnel once connecting the cellar with the rest of the network. The direction had been written in white chalk on one of the bricks, just like he had seen before.

To the Old Rectory
To Vineyard and Orangerie

Enrico recognised the reference to the vineyard and orangerie from his first visit to the tunnels, except he was now on the other side of the blocked path. A way to the vineyards now seemed plausible after finding wine in the depths of Wimbledon hill. The reference to the Old Rectory, though, is what made his head buzz with excitement. There had been indeed a path to the Old Rectory from here. Enrico could not tell how long ago it had been blocked. Enrico was eager to find out and wondered if they would ever find a way out to tell everyone about it.

Viviane was doing the same, staring at cobwebs and broken bottles. She had been staring for a few minutes when she saw in one of the corners another heap of debris. She noticed a few broken beams sticking out of the wall. She moved closer. A slight draught came through, almost blowing directly at her. Yet, she could not spot exactly where the cold air came from. Something was not right. Amid all the debris, she could make out a wide square opening; definitely man-made, as the shape was too precise. She then noticed a wooden beam supporting the square entrance, similar to those found in mines. It must have been an entrance that had been walled up at some point in time and had collapsed just now with the explosion.

'There is something behind here.' noted Viviane.

'What is it?' said Enrico.

'Come and look at this. I can feel air coming through here. A cold draught, as described in those notes we've just read.'

Enrico joined her and looked closely at the rubble. He could feel a slight draught at the height of his neck. They both touched the debris here and there looking for loose sections. The beams stuck fast, and it took Enrico some strength to move one and pull it to one side. Viviane moved pieces of rock one by one. After ten minutes, a gap in the rubble widened and the draught turned into cold air flowing in from the other side. Enrico dried his sweat and Viviane pulled the hair from her face. Their theory proved to be correct: the cellar did expand further to what could be a smaller chamber or another tunnel of bigger dimensions. Somehow, though, access to it had been blocked completely.

The gap became a hole big enough for them to peer inside. The scarce light coming from the large cellar gave a hint of what was inside: a squared confined space with only some rough-cut wooden furniture, like chairs and tables, stacked to one side. The cobwebs covering them showed they had not been used in a very long time.

'I am going in.' said Enrico.

'Wait! Let's use one of the surviving lanterns to guide us through it.'

Viviane went to pick one up and passed it to Enrico while he put one leg through the hole, then his arm and his head.

'Be quick. Not sure how stable all this is.' warned Viviane with a concerned look at the small room and the collapsed cellar.'

Enrico returned a gaze instilling confidence. He nodded and then waved the lantern ahead of him to see more clearly in the dark.

The room was more an additional section than a room per se. Yet, there were no signs of wine barrels or why the place had been walled up. The structure though seemed different. The stones were a darker colour and a rougher cut than the cellar. Probably an older part of the cellar, once used as storage. Nothing seemed to indicate its purpose. Enrico lowered the lantern to illuminate the floor. A bulky chest was tucked away to one side, under a table.

'Found anything?' asked Viviane.

Enrico waited before answering and looked more closely. Thin dust still hung in the air. Inside the room, there was another pile of rubble to Enrico's left. Another wall had also caved in. Enrico flashed the lantern to reveal a narrow opening, which cut through the wall and led deep inside. Another tunnel; this time so narrow he and Viviane would have to walk in line to squeeze through it. The draught felt stronger here. The pitch-black staring back at Enrico felt like an ominous presence watching him.

'This place is a labyrinth.' said Enrico thinking out loud.

'What do you mean?' asked Viviane sticking her head through to see where he was.

'Found another tunnel.' he added, unsure whether he should share his enthusiasm given their current situation. 'The flow of air here means that maybe there is a way out for us.'

'Would you mind helping me get inside?' she asked.

Enrico moved back and helped her climb through. She took a look at the room and the new possible way out.

'It is a big gamble.' sighed Viviane. 'I guess we will have to take it.'

The claustrophobic settings they found themselves in were starting to take their toll. The dust had settled, but they both knew it would not be long before the air became suffocating.

'What is the plan then?' she continued. 'We take this new tunnel and stick together hoping for the best?'

'Wait one second. There is one thing I want to check.'

The Italian baker kept looking at the old chest under the table. There may not be another chance to trace back their steps and he wondered if it would answer more of his questions. His curiosity was raving.

The trunk was heavy to pull on the uneven stone floor. It took help from Viviane to bring it out from under the table. The lock was rusty and weak enough to break with a rock. Some of the wood was also rotten and the lid fell off when pulled up. Inside, mouldy parchments rolled into long tubes piled up on top of each other. There was also some silverware, cutlery, chalices, candelabra, all mixed together as if ready for a jumble sale. Signs of age and mould clouded the metal's original splendour. The parchment rolls were in a worse state. Too fragile to unfold and turning to powder at the slightest touch.

'What is all this?' asked Viviane in awe.

'I have no idea.'

Enrico peered under the lid. He learnt from his grandma that owners used to mark the inside to brand their property or whoever they had stolen it from. A tiny name appeared carved in the rotten wood.

T. Janssen 1740

'Janssen? Another familiar name.' commented Enrico. 'Miss Viviane, care to refresh my memory?'

'I wish I had paid more attention to Dr Watkins's lecture.' yearned Viviane.

She did not feel in the right state of mind for a history quiz after all they had been through that day.

'I think Janssen was one of the many Lords of the Manor, if I remember correctly.' Viviane guessed. 'The one who took pieces of the second manor house to build his own. He probably found Edward Cecil's tunnels in the process of dismantling the Elizabethan House.

'It seems everyone has walked through these tunnels for centuries!' exclaimed Enrico. 'Janssen probably came here and I wouldn't be surprised if he hadn't drunk some of the wine Edward Cecil did not manage to drink!

Janssen must have known about the wine, and probably all other Lords of the Manor did. Who is the Lord now?'

'We don't know. Dr Watkins noted the title was sold to an anonymous bidder recently. Remember?'

'It sounds too convenient. I mean, in light of what we've learnt so far, there is something deep down here that is attracting a lot of people's attention.'

'Check what else is inside.'

Enrico dug deeper. He looked carefully under the silverware. Sandwiched between two silver trays, he found a leather-bound folder. The pages in it were in a better condition. The numerous lines scribbled on each showed they were diary entries, with some images included in the blocks of text. The same name as the chest's owner was written on one of the first pages. Thomas Janssen. The diary entries covered almost a decade. Enrico pulled it out slowly and passed them to Viviane who gently spread them on the table where she could find space. In doing so, a sketched map caught their attention.

'Is this showing where we are?' said Viviane raising the lantern above it for more light.

'Let me see.' Enrico replied. 'This small square is us. This large room adjacent is the cellar. Look at Janssen's side notes on the map. They clearly explain the locations.'

'Yep, what we found is indeed the Cecils' wine cellar.' she said out loud. 'From the cellar, you can see a blocked tunnel branching out. It is the one we just saw back there, the one leading towards the Old Rectory and all the way to Arthur Road towards a big mansion and St Mary's. I suppose this is part of the tunnel you explored.'

Enrico bobbed his head. Viviane kept tracing the faded drawings on the thin, silky pages.

'The tunnel we see branching out from this room is marked as a very thin path with a dead end.'

'Why do we feel a draught?' suggested Enrico.

'I guess there is only one way to find out. What are these strange drawings next to it?'

There was a small group of tiny, hand-written symbols neither had ever seen. No text. A jumble of curved lines and circles without meaning. The longer you stared at them, the more Enrico and Viviane thought they could see wild animal eyes and evil human-like faces. The whole thing gave them an eerie feeling.

'Anything in the diary we should read first?'

Viviane rolled her eyes and scanned the pages.

'Hardly legible in this light. Let's see. He tells of his arrival to Wimbledon as a refugee… He becomes director of Bank of England. The purchase of the Cecils' house. Ah, here he says he exposed the cellars during demolition.'

'Does he mention the wine?'

'He says the wine was nothing special but was as good as what he had tasted back in France.'

Viviane skimmed through.

'He then mentions a dispute with a local vicar and his Jacobite wife… He rambles on with moans and complaints about trivial matters in Wimbledon…'

She flicked again. Arguments with the local vestry, financial troubles with the South Sea Company.

'Nothing really exciting, Enrico…' confessed Viviane.

She kept on scanning quickly. The writing was pretty ordinary. Then a few words here and there made her slow down. Little by little, she stumbled upon pain, sorrow and anguish. History became interesting all of a sudden.

Toby woke up in the penumbra. The lights of the chamber were a soft glow. Calm. He was crouching by the table; his face buried in his hands. He did not know how long he had been sitting there. Paranoid thoughts circled in Toby's head as he sprung to his feet, flat against the wall, looking around with fear and suspicion. He forced himself to remember what happened.

The chamber was as he had left it. The tremors had not caused a single crack to it. The round stone basin was cold and lifeless. Toby felt someone, or something, was looking at him again. He glanced at the bird-like statue standing stern on the edge of the pool. Its eyes seemed real. The pool was filled with the usual thick purple sludge left from the experiment, shimmering with crimson reflections at the bottom. Toby felt a strange attraction to its magic glint in the poorly lit chamber. Toby's nose itched a little and he could sniff the remote stench of the fermented juice crawling up at the back his mouth. The short man gagged for breath and rushed out of the chamber, feeling sick and breathless. In the basement, he stumbled across the body bag and Reginald lying unconscious alongside it.

'…Power and revenge…'

Toby stopped in doubt; his body held in the grip of sudden terror. He heard the voice again, and for a minute he thought it came from the bird-like statue. The same voice he kept hearing in the cellar and around the tunnels. The same voice that had chosen to speak to him and not his brother. The same voice he had heard rising from the purple sludge inside the pool, calling him. Toby knew the voice had always treated him special. He could trust the voice.

'…Find me…'

Toby then remembered, memories flooding back to him. He had found the bottle of fermented juice and those two ripped pages, and it had been like a revelation. Henry had been a fool in not taking him seriously about the ritual. His brother still called it a mere experiment, even when the two anonymous writings said otherwise. The voice had spoken to the unknown author of those pages the same way it had decided to speak to Toby. When Henry started planning their escape, Toby could not let him. All the money from the sale of the vintage Cecils' wine could not compensate the rewards the voice said the ritual would offer. Finally, Toby had convinced Henry to run the ritual once more, just before they left, and had given Henry explicit instructions about how to perform it, but Henry thought Toby was mad and deliberately forgot to pour the fermented juice, the so-needed *alkimiae mulsi*, into the Pool of Elixir. Henry had done it to spite him and had paid the consequences. Henry never believed or supported him; he slapped him around like the village idiot, bullied him just like Lord Awlthorp and Reginald did. Do this, do that. They all made him feel inadequate, sorry for himself. But not the voice and its cries of power and revenge. It belonged to someone who promised to give him power beyond his wildest dreams. This someone had to be found so that it could give Toby the help it promised.

'…The ritual…'

There was no time to waste. He now had the opportunity to perform the ritual as it should be done, but it had to be quick before Lord Awlthorp or his driver turned up. He went to check the machine by the wall. Burnt patches showed it had suffered damage, but it had been mended and was now fully working again. Toby pushed the ignition button and let the buzz, so familiar to him, fill the basement and his ears once more. The machine was working; it rattled for a few seconds and then the invisible sound of high tension growing inside it meant the voltage was ramping up at the right speed and intensity.

Toby quickly gathered all ingredients running between the chamber and the basement. First, the chemicals and herbs to recreate the *juleep* and the

Manus Christi Pulvis. He then grabbed the bottle of *alkimiae mulsi* that Reginald had left by the machine. Toby swirled it around to check how much was left. Not much; enough for one last run. One last ritual, and he had to get it right this time. Then for the last ingredient, the *sangui venerarius,* he glanced at the body bag. His brother could not be of use anymore. His burnt flesh and blood had served its purpose although it had been a waste. When Toby had pushed him into the pool, to complete the ritual for the first time by making a sacrifice with his brother's blood, he did not realise his brother Henry had not poured the fermented juice. The machine and the whole apparatus had gone haywire, burning Henry to death. Toby then glanced at Reginald lying on the basement floor. Fresh blood, he thought. He tied up Reginald's wrists and ankles and dragged his unconscious body into the chamber. Toby grinned at the idea the bully himself would help him complete the ritual; he even wished Lord Awlthorp himself were there so he could inflict him with the same fate.

Toby put the first three ingredients into the purple sludge. With a paddle, he drew circles on the surface of the crimson liquid. It now had a gelatinous consistency and was bubbling on the thick surface. He glanced at the crimson liquid over and over; eyes seemed to float just below the surface. He thought he could hear screams echoing from the basement and the tunnel. The liquid in the pool turned from crimson to maroon and purple and then shades of crimson appeared again. The dosage levels on the laptop by the table blinked green. Toby knew he was on the right track. It was time to get the electrical charge going; let the electrolysis run its course. He put the cables together and let the extremes touch each other to ensure there was no electricity running. No spark. Good. He then went to the machine in the basement, turned the control knob up a notch, and walked back to the edge of the basin. He glimpsed at his reflection in the liquid. His face looked different, older, deformed.

'…Power and revenge…'

The voice was in his head again. Toby felt sweat on his forehead. He glanced to his left. Reginald stirred. His eyes twitched; he was about to wake up and the electrolysis had not yet started. Toby rubbed his eyes and stared at the crimson liquid in a vain attempt to focus. Sanity, or what was left of it, was slipping away from him. The trance clouded his thoughts and judgement. Instead, the soothing feeling of surrender from the voice gave him the sense of relief he longed for. Toby smirked nervously and rubbed the extremities of the two cables, causing a spark. He then looked up. Toby's eyes landed on the small bird statue standing on the pool edge. That weird Anglo-Saxon figure gave him the creeps the first time he had seen it. Now, he wondered if the voice came from inside it. He stared for a second and a glint in the jumble of signs on the statue's surface caught his eye, instilling an eerie confidence in him.

'…It is time…'

Time to start the charge, thought Toby. He could almost taste victory in anticipation. He would finally find the voice that had been calling him in the tunnels all this time. The voice of the Wynnman. He then dropped the cables in the pool and the earth shook wildly.

Enrico held the lantern high. The path was so narrow he kept scraping his arms against the ragged edges of natural rock. The walk felt like a journey to the centre of the Earth. They both realised they were passing through a primordial layer of rock underneath Wimbledon Hill. No bricks. No cut stones. The earth on the ground felt soft under their feet. Bunches of straw were scattered along the path, almost creating a natural carpet leading the way. It was proof the tunnel dated to well before Victorian bricks, well before medieval stone cutting.

Both Enrico and Viviane walked carefully in single file, each alone with their thoughts. The few lines Viviane had read from Janssen's diary left her troubled. It may have been the cold, the dark, the silence. Or perhaps Janssen's narrative which had used such striking words that could frighten any reader. However, what Enrico and Viviane found unsettling were the explicit references and the thin veil the pages raised between reality and fantasy.

It became apparent the French Huguenot spent most of his last years between his small house on Church Road and these old tunnels he had grown accustomed to when building Belvedere House, the third manor house. After losing all the wealth he had accumulated and even the manor house itself, he seemed to have lost his way and taken to the bad habit of drowning his sorrows in some of the Cecils' aged wine. He used to come down to the abandoned cellar after the sermon at Saint Mary's Church and take time to reflect, holding onto the last shreds of faith he had left.

Viviane also read about a new tunnel Janssen had discovered by chance, one which had nothing in common with what was built at the time of the Cecils. In his diary he explained how the path cut into the rock and after a while led inside a circular ritual site full of symbols of the devil. These were terrifying figures and drawings cut in the stone that would make any God-fearing man tremble like a leaf. He went on talking about bronze urns of different sizes he had found on the floor right below the drawings. Most had been knocked over or were empty. Only one was full and sealed. Its contents were a thick crimson liquid, dense like molasses but not as sweet. The smell was so foul and unbearable Janssen did not dare touch it or taste it. It was as foul as the devil, and he kept repeating he was in the presence of a demon each time he opened that urn. Still, Janssen spent a few times praying in that devilish refuge. He seemed obsessed by it, as if called upon it by some unknown force. His writing became more erratic, telling how he sometimes spent time there crying for his failures, sometimes shouting in pain for the voices he heard. Janssen's story was somehow colourful, a one-sided view coming from a deeply religious man.

'What are we meant to find at the end of this tunnel?' said Enrico.

'I don't know. I would prefer to find the way out!' yearned Viviane.

'What about these symbols? This liquid?' he insisted to feed his curiosity. 'Do you make any sense of what this Theodore Janssen is writing about?'

'Leave it to Dr Watkins, if we ever survive to tell him.'

She then shivered.

'It's getting colder. The further we walk, the further the temperature drops.'

The place they were in was damper than the cellar they had left behind, and colder than the tunnels Enrico had been through. They could feel it deep in their bones, and both Enrico and Viviane's teeth chattered.

They both soldiered on, retracing Janssen's steps with his words and description in their minds, eager to get out. The tunnel at some point widened as expected. It opened up into a circular shape wide enough for up to four people to stand. The space was bare, with only larger patches of straw on the floor. The tunnel carried on further, back to a narrow slit in the natural rock.

'Is this the ritual site Janssen mentioned?' double-checked Enrico.

'I believe so.' said Viviane, dreading their discovery.

She stepped aside and opened the leather-bound folder, sifting through the diary to find the map.

'Here are the symbols.' she added, pointing at Janssen's drawings he had carefully reproduced on paper.

She then pointed her finger to the curved wall where the same symbols were carved in the stone. Under the light of the lantern, the carvings almost shone with silvery hue against the grey natural rock. Viviane could not help but see what Janssen believed he had seen. The harsh lines and mean curves were almost like eyes staring back out. They felt alive in the coldness of the rock. Demonic, otherworldly.

There were seven symbols laid out symmetrically in a circle. They were all graphic representations of an item whose harsh lines gave them a hideous look. Time had not been kind to some, and some lines had worn out turning three of them into something incomprehensible. Enrico focused on the other four. A flower, an urn, some sort of fruit, a dagger. In the middle, a bird-like drawing stood out with its wings or arms spread out. It could have been a bird or a cross.

'Isn't this an azalea?' queried Enrico pointing at the flower.

Viviane checked from a distance.

'Yes. That's weird. It looks like the one we found in Cannizaro Park but more sinister. It is freaking me out just by looking at it.'

'These symbols are ugly, aren't they?' said Enrico stroking them with his fingers.

The carving of the azalea was precise and still sharp. He felt his fingertips prickle and for a minute he thought he had cut himself.

'Ouch!' he yelped.

'Careful, Enrico.'

Enrico sucked his finger and then shook his hand to ease the pain.

'What happened to the other symbols?'

'Janssen does not say if they were like this when he found them. However, they must have been. His drawings in the diary are limited to the four we see clearly on the wall plus that bird-like figure. It appears the rest have been scratched out. Whoever did it, must not have liked them.'

'Janssen mentioned an actual urn, didn't he? Wasn't it supposed to be here?' he continued taking his attention off the menacing symbols.

They looked on the ground around them but there was nothing. Viviane recalled a few things from her reading as she faced the creepy site mentioned by the French Huguenot. Janssen's health seemed to be in decline towards the last pages. He was more and more bitter about losing his seat in Parliament and he claimed he had been framed for the South Sea fraud that made him lose all his money. Maybe all this gibberish was the wine talking, or just the despair for the miserable end of his life. Yet, the French Huguenot insisted the devilish symbols spoke to him when he ventured to the ritual site. They spoke of revenge, of power. Viviane sifted through the page again. As she read the words, she felt those same words echoing in her head and all around.

'…Power and revenge…'

Enrico glanced up from staring at the symbols and the walls in silence.

'Are you mumbling something?' he asked.

'Me? No.' replied Viviane not looking up from the diary.

Enrico hesitated. He thought he had heard something.

'I've found something.' mentioned Viviane. 'The urn is last mentioned in a later entry towards the end. One day Janssen, alone in the cellar as he was used to, encountered a couple of masons and servants coming from Marlborough House. While setting up servants' tunnels for the Duchess of Marlborough and her manor, the masons had stumbled onto the old tunnel network. OK…There was an argument between Janssen and the masons, a territorial dispute since he was no longer Lord of the Manor, although neither side legally owned the underground passage. Here Janssen comes across as more bitter and grumpier in his old age, and his sanity is indeed wavering. He writes again that an evil voice coming from this ritual site and the symbols themselves, kept talking to him. The voice implored him to take the urn… use it to avenge his miserable life and… reclaim what is rightfully his. Charming! Unfortunately, after that, the diary does not say what he did with the urn. The pages end abruptly around 1740. Hold on…

Viviane flicked through the last pages.

'Something is missing. The pages are all bound to the leather folder. The sentence on the last page is meant to carry on. He is starting to talk about a recipe and a ritual, and then it stops just like that. Two pages are missing at the end. They have been ripped out!'

'Bit of a madman, in my opinion.' joked Enrico in light of Viviane's quick summary. 'Something you probably don't read about in the official history books. Do you think he took the urn with him then? Stored it somewhere else?'.

'Well…' summed up Viviane. 'Janssen thought he believed it to be evil inside. He probably destroyed it. Maybe others came down here and pillaged the place.'

'What? Another great relic of Wimbledon plundered and destroyed? Dr Watkins would not be pleased. Anything about this bird-like image in the middle of the seven symbols?'

Viviane searched the last pages. She tried to make sense of the writing. The sentences and even the words used had become more and more erratic, as if written by someone else. Janssen was plagued by this conviction of a demonic presence. She then noticed how the words 'devil' and 'demon' had become more infrequent. Another word had started popping up. Reference to a sorcerer from ancient times.

'What was the name of that sorcerer?' checked Viviane with Enrico. 'The one of whom Dr Watkins did not like to hear the story about?'

'The Wynnman, I think. Is that what this bird-like figure represents?'

'Just a wild guess. If you believe in this kind of thing. Isn't it all just fairy tales?' summed up Viviane.

'…Power and revenge…'

Viviane thought she heard a voice from the darkness of the tunnel.

'What did you say?' she added.

'What? I did not say anything.' said Enrico.

Viviane frowned unsure for a second.

'Do you think this has something to do with what has been happening?' carried on Enrico. 'The disfigured body. Toby Claymore. This Agent Bickingham.'

'They were stealing the wine. I don't see the connection.' reminded Viviane.

'Well, one of the Claymore wrote they were running experiments down here somewhere.' recalled Enrico. 'This Toby Claymore insisted on running it one more time. Perhaps this is the ritual Janssen mentioned on the missing pages. I figure that if we carry on in this tunnel we may find where these criminals have been hiding, so we can finally ask them face to face.'

'Baynard said they were dangerous. We ought to be careful, Enrico. I'd rather get out first. This place is giving me the shivers.'

'Yeah, I agree. This place may drive us insane like this poor Janssen. Better get out!'

The Italian baker followed the florist, who was already on her way out where the space narrowed down again to a tiny path. They hoped there would be an exit ahead. Maybe a way into the Old Rectory. The aura of mystery fogged Enrico's and Viviane's thoughts while delving deeper into the unknown. It was only after a few metres into the dark that the earth shook hard. Enrico had felt the tremors before, but they still caught him unaware as the earth pushed and pulled in all directions. Viviane screamed and grabbed the ragged natural rock to hold steady. Tiny stones tumbled down from the side walls and rattled against the hard rock. Enrico held still, waiting for the tremors to end and go away. Then a loud rumble came from behind them. Viviane and Enrico glanced over their shoulder in terror. Larger rocks had started to fall and block the way they came from.

'Run!' shouted Enrico.

The two started running ahead in the dark. They feared for their lives, worried the whole tunnel would collapse over them.

Dr Watkins followed Inspector Baynard up to the big door of Julian Alberon's mansion. He had been here just recently. This time though Baynard was leading the way, ready to warn Sir Alberon of the danger he was up against and get him on their side to gain access to the Old Rectory. The inspector hoped he would be able to by-pass formalities, but he did not want to cross an important man like Julian Alberon.

This time one of the house staff opened the door and invited the two inside. He led them through the hallway and into the same living room where Dr Watkins had engaged with Julian Alberon about Wimbledon history. The evening outside started to darken the mass of trees visible across Parkside against the dying light in the clear night sky. The lamp shades in the living room shone with a suffused light. The audio system was on a low volume, playing an imperceptible melody of classical music. The atmosphere was slowly winding down to the promised calm and silence at the end of a long day, but Baynard's day was far from over; it had just started.

Dr Watkins and Inspector Baynard were seated on one of the sofas. The inspector reminded the domestic of the urgency of their visit. Their arrival had been unexpected by the local tycoon, as they were calling without notice or without giving any clear reasons for their visit. The curator thought it would be a gamble. Julian Alberon had a busy schedule. In this case, though, a call from Wimbledon's finest inspector would probably have a reason of its own. The domestic did not argue and a few minutes later Julian came into the living room. He wore a dark red pullover and a white shirt with a pair of black chino trousers. He was checking his phone one last time before turning his full attention to the two new guests.

'Oh my, an inspector calls.' humoured Julian with his warm smile. 'Nice to see you, Inspector Baynard. It has been a while.'

He shook hands with the inspector and gave a nod at the curator of the museum.

'Dr Watkins, second time we meet. And on the same day.' he commented as they all sat down. 'I shall take it as a coincidence until we meet next time. How can I help you gentlemen?'

His words met the grim and stern faces of Dr Watkins and Baynard. He could see their troubled expressions.

'Something tells me your visit is of a serious nature.' added Julian. 'Please, speak at once.'

'Sir Alberon,' started the inspector. 'we require your assistance with a delicate matter. As I briefly mentioned on the phone, it is about a property you currently own, the Old Rectory building.'

'Yes, inspector. I believe it has already been object of speculation for Dr Watkins here and his friends. However, the fact the police calls me about it, worries me further.'

Baynard bit his lip in search for words on how to break the news. It was not just a matter of being gentle; he was careful not to be misunderstood. After the Chief Superintendent and his infuriated calls that day, Julian Alberon was probably the second most important person in Wimbledon he should be careful not to cross. They needed him on their side.

'We believe one or two men may have gained access to your property illegally. Motives are unclear, but we are fairly confident these criminals were involved in the recent accidents that have rocked Wimbledon Village in the last few days.'

'Are you referring to the disfigured body near Saint Mary's?' interrupted Julian, showing he was up to date with local news.

'Yes. It also appears to be connected to the events at 24 Arthur Road, not to mention the breach of Wimbledon Police Station today and the explosion at some garages near Durnsford Road.'

Julian Alberon could not hold back his stupefied look.

'Who would do such a terrible thing? These criminals need to be caught now!'

'This is why we are here.' confirmed the inspector composing himself.

'Should I take it, Dr Watkins,' asked Julian turning to the curator. 'your visit today may also have links to these police matters?'

Dr Watkins hesitated for a second, caught off guard by Julian's direct question. He preferred not to get dragged into questions about what information they were withholding from him. He too had a working relationship to maintain with the local tycoon that was Julian Alberon.

'We don't think….' he started.

'Dr Watkins here has helped me on a few historical clues from the area.' intervened Baynard to cut him short. 'We believe though these criminals may have taken or hurt his friends.'

'Miss Leighwood? And that funny baker?'

'Precisely. The two may have stepped on a hornet's nest without knowing.'

Julian rubbed his chin, deep in thought. He looked at both Dr Watkins and Inspector Baynard.

'Who are these people?' he asked after a brief pause.

The inspector gulped. He read his notes again to be extra sure of what Jeremy had found out. He had to be sure before he accused the man hired by Julian Alberon's company of being a criminal who probably worked with the Claymores.

'We identified one of them as Toby Claymore. His brother, Henry Claymore, was the man found dead near Saint Mary's. The other man is Reginald Bosham, but you may know him as Agent Bickingham.'

'Excuse me?' blurted out Julian, incredulous. 'I take pride in my company for being safe and able to guarantee safety at all times, Inspector Baynard. To my staff and to Wimbledonians. Are you saying Alberyx Enterprises may have hired a criminal to look after one of Wimbledon's oldest buildings?'

'From what we know,' continued the inspector. 'Reginald Bosham may be using his role as security guard as a cover. Did you ever suspect anything? Or did anyone report something out of the ordinary to you?'

Julian's attention drifted off slightly. He took his time to process it all. Dr Watkins and Inspector Baynard noticed his look of disappointment and indignation. Julian Alberon was known to dislike illegal activities that could tarnish his image, his role and Wimbledon itself. The tone that followed was drier, sterner and determined.

'This is not good news.' he said. 'I don't track every single employee at Alberyx Enterprises but at the same time I don't condone mistakes and take full responsibility. What exactly are you accusing them of?'

'We identified Mr Bosham's presence at various locations. The list is currently increasing although we are struggling with motives and we want to arrest him for questioning. At the moment we believe he may be involved in food fraud, or he may be stealing something of value that could belong to Wimbledon.'

'The tunnel network points at something under your Old Rectory.' added Dr Watkins. 'This is what I came across with Mr LoTrova and Miss Leighwood. It looks like these criminals may be onto the same thing.'

'Which is?'

'We don't know for sure, but you know as much as I do, Sir Alberon, what the Old Rectory represents for Wimbledon. We cannot let anything of historical value be taken away or destroyed.'

Julian Alberon held his gaze on the curator. Dr Watkins was calling him on the values they shared. Doing nothing meant letting the image of Wimbledon or its history get tarnished.

'So, do you expect me to tell you where this Mr Bosham lives?' asked Julian with renewed resolution.

'He no longer lives at the registered address we have; nobody has lived there for almost a year. We believe though he and perhaps even Toby Claymore may be using the Old Rectory to hide.'

'Are you here to serve a police search warrant?' exclaimed Julian.

'It may take too long. We were hoping in the meantime we could ask your permission to storm the building before things worsen. Especially now that we think there may be two civilians' lives in danger.'

'I understand, inspector, and I respect your decision. You did the right thing to warn me first. I would like to quickly call my board to inform them of the situation.'

'We are pressed for time but…'

'It won't take long.' objected Julian with a raised hand. 'Please consider my permission given though. On the condition I come with you in person. I know the house well and I will ask the chief engineer to bring plans of the house right away. I will also ask my staff to get my car ready.'

Julian Alberon made his decision without the hint of a doubt. He showed his naked trust to Baynard and Dr Watkins, who could only smile in appreciation of his honest collaboration.

The businessman then stood up and moved to the hallway to make his call. Dr Watkins turned to the inspector while they waited for him to return.

'When Julian Alberon took us to see the Old Rectory, we saw all the rooms and the basement.' he said. 'Where could these criminals be hiding?'

'Everything points to that damn Old Rectory!' started Baynard before he refrained from swearing more. 'You showed me what you and your baker friend found, Dr Watkins. Do you have an idea what would be of such importance down there?'

The curator shrugged his shoulders to show he was at a loss too. Despite his wanting to know more than ever, he could not see how all the pieces joined together. Baynard recognised how Dr Watkins felt powerless. He could not blame him. The tremors, the wine, a body burnt in blood and alcohol. So many unusual things happening that he himself wondered if he had missed some detail along the way.

Julian returned with a puzzled look on his face.

'I just managed to get in touch with the board as well as the chief engineer from the building company helping with the restoration.' he started to explain. 'I just mentioned the name "Claymore" to the chief engineer. Apparently, his building company had them on the payroll as freelancers for standard residential work. Agent Bickingham too appears on their payroll as a contractor to help with security at the Old Rectory. Alberyx Enterprises was not aware of their recruitment process and will follow up with the agency or whoever vouched for this criminal. This does not mean we do not take responsibility. I must say I am very displeased with all of this!'

The local tycoon hardly flinched finding the situation unacceptable. He stood up by the sofa staring down at the inspector and the curator with the look of someone demanding answers. Julian Alberon was a determined man who would chase it down to the very end to find where mistakes had occurred. Dr Watkins briefly recognised in him that same desire to look for answers that had pushed him and Enrico.

'We'd better get going.' exclaimed Julian. 'The board gave me their approval to let you in. The chief engineer will meet us at the gates.'

'Sir Alberon, I have my men ready to reach the Old Rectory within minutes.' proposed Baynard.

'Yes, we should get moving.'

Julian nodded and called out again to his staff to check if the car was ready.

His off-road was ready in a matter of minutes. Baynard radioed Jeremy to update him and asked Dr Watkins to join Julian in his car.

'Better if you two stay behind until my men deem the area safe.' he advised.

'Don't worry, inspector. Please be careful with our Old Rectory! We do not want it to get blown up!'

Julian gave Baynard a knowing look and the inspector understood the businessman had offered his collaboration on specific terms Baynard could not ignore. Access to the property while he was present. It would suffice for the inspector until a formal police search warrant was drafted.

Julian started the car and his headlights flashed on Baynard's car as it skidded on the gravel of the driveway and drove out onto Parkside. The businessman followed him in the light traffic, keeping his distance.

'What are we dealing with here?' asked Julian while on the way.

'What do you mean?' replied Dr Watkins.

Julian kept an eye on the road and glanced sideways at the curator.

'What are we really going to find there? Nothing was ever found under the hill, not even after the tunnels were first discovered. Are we sure there is something under the Old Rectory?'

The businessman was asking for his opinion as trusted historian, whether they were pursuing fact or fiction. Dr Watkins was overwhelmed by the question. He wet his lips, trying to put a clear answer together. Then his phone rang.

Enrico and Viviane reached the end of the narrow tunnel after a manic run for their life. The rumbling noise was fresh in their memory, amid fears of being buried alive. The whole tunnel they were in had started collapsing behind them like a row of falling dominoes, crushing the ritual site and chasing them down the never-ending tunnel. Their escape had seemed impossible until they both jumped out to safety through a slit in the rock at the end of the tunnel. Enrico and Viviane had to squeeze through to get to safety and they were out in the nick of time before the tunnel behind them caved in and buried its secrets forever. Sweat ran across their foreheads as they looked at each other, their faces lit by the lamp still intact. Their legs trembled even after the earth had stopped shaking under their feet. It was time to check where they were and get out of here.

The tunnel exit only came out onto another tunnel made of brick and running perpendicular to their path. Enrico dreaded these tunnel walls; they all looked the same.

'I'm starting to hate these tunnels.' confessed the Italian baker, feeling frustrated.

'Isn't this where you wanted to get?' exclaimed Viviane in a useless attempt to wipe the dirt from her trousers.

'Yes, but where are we?' replied Enrico.

'Here, hold the leather-bound folder.'

Viviane took hold of the situation and shone the lamp around. Both ends of the tunnel led to dead ends.

'A lot of rubble here. It looks as if the tunnel has…imploded.'

She then shone the lamp above her head. An old tile came into view, just like the ones Enrico had described. She read it out loud.

To the cellar

'I didn't come across that sign last time.' noted Enrico.

Viviane squinted in the direction of the sign to see where the tunnel went. It was another dead end, filled up with rubble. She was about to get closer when she felt one of her legs give way, and before she realised, she slipped.

'Viviane!' called out Enrico.

Enrico grabbed her and held her tight. Viviane gasped and shone the lamp down to her feet. She had almost fallen through a crack in the ground wide enough for one person to climb down.

'Are you ok?' asked Enrico pulling her up.

'Yes… Look here. There is a hole in the ground. Looks like this is the only way out!'

Enrico looked down the crack and the light of the lamp revealed another path running underneath. He wondered if this reconnected somehow to the tunnels he had visited.

'But…' hesitated Enrico.

'But…what?'

Enrico spun around mumbling to himself.

'I still don't understand. Where did the burnt body come from?' he muttered. 'This section of the tunnel we are in is all walled up.'

'Can't we do this outside?' pleaded Viviane. 'We've found our way out!'

Enrico was not listening.

'One second. I need to check Janssens's map. Pass me the lamp!'

He grabbed it and held it a few inches from the ground, holding the leather-bound folder close to his chest. His eyes fell on the ground. New dry crimson traces appeared in the golden glow turning a macabre bronze colour. Enrico's eyes widened with anticipation and started following them. Yet, the trail seemed to have no beginning or end; it just disappeared into a wall. The Italian baker scratched his head. He put the lamp down and half-kneeled to take a closer look at where the trail was interrupted.

'Come on, Enrico! Let's go!'

'One second…'

Enrico placed his free hand flat against the wall to hold himself. He looked closer at the trail, which seemed to disappear under the wall. A click followed. Before he knew it, Enrico felt his hand and arm give way. Something was moving. He heard the lamp fall and the light slowly faded away.

'Enrico…' called out Viviane.

Viviane reached for the wall, but it was too late. She cried out Enrico's name again, hammering the wall with her fists. Nothing. She could not hear Enrico at all despite her cries to him. She picked up the lamp and checked the bare wall in front of her. She touched every inch of its surface to maybe find a loose stone acting as lever. Nothing. Whatever had sucked Enrico into the wall was no longer working. She spun around and her eyes met the solitude of the tunnels. Alone, she could feel the same pain and anguish Thomas Janssen had spoken of in his diary. She could almost hear those words again. Power and revenge. The power of suggestion in the nightmarish darkness was now unbearable. Viviane hoped the newly found hole in the ground would take her out of here as soon as possible. She had to find help; she wanted to get herself and Enrico out alive.

The vibration suddenly ran through his body. Reginald woke up startled. The stone walls of the chamber were shaking too. Alarmed, he started to move only to realise his wrists and ankles had been restrained. He wobbled to his left, pushing against the wall from time to time. He was then able to see Toby standing by the table on the other side of the pool, checking the voltage graphs on a laptop. His gun was there, next to the laptop.

'Claymore!' shouted Reginald on top of the rumbling sound of the vibrations. 'You bastard! What is the meaning of this?'

Toby turned. He had sweat across his forehead; his face looked delirious.

'Be quiet! I am working…'

He fidgeted with his hands. His neck craned back and forward between the laptop and Reginald. The electrolysis was not yet completed.

'What is happening?' shouted Reginald, unable to explain the tremor.

'The ritual…is finally happening…' answered Toby absent-minded.

'What? Do you mean the experiment?'

'The ritual!' Toby lashed out. 'It is a ritual!'

Toby looked hysterical. Reginald was stumped by his looks. His hair was a little messy, his eyes wild, his face twitching. Reginald quickly took in his surroundings. The tremors in the chamber were more prominent. Handfuls of dust dropped occasionally from the ceiling as if the whole hill were vibrating. He noticed how Toby had put more lamps around the pool, creating a brighter view of the chamber. He saw platinum or silver streaks running alongside the border of the pool which intensified around the abstract bird statue.

Toby moved away from the laptop. He picked a wooden paddle and stirred inside the pool. His transfixed gaze was out of the ordinary and raving mad. He observed Toby going through every step as if he knew it by heart. Reginald stood on alert. He could not see well over the edge from where he sat. The cables had been dropped inside the pool. At every swirl of the liquid by Toby, the signs carved into the small statue almost came to life like fireworks in the night sky. It was as if the pool was alive and not entirely made of stone. Reginald thought the atmosphere down here had taken a strange turn.

'What are you doing, you mad chemist?' he shouted again, wriggling to break free. 'What did you and your brother do down there?'

'Leave my brother alone. He was stupid not to understand what we could achieve. This is my doing, mine alone!'

'What?'

Toby pointed to Reginald's side. Reginald followed Toby's gaze. The body of Henry Claymore lay on the ground in the open without its body bag.

'Your fate, Reggie, will be a better one, once you immerge yourself in the pool. Trust me!'

'Don't call me, Reggie!'

Toby chuckled.

'Your offering will not go to waste the same way it happened with my brother. He did not listen to me!'

Reginald looked at Toby confused first, then he glanced at Henry's body again before realising what had happened.

'A bit slow, Reggie. What's the matter? Cat got your tongue? I killed my brother Henry. I pushed him into the pool to use his blood.'

'And the wine? The planned escape?'

'That was my brother's plan for a better life. The one he had forced the docile Toby Claymore to follow. Well, that Toby's gone. The new Toby has already laid his eyes on something else. That bully of my brother spoiled my plans when he did not put the ingredients I asked for. Now, there is no-one to stop me. Almost all ingredients are there – only fresh blood is missing…'

Toby put the paddle on the floor and crouched closer to see Reginald eye to eye. He licked his lips, savouring that moment of power over those who had bullied him.

'Soon I will hold a power beyond anyone's imagination…' he added.

Reginald thought fast and swung his joint legs to try and hit Toby. The short man lost his balance but leaned back enough to miss being knocked out. Toby stood fast, holding steady by the edge of the pool. His wild eyes met Reginald's angry ones. Toby then huffed and returned his attention to the laptop.

Reginald grinned. He could now see the blade sticking out of his boot. He would make Toby Claymore pay. He may not kill him straight away, not until he informed Lord Awlthorp. He freed his hands and ankles and was on his feet again. He crouched like a tiger not making a sound. The tremors and the machine buzzing the basement covered for him. He grabbed the paddle on the floor and moved an inch closer.

Toby thought of his revenge plan, staring at the voltage charts, waiting impatiently for them to complete the process. The swing of the paddle hit him hard on the cheek and pushed him against the wall. A few of his teeth flew off in the process. Reginald dropped the paddle and grabbed his gun, quick at pointing it at Toby before he got back on his feet. The short man had slid against the wall and crashed near some empty crates. Reginald searched his trousers. He was looking for the phone. He checked the table where he had spotted the gun. The laptop flashed a series of lines tracing voltage and chemical composition, nearing a green threshold bar. Next to it, there was a bottle of Cecil 1590 wine and then near it there was his phone. Reginald had to warn Lord Awlthorp.

'Hello?'

'Sir, it's me.' said Reginald, eyeing Toby's body.

'What on earth happened?'

'Toby Claymore has lost it, sir. He ambushed me, knocked me out but I just managed to take back control of the situation. For the time being at least, I think.'

The tremors then stopped. Reginald heard himself shouting down the phone. He then heard a ping sound from the laptop. Green lights flashed on the screen. Whatever preparations Toby was making, they were now done.

'What is that noise? Is it what I think it is?' questioned Lord Awlthorp recognising sounds he had heard before.

'He has been running the experiment, sir. From what I see around here, he prepped it all up. He was planning to throw me in the pool. His last ingredient, apparently. What the hell is going on?'

Lord Awlthorp thought carefully what to say. The timing was not right. Everyone was converging into the Old Rectory. Yet, that ghostly voice he heard on the phone made him realise he was on the right track.

'And has he done this all out of his own accord?' asked Lord Awlthorp.

'He killed his brother, sir. His brother Henry tried to sabotage him the first time round and Toby was the one to throw him in the pool. He keeps talking about a ritual. He is mad!'

'He may be, but we may have some answers now.'

Lord Awlthorp spoke coldly, detached. Reginald could hear traffic in the background.

'Are you coming here, sir?'

'I am but…'

Lord Awlthorp's voice trailed off, as if he could not speak freely.

'Go ahead!' he then cut short. 'But he goes in instead of you!'

'Into the pool? You want me to throw him into the pool?'

'Yes. I will be there as soon as I can but…'

The hint in his voice said it all. He would soon arrive at the Old Rectory, but the police would be there too. Lord Awlthorp had to stay under cover, which meant Reginald was on his own.

'We will come for you.!'

Then Lord Awlthorp hung up. Reginald felt a tinge of betrayal. They had used him and now they had to cut him loose for precaution. Just like that. Even if Lord Awlthorp could help him with the police, Reginald knew the future was grim and there was only that much he could do to cover up his involvement and avoid prison time. He thought quickly how he could get out of this mess, whether he could blast the trap door open. Chances of success were slim.

He swore under his breath. He then cursed the Claymores for the mess they had done. Reginald then stared at Toby's body on the ground and noticed he was slowly stirring in the dirt of the chamber. The mad chemist was waking up.

'…Power and revenge…'

Reginald thought he heard something. He then clenched his fists and promised to himself there and then he would do what Lord Awlthorp had asked, but at the same time he would seek his own revenge and take pleasure in killing Toby Claymore.

Viviane's voice died the moment Enrico tumbled forward. He had slipped into darkness and found himself on a sloping path. He wondered where he was. He must have come through a trap door.

Enrico strained his eyes looking at the ground around him. There were traces of blood and maroon patches, this dried crimson gelatine that had taunted him for days. They led up the sloped path, now mixed with the accumulated dust and dirt of past centuries. The burnt man must have come this way. Curiosity started to tingle Enrico.

He tried to open the trap door again, to find the mechanisms he had hit by mistake. He pressed random spots on the wall. Nothing. It did not seem to work anymore. He could not hear Viviane and her voice through the wall. He was alone in the tunnels once again. Then, a distant chatter caught his attention. He stood up, half-bent in the tiny cranny, keeping quiet. The chatter was not so far away. Muffled noises but surprisingly human.

'What the heck was that?' said one voice, panicky.

'You are a dead man, Claymore!' said another.

Claymore. There could only be one Claymore. The Italian baker knew he was getting close to where the brothers had been hiding. He did not have a torch. Only the feeble glow ahead, where the chatter seemed to come from, allowed him to see in the penumbra. He tiptoed up the sloped path, crouching to one side of the wall and keeping the source of light ahead of him with the leather-bound folder close to his chest. The natural rock here was identical to the one Enrico and Viviane had seen in the ritual site, when they were comparing Janssen's symbols on the wall. He was surprised how these tunnels took on different shapes, revealing new entrances, blocking old ones, covering past tracks and then building new ones again, as if a living entity had taken hold of Wimbledon hill. The Italian baker hoped Viviane had found her way out to get help. He knew they were getting close to something.

Enrico stopped for a second. It was too dark to check Janssen's map. He could easily be under the Old Rectory or way past it. Enrico bit his lip nervously at the obvious outcome. Even if he were close to a way out, there was no guarantee he could get out unless he faced the two voices ahead first.

He moved on with stealth, keeping to the side wall, taking advantage of the darkness before approaching the light. The chatter became more distinct. Two male voices. Both interwoven with a low buzzing background sound. He squinted to focus ahead. The path widened to a round space with a round stone pool in it. It was definitely man-made and not natural. On the edge, a small bird-like statue stood over it. Enrico thought it vaguely resembled one of the symbols back in the ritual site.

The click of a gun made Enrico suddenly wary. He ducked and swiftly took hiding behind a large crate close to him. Two men stood in the small round chamber. Enrico recognised the first man as Toby Claymore. This time he could see him in a better light. Short and stocky, he wore dusty overalls and he appeared a little under the weather by the looks of his hair. He hunched over a laptop screen, tapping furiously on the keyboard, while the second man held him at gunpoint. The second man watched him carefully. He had a square jaw, large shoulders, and strong muscles. Enrico widened his eyes, surprised to cross paths again with Agent Bickingham. His corpulent figure, dressed as usual in black shirt and trousers, looked scarier, more severe in the scarce light. Enrico presumed the two were working together, but clearly the burly man was now calling the shots and Enrico felt tension rising in the room.

He scanned the area. Opposite the pool, Enrico could see a dust sheet hung over the entrance to a short corridor. To one side, there was a table with a laptop and a bottle of Cecil 1590. The little red-looking liquid left inside it looked like wine. Wine again. Enrico wondered if it came from the Cecils' wine cellar. He then spotted an intricate web of cables ending up inside the pool. Enrico felt itchy all over by the sight of all this electronic equipment. He tried to peek over. Inside the pool, a dark liquid brewed and bubbled gently. The soft light from the lanterns all around the pool reflected beautiful crimson colours on the surface. It was a mesmerising spectacle and for a minute he thought shining streaks called out towards him. He quickly crouched back down. Now that he was here, he wondered how he would get out. He hoped Viviane was already out and had found Dr Watkins or Baynard.

'Don't delay, Toby.' spoke Reginald. 'Time for you to take the plunge!'

Toby moved cautiously from the table to the pool.

'It won't be long before the crimson liquid is split.' he explained nervously. 'You can see the shining dregs coming up to the surface.'

'Don't fool me, Toby! Or I will fill you with lead and dump you myself in that stinking crimson stuff.'

Reginald eyed Toby suspiciously, checking everything he was doing, making sure he was not stalling. Toby Claymore had been acting less cocky ever since Reginald had woken him up and forced him to get ready to finish the ritual. Yet, Toby still acted strange, as if he were a different person and not the dim-witted brother. Reginald did not understand where that unnatural confidence came from. He looked again at the odd-looking crimson liquid in the pool; its thickness, its colour. He had never seen any contents like this in the pool before. He wondered if this *alkimiae mulsi* had anything to do with Toby's behaviour. He moved closer to the pool, twitching his nose in disgust at the unbearable stench coming from it. The same stench as the bottle he forced Toby to drink.

'What is this stuff anyway? It smells awful...' commented Reginald.

'You would not understand...'

Toby moved to the edge of the pool with the laptop. The crimson liquid in the pool had now formed a thick foam and emitted small sparks of electricity all over the surface. A strange smell filled the air. Ethanol, honey, rotten eggs, iron. Reginald covered up his nose and mouth with his arm. The smell got stronger, and even Enrico could sniff it from where he was hiding. It was so foul he nearly wanted to throw up. Toby did not look affected by the smell. He did not flinch; he just kept grinning at the pool. Enrico found it unsettling. He stayed crouched against the crate and tried to slow down his breathing. His heart was racing out of control. The two men in front of him were definitely up to something more sinister than stealing wine. It was an experiment for some unknown purpose. His curiosity was gnawing at him. He then recalled what he and Viviane had been reading. He glanced at the leather-bound folder he clutched under his arm. Janssen spoke about a ritual site. He spoke about an urn whose contents were a thick crimson liquid, and whose smell was so foul and unbearable. As foul as the devil himself. Those were Janssen's words. Now he really hoped Viviane was already talking to Dr Watkins or Baynard, telling them where he was. Enrico checked his escape routes. Beyond the dust sheet, there was another room. It was the only way out. Yet, any possible scenarios for escape seemed improbable, having no idea where the corridor led. The Old Rectory maybe, or somewhere else new.

'Finish the experiment, you idiot!' yelled Reginald.

Toby did not answer. He turned to Reginald and showed his wild-eyed grin.

'Did you hear what I said?' insisted Reginald.

He checked his watch. There was not much time left; the police would be here soon. He slashed his gun, raking across Toby's face. A trickle of blood formed on the corner of Toby's mouth, together with foamy saliva as if he had become suddenly rabid. The crimson liquid started bubbling here and there; its surface almost as thick as the ice over a winter lake, beyond recognition of the wine or any of the other ingredients Toby had poured in.

'Finish the experiment!' repeated Reginald.

He placed the gun barrel on Toby's cheek and then hinted at the laptop and the pool to remind Toby what he had to do. Toby tensed a little and did not say anything. Reginald then moved slowly behind him, about a foot apart. Toby could feel Reginald's heavy breathing.

'…Power and Revenge…'

Toby knew then it was time to react. The voice told him it was time. Time to unleash power and revenge. He quickly grabbed the laptop and hurled it backwards hard enough to hit Reginald's face in full. Reginald staggered. The gun fell out of his hand. Reginald felt the blinding pain in his teeth and jaw. He felt something break and a burning sensation on his cheeks. He let out a groan of pain and put his hand on his face while lashing out at Toby with the other. Toby tried to hit him a second time, with the same extreme violence. This time though he miscalculated the space in between and bumped into Reginald's muscular torso instead. Reginald took his hand off his face; it was stained with blood. He then looked at Toby in anger and punched him hard on the chest. The short man gasped, and the laptop fell out of his hands. Reginald grabbed Toby's shoulders to counter-attack. He squeezed them hard and clasped his hands hard enough to make Toby squeal with pain as if his shoulder blades were about to crack before reaching Toby's neck to strangle him. Enrico could not believe what was happening and was in shock to see Reginald's real strength. In just a few seconds, he had almost lifted Toby's short body from the neck and his feet were dangling a few inches from the floor.

'You little bastard.' Reginald shouted through broken teeth. 'You will pay for this! I will throw you into the pool myself!'

'No!' yelled back Toby. 'I am the one who has to decide… The voice spoke to me… I will be the one who pushes the person chosen for the human sacrifice!'

'Mad like your brother!' spat Reginald.

Reginald tightened his grip around Toby's throat. Enrico knew Reginald would either strangle him or throw him into the crimson-filled pool, or both. He could not let the short man die, especially if he held any answers. He acted on instinct and crawled out of his hiding space. He leaped forward and he jumped on Reginald's shoulders from behind grabbing his face in a headlock. Reginald released his grip and Toby fell hard on the ground. Toby groaned in pain. He then glanced up to see the odd man in the chef jacket, who was trying to knock Reginald out. He thought he had seen this man in a chef jacket before, but his mind was getting foggier and foggier. He had to finish what the voice had told him to do. Toby looked for the laptop. The moment he saw it he crawled towards it. His chubby thumb pressed 'Enter' and suddenly the low buzzing sound in the chamber increased until it became a deafening noise. The crimson liquid started emitting larger sparks off the surface. The voltage was now beyond the safety limits.

Reginald growled at his unknown attacker, swaying left and then right, using all his weight to push him off. Enrico could not believe how strong the man was. Reginald's arms reached backwards and tried to grab Enrico around his neck. Enrico tried to pull his head back but like a game of arm wrestling he started to lose grip and could no longer hold him still. Reginald twisted his torso a few times with great force. He could hear the deafening noise and the electric current being discharged into the pool. The ritual was kicking in and he could not see Toby. He had to act quickly and not let him get away. Reginald slipped out of Enrico's headlock, and sprinted back into action by hitting Enrico on the chin with his head. The Italian baker, almost knocked out, lost his balance. Reginald took this opportunity to take a step backward and crush Enrico's body against the wall. He hit Enrico's body time after time. Enrico felt his back was about to break and fell down exhausted. Reginald turned around wiping the blood smears from his face and looked at his assailant, now leaning against the wall in pain.

'You? Again?' shouted Reginald. 'You little crazy baker, have you got nothing better to do? This is the last time you stick your nose where you shouldn't.'

Enrico was taken aback by Reginald Bosham's furious comment. Reginald grabbed him by the collar when a loud clicking noise echoed in the chamber. He glanced round, while keeping Enrico pinned against the wall. Toby stared back at them, his legs spread apart, and his arms stretched towards them with Reginald's gun pointing at them.

'Time to finish the experiment! On my terms!' Toby announced.

Reginald blinked.

'Don't be a fool, Toby!' he said.

Toby kept his gun aimed at them and slid next to the edge of the pool. He then nodded to it.

'I need the *sangui venerarius*, the blood offering. Either of you would do. Just don't make me pick by shooting one of you two.'

Reginald smirked and turned to Enrico. He was quick to jump at the opportunity.

'I guess we have found a good replacement!'

He pushed Enrico forward towards Toby.

'What blood offering?' quivered Enrico, his blood curling.

'Shut up!' barked Reginald with a hard slap on Enrico's back that sent him an inch from the gun barrel.

'My peace offering to you Toby!' he then added.

Reginald spread his hands, as if to break free from Toby's maniacal fixation. Once the Italian baker was out of the picture, he would be able to kill Toby once and for all.

'I don't understand…' stammered Enrico, who suddenly found himself thrown from the pan into the fire.

'You don't need to.' answered Toby in a trance. 'This time, I will follow the steps of the ritual to the letter, as the voice told me over and over.'

'The voice? The one your brother wrote about?' mentioned Enrico, remembering the notes folded in his pocket. 'He did think you were mad. I bet he did not expect you to use him as a guinea pig for your ritual!'

'What? How do you know about the ritual?' retorted Toby.

Enrico had to improvise with the little he knew from the notes and Janssen's diary.

'The voice. It is from…the demon… He…erm…he spoke to me…'

Enrico swallowed hard, hoping his lie would buy him enough time. He wondered where Viviane and Dr Watkins were. And Baynard. How he wished the police were here to help him out of this mess.

'Hold it here, crazy baker.' snorted Reginald. 'You are not fooling anyone…'

'Silence!' yelled Toby. 'He may know something I need to know! He needs to tell me…'

'Hold it there!' ordered Reginald, making a small step forward.

'Don't move!' reacted Toby. 'Or I will shoot!'

His mad eyes stared at them but seemed to look beyond, through the walls. Enrico knew something was not right with Toby Claymore. He had to wait for the right moment to get the gun, but at the same time keep a tab on the big man behind him. Enrico looked at the gun, then at Toby, then at the pool behind. The gooey crimson liquid was now churning, becoming thicker. Soft peaks emerged from unnatural waves forming on the surface of the mixture. For an instant, the Italian baker thought they looked like little arms out there to grab who would fall into their embrace.

Then a door slammed upstairs. Loud voices could be heard. They came from behind the white sheet. Someone was coming. Toby glanced in the direction of the basement.

'Oh no!' he muttered. 'They are here. I must act now!'

Enrico knew this was his chance. He leaped forward and went for Toby's gun, pushing it away from him. Two shots fired and went amiss to the ground. Toby tried to resist Enrico's grapple. He then pushed the Italian baker back against the table. Toby was about to aim and shoot again when something pierced his hand, forcing him to jerk backwards and spin half-way around. The chubby man let out a cry of pain and the gun fell somewhere to the ground. He grabbed the edge of the pool with one hand and then looked at the one which had been holding the gun. Reginald's knife had cut through the palm of his hand and had started bleeding. Toby's blood dripped quickly from his hand and into the pool one drop after the other.

Reginald was about to run forward and push Toby into the pool, when something forced him to stop in his tracks. Enrico, next to him, stirred from the pain in his body and squinted at the scene developing in front of him. He watched the events unfold as a spectator strapped to a chair, unable to move or run. Reginald felt the same; his full attention also on Toby Claymore. Everything unfolded as if it were inevitable. The basin of the pool had become a brighter ivory colour, as if shining from within, and the content of the pool had increased its mass. Both Enrico and Reginald looked dumbstruck as the gooey crimson liquid came to life and the soft-like peaks of the strange mixture rose from the pool as if they were fluid tentacles which had been hiding underneath the surface. They wrapped themselves like algae around Toby's body and slowly formed a coating on his hands, arms and upper torso. The strange tentacles started pulling him into the pool. Toby put up some resistance, with one foot against the pool's edge. New tentacles jumped out and grabbed his foot. They seemed to move on their own, having picked Toby as their victim. Then the crimson liquid caught fire, and the tentacles burst into flames engulfing what flesh they had grabbed. Toby's cries of pain followed. Terrifying screams rang in Reginald and Enrico's ears. The screams of power and revenge.

Viviane made her way up into the tiny niche and pushed the loose panel, which led back into the spooky crypt. She then climbed up the stairs and was finally out of the claustrophobic tunnels. The crack she had found with Enrico had been a godsend. She had dropped in one of the dead-end tunnels Enrico had originally explored and was able to find her way back to Saint Mary's Church. Viviane did not mind the site of the graveyard on the cloudy night. She ran out onto the soft, damp grass, enjoying the open, cold air. Her lungs felt so out of practice that the short run almost left her out of breath.

'Help!' she cried out, not sure who she was calling. 'Help!'

She ran further down the gravel path towards the entrance of the church. Upon turning around the corner, she stumbled into something. A torch was flashed in her face. Viviane screwed her eyes and put her hand forward, irritated by such a bright light.

'Miss Leighwood? Is that you? Oh lord, what happened to you?'

Reverend Green looked Viviane up and down in shock. Her hair hung loose on her dirty and sweaty cheeks.

'Help! Enrico needs help. We need… Baynard… and Dr Watkins…'

Viviane mumbled on and Reverend Green struggled to follow. He was not wearing his religious robes. He had just come out of his house next door, in a plain t-shirt and jeans, upon hearing her cries. He was suddenly alarmed.

'Where are you coming from?' he asked.

'The…crypt…' she stammered taking deep breaths of fresh air. 'We found…wine…rituals… Agent Bickingham. The… security guard… at the Old Rectory. Call… Dr Watkins!'

Viviane blurted out the clues, in the hope the reverend would understand.

'Let me help you!' said the reverend.

Reverend Green grabbed his phone and searched his contacts. He found Dr Watkins's name and quickly dialled the number. He put his other hand around Viviane and started walking her to his car. Dr Watkins answered the phone.

'Dr Watkins, it is Reverend Green.' spoke the reverend. 'I have Viviane here. She is ok but I must say I have seen her in a better state.'

'Oh, thank goodness! How is she? Is Enrico with her? The police are looking for them.'

'She just came out of the crypt, alone. She is talking about tunnels, wine, rituals, and a man named Agent Bickingham.'

There was silence. Reverend Green realised Dr Watkins was in a car and was talking to someone. He then came back to the phone.

'Bring her to the entrance to the Old Rectory. We will meet you there. We have police on their way too if they are not there already. What about Enrico?'

'I don't know. She says he needs help. What is going on, Dr Watkins?'

'I will explain later. It could be linked to the dead man we found on Sunday.'

Reverend Green understood the situation, and by the time the call was over, they had reached his car. Saint Mary's Church stood silent next to them as a witness of the events unfolding on one of Wimbledon's seemingly quiet nights. Reverend Green felt a little uneasy. Dr Watkins's interest in the tunnels did not seem to relent and now even Enrico and Viviane had been involved. He wondered if things were repeating themselves.

The short drive via St Mary's and Church Road brought them to the gravel path leading to the Old Rectory. Three or four police cars blocked the way and there were police constables standing outside the cast iron gate that led into the driveway. The sirens shone their light without sound. The blue light started to tinge the trees and houses. Another police car and an off-road arrived at great speed. They screeched on the gravel and came to a halt behind Reverend Green's car.

Inspector Baynard was the first to get out. He spotted Viviane next to Reverend Green with a blanket around her. She smiled weakly through her fatigue. She also felt a little embarrassed about what she was going to say to the inspector after what Enrico and she had done. Dr Watkins appeared from the off-road with Julian Alberon. He joined the inspector's side. They were both so shocked to see the state she was in. Dr Watkins though was pleased to see her and hugged her close.

'Miss Leighwood,' interjected Baynard. 'we have literally no time on our hands, but Dr Watkins explained me everything. Do you know where Reginald Bosham is? What about your baker friend?'

Viviane caught her breath. She had gained some of her strength back under the warmth of the blanket.

'Reginald…Bosham…?' she gasped.

'The security guard here at the Old Rectory.' said Baynard to reassure her and to convince himself they were on the right track. 'You know him as Agent Bickingham. His real name is Reginald Bosham. He may have been working with the Claymores. We still are not clear on what criminal offense they have been perpetrating.'

'And we are here to sort this mess out!' added Julian Alberon.

The businessman had joined them to Viviane's surprise. He smiled at Viviane, sharing his relief seeing she was ok.

'You will not believe… what I have to tell you…' Viviane explained. 'This Reginald Bosham… has been stealing... wine. With these Claymore individuals. Real wine, Dr Watkins, from under the hill! We followed him after he escaped from the police station and he led us to another entrance to the tunnels. We got stuck underground after the tunnels collapsed and tried to find a way out.'

'Good grief.' exclaimed Dr Watkins. 'And Enrico?'

'He is still down there. He fell through a trap door.'

'Where did it lead?' asked Julian.

Viviane shook her head. She told them about the lost diary they had found and Janssen's map. They hoped they would reach the Old Rectory, but never did.

'Where is the diary and the map?' asked Dr Watkins, eager to know more.

'The diary is in Enrico's hands.' she replied.

'Miss Viviane,' replied Baynard. 'we need to act quickly. Can you lead a handful of my men to this "trap door"?'

There was a certain haste in Baynard's voice, pressed for time and pressed for truth.

'Inspector,' interjected Reverend Green. 'I don't think Miss Leighwood is in the right state of mind to…'

'I can!' interrupted Viviane with renewed determination.

Behind her tired eyes, a fiery sparkle challenged the four men. She pulled back her dirty hair, awaiting instructions.

'I will go with her, inspector!' added Dr Watkins.

'I don't think it is a good idea…' stepped in the reverend, not shy to show his concerns at such a delicate time.

'We have no other choice!' replied the curator. 'Inspector Baynard, what is the plan?'

The inspector summoned Sergeant Jeremy. The young man had been waiting by the gates to the Old Rectory.

'Inspector, the Old Rectory has been surrounded by snipers.' confirmed the sergeant with added confidence. 'At the moment the building looks empty, but they spotted a green van parked on the grass, off the driveway. We can see if anyone tries to come in or come out!'

'Good.'

'You may want to know in the last hour we have received a testimony from a wine shop on the Ridgeway. They recognised Reginald Bosham as someone who visited regularly, buying cheap wine, and the last time was yesterday.'

'Wine again, just as Miss Leighwood mentioned. We'd better move fast and find out what this man and the Claymores are up to. Here's the plan. Jeremy, you will lead a few men to the crypt at Saint Mary's. Miss Leighwood will take you to where she lost the baker. Here's a tracker. Keep it on!'

'What about you and me, inspector?' asked Julian Alberon.

The businessman had already included himself in the police search team. Baynard hesitated.

'Is your chief engineer here?' asked the inspector.

Julian nodded pointing at a man guarded by police a few metres before the gates. He had the planimetry of the Old Rectory ready on the bonnet of one of the police cars.

'We will check the house plans for anything unusual.' continued Baynard. 'We will make our way inside the house taking advantage of the darkness. Jeremy's tracker will be able to transmit from underground. His team can then confirm if their path leads under the Old Rectory. It can help us determine whether there are any links between the Old Rectory and the tunnels. If there are, Jeremy will block any chance of escape from where they are, while we guard the exit from the Old Rectory.'

'Do you think this Reginald Bosham is hidden inside?'

Baynard gave Julian Alberon a reserved look. He did not want to upset the man who had made most of his search possible so far. The Chief

Superintendent's warnings about involving civilians had been thrown out of the window now. He then glanced at Viviane and Dr Watkins.

'Let me remind you this is a police operation. Sergeant Jeremy and I are in charge and will lead the men in front. Always. Please stay behind, to keep away from any danger. We don't know who is in there, how many, and if armed.'

Baynard's inquisitive stare looked around the circle. He wanted his intentions to be clear from the start. This was his show now.

'Sir Alberon, all clear for us to go ahead? Not that we need to waste any more time...'

'All clear from me and the Board. Could we please ensure minimum damage to the property or any item of historical value?'

'I cannot guarantee, Sir Alberon!' replied Baynard.

The group split up. Jeremy and a handful of police constables left with Viviane and Dr Watkins. Upon seeing the dark shadow of Saint Mary's Church and its steeple, Viviane regretted briefly for volunteering to return. She then thought of Enrico. She had to save him.

The tunnels looked less scary thanks to the full support of police equipment. Bright torchlights lit up the vaulted low ceiling, stripping off the shadows and showing the dull mouldy brickwork. Viviane felt less intimidated, despite dreading the claustrophobic environment. Dr Watkins, however, had a buzzing excitement all over. He could not hide his excitement. She could tell by his pace, his breathing. He was eager to see or find something. He had never ventured in the tunnels and had waited for this moment for a long time. Even though there was nothing special to see in the decay of these tunnels forgotten by history, the curator felt he was part of something. He was walking through Wimbledon history.

On the surface, by the gate to the Old Rectory, Baynard and Reverend Green listened to the chief engineer while he discussed the house plans with Julian Alberon. Next to the house plans, one of Baynard's men kept a tablet in full view for the inspector to track Jeremy's movements underground.

'Were you aware of the tunnel stretching from the crypt, reverend?' asked the inspector.

'Not at all. Crypts and tombs outside Saint Mary's are old enough; we do not wish to disturb them. My skin crawls at the thought of how many people have walked through someone's tomb to get to the tunnel in the last few days…'

'We will put an end to all of this madness.' replied Baynard, wishing to bring Wimbledon back to the normal neighbourhood it was.

His eyes monitored Sergeant Jeremy's movements. His ears listened to what Julian Alberon and his chief engineer had to say.

'There is no other basement, sir.' commented the chief engineer.

'Are we sure nothing has been walled up?' insisted Julian for the third time.

'We would have noticed.'

'How about the initial reconnaissance?'

'We have the first security check and first survey of the house.'

'Who did that?'

'Reginald Bosham.'

Julian frowned. He did not like the sound of that. And neither did Inspector Baynard.

'And this Mr Bosham,' asked Baynard. 'did he ever do anything suspicious? Like hanging around one room in particular. Anything…'

The chief engineer thought for a moment.

'Well, as part of his job as security guard, he had to stay in the entrance hall most of the time. He was always there, most of the time. Now that I think of it, he never walked away from the wooden panels under the stairs…'

'That's right. I noticed that too on my last visit.' agreed Julian.

'Check here!' interrupted Baynard.

The dot representing Jeremy on the flat touch screen moved from Saint Mary's Church towards a point between Wimbledon Park and the Old Rectory. It then made a sharp turn back towards them and stopped. Exactly under the driveway.

The inspector was about to alert everyone when another dot appeared on the radar. It was a quick flash and it grew bigger into a wider circle until it faded away like a bursting bubble.

'What was that?' he exclaimed.

'Not sure, sir.' confirmed the police constable next to him who had witnessed the same thing. 'A strong electrical current has just been registered. Very unusual. It cannot be a glitch.'

The tablet screen started to blur, showing some interference. Baynard's radio crackled. He picked it up.

'What is happening?' he said alarmed.

Jeremy's voice came through broken, drowned by radio interference.

'Inspector!… found… trap door… leading northward. Permission to blow it up!'

Baynard glanced at the radar. Northward meant towards the Old Rectory. He snapped his fingers at the police constables around him, ready to stand-by.

'Ready to move in!'

He then turned to the radio.

'Sergeant Jeremy. Blast your way in ten minutes!'

The confirmation came through, clear enough for Baynard to understand his sergeant was ready. The inspector walked away from the car and issued to his men the order to move in.

'Will you at least let me come with you as agreed?' reminded Julian, grabbing Baynard by the arm.

'Yes.' nodded Baynard reluctantly, keeping his word. 'Just you, though. And please stay behind me! Reverend Green and your chief engineer will have to wait here with the agents staying back.'

The inspector informed the police constable next to him to give Julian Alberon a bulletproof vest. He made it clear it was important to keep civilians out of danger. Last thing he wanted was the most notorious man in Wimbledon to be killed during police action. He then glanced at his phone. Ten minutes. Ten minutes before Jeremy blew up the trap door. Ten long minutes before he knew whether he was closing in on Reginald Bosham and Toby Claymore. Deep inside, he hoped he was not wrong or too late.

The gate opened silently inward and Baynard led his small group of police constables into the driveway. The snipers had narrowed the circle and cleared the gardens, including the Fig Walk. Baynard beckoned sending one group to the side entrance by the kitchen and then he led the rest through the main entrance.

The two policemen opened the main door and rushed inside. The building was indeed quiet, abandoned. Baynard flashed his light inside, moving to the left and to the right, and turned the lights on as the whole team flooded inside the Old Rectory on both floors.

Julian Alberon was still in the driveway and could see inside the hall. His eyes focused on the point where Reginald Bosham always stood. Both he and his chief engineer agreed he must be hiding something there. Julian inched forwards, up the steps and over the threshold.

'Not safe yet, Sir Alberon.' halted Baynard at the door.

'Inspector, you may want your men to look there!'

He pointed to one of the wooden panels under the stairs.

'The chief engineer thinks there could be something hidden by the wooden panels under the stairs.'

'I don't see anything.'

'Let me have a closer look!' whispered Julian rushing past him.

Baynard wanted to wait. He tried to hold Julian back, but he was wary the ten minutes were almost up. He could use all the help he could get. He joined Julian standing next to the wooden panels. The businessman was tapping them one at a time.

'This one is void!' he confirmed.

Baynard started looking for one of his men to help knock it down.

'There is no time, inspector!' exclaimed Julian. 'You will have to trust me!'

'No! Stay back!' cried the inspector.

Julian Alberon slammed the panel twice with his shoulder. Despite Baynard trying to hold him back, the damage had been done. The banging echoed in the silence of the Old Rectory and the panel gave in to reveal a secret door. The stairs led down into the darkness. They expected silence to welcome them, but suddenly an ear-piercing scream broke through the hall from the darkness below. Julian and Baynard shivered on hearing it.

'Move in!' cried out Baynard to his policemen.

Julian went in before them.

'Sir Alberon…' shouted Baynard in vain.

The inspector rushed inside cursing after the careless businessman. As he made his way down the flight of stone steps, he listened to the earth-shattering scream. Someone was being tortured. The voice he heard in the dark was nothing he could recognise.

By then, the ten minutes were up. The roar of Jeremy's contained explosion rose from the bottom of the stairs and drowned the horrible screams for a few seconds. The stone steps shook under his feet and Baynard balanced himself while running down after Julian Alberon.

When Baynard reached the ground below, he was welcomed by a cold, abandoned basement. In the confusion, he glimpsed at the open space, cluttered with crates, tools, broken bottles, sleeping bags, and a buzzing machine. He tried to make sense of it all. He could not yet identify the source of the screaming. Ahead of him, he saw Julian Alberon stop by a side entrance and peer inside. There was an opening cut into the basement wall. A white sheet hung over it, blowing in the wind, its edges were half-burnt and burning ash fluttered in the air. Baynard focused on Julian's face. A strong orange glow washed his face. Unspoken horror flickered in his eyes. Suddenly there was heat.

Jeremy on the other side had waited impatiently before pressing the remote button at a safe distance. They had placed C4 explosives by the trap door and found shelter. Jeremy had to fight against Dr Watkins who insisted on being with them when they forced their way into whatever lay behind the trap door. Jeremy was not sure how to handle it apart from warning him of the dangers. The curator had been behaving wildly, ecstatic and overexcited ever since setting foot in the tunnel. Even Viviane struggled to handle him.

'We are close. I know it!' kept repeating Dr Watkins.

'We also want to stay alive!' commented Viviane.

'I insist. For your safety.' added Sergeant Jeremy. 'The ten minutes are almost up but you can still leave…'

'We are staying!' insisted Dr Watkins peering round the bend, anxious to get access to the trap door.

Viviane and Jeremy looked at each other. The florist agreed with the sergeant's advice and yet she could not leave Dr Watkins behind. Seeing the state the curator was in made her worry more about him. His bewildered eyes alarmed her, and she knew nothing would make him budge.

Jeremy rolled his eyes and waited. When the ten minutes were up, he finally ordered the blast. The walls around them shook temporarily. The sergeant and his men did not waste any time and pushed on to get through the blasted opening. Dr Watkins stood up and Viviane tried to grab him.

'Where do you think you are going?' she cried after him.

'I need to see…' he protested.

'Sir, please stay here. For your safety.' said the police constable left to look after them.

He tried to calm Dr Watkins down, but the curator's zeal was out of control. He wrestled with the policeman and during the scuffle Dr Watkins slapped him hard to pull away from his grip. He then rushed in the direction of the blasted opening, without looking back. He could not hear Viviane's shouts, or the policeman's. His ears, like everybody else, were still ringing from the nearby controlled explosion. He also had a valid reason to be down there, ahead of everyone; he had to find out the secrets that lay under the Old Rectory.

Dr Watkins covered his mouth so as not to cough and squinted through the hazy cloud of dust left by the blast. Beyond, a sloped path led ahead. Terrifying screams of pain echoed and sent shivers down his spine. He rushed to join Jeremy and his men standing by a small round opening.

The scene waiting for them was pure horror. Thick smoke filled the air. A round pool was in the middle of a domed chamber. A darkened crimson ooze swirled around inside it, and high flames rose from it like liquid fire. At the edge of the pool, a human-like shape was bent over it with its arms into the fire, screaming in pain. The crimson ooze surged upward as if it were alive, wrapping the body like deadly ivy, like ancient roots from the depths of the hill. The whole body was quickly covered in the crimson ooze from head to toe and only the dark shadows around the eyes and mouth gave a faint reminder of the man underneath, staring at them, pleading for help. The human-like shape was suddenly pulled forward. As it struggled to break free, the screams quickly turned into a suffocated gurgle, a beastly sound. Then, a surge of heat coming from a burning body overcame Dr Watkins and Sergeant Jeremy.

Thick smoke had filled the chamber. Enrico squinted through his blurred vision. He struggled to see what was happening to Toby Claymore. He could still not fathom what he was witnessing. Whatever unnatural force was in the pool, it was trying to pull Toby's body into the pool. The crimson ooze was rising to Toby's legs and had started to cover his right shin.

Enrico naturally moved forward to help Toby and grab the one part of him still not covered by the hazardous liquid. Reginald caught him out of the corner of the eye and bashed him on the head with his bare hand. Enrico's head ached as he stumbled back against the table. The Italian baker rubbed his eyes and he was suddenly face to face with the burly figure of Reginald Bosham against a background of flames.

'Let him die. One down, one more to go.' sneered Reginald. 'I will now have the pleasure of killing you too, crazy baker!'

Whatever the reason, the burly man in front of him had made this very personal. Reginald threw the first fist. He punched Enrico on the cheek. Enrico almost lost his balance and fell again a few steps back towards the table. He shook his head. Reginald then went for a second punch. Enrico dodged it and returned the punch in Reginald's stomach. Enrico's fingers cracked against the steel abs. The burly man grinned.

'No more games!' shouted Reginald.

Enrico glanced around. In the smoke, he spotted the laptop on the floor. Perhaps he could use that and smash it on Reginald's face. It seemed to have worked for Toby. Enrico hurled himself intentionally towards Reginald.

The burly man tried to hit the baker again, but Enrico rolled to one side. He swiftly grabbed the laptop and turned towards Reginald throwing it at him as if it were a frisbee. Reginald ducked to avoid it and the laptop smashed against the wall. The distance echo of the electrical discharge suddenly stopped. Reginald stood and looked back at Enrico's baffled gaze, but his grin had disappeared. His face was now lit up and the chamber seemed brighter. Enrico turned around. The crimson ooze had suddenly flared up and turned into a liquid flame. The vapours of the ooze filled Enrico's nostrils. An acrid smell mixed with ethanol and blood. Toby Claymore's body was burning.

'We need to help him!' shouted Dr Watkins to Jeremy pointing at the body in flames.

'What are you doing here, Dr Watkins? Stay back!' warned Jeremy, unprepared for what was in front of him.

The sergeant pulled his gun out and ordered his men to do the same. They all stood speechless; their faces contorted in disgust. Jeremy spotted Enrico struggling with a man twice his size. The smoke made it harder to see. Dr Watkins then made a few steps forward.

'Wait...' warned Jeremy.

The sergeant was too late. Dr Watkins ran ahead and put his foot on the edge of the pool, stretching out his hand. The human-like shape covered in the crimson liquid stiffened and Dr Watkins thought it was staring at him. The void eyes narrowed as if the shape had recognised him.

'We must do something! Help him!' shouted Julian Alberon.

He was standing at the end of the corridor, on the opposite side of the pool, watching the body burn alive.

'What is this? What is he doing?' gasped Baynard, next to him.

He held his gun high and kept one hand forward to block the strong heat coming from what appeared to be a pool filled with a burning liquid. He could not see well. The vapours had started to fog the chamber. He could not even see Jeremy beyond. According to the tracker, he should have been in the vicinity. A handful of policemen joined them at the back and Baynard turned to give quick orders. Julian Alberon then made a step forward.

'Wait...' warned Baynard.

Baynard was too late. Julian ran towards the pool, hoping to save the human-shaped mass covered in the burning crimson liquid. He could see two hollow eyes starting at him, as if the shape had recognised me.

'Sir Alberon, stay away!' the inspector called out.

'No...' whispered Julian.

He stretched forward with a foot firm on the ground, careful not to slip into the pool. Dr Watkins did the same on the other side. Unaware of each other's presence, they both reached out to grab each of Toby's shapeless hands nearest to them. Those shapeless hands seemed to call for help.

In the meantime, Reginald had grabbed Enrico by the neck to strangle him. Enrico could feel the deadly strength in his hand. He tried in vain to tame the angry Reginald Bosham, pulling him in all directions to shake him off. The Italian baker then glimpsed at Dr Watkins and Julian rush forwards, both reaching out for Toby's burning arms. He was dumbstruck by what they were about to do.

'Don't...' gasped Enrico with the little breath he had left.

As soon as Dr Watkins and Julian's hands joined with Toby's, the flames in the pool picked up strength. In an instant the fire rose to the ceiling and through what was once Toby's body, up to his face and then down through his arms before discharging onto Julian's and Dr Watkins's hands. The two felt something warm in their hands. Then a flash blinded them and everyone else in the chamber. The heat became unbearable.

'Get back! Call emergency services…' ordered Baynard through the radio.

He could not finish the sentence before the flash turned into one last intense burst. It died out all of a sudden and a sonic boom ensued. The shock waves travelled fast, knocking everyone to the ground, crippling any light or machine in its way. One last violent shake of the earth in the bowels of Wimbledon Hill.

Enrico felt the back of his head thumping with pain against the cold, hard stone. His neck was sore from the whiplash of the blast. He could not tell how long he had been unconscious. His eyes opened up to what he expected to be a dark chamber. Instead, a bright, crimson light flickered in front of him. The only one in the pitch black surrounding him. He could not tell where he was or where the others were.

The light resembled Toby's human-like shape, going up in flames in the middle of the pool. The screams had faded now. Maybe his hearing was not yet back, Enrico thought.

The human-like shape stood still, unaware of Enrico's presence. There was no pain. There was no fear. It floated peacefully, and the flames had now become ghostly apparitions about to fade away.

'…Power and Revenge…' the ghostly shape called out.
Enrico heard the words echo in his head. He watched the shape dissolve until his eyes closed again. Then he slipped into a deep sleep once more.

An eternity passed until Enrico's feeble eyes opened again. The fire and heat had vanished, leaving a cold, thick cloud of smoke in the air. Enrico's eyes burnt and he could not open them wide enough. He moved his hands and arms around to touch the hard rock floor beneath him. Shrieks echoed in the distance. He then saw a shadow emerge from the cloud. The shadow approached him quickly and then Enrico felt his weight being lifted up through the layers of smoke that filled the chamber.

Baynard pulled Enrico's arm around him, ready to walk him out. He kept calling out at Enrico, to keep him awake. The Italian baker was not able to turn his head to look at him. He could barely stand on both feet. His legs ached badly and trembled like jelly. Baynard dragged him out of the chamber with force. More people started to appear, brushing past them. Enrico wanted to call out for Viviane, Dr Watkins, Julian. His mouth was dry and his throat croaky. Images of the burning body in the crimson liquid flashed before his eyes, causing him to lose balance. Baynard held him up and pulled him through the corridor and into the basement. Enrico spotted a larger crowd of police constables, firemen and paramedics around them. Their torch lights filled the room and blinded Enrico. Baynard then disappeared and two paramedics checked Enrico before escorting him up some stairs and into a vaguely familiar hall. And then he was out in the fresh air.

The blue siren of the ambulances glared against the stern façade of the Old Rectory. The driveway was no longer silent. It was now crowded with extra police, emergency medical services and the crime scene investigation unit. The chattering of voices, the constant stamping of feet on the gravel and the stairs outside the main entrance, they all brought back a strange rhythm to Enrico's ears. At first, he thought his head would explode. Then his foggy memory desperately tried to nail down the events that had led to this, to put each detail in order, and each time his head hurt. He wondered whether everything he had seen had been real or just a dream. Then the paramedics sat him down on a hard cushion and Enrico found himself at the back of an ambulance where the paramedics flashed lights into his eyes, asking questions, moving his limbs, tilting his head.

Enrico sat upright on the stretcher following each of the paramedic's orders. He opened his eyes to let the small torch check his pupil movements. He moved his head from side to side each time they needed to check one of the burns on his face. They monitored his heart rate and blood pressure. Enrico stared ahead impassively at the chaos running wild in and out of the Old Rectory. He caught a glimpse of Baynard running back and forth; the others who had been in the basement were not in sight.

'Viviane…' he murmured.

His mouth was dry. He could still taste the bitter smoke.

'She is fine, sir.' said the paramedic.

'Where is she?' insisted Enrico, stubborn even at his weakest point.

'Here, Enrico!'

Thin, delicate hands wrapped around Enrico's dry knuckles. Enrico felt their warmth spread through his body and wipe out the cold of the chamber from his bones. He finally opened his eyes and there she was. Viviane stood by him with a bag of ice on her head. She looked a complete mess. Clothes torn, plasters stuck on her face and arms. Yet, her weak smile beamed with a sigh of relief. Enrico squinted in the bright multi-coloured lights flooding the driveway of the Old Rectory behind her.

'What happened?' moaned Enrico, while the paramedic stuck a large plaster on his forehead.

'I don't know.' Viviane replied, taking a seat next to him. 'I was brought here and told to stay put. I asked about you and wanted to know you were safe.'

'How come…weren't you supposed to get out?'

'I did. I found a way out that led me back to the crypt. I called for help and came back with reinforcements!'

'Are you ok?'

'I'm fine. I was further back from the blast, with Jeremy's police constables. We traced back our tracks and escapes through the tunnels and the crypt.'

'Ah…the bloody tunnels…'

Enrico winced, unsure if it was due to the painful memory of the tunnels or one of the bruises from his fight with Reginald Bosham.

'The others? Where are they?'

Viviane bit her lip. Enrico recognised sadness in her pale face.

'Dr Watkins and Julian Alberon have both been rescued and brought out to safety.'

'Are they alive?'

'Sort of. They are badly burned, and they lost consciousness. Electrocution, maybe. Details are not clear. They were taken away to Parkside Hospital straight away.'

Enrico stood up to get a better look of the busy driveway. One of the paramedics watched him warily. The Italian baker gave him a half-smile, promising to stay put, and then he looked at his chef jacket, completely torn and burnt at the edges. As he checked the damage, Enrico remembered something and felt his pockets.

'What is it?' asked Viviane.

'The Claymores' notes. The ones we found in the Cecils' wine cellar.'

He pulled them out, all crumpled in a ball of paper. Both he and Viviane were surprised to see they were still intact.

'What about Janssen's diary? The leather-bound folder?' wondered Viviane.

Enrico searched his jacket by reflex, even though nothing of that size could fit anywhere; he looked around in vain. He knew what may have happened to it.

'I left it by the large crate…' mumbled Enrico tracing back his actions. 'When I jumped out to save Toby Claymore…'

'I don't believe much survived down there.' commented Reverend Green.

The reverend peered at them from the open door of the ambulance. His pious nod told Enrico and Viviane he was pleased to see them.

'Reverend Green!' asked Viviane.

'I have been told to stay put by Baynard as well.' he added. 'Security, I presume. What is important is nobody died. You two seem to be all in one piece, thank goodness. I wish I could say the same for Dr Watkins and Julian Alberon…'

'Did you see them?' asked Viviane.

Reverend Green gave a sombre nod, his head low.

'The explosion does not seem to have harmed them. For now.' explained the reverend. 'Their vitals are weak but stable. It wasn't clear if anything was broken. However, I heard talks of severe burns when I saw them being put on a stretcher and into the ambulance. It seems both their hands were severely burnt, and the skin scorched up to the wrist. What happened down there?'

Enrico and Viviane looked at each other, questioning each other whether they saw the same thing.

'They both tried…to save…that man!' muttered Enrico.

'Who was he anyway?' asked Viviane.

'Toby Claymore…' confirmed Enrico.

'That was Toby Claymore? They were trying to save…*him*?' Viviane frowned.

'What were they thinking?' exclaimed the reverend. 'I hope they will be ok. How are you two feeling?'

'We will survive…' replied Enrico. 'What happened to the rest of the people down there?'

Enrico massaged his jaw and his stomach, reminded of the pain from Reginald's heavy blows. He took a good look at the busy driveway. Policemen were placed everywhere, at the gates, at the entrance to the building. Others came in and out of the Old Rectory, busy wrapping up the most bizarre case ever encountered. He then noticed the inspector walk out with Jeremy on his side. A team of firemen went past them, ready to check the building and the basement to make sure they were no longer at risk.

Baynard had been on his feet for a while despite his cuts and bruises. He guided the teams in and out of the Old Rectory relentlessly. His movements were a little slower but his stare still attentive, focused. While he briefed Jeremy, the inspector caught Enrico's eye. He issued a few last orders and then quickly parted to join the three by the ambulance.

'How is everyone doing here?' asked the inspector.

'I must say I have been better.' admitted Viviane.

'And you Mr Liriva?'

Baynard reserved his inquisitive stare for the baker that caused him so much trouble.

'LoTrova!' corrected Enrico. 'Ready to be back to baking!'

'What makes you think that, Mr Lirtova?'

'LoTrova!' repeated Enrico, coughing in between. 'Am I under arrest?'

'Gain your strength while you still can. You are not off the hook, yet. I will need you to explain what happened here and make a sense of all this mess.'

'So, this was not your ordinary robbery, was it?' interjected Viviane, hinting at the last conversation she and Enrico had with Baynard.

The inspector leered at her unexpected comment.

'The baker's curiosity may be starting to become contagious. Mr Lariva here…' he told her.

'LoTrova!' added Enrico.

'…plays dangerously.' carried on Baynard not listening. 'He is lucky to be alive after what happened down there. You should also thank me if I don't decide to throw both of you in jail for obstruction of justice. If it wasn't for Dr Watkins and Julian Alberon…'

Enrico swallowed hard at the comment. If he had the strength, he would protest. He was the one who had ventured down the tunnels in the first place. Viviane and he were the ones who had risked their lives to follow those criminals and find the cellar.

'The cellar!' exclaimed Enrico.

'What?' replied Baynard.

'We found an old cellar, belonging to the Cecils. Deep underground.'

'Miss Leighwood told us about that.' confirmed Reverend Green.

'Then you may want to have a look at it!' said the Italian baker.

Enrico showed him the palm of his hand with the crumpled half-ball of paper in the middle.

'What is this?' asked Baynard.

'Proof!' exclaimed Enrico again.

'Of what?'

'Of what the Claymores had been doing.'

Baynard watched Enrico with suspicion.

'It is true, inspector.' joined Viviane. 'We both found these notes in the cellar. You can go and check…'

'The tunnels beyond the chamber have all collapsed!' announced Baynard, knowing he could not hide everything from Enrico and Viviane. 'You were lucky, Miss Leighwood, to get out of the crypt in time. You and Jeremy would have been buried down there. Unfortunately, the shock waves from that weird blast in the chamber caused the earth to shake throughout the hill. While it did not harm anything on the surface, almost all the tunnels have collapsed, including the one accessible from the crypt.'

Enrico and Viviane were left speechless.

'The chamber sustained the impact from the sonic boom, as they called it.' carried on Baynard, struggling to remember the many details he heard from the fire brigade. 'The few cracks in the stone walls have been confirmed as safe by the firemen. The chamber is still accessible, but the rest of the tunnel network is now completely sealed by tons of rubbles.'

'Collapsed?' gasped Enrico and Viviane in unison. 'The ritual site… Janssen's furniture…'

They both realised most of their proof was now buried forever.

'What are you two mumbling about?' asked Baynard. 'Is your head ok?'

'Inspector Baynard, did you find a leather-bound folder down there? Or a bottle?' asked Enrico.

Baynard kept his inquisitive stare.

'This is all an open investigation…' he said.

'Did you at least find out what the Claymores and that man…Bickingham…were up to down there?'

'No comment. Don't push it, Mr Lareva!'

'LoTrova! I think we ought to know after what we've been through. Happy to keep these notes for myself!'

Enrico showed the crumpled notes. Baynard stalled for a minute. He sighed. He could not keep all the truth from them. He had to give them something. No matter how much he despised Enrico's intrusion, it was thanks to him and Viviane that he had been able to arrive on time before something worse happened. With a gentle stroke of his goatee, he thought carefully of what he could share.

'In one of the rooms upstairs we found bundles of letters, documents and a hard drive belonging to the Claymores. They seem to point everything to our two fake builders. We will find out what they were up to once we read them all and logged them as evidence. The man you refer to as Agent Bickingham goes by the real name of Reginald Bosham. Ring any bells?'

Enrico shook his head. He remembered the burly man's antagonism and how he had found it odd, as if this Reginald Bosham had dealt with Enrico before.

'And what is Reginald Bosham's involvement in all of this?' asked Enrico.

'He was just a pawn probably. We'll take time to interrogate him. He was in a worse shape than you after the blast. He is now heavily sedated and heavily guarded at Wandsworth Prison while the doctors look after him.'

'A pawn? Yeah right…' groaned Enrico. 'He tried to kill me. He acted like he knew what he was doing.'

'You just said this crumpled piece of paper points to the Claymores.' pointed out Baynard. 'Do you have your facts straight or shall we wait until things are clearer?'

The inspector looked at Enrico and Viviane in the eye. His inquisitive stare put an end to any further question. He was not going to make a scene in public. He had told them enough already.

'In any case,' continued Baynard. 'we are holding Reginald Bosham for further questioning as we have some evidence against him. Maybe he knew what the Claymores were up to, and maybe he wanted a share of the money.'

'How about the chamber and what we saw down there?' asked Viviane. 'I am sure Dr Watkins will want to ensure what we found is safeguarded.'

'Viviane is right.' said Enrico. 'And you have not yet asked me what I saw down there…'

The imagery of Toby Claymore near the pool, engulfed by crimson tentacles and strong flames, flashed before Enrico's eyes. He had to tell them about the ritual, and what he and Viviane had read about in Janssen's diary.

'In due time.' answered Baynard impassive. 'We are all under shock. We've all seen things. Your statements will be treated as evidence to clarify and hopefully close this case. The police will be in touch once everything we found has been properly analysed and reviewed. This time, though, if we ask you to come down to the station, please avoid causing unrest like last time!'

Baynard's last statement was suddenly drowned by the sound of wheels breaking hard on gravel. It caught the group's attention and all the emergency staff at the site. The gate to the driveway then opened and a slick Jaguar drove in. It slowly moved inside the driveway as far as it could until it came to a halt in front of the building. The driver did not get out. The rear passenger door opened, and a small man got out. He wore a freshly pressed grey suit and a white striped shirt. His body stance was curved as if he had a hump. He had a bald patch with few hairs combed over and his eyes looked grim through round rimless glasses. No one else followed him out of the car. He seemed to be looking for someone and it took a few seconds to spot Inspector Baynard in the crowd. The inspector felt nervous. None of his men seemed to intervene.

'Inspector Baynard, I presume?' asked the bald man politely.

'Yes?' said the inspector hesitantly. 'Do you happen to know this is a crime scene at the moment?'

'Yes, inspector. I am Mr Sanders, Sir Alberon's lawyer. You were expecting me.'

'Was I?' wondered Baynard confused.

'Yes, Mr Sanders. We were expecting you.' boomed a third voice.

The Chief Superintendent appeared among the crowd. He walked briskly to them while asking everyone in the driveway to resume the rescue operation and continue the investigation. Baynard's icy stare became colder. The presence of the Chief Superintendent, very rare in the worst of cases, made a big difference.

'Inspector Baynard,' continued the Chief Superintendent 'Mr Sanders is here representing Alberyx Enterprises. Glad he arrived now rather than earlier.'

'What is the meaning of this?' interrupted Baynard.

'Inspector, I could not get hold of you. Things moved pretty fast. Mr Sanders, please proceed.'

Baynard sensed a humble reverence in his superior's attitude towards the lawyer. Mr Sanders looked like the corporate-type lawyer. Baynard did not know what to expect but at this moment in time he was ready for the worst.

'This is just a formality, Inspector Baynard. I am required to talk to the active inspector directly. I am terribly sorry to learn what happened here. I promise I will be swift.'

'Swift with what?' asked Baynard not picking up the sense of the conversation.

'Sir Alberon requested Sanders Ltd. to provide full legal cover for the heritage of great historical value found and residing on the premises of the Old Rectory, above and below ground.'

'I am not following.' went on Baynard bemused.

Enrico, Viviane and Reverend Green lent their ears in order to make sense of the legal jargon.

'Sanders Ltd.,' continued the lawyer almost in automatic pilot. 'kindly requests Wimbledon Police not to move or displace any of the items discovered as part of their investigation. In an absence of a formal search warrant, all items, including relics, realty, equipment, belong to the property owner, Sir Julian Alberon, and will by default fall under his jurisdiction.'

The lawyer did not seem to breathe. He carried on. Baynard was stupefied.

'Wimbledon Police is kindly asked to perform their investigation on site under the supervision of Sanders Ltd. to allow justice to be carried out while the wishes of Sir Alberon and Alberyx Enterprises are met.'

Inspector Baynard could not believe his ears. His light grey eyes were fuming behind the icy stare.

'I don't understand., What is the meaning of this? Sir Alberon gave us his approval.'

The lawyer adjusted his glasses.

'As Sir Alberon is now unconscious and his safety at risk, Protocol B is automatically triggered to safeguard any property or asset of his. Since the Old Rectory currently belongs to him, we had to intervene to follow his wishes. Alberyx Enterprises steps in as the temporary owner until Sir Alberon is fit for work again. We are not here to make your job harder, inspector. We are here to ensure nothing is broken or misplaced in the process.'

'Inspector, nothing to be worried or angry about.' added the Chief Superintendent. 'The formality here should not hinder the process and Alberyx Enterprises is here to cooperate. They simply ask that nothing is removed from the site and preferably it is analysed here rather than the police station, especially if it is of historical importance. Your men can still carry on their investigation work.'

'I appreciate that!' replied Baynard, not at all pleased. 'I wish I had known earlier though. Nothing of this came out in our discussions earlier.'

Baynard was caught unprepared by the move from Alberyx Enterprises. Julian Alberon was not there to vouch for him and confirm their friendly agreement before accessing the Old Rectory, and now it was Baynard's word against this lawyer's, Sanders. He remembered he was expected to tread carefully when dealing with Wimbledon's number one business.

The inspector felt his head spinning. He had tried to show strength in the rescue effort, but he was still weak after the mysterious explosion underneath the Old Rectory. The strength to go on and even protest was feeble. He sighed; his icy stare though did not flinch. Only the ridges of his crinkled forehead deepened to a maddened frown. His frustration in front of no options to choose from was clear. His hands were tied.

'Fine, Mr Sanders. Sir. The police force will comply.'

He paused looking at both the lawyer and the Chief Superintendent, who showed a pleased face. Baynard then addressed Mr Sanders more directly.

'I don't want any obstruction while we finish our work. Clear?'

'Understood.' confirmed Mr Sanders with a gentle bow of his head.

'Glad we could come to an agreement.' added the Chief Superintendent. 'Let me also congratulate with you for the fine work, Baynard. I am sure we will close this case for good very soon.'

The Chief Superintendent winked. Baynard glared at his boss as the inspector's last grip of authority slipped away. He then smiled as he remembered the Chief Superintendent's wishes. Bring back order, close the case, and avoid messing up the status quo. Baynard was sure this included not going against influential people like Sir Julian Alberon.

'My pleasure. If you will excuse me now,' the inspector concluded. 'I have a job to do.'

He quickly excused himself. He was set to leave the group and join the busy traffic of policemen and firemen, when Jeremy rushed to them with a few firemen following behind.

'Inspector. We've found something!' he called out.

Everyone turned their attention to him. Enrico jumped off the ambulance to get a better look. Together with Viviane and Reverend Green, he took a few steps closer to Baynard. They saw each of the firemen holding two fuming objects, blackened.

'Inspector. These items were found just now. One is a burnt leather-bound folder. Whatever was inside is all burnt…'

'The diary…' gasped Enrico and Viviane exchanging looks.

'What's the other thing?' pointed Baynard. 'Is that what I think it is?'

The fireman lifted it up. It was obvious it was a bottle, although the thick green glass was discoloured. Baynard and Enrico could not believe their eyes.

'The bottle…' they both exclaimed.

'It is intact!' added Enrico.

Baynard spun around, his icy stare demanding an explanation.

'This was evidence Mr Bosham took from the station.' he said. 'How come you know about it?'

Enrico gulped. He did not want to get the wrong impression.

'I...I saw it in the chamber... It was on the table when I found Toby Claymore and Reginald Bosham arguing...' explained Enrico.

'Wimbledon Police and Alberyx Enterprises will make sure they take care of both items!' interrupted the Chief Superintendent, cutting short the conversation.

Mr Sanders nodded. Enrico was puzzled.

'If Dr Watkins's were here, he would want all this to be part of the museum...' told Enrico.

'True.' added Viviane.

Both Viviane and Enrico felt they had to defend Dr Watkins's love for Wimbledon history, no matter how valuable the charred bottle in the fireman's gloved hand was.

'We share the same goal, Mr LoTrova.' spoke the Chief Superintendent. 'Our intention is to ensure it is safely stored and not mismanaged, as Mr Sanders here confirmed. Isn't that case?'

'Of course!' added Mr Sanders. 'Alberyx Enterprises intends to follow through with Sir Alberon's wishes, which he shared with all Wimbledonians: safeguard our history and our community.'

Baynard knew the Chief Superintendent was trying to cover up the fact the police had failed to keep evidence safe. They still had not figured out how Reginald Bosham had been able to steal the body and the bottle. He saw Enrico moving closer, joining to his side.

'Is anyone wondering what for the Claymores were really up to underground?' complained Enrico. 'Who is going to check they have not stolen something we don't know? And what about the wine they smuggled out?'

'Be careful, Mr LoTrova!' spoke the Chief Superintendent, raising his voice. 'We know what you have been up to! I would like to remind you that you have no jurisdiction here. This is a matter between the police and Alberyx Enterprises. I think it is time for you to leave!'

The Chief Superintendent summoned a couple of policemen to keep Enrico in check. The Italian baker became more agitated. Enrico feared they were overlooking something. They must all have seen Toby Claymore burning in the pool. He closed his hands in a fit and then felt Baynard's grip on his arm.

'Step back and don't do anything foolish!' Baynard whispered to Enrico. 'You are lucky we are not putting you behind bars for the chaos caused! You do not want to irritate the Chief Superintendent, or next time you may not get off so easily, sticking your nose into police matters.'

His icy stare met Enrico and forced the Italian baker to stand down.

'Listen to the inspector!' warned the reverend. 'We do not want to make things worse than they already are. Let's pray for Dr Watkins and Julian Alberon!'

Reverend Green and Viviane pulled Enrico back under the watchful eye of Baynard and the Chief Superintendent. The tension took a while to ease.

'Ok. Sergeant Jeremy!' ordered Baynard snapping back to work. 'Please ensure all the material found here at the Old Rectory follows the instructions given by Mr Sanders here.'

Having witnessed the brief face-off with the Italian baker, Jeremy knew this order was something he should not disobey. The sergeant then dared to ask one last question.

'What about them?' he asked.

'Who? asked Baynard.

Jeremy pointed at the middle of the driveway. Paramedics had come out of the Old Rectory carrying two stretchers across the driveway. Each stretcher had a transparent plastic body bag on it. Toby Claymore's carbonised body lay on one, and Henry Claymore's on the other. They were completely charred and hard to distinguish if it were not for their difference in height. The group gasped in horror at the macabre sight.

'It appears Henry's body, being closer to the flames, suffered a second combustion.' added Jeremy. 'I am told we should take both back to the forensics lab.'

'Take them away, Jeremy!' said the inspector. 'We have seen enough.'

Baynard's inquisitive stare turned to perplexity. He feared this case would haunt him again and again in the days and weeks to come.

'God rest their souls!' proclaimed Reverend Green, making the sign of the cross.

Enrico could not help staring. Despite the moon-less night sky and the bright lights of the emergency vehicles, Enrico thought for a minute he could see fluid reflections of crimson hovering around the lifeless burnt and disfigured bodies. It was just his imagination. The two bodies, who were once brothers, were now just motionless, black shapes. The purplish reflection he had seen on Henry's dead body had disappeared. He then remembered the dried crimson gelatine he had found in the tunnels. He glanced at the burnt bottle at his feet and his thoughts went back the texture of those crimson tentacles almost devouring Toby Claymore. His gut feeling told him there was a connection he could not put his finger on. Yet, the more Enrico thought about it, the more his head hurt.

Baynard closed the door behind him to meet Jeremy's doubtful face. The sergeant put his hand through his ginger hair and then looked through the one-way mirror in disbelief. In the room on the other side, Reginald Bosham sat handcuffed at the table, guarded by two police constables at the door. It was an image they had grown accustomed to in the last few weeks of police investigation.

'So, you heard everything again?' said Baynard.

Sergeant Jeremy nodded.

'And what do you make of it?'

'It kind of rang true when he first told us, inspector.' expanded Jeremy. 'Now, the hospital records I have show that Toby Claymore was indeed schizophrenic. This proves what Reginald Bosham told us, and we have the notes Enrico LoTrova found. Toby Claymore killed Henry Claymore in a frenzy of jealousy or greed.'

'Bit of a sadistic way of killing, isn't it?'

'I don't know why you are surprised. The documents we found in the upper floor of the Old Rectory profiled Toby Claymore as a fanatic of occultism. We tested the few dredges of liquid found in the pool and they match what we found on the Claymores' bodies. But you know this already, inspector, so why are you asking again?'

'How does he fit in?' said Baynard hinting at Reginald.

'He claims he was working for the Claymores and that the two chemist brothers were trying to create fake vintage wine to sell. Your food fraud angle now make sense, inspector. The documents we found in the Old Rectory confirm all that. After all, the rented garages are all in Henry Claymore's name and they all contain equipment for making wine. That was their experiment. The Claymores were the ones who gave Reginald Bosham his cover at the Old Rectory through the company hired by Alberyx Enterprises. He was the one buying cheap wine and other stuff for them.'

'Why go against Toby Claymore though?'

'The statement from your friend Enrico LoTrova says he found them both arguing in the chamber. I guess Reginald was scared after he found out what Toby had done to his brother and what Toby's real intentions were. Plans had changed the moment the Claymores found the real vintage wine. Toby was so off his head he killed his brother to keep the vintage wine for himself, but he needed to kill off Reginald Bosham too before making a run for it. As we know now, things did not go as planned. Enrico LoTrova was just collateral damage for them.'

'What do you make of his statement?'

'The baker?'

Sergeant Jeremy grimaced. He walked towards the one-way mirror, sipping his morning coffee. Jeremy could not put his thoughts in order. Enrico LoTrova's talk of rituals and demons was laughable and terrifying at the same time. Jeremy thought he had seen something in the pool, but the smoke had been thick and his vision hazy. All he remembered, while trying to hold Dr Watkins back, were the flames and the screams.

Jeremy glanced at Reginald, who was unaware of being watched. He sat still, facing the wall in front. He had been calm in telling his versions of the facts. He had denied everything Enrico LoTrova claimed to have seen.

'I don't know…' he muttered.

'Exactly. Burning ghosts? Tentacles coming out of a pool? Please! I can only conclude Toby's love for occultism really had an effect on impressionable minds. He was playing tricks with everyone until the trick was on him.'

'Why are you checking with me again? Why interview Reginald Bosham a second time? We have it figured out, inspector!'

Baynard sat at the large desk, in front of a pile of notes and the monitors which had recorded each police interview over the last couple of weeks. He took a gum from his pocket and put it in his mouth, chewing intensely with one eye on the one-way mirror.

'I have to be sure, Jeremy.' he then admitted. 'I have to be sure what I am going to tell the Chief Superintendent, and the Council and the general public. It has to make sense to me first before we present the case to the judge. I know Reginald Bosham may not be sentenced to prison if his lawyers go for involuntary manslaughter. There is little proof he wanted to kill. I presume you've read the papers?'

Baynard grabbed hold of a newspaper and threw it flat on the desk. It was a copy of the Wimbledon Gazette from a few days ago. Jeremy recognised the page and the article. He had of course already read it. Every Wimbledonian had had the opportunity to read it.

'Where does he get some of those ideas?' protested Baynard. 'I would just throw him in jail for defamation.'

'Don't let Nathan Glenn get to you, inspector. He is an opportunistic journalist. I mean, have you seen how he barged into the police station just to make a scene? People will gossip but won't take him seriously.'

'Right! Well, before this case comes back to haunt me, let's wrap up all the evidence and put it before the Chief Superintendent. You can send Reginald Bosham back to his holding cell. I will join you in a minute.'

Sergeant Jeremy nodded at the inspector and grabbed all the papers in the thick file folder before leaving the viewing room quietly. Baynard sat in his chair, watching Jeremy and the police constables taking Reginald Bosham away. Three men were enough to keep the burly, strong man in check. At least the baker had told the truth about that; the bruises on his face and body were further proof. He then recalled something else the Italian baker had said. Something that did not add up.

He went to the nearest monitor and accessed the police cam recordings. Each police constable had a camera on their shoulders for in-action video recording. The quality had not been great due to the poor visibility in the chamber. Still, Baynard fast forwarded to the few seconds before the sonic boom knocked out all the equipment. It was Jeremy's camera. He pressed the 'zoom-in' option, closing in on the area of the screen where Dr Watkins's hand could be seen and beyond it another hand, presumably Julian Alberon's; each grabbing the burning hand of Toby Claymore.

Apart from being outraged with their disrespect for police orders, Baynard could not fathom what they had been up to. Their testimony, taken at the hospital, had been justified as an act of charity, pure and simple; to help the man in excruciating pain. The inspector dropped that line of inquiry once the motives attributed to the Claymores and Reginald Bosham became clear. Baynard knew putting pressure on those people who had been helping would not be seen in a good light by the press. He thought it wise to check the video recordings again.

Baynard hit pause. At the highest zoom, the scarce, pixelated quality did not say much. The freeze frame shot was just blob of colours. The colours roughly highlighted where the sleeve and the hand belonging to Dr Watkins and Julian Alberon appeared and met with Toby's. Baynard went back and forth the same range of seconds a few times. It was probably just a trick of the mind, he thought, especially after watching it over and over. He rubbed his eyes. It had been a long two weeks and he deserved a break. Time to let go. Inspector Baynard knew each time he looked at that freeze frame and rewound it to watch it again, he would have the same impression: that each set of hands were not grabbing Toby Claymore, but actually pushing him into the pool.

From the Wimbledon Gazette:

GRUESOME DEATHS BRING THE OCCULT TO WIMBLEDON
Opinion Column by Nathan Glenn

Wimbledon has always been a peaceful place to live. It is our pride and joy. The shocking events that have rocked our village this year, have reminded all Wimbledonians that we need to be vigilant to preserve the calm and tranquillity we so dearly enjoy.

Details of the Claymore brothers' seedy activities are now public to everyone living in SW19, thanks to the great press coverage from a month ago. Great journalism is what has allowed the paper to reveal how underground basements in our conservation area were used for illegal experiments, right under our noses. But who are the Claymores? They are simple chemistry fanatics who enjoyed taking advantage of poor folk, hoping to sell us fake wine concoctions masked as aged wine. Their horrible, gruesome death is a clear punishment for their actions. It does make me wonder though what really went on there, in the depths of our lovely hill. Police information has been sketchy but unofficial reports talk about vats and machines to mix secret ingredients. Yet, Toby Claymore's schizophrenia and his love for occultism could not be kept under cover. What happened underground is true modern witchcraft, I say. More shockingly, under one of our sacred sites, that of Saint Mary's Church.

For those who care to remember, it is only a few months since our lovely Wimbledon was plagued by explosions and poisoning at Cannizaro House. Is this what will become of our idyllic village? A place of death and violence? Who are these people coming here to cause unrest? Why are the police not doing more to prevent it? Most of you, dear readers, will know my position on this. The incompetence of Wimbledon Police, and in particular Inspector Baynard, should be raised to the higher authority. Their poor management of the Cannizaro House explosion first caught my eye, but it was their handling of the Claymores' case that really showed me their ineptitude. Take Mrs Biggins, a lovely housewife who has lived in Rectory Orchard for decades. For months, she reported strange disturbances, and nobody listened. Nobody cared. Until things got ugly. Until burnt bodies came out of the gutters, literally. Wimbledon Police took their time to track all these events in an area the size of Wimbledon AFC football stadium. Not really a needle in the haystack, is it?

Perhaps there is more to this than meets the eye. There is more for us Wimbledonians to worry about. I came to the conclusion the police are just a pawn in all of this; clueless as they are. I turned to Alberyx Enterprises, instead, and challenged our number one local business and benefactor on their hiring procedures. How could they hire criminals like the Claymores and Mr Bosham as part of their construction and security staff? It has never been clear how Alberyx Enterprises manages their organisation and I think there should be more open scrutiny. As a journalist, I took the liberty to find out more by spending time at the Council's town hall and checking public records. What did I find? The Lord of the Manor of Wimbledon has recently given a large donation to Alberyx Enterprises, as well as the Wimbledon Museum. With that money, Alberyx Enterprises promises to make many radical improvements across Wimbledon. If you have not realised yet, that plan is already in motion with the Old Rectory, which they rightfully own. The infamous crime scene has now been walled off and turned into a protected archaeological site. What else will Alberyx Enterprises buy or control next? Our peace? Is this the price to pay for funding our local business, our community?

Talking about buying, my research went a little further. I was surprised to find out the local title of Lord of the Manor of Wimbledon, a century-old decoration which is now mainly a piece of paper, was bought off the last Earl of Spencer a few weeks back by an undisclosed individual. A piece of Wimbledon has been sold to strangers, just like that. Whoever this person is, he now owns some of the land in Wimbledon. This includes buildings like the Artesian Well that almost collapsed because of the tremors, remember? Who else will come next and take a piece of Wimbledon from under our noses?

As you can imagine, nobody from Alberyx Enterprises, the Council or Wimbledon Police were available for comment. Wimbledonians need to rise and stand up to protect what is dear to them. Our village, our community. Together we can put a stop to the mysterious havoc created by dangerous criminals who do not belong here. This is only the beginning of a long fight. Nathan Glenn will not stop here; I will keep bringing you the news before they happen.

Lord Awlthorp woke up in the middle of the night, calling out incomprehensible names. His forehead was drenched in sweat. His eyes wide open, awake, alert. His look was feverish, exhausted. He called out in the darkness of the room. A hand emerged out of darkness, holding a moistened cloth, to wipe Lord Awlthorp's forehead.

'Are you ok, sir? You need to rest!' said the driver's voice, hidden in the dark, behind the caring hands. 'The doctors said you may get some restless nights once discharged from Parkside Hospital.'

'The second test! The second test!' babbled Lord Awlthorp staring up as if the heavens had opened.

'You are delirious, sir. The second test, whatever that may be, failed. We never completed it!'

Lord Awlthorp cackled, followed by choking sounds and eerie silence that seemed to drain blood from his feverish face. He started shaking his head.

'No…no…you have not seen it…'

'What, sir? All I know is that Toby Claymore threw himself in the pool and you could not do anything to stop him!'

The calm voice withdrew his hands, wringing the wet cloth before he placed it back on Lord Awlthorp's hot forehead. The driver knew this was a side effect of the fever. It was the third night he had woken up, disillusioned about the second test. He looked at Lord Awlthorp's eyes, fearful and bewildered at the same time.

'What, sir?' asked the driver again.

'The second test…' giggled Lord Awlthorp. 'We did it!'

The voice next to him sighed.

'We never did it, sir. The Claymores are both dead. Reginald is under investigation; not sure if we will be able to bail him out. You barely survived the flames. You should have never showed up in the chamber with the police. That was a big risk you took. We now lost everything we had on the experiment, and there is nothing left for us to do!'

Lord Awlthorp did not seem to hear. He stood motionless under the covers pulled up to his neck to keep him warm. He kept looking up and whispering things to himself.

'That little Italian baker put a spanner in the works again.' continued the driver. 'I told you we underestimated him. We should have kept an eye on him.'

Lord Awlthorp carried on with his mumblings, not paying attention.

'I don't understand you, sir. What are you saying?'

'It's the beginning…' repeated Lord Awlthorp.

'Of what, sir?'

The driver played along, recalling what the doctors had advised. Keep the conversation going; let the patient say what is on their mind.

'I heard. I saw. The mightiest power to move seas and mountains. I heard his voice…'

'His voice? Whose voice?'

'He made me see… the future…'

'You are still in shock, sir. You were badly injured. You need to rest.'

The driver pulled back the covers to check Lord Awlthorp's bandaged hand. The bandage covering his burns reached up to his forearm.

'What were you thinking?' he muttered.

He then leaned forward, to check Lord Awlthorp's temperature. The man in black was lost in his reverie.

'You are burning with fever.' warned the driver, rummaging the bedside table for some paracetamol. 'Time for you to rest. Enough with this nonsense! There was no potion. There was no ritual. You have been fooled, sir. We all have. The power of the Wynnman does not exist!'

'No!' shouted Lord Awlthorp.

He grabbed the driver by the neck with his injured hand. His grip was firm, strong, enough to cut out the air completely. The coarse bandages around his burnt hand grazed the skin on the driver's neck. Lord Awlthorp turned to him, his corvine eyes now blood-stained, his hair all ruffled like a madman.

'Sir… you are strangling… me!' gasped the driver.

'You need to believe!' hissed Lord Awlthorp.

'Yes…yes, sir…but…' nodded the driver, fearing he would soon pass out.

Lord Awlthorp released his grip and the driver fell back on the floor gasping for air.

'You don't understand. Nobody will ever understand.' Lord Awlthorp warned.

He sat up in his bed and enjoyed the blackness around him. The driver thought he was looking at a stranger. He had never seen his employer like this before. Lord Awlthorp fixed his eyes on one corner and stared into the darkness as if talking to an invisible presence.

'Toby Claymore understood the ritual.' rambled on Lord Awlthorp. 'He knew the person who would push the human sacrifice, the *sangui venerarius*, into the pool would be the one to awaken the Wynnman. He wanted to push Reginald in the pool for that reason. But that didn't happen…'

'Toby fell into the pool on his own, no?'

'No.' grinned Lord Awlthorp. 'I pushed Toby into the pool. I was the one to complete the ritual. And when I did, I saw a bright light before me. It was a spirit. It spoke to me with its talks of power and revenge. The instant we connected he let me see the future.'

'Who?' asked the driver confused.

'Fairy tales are true, my friend. The legendary power I have been seeking to prove exists. The spirit told me to look for him, and now I know where to find him. He asked me to bring him back, whatever it takes. He promised me that together we will help Wimbledon regain its old glory!'

His words could have been the words of any madman except they carried a stronger conviction. Lord Awlthorp spoke as if he had just forged a new alliance and built a mysterious bond that could never be broken.

'Who…are you…talking about, sir?' asked the driver.

'The spirit of the sorcerer himself.' said Lord Awlthorp. 'The Wynnman!'

Enrico threw the copy of the Wimbledon Gazette on the table. He then looked down into his espresso cup. The coffee he had just made tasted bitter all of a sudden.

'Stop reading that trashy article!' reminded Viviane across the table, sipping her own *caffè latte*. 'It will drive you crazy!'

'I can't stop thinking about it, Viviane.' moaned Enrico. 'This journalist writes about conspiracies and everyone talks about it. I tell the police everything I remember, what we found in the cellar, and also shared my suspicions, and what do they do? Nothing! They just brush it off with a "thank you"!'

'They caught the people responsible for what happened, Enrico. What more do you want?'

'I don't know. Something does not add up…'

'Here we go again! Something does not add up because you are trying to explain the actions of a mad man. Just because you can't explain what ritual Toby Claymore was talking about, doesn't mean it is real. He was mad! Just like Janssen in his diary. It could have been anything popping into his head from one day to the next! Satanism. Aliens…you name it. It does not make it real!'

Enrico crossed his arms and stared out into the high street. The third Sunday of the month had come round again and Enrico and Viviane were getting ready to make their way to Saint Mary's Church. Weeks had gone by and the bustling rhythm of Wimbledon Village took hold of *The Wynnman* bakery once again. Enrico felt time had just flown by. He had found himself with a backlog of requests due to the few days he had stayed closed. He had been working round the clock ever since in order to get his bakery up and running again. The more fairs he attended, the more he made a name for himself. More and more Wimbledonians flocked to *The Wynnman* bakery, and his mind was filled daily with order numbers and customer faces, from Mrs Rochdale's order of *sfogliatelle* to Mr Wyczsenki's daily request of five loaves of bread for his team.

Enrico though had not forgotten about the 'Old Rectory and the mad experiments', which is how the local news had described the events. For a while Enrico's sleep had been disturbed by nightmares. In each of them, the image of Toby Claymore burning up in the pool chamber was a recurring theme, and Enrico could feel the heat on his skin to the point he would wake up in his bed in a pool of sweat. It worsened a few days after he had to give his statement to Inspector Baynard and Sergeant Jeremy. Recalling what he and Viviane had been through was a painful exercise. Enrico still remembered the stupefied look from the two police officers. They did not believe what he claimed to have seen. He himself was embarrassed to describe something that looked like tentacles rising from the pool and grabbing Toby Claymore. The whole statement seemed surreal when written up; Enrico was not surprised the police had kept a few things he said out of the final report in order to close the case.

Viviane slid her chair closer to Enrico and wrapped her arm around him. Enrico peered at her suspiciously.

'Listen, Enrico.' she spoke kindly. 'You now have a successful business here. Why ruin it with fairy tales? Do you really want to be at the same level of this Nathan Glenn and his conspiracy articles?'

'You are not the one still having nightmares!' Enrico sighed. 'I dream this ghostly image burning before me, right after the blast. I even told Baynard I had the impression Dr Watkins and Julian Alberon deliberately pushed Toby Claymore into the pool!'

'And why would they do that? It is all in your head, Enrico, and only time will heal. I had quite a few nightmares in the days after what happened.

After running in the dark through those forsaken tunnels, and reading about Janssen's demonic experiences, it is completely understandable to imagine things. It does not make them real!'

'You sound like Dr Watkins and his need for historical facts!'

'Which reminds me…' noted Viviane, glancing at her watch. 'Dr Watkins is coming by soon so I can drive you both to the Sunday fair at Saint Mary's. He has been looking forward to it ever since he was discharged from Parkside Hospital. Reverend Green was keen for everyone to come. It would help bring joy back to the community.'

Enrico smiled at the nice thought.

'See? That's the spirit!' exclaimed Viviane.

The curator joined them a little later in his best Sunday frock. Dr Watkins walked slowly in front of the bakery with the help of a walking stick, saying hello to passers-by. His white wavy hair and his blue eyes were alive as always. His charming smile did not look beaten against his tired skin. One of his hands was heavily bandaged, including part of his wrist and forearm. The only visible trace of his reckless act to save Toby Claymore. He saw Enrico and Viviane through the window and lifted his stick to greet them He then walked in with renewed confidence and Enrico and Viviane stood up to hug him.

'Morning!' said the curator.

'Morning!' echoed Viviane.

'*Buongiorno!*' answered Enrico. 'You are still alive!'

Viviane rolled her eyes at Enrico for his usual lack of tact. Enrico shrugged and laughed. They both glanced at Dr Watkins's face. From his expression, they knew the curator could handle Enrico's amusing spirit. He chuckled.

'How are you getting along, Dr Watkins?' asked Viviane.

'I am perfectly fine. Never felt better. Thanks for the flowers, Viviane, and for covering for me at the WAIS meetings.'

'I am glad.'

'How's your sleep?' checked in Enrico.

'Still a bit troubled.' replied the curator. 'I get tired more than before. The burnt hand wakes me up from time to time. It is mainly scar tissue now. It itches badly though so I need to take some pills. Doctors were at first surprised I survived, but they now say it will go away in a few weeks. Soon I will have fully recovered!'

Dr Watkins paused to take a deep breath. A grave look flashed across his face.

'I know Sir Alberon and I both paid dearly for our selfless acts.' sighed Dr Watkins raising his bandaged hand. 'I know it was foolish of us to do what we did. I am sorry. We both are.'

'You don't need to apologise.' said Enrico. 'You are here with us now! Just take it easy from now on!'

Dr Watkins smiled at them.

'Have you heard from Julian Alberon?' asked Viviane. 'How is he coping since you share the same injury?'

'I must say it was nice to share the room with him at Parkside while we were both recovering.' replied the curator. 'He was in good shape when we were both discharged. I heard rumours he may make an appearance today at the fair.'

'Really?' exclaimed Viviane in astonishment.

'And how do you feel about his plans for the Old Rectory?' interjected Enrico. 'I suppose you heard what Alberyx Enterprises did after the blast in the chamber.'

'Enrico!' exclaimed Viviane about to elbow him. 'Give it a rest! Stop thinking about that newspaper article, will you?'

The curator raised his bandaged hand to stop the two bickering. As strangely as it sounded, he was somehow pleased to hear them.

'If it is in Julian Alberon's hands, Wimbledon history is in safe hands. As I understand, he plans to fund the opening of an archaeological site to find out more about what lies under the Old Rectory.'

'And you are happy with that?' insisted Enrico. 'Are you sure he is not going to take it all away?'

'Why would you think so negatively of Sir Alberon?' commented Viviane. 'He is a benefactor!'

'All I am saying is' insisted Enrico. 'we had on our hands one of the most extraordinary discoveries. Now, they are either burnt or buried underground...'

Dr Watkins put his bandaged hand on Enrico's arm.

'It's ok, Enrico!' he said. 'I am fine with it!'

His blue eyes met Enrico's, dark and restless. Dr Watkins then frowned and winced as if in pain. He gasped and pushed his bandaged arm away from Enrico's.

'What's the matter?' cried Viviane.

'Are you ok, Dr Watkins?' joined in Enrico.

'I am ok. I am ok.' repeated the curator, catching his breath. 'I just need to be careful when I place my hand here and there. Nothing to worry about.'

The two stared at him, still concerned.

'Stop looking at me like that!' groaned Dr Watkins. 'Shall we make a move? We're going to be late!'

The bells of Saint Mary's Church rang again across the hill, but their sweet melody was lost to a cold wind, announcing the arrival of Autumn in full swing. The golden rooster on the church steeple rotated furiously, a manic shape against the grey sky. The congregation, led by Reverend Green, left the church on time. Their murmur somehow brought the top of the hill to life as the crowds flooded once more the green space in front, lined up with market stalls.

Enrico and Viviane made their usual theatrical entrance shortly after. Viviane was the one driving this time, feeling Enrico's might be too reckless. The yellow Fiat 500 skidded once again over the grassy parking space and played the cheery jingle through the crackling speakerphones to announce their arrival. Enrico showed himself through the passenger window, while Dr Watkins held himself tight until the car had completely stopped.

Enrico and Viviane had opted for two quiet stalls in one of the corners closer to the church. To their surprise, their stalls was next to the shopkeeper who sold wine on the Ridgeway. He had a few leaflets advertising the upcoming exhibition on the Cecils' wine, sponsored by Alberyx Enterprises. Apparently, once the case had been closed by the police, Alberyx Enterprises had bought all the vintage wine stolen by the Claymores and safeguarded it as local heritage. Dr Watkins stood by the stall, admiring the photos of the gorgeous-looking old bottles.

'Glad these have not left Wimbledon in the end!' praised Dr Watkins, pointing his stick at them.

'I could not agree more!' said Reverend Green.

The reverend had left a small group from his congregation to join the Italian baker's stall. His jovial, clean-shaven face lifted Enrico's and Viviane's spirits.

'Reverend Green, nice to see you!' said Viviane.

'I hope you have been well.' replied the reverend. 'Staying out of trouble, I hope.'

Enrico smiled nervously, not saying much. He realised his fame as a troublemaker was getting known beyond the private circle he shared with Viviane and Dr Watkins.

'We try.' joked Viviane. 'And how have you been, reverend?'

'I am glad we finally fixed the broken slabs in the crypt and sealed what was left of the tunnel. Police and council were adamant to fix any hazards before another child got lost in there.'

He exchanged a knowing smile with Dr Watkins and then he watched him wander away through the stalls, greeting old acquaintances, catching up on what he had missed.

'How is he?' asked Reverend Green, his gaze still on his old friend.

'Getting better.' replied Enrico as he tidied up some of his bread baskets. 'He still has troubles with sleep, worse than before the accident …'

The reverend held his gaze on Enrico, taken aback by the innocent comment.

'Trouble sleeping?' he said curiously.

Enrico nodded still carrying on his work. An older gentleman passed glancing at the bread on offer.

'You know, reverend, how Dr Watkins gets excited about Wimbledon!' teased Viviane addressing her floral decorations.

'Indeed!' replied the reverend moving closer to their stalls. 'Now, I know you two are very keen to ask Dr Watkins many questions…'

Reverend Green gave a knowing smile.

'I am referring about getting him involved in your adventures or escapades.' he added.

The reverend was now looking at both Enrico and Viviane with concern. He glanced sideways before speaking openly.

'Dr Watkins looked very tired when I saw him.' said the reverend. 'He easily gets very excited and you ought to take care he does not get too carried away.'

Viviane bit her lip and glanced at Enrico. She then addressed Reverend Green without looking too embarrassed.

'We try, reverend.' she explained Viviane. 'The recent discoveries here in Wimbledon have been unexpected. We did not know Dr Watkins would get so involved. You should have seen him how odd he was in the tunnels when we went in with the police to save Enrico. He disobeyed the police completely!'

'And then you say I am the troublemaker…' joked Enrico.

'You need to know…' resumed Reverend Green, his voice now taking on a softer tone close to a whisper.

He glanced sideways again, so as not to be heard. He checked Dr Watkins was far away.

'You need to know' he repeated. 'Dr Watkins has been a fan of Wimbledon history for longer than I can remember. You know that already. He has been involved in every single research and expedition. Then, when the 1984 speleological expedition into the tunnels was organised, he was the first one to lead in.'

'I thought he had never been down the tunnels. That is what he told me.' said Enrico.

'He went but he had an accident along the way. He fell somewhere and knocked his head badly. We found him unconscious a few hours later, and when he woke up, he did not remember a thing. Despite what had happened, he couldn't wait to go back into the tunnels. As if nothing had ever happened and it was his first time ever. We decided not to let him go in and made him believe he had not been selected. He still gets excited about the tunnels in ways we cannot possibly imagine. If we could avoid the subject of the tunnels or new discoveries in the future, I think it would be better for his health. He is not a youngster anymore!'

Enrico and Viviane nodded in agreement. As they had listened, something in the way the reverend spoke made it clear the reverend regretted sharing a village secret that had been kept for so long.

'I was worried when the tunnel entrance under the crypt was exposed.' he continued. 'I was even more worried when, the day after Henry Claymore's body was found, Dr Watkins came to see me about the Old Rectory. Again, sorry if I repeat myself, but let's keep things quiet. Please.'

Enrico and Viviane looked at each other, baffled by the revelation. Yet, there was little time to cherish Reverend Green's open secret. Viviane looked up. She pulled at Enrico's white chef jacket, and Reverend Green turned around as well. Dr Watkins was returning, over the moon with himself. Wimbledonians at the fair had been kind to him and he had a plastic bag full of goodies.

'Nice to be here! Hold this bag, Viviane, please.' he asked all excited, leaning on her stall to catch his breath. 'You have to try that Cecil 1590 vintage wine. Beautiful. We need to do something about it at the museum. An exhibition perhaps!'

'We can see you are getting back into shape.' commented Reverend Green. 'You have not lost your organisational skills, Dr Watkins!'

The curator chuckled. He then glanced over Enrico's shoulder and made a sign to the baker to alert him about something. Enrico turned around. An elderly lady with a young mother and baby waited anxiously at the opposite end of his stall.

'*Buongiorno!*' said Enrico. 'How can I help?'.

'Aren't you the man who saved that little girl?' queried the elderly lady with a nosey attitude.

Enrico was caught by surprise by the sudden claim to fame.

'Yes, ma'am. It is me.'

'What a wonderful gentleman! You should be proud!' she continued without sparing on compliments.

'*Grazie…*Thank you!' replied Enrico a little embarrassed.

'You are the man from the tunnels?' exclaimed the young mother. 'How heroic! I heard how you drove out those wine fraudsters!'

'It was…my pleasure.' answered Enrico with little to say.

He took their bread orders and worked quickly to shove bread after bread into a brown paper bag. The sweet eyes of the elderly lady and the young mother stayed on him all the time and Enrico felt the discomfort that comes with fame.

'Look, Enrico!' whispered Viviane moving close him. 'They may ask you for a selfie soon. Perhaps you can take one with your Nokia 3310.'

Enrico nudged her with his hip and handed over the brown bags to two newly found fans. He could see them gossiping between each other as they moved onto other stalls.

'What was that about?' said Enrico aloud.

'Something tells me they were not here just to buy bread.' pointed out Viviane.

'It seems, Mr LoTrova, you are making a name for yourself.' said Reverend Green.

'Not really because of bread, though.' joked Viviane. 'See, you have a bright future, Enrico! I told you!'

Viviane's words reassured Enrico that everything would be alright and soon back to normal. A chilly breeze then picked up through the graveyard behind and made him shiver. A cheer from somewhere among the stalls caught their attention. The sound of a crowd gathering echoed in the air. Enrico and Viviane saw everyone running towards it, some shopkeepers leaving their own stall.

'What is going on?' said Viviane.

Followed by Dr Watkins and Reverend Green, they pushed forward through the crowd to the opposite end of the fair, used as a temporary car park. A large black saloon car stood there in the middle of the short grass, and Julian Alberon had just stepped out to thank the welcome party. Enrico witnessed for the first time how Wimbledonians loved the local businessman. He was standing there in his perfect image. His hand waving at them, white smile, a bright-coloured suit jacket and casual jeans. The moment he moved towards the stalls, a few men, women and children stopped to ask for an autograph or even steal a selfie with him. Julian did not mind them and did not rush. Even though they called him 'sir' or treated him like the special tycoon he claimed to be, he was a kindred spirit to all Wimbledonians. Enrico looked at the scene with a little envy, wondering if he would be in his place one day. He glanced at Viviane next to him. She was pleased to see Julian again, and so were Dr Watkins and Reverend Green. They looked up to him as a man who gave Wimbledon hope.

Julian saw Dr Watkins first, and gently pulled away from his last admirers to join the curator and the others. He made his way forward, and only when close enough, did Enrico notice an imperfection in the businessman's image. Julian's other hand had been in his pocket all the time, and now that it was out, Enrico could see the same bandage as Dr Watkins. Julian's burnt hand was also bandaged up to the forearm. The Italian baker thought how Julian as well as Dr Watkins had risked their lives to save Toby Claymore, and then the nagging thought at the back of his head made him wonder again whether he had really seen the two pushing Toby Claymore into the pool. He brushed the crazy idea off, remembering Viviane's advice. They were all alive and that was what counted.

'Hello, my friends. Very nice to see you all!' exclaimed Julian with his friendly, boisterous voice. 'I was told you would be here, so I had to arrange a visit and make the short trip here. I have something for you.'

Enrico, Viviane, and the others looked at each other not following. Behind Julian Alberon, Mr Sanders made an appearance and the gloomy lawyer stood next to Julian with a brown case in his hand.

'This is something that you may find of interest for the museum.' added Julian.

Dr Watkins picked it up under the curious eyes of the others. He opened it and saw the old wine bottle. The curator recognised it as the same bottle the police had found in Arthur Road and Baynard had shown to him. Even Enrico could not mistake the old label of the very same bottle he had seen on the table in the chamber, next Toby Claymore. The bottle with the foul-smelling liquid.

'I thought it had been charred by the fire…' mumbled Enrico.

'My staff at the Alberyx Enterprises lab in Warren Farm tried to restore the glass and salvage it.' explained Julian. 'This is an older bottle from the Cecils' wine cellar. We could not let it go to waste and rot in an evidence box at the police station.'

Dr Watkins lifted the bottle from its cradle. It was sealed with a silver cork. The curator shook the bottle to see what was inside. There was a small residue at the bottom.

'What happened to its contents?' asked the curator remembering the foul smell.

'The bottle was found in the chamber. Toby Claymore may have wasted its contents on whatever ridiculous experiment he was up to.' Julian replied. 'There are some dregs left at the bottom, still with the same repudiant smell. We sealed the bottle for safety with aluminium steel.'

Enrico gazed at Sir Julian Alberon with an enigmatic smile. He had to admit he was kind and generous; he ought to change his mind about him. Julian caught Enrico staring at him and smiled back. He lowered his eyes for a second, escaping the attention of the crowd, and then glanced at Mr Sanders's gloomy face who did not seem to react.

'I know some of you may have felt cheated by my…what was it called?... Ah yes, Protocol B.' Julian started explaining with regret. 'However, like all businesses, I need to have a failsafe in place to protect my assets. This was by no means a disregard of your interest or wishes. Especially you, Dr Watkins.'

'We owe you a lot already, Sir Alberon.' replied Dr Watkins with a smile. 'There was no need to apologise…'

'I think there is.' Julian interrupted, taking a moment to look at Enrico, Viviane, and even Reverend Green, to make his public apology heard by all. 'You see, we are about to turn a new chapter in Wimbledon history. Now that Wimbledon police have closed the case, I have specifically requested that the Old Rectory be setup as an archaeological site. We need to explore what lies below. What we have found already opens new doors.'

'But Baynard, the police, said all tunnels collapsed…' added Enrico.

'Don't despair, Mr LoTrova.' reassured Julian. 'Mr Sanders informed me of the status of the Old Rectory above and below. The chamber with the pool is intact and that's a good start. I am scheduled for an archaeological meeting next month to better assess the historical evidence readily available, once the police have removed all seals.'

'Do you have the funds to do so?' wondered Dr Watkins.

'The funds definitely, but I also managed to grab the attention of the British Museum. I know you have been quite unsuccessful on that front, Dr Watkins.'

Dr Watkins was baffled.

'How did you convince them?' asked Reverend Green, as bewildered as Dr Watkins.

He was more concerned the curator may get too excited, knowing his history. Julian paused in anticipation of what he had to say. Enrico and Viviane recognised the same school-boy excitement in Julian Alberon as Dr Watkins. The two, now in front of each other, both with their bulky bandaged hands, both with their eyes shimmering with excitement, shared something that went beyond their looks.

'Preliminary observations say we may have come across evidence of an Anglo-Saxon site.' revealed Julian. 'Incredible! You know the irony of all this, Dr Watkins? I recall your views on everything that is fiction, or not historically founded.'

Dr Watkins was taken aback by Julian's words.

'What do you mean?' he said, blushing a little.

'Our talk in the gardens of the Old Rectory, by the Fig Walk. I still remember it!'

'I remember our discussion...' repeated Dr Watkins still unsure what the tycoon was getting at.

'Exactly. I put my case forward again that local legends could help where our rational minds sometimes fail. We should not ignore the existence of Anglo-Saxon settlements on Wimbledon Hill, Dr Watkins, the same way we should not ignore the legend of the Wynnman.'

'Anglo-Saxon, yes. I would not say the same for sorcerers and potions.'

'Excuse me, gentlemen.' interjected Reverend Green. 'What is this discussion you are referring to?'

'Saint Mary's.' interjected Sir Alberon, all excited. 'The Old Rectory. All the houses on Belvedere and Marryat Road. This hill may stand on old Pre-Christian burial sites. This is what the legends hint at. However, the question is whether what is down there could confirm the legends to be true. We now have the opportunity to explore. The Cecils' wine bottles may be just the tip of the iceberg. We probably do not realise we have come across something of more value.'

'Which is?' insisted Enrico.

'Traces of Wimbledon's past we never knew of before, that we could only dream of until now. Tell them, Dr Watkins. How many Anglo-Saxon remains do you have in your museum?'

'Almost none...' replied Dr Watkins, his face suddenly lit up.

The curator could not argue with Julian's position. Julian's move to save the Old Rectory could help find and keep new relics before they could get lost again. Julian's plan was clear. An opportunity to safeguard a newly found historical heritage. It would mean more material for his museum and more evidence of the local history he loved, all funded by Julian Alberon himself.

'You are right.' he murmured. 'This is an opportunity!'

Enrico had been watching the dialogue between the two, not sure if his own curiosity had been satisfied. He never accepted Julian's Protocol B and the way it had snatched everything out of their control. He remembered Dr Watkins's tales of Wimbledon history, forsaken and buried over the centuries. He was worried history may be repeating itself, leaving Dr Watkins cheated again for looking after Wimbledon's past.

'Are you sure Dr Watkins?' the Italian baker interrupted. 'I mean, what are we really talking about here, Julian? Is this just a way for us to approve another plan to take over the Old Rectory?'

'Enrico…' hissed Viviane.

'I mean, shouldn't the Old Rectory be part of the Wimbledon Museum?' carried on Enrico to make his point, aware of the few frowns in the crowd. 'Shouldn't Dr Watkins be aware of what he is agreeing to?'

'Stop making a scene, Enrico…' repeated Viviane.

Julian raised his bandaged hand. He chuckled.

'Not to worry!' said Julian in calm tones. 'You all came to me for support. I provided access and pulled resources. Yet, it is in the interest of Wimbledon, and not just mine, to work together and ensure we do not lose sight of the great source of archaeology we have found below this hill. Dr Watkins, wouldn't you agree?'

Dr Watkins weighed his answer.

'As curator of the local museum,' he said. 'I share Julian's interests of Wimbledon history. I do approve of his plans and I believe his arrangement works for all of Wimbledon.'

'This is why you will be my lead here, Dr Watkins. With immediate effect.'

Dr Watkins looked up and met Julian's eager eyes.

'What do you mean?' he dithered.

'I want you to be the local chief archaeologist.'

'Are you serious?'

'Yes. I am not the expert, you are. And I am sure you want to keep an eye on what the British Museum does!'

Viviane elbowed Enrico again. This time with a knowing smile which seemed to shout at him 'I told you so!'. The Italian baker was embarrassed and struggled to find what to say. He blushed not sure what the right thing to say was. Julian was truly Wimbledon's most beloved benefactor.

'Mr LoTrova,' resumed Julian to find the words Enrico could not. 'I must congratulate you on your perseverance and defiance. Not that I support your unconventional approach towards law and order... It goes without saying that it is you who have done me and Dr Watkins a big favour. Who would have thought under the Old Rectory lay all these secret chambers and tunnels, unless you had ventured down there?'

Enrico smiled nervously. Julian's compliments took him by surprise, and he blushed again.

'I don't know what to say... Thank you, Julian.' answered Enrico returning Julian's compliments. 'You can call me Enrico.'

'And I will make sure your bakery gets what it deserves. Publicity!'

He then turned to the crowd by the stalls nearby.

'Everyone here!' he shouted clamping Enrico's shoulder. 'Don't forget to buy your bread from this man. *The Wynnman* bakery, on the High Street. Approved by Julian Alberon himself.'

Enrico was overwhelmed by the tycoon's generosity. His ears buzzed with the cheers of the crowd, emotion swelling inside as he became the centre of attention for all the good reasons.

'Proud of you!'

Viviane's whisper was the only thing that reached him loud and clear. She gave him another peck on the cheek and Enrico felt hot and confused.

'Well,' announced Julian once the excitement was over. 'I would love to spend time here but need to go back home and get some rest.'

He coughed and turned to Mr Sanders urging him to get going.

'Exciting times ahead.' he added. 'We should definitely have dinner together sometimes. To celebrate properly.'

'We will be there!' confirmed Viviane holding both Enrico and Dr Watkins under the arm.

Julian Alberon left a few minutes after, again followed by a small group of fans who wanted to catch a glimpse of the self-made businessman. Enrico watched the man go and for once he could not criticise the man who had just put him one step up on the ladder. Hours before he would have asked why he had to save, or maybe push, Toby Claymore, but now he felt it was not the time nor the place. Everything was getting back to normal somehow. He saw Viviane out of the corner of his eye. She was staring at him with a smug on her face.

'Yes?' he asked, catching her in the act. 'Are you waiting for that 'thank you' you always expect?'

'I am just glad Baynard did not arrest you. You would have missed the opportunity Julian Alberon just gave you.'

Enrico thought of the inspector. Baynard's icy stare could not be forgotten and he recalled the inspector's serious warning to him. He told him the police may not go easy on him next time he was caught meddling in police business. The Italian baker hoped he would not need to, and it would be only bread and pastries from now on. He had never thought life in Wimbledon Village could be so adventurous and dangerous.

Enrico then looked at Reverend Green. The reverend was staring at Dr Watkins, who toyed with the old bottle in his hands and looked overjoyed about the upcoming plans for the museum. The perplexed look on the reverend's face daunted Enrico. He remembered the story he had been told, about what had happened to the curator in the tunnels. Perhaps this was all too much for Dr Watkins. Enrico realised he and Viviane would need to keep an eye on the curator.

'Everything ok, Dr Watkins?' asked Enrico.

The curator blinked and took his eyes off the bottle. He pulled a weak smile and then closed his eyes to massage his temples.

'Yes. Tired, I must say.' he responded. 'All this good news at once was a bit too much.'

'Well, save your energy.' reminded him Enrico. 'The British Museum may finally get back to you. Busy times ahead for all of us!'

'That means you too, Enrico.' stepped in Viviane.

'I can handle it.' protested Dr Watkins. 'Looking forward to it.'

'How are you going to display the bottle in the museum?' asked Viviane.

'Not sure yet if I will display it right away. If I do, though, I may display with one of the Cecil 1590 bottles. It will be an example of how miracles can happen. Wine made in Britain!' said Dr Watkins.

'I thought you said you didn't believe in magic.' joked Enrico.

Dr Watkins grinned. He yawned and stretched his arms and legs.

'I don't.' replied the curator. 'We should take the past as face value. History as facts.'

Sunday afternoon on Wimbledon High Street dragged on. The lazy strolls of the locals and the liveliness from the pubs somehow pushed away the blues from the grey, cold autumn sky. Enrico, Viviane and Dr Watkins enjoyed the walk back from the fair after it was over. As the evening crawled back up, sunny spells pushed through the clouds. They plotted bright circles on the grey asphalt and on the dull façade of the low buildings facing the high street. The three stopped in front of *The Wynnman* bakery to bid each other farewell.

'So, the journey ends here.' said Enrico pushing through the door to drop the boxes of *sfogliatelle*. 'Back to normality, I suppose.'

'You'd better be!' said Viviane. 'Now that Julian Alberon has endorsed you, get ready for business! I know because that is what happened to me.'

'*Speriamo in bene!* Let's hope for the best! We should have dinner some time. The three of us. Pick a date.'

'Need to check my calendar.' teased Viviane.

Enrico grinned.

'How about you, Dr Watkins?'

'Well, I would not say no. Hopefully it will be before the museum is overwhelmed by tons of new material. God only knows what Alberyx Enterprises and the British Museum will recover from the Old Rectory.'

'Take it easy, doctor!' laughed Enrico as he patted the old man's shoulder.

'Enrico is right!' added Viviane. 'Make sure you get plenty of rest. Starting now!'

Behind their cheerful comment, the Italian baker and the florist could not hide their deep concern for the curator's health. His tired face, a little worn after the accident, and his bandaged hand made him look like a wreck if it were not for his occasional weak smile or the moments of joy as he heard Julian's offer for him to look after the archaeological site.

'It will be fine. It is not the first time I catalogue new relics at the museum. I have been here longer than you two, you know!'

'Sometimes I wonder if you will have room for all your stuff in that small museum.' continued Enrico. 'First the black azalea, then this bottle. You also have that sample of crimson gelatine I picked up for you. If we keep finding relics at this rate, there will be no more room left in the museum. Anyhow, I look forward to that dinner.'

The three parted ways returning to their daily routine, preparing for another ordinary week in Wimbledon, to enjoy the long-deserved quiet after the storm. Enrico stood by the counter glancing in horror at the long backlog of orders he had to work on for the week. He kept his jovial appearance. The worries for an instant hid behind the warm brown eyes and ruffled hair tinted with dustings of flour from the morning bake.

Viviane waved goodbye and returned to her apartment, stopping a moment in her shop to check upon her flowers. Their colourful petals looked back at her with a pure innocence she found comforting and rare. She realised normality probably had never left the quiet surroundings of Wimbledon Village. Shops still sold their goods, passers-by met friends up and down the streets, locals stopped for a drink at the Dog and Fox or the Rose and Crown. Ignorance was bliss and all the rumours on the secret tunnels or the scary tremors or the fake wine splashed over local media only fuelled the locals' imagination over a cup of tea. Viviane wanted to return to normality as soon as possible. She brushed away her worries and gently watered her flowers, thinking of a bright tomorrow.

Dr Watkins made his way towards the Ridgeway. He did not want to go back home. Not yet. A cold wind picked up and blew from the High Street in his direction. It swept away his thoughts from the joyful day and left him void and uncertain. In his years as curator, he had never seen Wimbledon Village shaken by such chaotic events one after the other.

The curator arrived at the Wimbledon Society building. He ignored the chatter coming from the bar and walked up the stairs to the museum. The thought of the work coming his way filled him with dread. Approval requests for funding excavations, press conferences for local newspapers, local council members wishing to be kept up to date on any new developments. A call from Alberyx Enterprises would come at any moment.

As he entered the modest room of the museum, Dr Watkins could not ignore the enormous possibilities he now had to refurbish and modernise the place, to make it a little more welcoming. He could afford new lighting, digital interactive tablets, less bulky glass cases. He dreamed on while he checked the post. He yawned again. His eyes felt tired and the bandage itched again. He wondered if Julian's itched too. He closed his eyes for the moment. The last thought he had was to remember where the doctor's pills were, before his eyes became heavier. He spun around in the artificial neon light and took a look at where he had set up the cabinet for the black azalea, the black rock from Cannizaro Park. Except the small polished rock was not there. The glass case was empty. He had told everyone he had lent it out for an exhibition. Same with Enrico's sample of crimson gelatine from the tunnels. He wondered if the British Museum would finally get back to him on that. Dr Watkins did not react or seem alarmed. He wanted to sleep now more than ever. He checked his watch and he still had some time left before going back home. He then locked the entrance and walked to the storage room at the back. The keypad was always there behind the fake panel. He placed his hand where a greenish beam scanned his fingerprints. The door whirred into motion and slid open for a few seconds, enough for Dr Watkins to jump inside and take the short flight of stairs to a separate room.

Cables, computer screens and server mainframes filled one corner of the room with their soft buzzing and beeping. Most of the desk space to one side was a cluttered mess of research notes except one area which was kept neat and cleared. Here, under a series of low hanging spotlights, there were two small pedestals. On one of these, there was the black azalea, the smooth lava rock found in Cannizaro Park, reflecting its pitch-black shine. Dr Watkins remembered the good polish he had given it recently. On the other pedestal, a small steel container held the samples of dry crimson gelatine. Dr Watkins walked to it and opened the wooden box Julian Alberon had given him. He pulled out the bottle. Dr Watkins knew it was probably older than the Cecils' wine. It was a gift he had to treasure dearly. He did not care to expose it to the public. The most important thing now was that the bottle was in his possession and in the safety of his room, where he could finally take time to analyse it in peace.

Dr Watkins squinted to get a better look at the bottom of the bottle. Under the spotlight, the dregs inside seemed as dark as the surface of the lava rock and at the same time crimson swirls shimmered all around. As he placed the bottle on the second pedestal, next to the dry crimson gelatine, the two substances started to move as if an invisible magnetic force pulled them towards each other. Then the black azalea started wobbling and whispers started to echo in the curator's ears. Dr Watkins pulled the bottle out of the way amid fear and awe. It was as if a faint tremor was starting to build up when the rock and the crimson liquid were in proximity of each other. There was a connection. Indeed, there was.

He then heard a voice over his shoulder.

'Are we ready?'

Dr Watkins closed his eyes for a moment, and then reopened them again.

'Yes' answered the curator. 'Time to find the Wynnman!'

Enrico will return in
"The Wynnman and the Silver Spectre"

November 2016 – September 2019